THE DEMON'S CURSE

Book Four of The Dark Angel series

COURTNEY LILLARD

ISBN: 979-8-9858212-9-1

Cover Design by Etheric Tales & Edits | MC Damon

ACKNOWLEDGEMENTS

This book is dedicated to everyone who contributed some fraction of their time to help shape the person I am today, including my parents, siblings, friends, teachers, and colleagues from across the country. I also must thank my husband, Darren, who not only gave me the push I needed to begin writing seriously and reads the drafts but who also listens to my ideas with honest, eager ears.

A NOTE FROM THE AUTHOR

The Dark Angel series has gone through several editions. This final version combines what used to be the first two books, The Shadow's Grasp and The Guardian's Deception, into Part One and Part Two of the former. The Demon's Curse also used to be the first book in The Yeluthian Duology, a sequel story meant to be two books. This book has been altered to continue The Dark Angel series as its fourth book. This decision was not made lightly considering the amount of effort it takes to rebrand a series, as well as my readers who were familiar with the original book order, but each part of the story has been kept the same. Chapter titles have also been added, and the rest of the series will follow a new order, so to speak.

This note serves as a notice for those of you who may see The Guardian's Deception, whether online or a physical copy. That book will now be considered the second half of The Shadow's Grasp, and the rest of the series will be numbered appropriately. The Yeluthian Duology is no longer its own entity since The Demon's Curse is now Book Four.

Other changes will be mentioned in future notes.

Contents

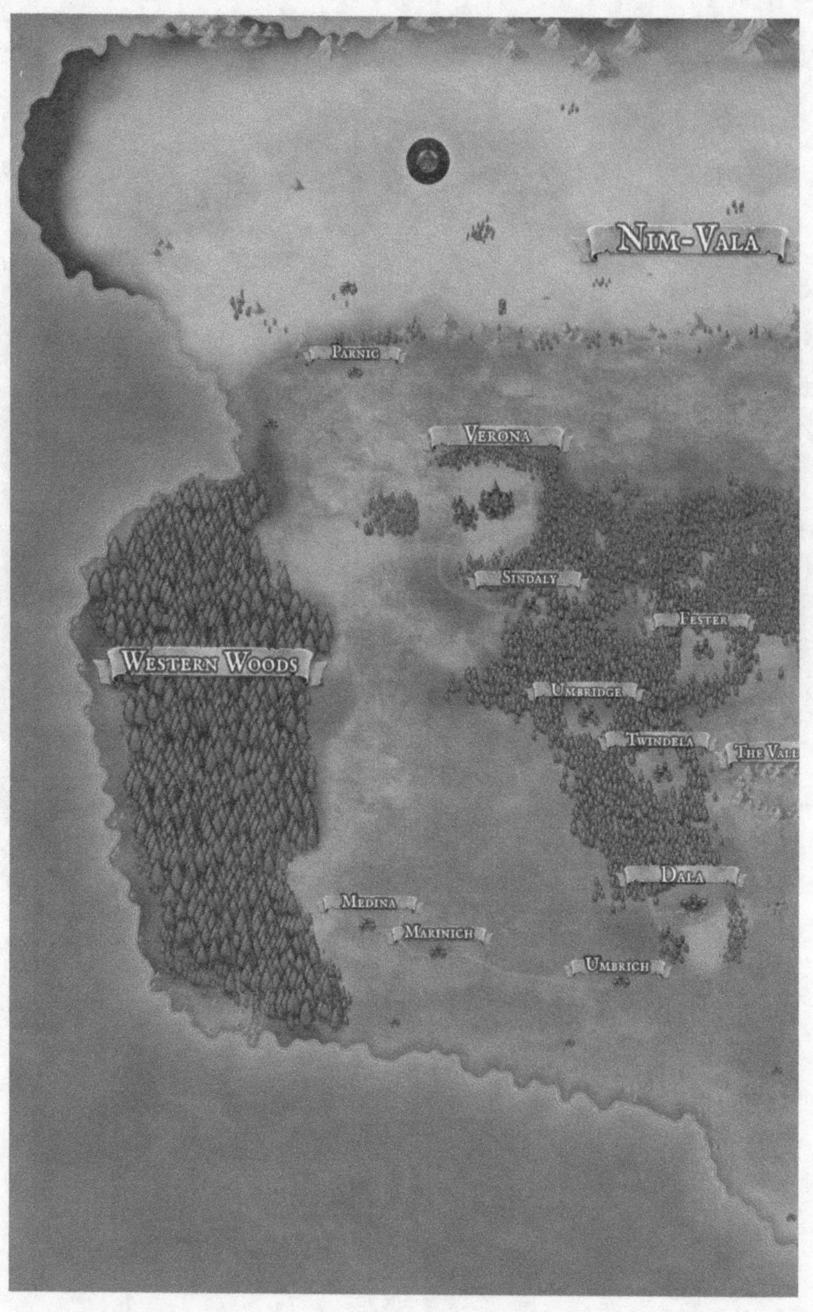

Nim-Vala
Parnic
Verona
Sindaly
Fester
Western Woods
Umbridge
Twindela
The Vall
Dala
Medina
Marinich
Umbrich

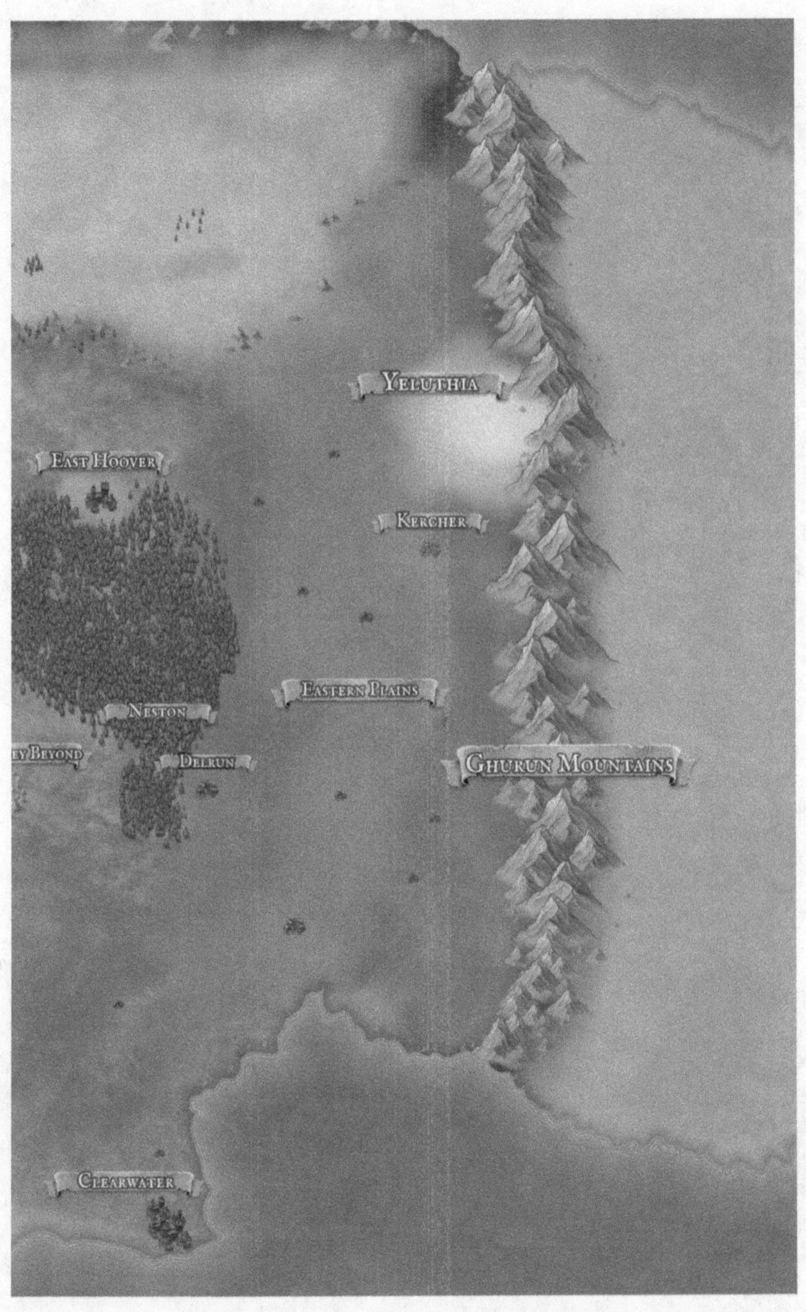

Yeluthia
East Hoover
Kercher
Eastern Plains
Neston
Ghurun Mountains
Ey Beyond
Delrun
Clearwater

Part One

Forward Progress

he weather in the city above the clouds seemed to always behave like a living presence. It acted of its own accord while somehow managing to take into account the creatures forced to submit to its will, often reflecting the people's emotions. At least, that was what Evern believed during his time in Yeluthia. Rain fell from the sky as more of a mist than a shower, so their people rarely experienced severe storms. The only days anyone could remember those taking place were during times of great stress; the most recent example had been two years ago after his return from Asteom's palace in the capital.

The chain of pleasant, normal weather that followed broke again when he awoke to a rumble of thunder shaking his home. He fully expected horrendous conditions, though, because of the controversial execution he would be attending.

As he peeked outside the safety of his home, Evern refused to cave into his desire to remain inside even as his wife wrapped her arms around his waist. No words were exchanged between them for minutes until he turned away from the window, returned to the bedroom, and donned his bronze suit of armor. Within the hour, he stood outside the capital building alongside his fellow commanders Isan and Detrix. Neither appeared pleased with the downpour and howling wind nipping at any bit of exposed skin.

This is far from summer weather, he thought as a shiver ran down his spine.

King Arval emerged from the upper level then and descended the staircase while eight soldiers trailed behind with the four prisoners in between. Chains bounded the traitors' hands and feet together with enough slack for walking, but cloth sacks covering their heads eliminated their sight.

They probably cannot breathe well either given all this rain soaking through the bags. I just want this to be over as soon as possible.

Commander Isan led the way to their destination, which was nothing more than the farthest edge of the plateau. As the procession went forward, Evern couldn't help but catch curtains flapping in the wind, pulling back far enough to reveal the residents' stares beyond.

An execution among Yeluthians proved rarer than dangerous storms; even the citizens who remained silent throughout the months of debating would look on as best they could. He had only been a part of one other case involving a murderer deemed too mentally unstable to be kept alive.

The traitors currently trudging behind were not as easy to judge. Their involvement in the turmoil within Asteom and the resulting battle could not be forgiven; however, many argued over the past couple of years about the most fitting punishment for such treachery. The usual procedure consisted of a lockdown period inside the prison, but that applied to petty crimes done by citizens who could learn from their mistakes. For others, like the four and their deceased friends, banishment into the mountains became the standard.

After all, who would willingly agree to be thrown into the unknown world below. That was what my people and I always thought...

Isan halted ahead of King Arval, who walked in front of Evern. "This is the spot," he announced in a shout; however, the pounding of rain against the ground grew loud enough to make it seem as though he had whispered the words.

The remaining commanders stayed at either side of their king as the soldiers escorted each prisoner forward one by one. Isan stepped in front of the first to be executed, slid a dagger out from the sheath on his belt, and addressed the crowd.

"Kline Galbourough."

A pause followed before he continued by listing the names of traitor's parents, grandparents, and great-grandparents. Then, the weapon slashed across the prisoner's shoulder blades before a final stab through the center sealed the ex-Yeluthian's fate. Blood poured forth to color the nearby puddles crimson, and a soldier shoved the body over the edge a minute later. Even if those in line to be executed had not been starved to deprive them of their energy, the added weight of manifesting their wings would be excruciatingly painful on such direct wounds. That, coupled with their restrained arms and legs assured that even if they somehow lived through Isan's final strike, they were destined to collide with the ground.

Evern caught Detrix's head bow in what he guessed to be pity and turned his attention to Isan once more.

How disgraceful, he reflected as the execution went on. *Their names and lineage will now forever be tainted by this day. Yeluthians' value our loved ones and the freedom this city brings more than anything else. To have a member of our family killed in such a way brings no greater shame to the household. What is worse, their bodies will never be buried on Yeluthian soil. I doubt I will ever hear about these four again, though this may haunt me for longer than I care to admit.*

The final traitor stood a head taller than Isan, yet he proved to be the only one to collapse after the commander removed the dagger from between his shoulder blades. It took two guards to haul his body away like a dead animal. No prayers to the goddess were offered for their souls to find peace; Isan just cleaned the weapon, stood in front of King Arval, and nodded.

"The execution is fulfilled," he said in a tight voice.

"Then let us dismiss this day," came their leader's automatic response.

The group retreated to the stone steps of the capital building and only broke apart when their king moved inside with his trusted guards. No one attempted a conversation or lingered around, especially since the clothing under their armor became damp over the course of the execution, chilling them to the bone.

It is supposed to be summer, right? Evern growled in his mind as he hurried home.

*

For all the gloom the morning brought, Paulina projected a shining picture of stability and warmth. Before he could even walk inside, she stuck her head out of the opening and ordered him to remove his armor, or else he would be drying the floors instead of eating lunch with the rest of the family. His hunger had been suppressed by the emotions from earlier but returned with a fierce vengeance, so he practically threw the bronze equipment into a pile against the wall to keep them as dry as possible until he could clean them later. After, he hurried inside, changed into the set of clothes his wife laid out, and emerged to the scent of a simmering, vegetable soup.

Odell and Jackie were already deep into their meals, and he soon caught up once Paulina set a steaming bowl in front of him. No one asked about what took place, though he didn't believe the children fully understood the execution, yet his wife commented on the rain, wishing it would let up. Evern did too.

He helped his wife clean up while the children went to study in their rooms once everyone appeared full. Although he hoped Paulina wouldn't bring up the past, her anticipated question filled the space when the two were alone.

"How did it go?"

"As I said it would," he answered curtly to show his disinterest for the topic.

Somehow, he figured she still didn't accept the verdict, mainly because she had been one of many citizens who voiced their displeasure with an execution.

"Was it as public as His Highness and the others wanted?"

Her tone sounded harsh, as if to remind him of the lack of a proper audience due to the weather. King Arval meant for the event to be more of a spectacle than anything, which those opposed to it felt was not necessary to enact the traditional, violent showing. He tried to explain the matter to her for the past week after the leaders reached a decision, yet his wife proved to be more stubborn than she let on.

Evern put an arm around her shoulders. "Enough, Paulina," he begged as he kissed her cheek. "What is done is done. Let the dead rest."

She leaned into his embrace and spoke softly and without the previous malice. "It is so barbaric and cruel. I thought I had seen the worst in Asteom, but nothing like this. Why make their families suffer even more?"

"You are not going to understand Yeluthian society as an outsider," Evern began only for her to pull away.

"I hate when you say that. We have lived here for over a decade, had children who only saw the surface for the first time a couple years ago, yet I am still an outsider. *You* lived in Verona for part of your life too."

"I embrace Yeluthian society and its customs fully. If King Arval and those he trusts decide the worst punishment is an execution that brings dishonor to the traitors' families instead of locking them away for the rest of their lives, I support them. Besides, I saw more savage behavior from those living on the surface than here. Perhaps all this alliance has done is influence Yeluthia in that way. Maybe we are destined to become cruel to one another."

Paulina did not answer for a while; in fact, Evern thought that was the end of their conversation and bit his tongue for speaking so foolishly. When she did comment, she used a strangely stable tone of voice.

"Yeluthia is being exposed to much that is new, and unlike you, I believe this is what needs to be done. Your people remained in hiding for decades in order to build their society and avoid the problems Asteom faced. Because of that negligence, the humans struggled against all kinds of creatures. This is a chance to merge with the cities on the surface again, but such an act includes embracing the changes forced upon us."

"I suppose you are right," Evern agreed after another, lengthy pause. He had never been one to want more than the simple pleasures in life, which he possessed for years.

Paulina put a hand on his cheek to catch his attention again. Her genuine smile assured him, even during their moments of disagreement, nothing could damage their love for one another.

"If you ever doubt Yeluthians here should not stay isolated, remember what happened to Coura and how needed you were then. Speaking of which, I assume we will depart when the weather clears up?"

He nodded as a wave of emotion cut deeper than anything else could while his wife walked toward the children's rooms. Despite how much he cared for Paulina, Evern despised when she sparked memories of that demon. No other being in the world could disgust him more than such a creature, not only because of what it was, but also because of what it had done to his eldest child. The lasting effects remained, whether anyone realized it or not; if they did, no one shared their observations with him.

His wife would always be blind to it as well, leaving him to reflect on the problem alone. No other person could understand the pain he felt every time he remembered her bloodied, damaged body beneath his hands that day. No one else utilized all of their power to save his daughter from dying. Ultimately, what led to the culmination of such destruction had been his lack of attention.

That was why he became determined to erase any trace of the horrific experience from Coura. During his suffering, he offered a silent vow to her and the goddess that if she lived, he would fully heal her from the demon's curse and welcome her home as a citizen of Yeluthia.

***

The woods where Coura found herself could hardly be viewed as such due to the trees being lean, stone structures and their leaves nothing but shadows. All around, unseen creatures laughed in place of chirping insects, setting her on edge as she crept along a dirt road. Every out-of-place sound had her glancing around until a stranger's silhouette blocked her path farther ahead. Although she had no indication of their intentions, a sudden, strangling fear caused her to spin around and run.

For a while, she continued in that direction, stumbling over puddles of a dark liquid and fallen debris that sliced open her hands and bare feet. Her eyes fell to the wounds spewing blood before raising and spotting a wide boulder in the middle of the road. Why she could not go around, she didn't know, yet she slid to a stop before the object. A moment later, a force from behind shoved her hard enough to slam her body into the stone wall where she reached upward for a ledge or crack to grab on to.

{*Face me.*}

The voice in Coura's mind sounded foreign, yet the growing cackling of the unseen beings off the road distracted her from considering the presence. She shifted herself around while keeping her back as pressed to the chilly boulder.

The figure came within reach and morphed into the appearance of her younger self, complete with the demonic markings and a serious expression. In the doppelganger's hand was a golden sword, yet unlike the real one, this did not produce any light to counter the surrounding darkness.

Her vision blurred and refocused.

The stranger's lips curved into a glee-filled smile, but a pair of endless voids replaced the eyes. Before she could consider more, the figure lunged with the point of its sword at her heart.

*

A crack of thunder pierced through Coura's nightmare just as the imaginary blade slid into the middle of her chest. She sat up abruptly in bed and found her hands clinging to the sheets tightly enough to make them ache. As she gasped for air, her whole body sweat profusely, even though she'd grown cold and trembled.

It was only a dream, she told herself once her mind could work again. After months of similar experiences, the resulting shock became a familiar sensation. *It's been so long since I had one of those nightmares...*

Another rumble from outside reminded her of the storm from the previous night, which still lingered. As she stretched her stiff legs to stand and wander over to the window, a line of clouds indicating the end of the rain became visible. She noticed some light beyond and realized dawn wouldn't be too far off. Sleep always evaded her when she woke like that, so Coura took her time getting dressed before moving outside to the training ground.

For months after sealing the demon away, along with its borrowed power, she had difficulty sleeping on her own. Even when she drank all the medicine the healers' claimed to be safe to consume in a single day, every once in a while a nightmare snuck up to remind her of what she lived through.

The best method for her to recover had been to find something that would distract her from thinking, which became weapons work. As usual, she proved to be the only person outside so early, aside from the regular soldiers on patrol. That morning, it probably had to do with the sprinkling at the end of the storm while the last flashes of lightning trailed off.

After selecting a stack of hay used for long-distance practice sessions and dragging it from the stable, Coura procured several knives kept in one of the iron bins inside before standing near her target. Because of her natural skill with a sword and elemental spells, she never considered learning to wield another weapon until her magical power disappeared. What light energy she possessed remained untrained.

This led her to find alternate methods of fighting to compensate for that loss. Thankfully, the Magical Arts Academy required its students to exercise with a variety of weapons in order to explore what they felt most suited for. Coura's leaner build limited her use of heavier items, such as maces, spears, or broadswords, though she rarely explored long-distance combat until recently.

Clearshot directed her through archery, which she wasn't too fond of, but she became rather accurate and grew confident that she could survive with only a bow and quiver of arrows. Because of her preferences, he recommended she try throwing knives next.

For at least an hour until the sun fully rose and people gradually made their way into the training ground, Coura continued to focus on the hunched bundle. She had no intention of stopping, though, until a voice from behind addressed her.

"You're getting scarily accurate with those."

She expected Marcus to make an appearance around that time since he began combat instruction courses most mornings. The last knife in her hand flew after she positioned herself to flick her wrist mid-swing, and the two watched as its blade sank into the top right corner of hay.

"I think it helps when the weather cooperates. That, and no one is around to distract me," she explained with a raised eyebrow at him.

His resulting chuckle lifted her spirits a bit, as did the humor reflected in his hazel eyes.

"How else are you going to get better without having to actually concentrate?" he asked while sliding a dagger out of its sheath located on the opposite hip from his sword. After a second to study the target, he released his weapon in one, swift motion, causing it to land in the center of the bundle's lower half with nothing more than a muffled thump.

Coura rolled her eyes. "Show off," she muttered before jogging over to retrieve the weapons.

Marcus attempted to hide a smirk as she moved away, yet he wore a suspiciously calm expression when she approached to hand him his dagger.

"You're out earlier than usual. Couldn't sleep?"

The question reminded her of the nightmare, causing her to grow tense and avert her eyes after shaking her head. At some point over the months following her life-threatening injuries two years ago, the assistant general had been one of a few people to catch on that she had difficulty sleeping through the night and came outside before the sun rose as a result. He would find her in the training ground and sometimes spend a few minutes listening to her explain the dreams or share her thoughts.

Over time, the incidents became less frequent; the last nightmare took place nearly three months earlier at the beginning of spring.

"You should visit Will or Emilea," Marcus continued in a sympathetic manner. His words coupled with the knowing look he wore confirmed his understanding.

"I will," she added before deciding to change topics. "What are you doing here? I thought you were leaving for the northern border."

"We pushed the departure back to tomorrow morning. The general wants to be sure no rain hinders our progress, which I guess I should be thankful for considering we'll be sleeping outdoors."

"That's true. It'd be unpleasant on the road, though if you're with Casner, you might feel miserable anyway."

He shot her an unamused look. "Just because you two didn't get along doesn't mean he's incompetent or heartless. I'm glad to be able to spend time with him on a practical assignment."

Coura considered mentioning how the expedition might give Marcus valuable experience when a new general would be needed, but that remained a touchy subject.

Her friend had been overlooked for the promotion twice due to his father's lack of faith in his ability to lead, and she remembered hearing an assistant general could only move up in rank if their supervising general deemed them worthy. Both of the previously empty positions were filled by older soldiers under Casner's command, which infuriated Marcus. Now, he seemed more determined than ever to earn his father's respect. She just made sure to keep her opinions to herself, especially since she dealt with an opposite experience regarding her parents' approval.

"Whatever," she said dismissively and inspected the knives in her hand. "Make sure to fill me in on the Nim-Valans when you return. I'm still curious about that message."

"So are the rest of us," he muttered.

She expected him to drop the conversation, yet as she went over to the hay bundle to bring it into the stable, he followed and continued, seemingly mumbling more to himself than to her.

"We hear nothing for over a year, but now that their capital city is a mess, they request Asteom's help. Did I tell you our spies returned all at once because the outer ring started ransacking their people's villages?"

Coura nodded. "This has to be the third or fourth time you mentioned it."

"Out of all the actions they could take, their leaders send a plea to Aaron requesting mages and troops. It sounds suspicious; at the same time, an alliance is on the table."

"They mentioned the alliance in their message?"

"Yes. In fact, it sounded like the only leverage they possess. My father said the council doesn't want to turn away the opportunity, even if it means risking the lives of a hundred or so Asteom soldiers and mages."

"That must be why Aaron requested volunteers for your assignment," Coura concluded.

Over the last month or so, several documents had been posted around the palace asking for a certain number of soldiers and mages to head into the northern country. Most everyone learned about Nim-Vala's inner turmoil then, though the details remained private.

Nothing about the journey appealed to her except the idea of exploring the area. Of course, if anyone with wings went along, they would not be allowed to fly unless the general gave his permission, which she doubted he would grant her in any situation.

They chatted about the squad until Marcus seemed to remember his group waiting farther away.

"Am I going to see you at dinner?" he asked by way of ending their conversation.

Despite her desire to disappear for the rest of the day, Coura assured him she would be there. She hurried to return the bundle and knives before moving inside for breakfast while contemplating the remainder of her day.

Evern, Paulina, Odell, and Jackie would be arriving with King Arval, Commander Detrix, and other Yeluthian guards and city leaders to assess the progress of the recent changes to the palace based on the angels' permanent place in Verona. Most revolved around new trading routes to be established or needing adjustments, as well as policies for citizens like her parents who wish to travel or live on the surface. The final additions were already in progress and include another training space to the south of the palace for mages and soldiers to use without crowding the northern one and the construction of a building to house the growing number of troops.

For the time being, the Yeluthian guests stayed in the palace on the fourth floor near Grace's quarters where their frequent visits provided them with enough knowledge of the capital to feel comfortable. She had no doubt they would move freely around the palace by the afternoon, ready to inspect every place with an outsider's eye.

When the Yeluthians' completed their business, Coura would be thrown into training with Evern until her parents' time in Verona ended.

As much as she loved her father, she dreaded those moments more than any others. Their combat styles proved to be drastically different, and he refused to be in the air until the ground maneuvers sharpened. Still, sword work remained easier to deal with than trying to cast light spells. Something seemed wrong with her magic, yet he could provide no direction and barked at her about continuing to practice.

She tolerated the exercises and what he attempted to accomplish with strengthening the magical energy from his bloodline because of their relationship. As the weeks flew by and Evern made his intentions to become her mentor clear, she learned the security of her family ties relied on keeping any negative emotions locked within herself.

*

The rest of the day proved uneventful as Coura followed her routine until the early afternoon. Normally, she visited the library to study, volunteered for guard duty around the city, or found another task to assist with; however, she agreed to accompany Grace to Lady Katrina's home before the private dinner that evening. For whatever reason, Aaron decided to limit the number of gatherings and guests, but he included the Yeluthian king, commanders, and leaders. Emilea once told her how the changes bothered the nobility until the lords and ladies realized what an honor it was to receive an invite, even though the majority did.

Coura, Grace, Will, and Marcus were also welcome, though Aaron personally reached out to let them know this once the dinners had been established. The foreign ambassador always attended in order to uphold her people's image, and the assistant general usually stood guard and kept his best friend company. Meanwhile, Will rarely found a reason to go, and Coura felt the same unless someone asked her to accompany them.

She didn't mind joining the younger Yeluthian, except it meant she had to escort Grace to Katrina's home as well. The noblewoman took pleasure in housing an important figure and offered to do their hair and makeup while chatting about those she interacted with on a daily basis. None of the information mattered to Coura, but her friend seemed to enjoy keeping up with the gossip.

The pair reached their destination, and the lady's butler greeted them, unlatched the silver gates, then led them inside through the decorated, floral walkway. Nothing looked to have changed since their last visit earlier in the year, yet the décor and cleanliness continued to impress her.

"You're right on time," came the chipper, high-pitched voice of their host.

A second later, Katrina emerged from the nearest hallway to curtsy in front of Grace. Her wide, cream-colored dress appeared gold thanks to the sunlight reflecting off the windows and her metal jewelry. Blonde curls sprouted from the back of her head underneath a matching, beige bonnet.

While the Yeluthian ambassador offered a similarly polite gesture, Coura noticed Emilea approaching from behind the lady. The master light mage dressed in an opposite manner, wearing a dark blue gown with ribbons laced at the waist and a silver, sapphire-adorned necklace. Unlike Katrina, her hair remained unbound, allowing it to trail over her shoulders in a natural position.

"Don't mind me," she commented with a friendly smile. "We were just catching up before you arrived."

Katrina giggled before shaking her head. "It's so difficult for us to meet, what with our busy schedules. Now, if we had the dinners every night, this wouldn't be a problem. I suppose I'll just have to accept this new direction."

Coura avoided the urge to roll her eyes as she followed the lady farther into the house. Once they reached the sitting room, she prepared to take a seat beside Emilea so the two could converse, but the cream-colored dress blocked her path as Katrina slid in front of her.

"You can't honestly be going like that," the woman began before eyeing her up and frowning.

"Why? What's wrong?" The words took Coura back, though she avoided the urge to glance down at herself. Out of the four, formal outfits she'd come to collect over the years, she selected the rose-colored dress she first wore during her time in the capital city and a pair of gray shoes with a slight heel she wouldn't struggle in. The lady usually fixed her hair, despite her reassurance that it would be fine tied back, and she didn't own any fitting jewelry.

Katrina made a tsking sound and placed both hands on her hips. "You wore the exact same thing the last time you were here!"

"Did I?"

"You don't remember? It was only a month ago."

Coura prepared to mention how she didn't care too much about her appearance since no one paid attention to her, yet she assumed admitting the truth would upset her host. Instead, she shrugged.

Unfortunately, her dismissal spurred a negative reaction. Katrina stepped closer, seized her by the wrist, and began dragging her out of the sitting room.

"Hey!" she snapped and half-heartedly attempted to pull her arm away. "What are you doing?"

The grip remained while the noblewoman grumbled a response. "I have plenty of gowns you can use just sitting in my closets. There's no need for you to settle on one of your older dresses."

"It's fine. I really don't mind-"

"You can thank me later."

As much as she hated being forced to change her outfit, Coura knew from past encounters and Emilea's stories how Katrina could throw a tantrum if she became truly passionate about a subject. So, despite her wishes, she allowed the woman pull her toward the opposite side of the building to one of the spare rooms. There, the lady dug through the closet while removing several dresses, which either wound up on the floor or on the lone bed.

Perhaps I should have argued more, she thought as she watched this take place. The amount of fabric on a majority of the outfits made her nervous for what the mad woman would select.

Finally, after about a dozen gowns had been strewed around the room, Katrina stood straight while admiring a maroon piece no more elaborate than what Coura already wore.

"This is perfect! Exactly how I remember it." The lady turned around to hold out the dress. "Put this on, then join us in the sitting room. You can leave your old dress here and pick it up another time."

With a sigh in resignation, Coura accepted the new outfit and changed once she was alone. When she returned to the others, Emilea had begun applying Grace's makeup, giving Katrina time to pin up her hair while they waited. She bit back several, spiteful comments and ignored the talk until every strand of hair had been pulled into a tight bun on the back of her head.

"You two look much more elegant than when you first stepped inside," the lady commented and laughed before adjusting her position to do Grace's hair.

This time, Coura did roll her eyes, earning her an amused smirk from the master mage. She expected Emilea to join her so they could talk until Katrina finished; however, the woman shifted around to face her instead in order to begin applying her makeup.

Coura leaned to one side a bit in order to move out of the brush's reach. "It's okay. I don't need you to do that."

Emilea tilted her head. "Why not? I don't mind."

Before Coura could respond, Katrina interrupted while waving the comb in her hand around to emphasize her words.

"Quit being difficult, darling. You should wish to be dazzling in front of good company!"

"They're tolerable at best," she muttered before allowing the master mage to continue.

After a pause, the lady responded in a kinder tone of voice. "When I was your age, I couldn't wait for an excuse to go and mingle with the noblemen."

"Or flirt with the guards," Emilea added.

"I don't believe I ever would have caught the eye of my husband if I didn't try to put in my best effort every time we encountered one another," Katrina went on while ignoring the extra comment. "If you don't get married when you're young, you'll need to work harder to secure a stable future."

This time, the master mage paused to address her friend directly. "Marriage isn't the only option. Don't confuse them."

"I already understand," Grace chimed in with a smile. "My parents taught me my decisions will reflect my image, so what I say and do are important to consider at all times."

"They're right, but life changes," Emilea replied. She switched brushes to begin applying a scarlet-colored powder to Coura's cheeks. "You can plan for everything except the unexpected. Besides, Katrina's a hopeless romantic."

The lady released a dramatic sob before agreeing. "You're right! I love nothing more than observing blossoming relationships and dreaming about their futures. Don't you ever imagine one of the soldiers fighting for your honor or rescuing you from a hideous monster hovering over the cliffside?"

Coura couldn't picture becoming enamored by one of her comrades and even had to force herself not to snicker at the idea. Grace had no such restraint, though her laughter sounded as though it was spurred by the ridiculousness of the scene.

"What's so funny?" the lady chided in a playful manner. "Maybe you'd love waltzing with the young king instead. He's been the talk of the capital ever since his last birthday."

While her friend continued chuckling, Coura recalled the first instance when Aaron asked her to dance during the Harvest Festival.

I didn't know him well back then, and the other women didn't hide their jealousy. I wonder if they all think like Katrina...

"It's difficult to get the shading right on your cheeks when you're blushing," Emilea said quietly to interrupt the memory. The master mage didn't remove her eyes from the brush, but the hint of a smile appeared on her lips.

Coura didn't notice her face heating up until that moment; it grew worse when someone pointed it out. Thankfully, Emilea ended the task there, grabbed the rest of the makeup, and left to presumably return it after.

Katrina and Grace's following discussion allowed Coura time to recover from her embarrassment. Then, she found herself reflecting on why she reacted that way.

No one ever discussed romantic relationships on a personal level when she was growing up, most likely due to her immature attitude toward those in her classes and others when she first arrived in the capital city. For that matter, romance could never be an option because of the discovery of her demonic and angelic abilities, which lasted until she sealed the demon away.

Now that she could explore her future, she wasn't certain what she wanted.

I enjoy the time I spend with my friends, especially because I never really had any, but it's different with...certain people. Maybe that's why I savor what opportunities I get with them. In fact, I desire those moments above any others. Is that what being in love means?

She contemplated asking Emilea the next time the two were alone and dismissed the question for another day once the group prepared to head to the palace.

An Ambiguous Relationship

During his younger years, Aaron never felt the need for fancier dinners with the nobility in the private dining hall. He knew his father had thought the same, yet being surrounded by them pleased his mother, especially when the guests brought their daughters along.

Any social gatherings throughout his life had been used as a means of setting him up with a bride and social network, which was why he tried to stay away from them at all costs. While thinking back on how he would do all that he could to avoid being present, Aaron had to laugh. The ploys usually involved Marcus, who found it amusing, or his father, who understood what the world of an unmarried prince was like.

As of late, though, Aaron grew fond of what the hall became. When the council's meeting chamber needed to be cleaned and the furniture replaced, the dining space took on an air of politics, financing, and justice as much needed to be reorganized. That lasted six weeks, but even after the group returned to their original room, no one felt compelled to reestablish the dinners his mother started. He had to wait for the noblewomen to complain about its absence before begging Lady Emilea for help.

In his mind, she seemed to be the perfect person to ask because of her position and familiarity with the lords and ladies, yet her disgust for the events surprised him. To hear he wasn't alone in his distaste for the previous system comforted him and ended up working in their favor.

From then on, the private dinners became monthly affairs, included invited guests only, such as the Yeluthians when they visited, and showcased music or various forms of entertainment in place of the downtime used for gossiping. This allowed for a peaceful atmosphere with less pressure to make conversation, though many left early in pairs or trios to talk outside the space.

Aaron took his place at the head of the table with King Arval to his right and Grace to his left. Marcus stayed behind as a guard while the generals, Byron, and Emilea occupied their own spots around the table. To the master mages' sides sat Will and Coura, who he always appreciated seeing. The nobility fortunate enough to receive an invite filled the rest of the seats.

As soon as he acknowledged the head attendant, the meal began. Servants scuttled in through side doors with steaming plates they set before the guests, though the head chef delivered the kings' plates for the rulers' safety. A quartet of string musicians plucked a lively melody that proved to be the perfect background noise for light conversations in between courses.

During their first meetings, the Yeluthian king intimidated Aaron, mainly because of his god-like appearance, but they soon grew comfortable with one another after multiple interactions. The angels acted friendly and polite, giving their own opinions without forcing them upon him or the council. It also helped that Grace was related to the king and Coura to one of the commanders; both of those facts had left him speechless when he found out.

King Arval discussed their uneventful journey and expressed his desire to see more of Asteom while Aaron smiled and added comments about the cities he visited over the years. When the final crumbs of their desserts had been licked up, the musicians reorganized themselves with a pair of female vocalists joining to perform a customary ballad meant for slow dancing between couples. It was no surprise that the center space filled with partners soon after.

Aaron always waited for the Yeluthian king to exit before participating or leaving, as it seemed rude to enact his own plans while the main guest remained at his side. Fortunately, the angels retired almost immediately, except for a handful who already began dancing. All three commanders and several, weary guards escorted their leader out of the hall, then Marcus slid into the empty seat next to Aaron so the two could chat. This also prevented any of the ladies from pulling him away before his stomach settled.

"Everything is the same, I take it?" the assistant general asked casually while glancing after their visitors.

Aaron's lips curved upward as he studied the fluid movements of the dancers in front of them. "It has been for a while."

"I'm glad to hear it. Are you going to talk to Coura tonight?"

His friend's devious grin stretched wider when Aaron felt his smile deflate.

"I don't know."

It was no secret between him and Marcus that he had felt something for her from their initial encounters. She could treat him as nothing more than another person living in the palace. This amazed him considering every time he requested that from others it took some amount of adjustment time, if his wishes were respected at all.

The two laughed without worry and acted as themselves when they could be together. She held him at the lowest point in his life and didn't judge him for being weak. What started as an attraction, one he believed had always been mutual, bloomed into more serious emotions after the incident that nearly cost Coura her life. Seeing his friend so frail and broken awoke those mature feelings, as well as a desire to make sure she would always be safe.

That, plus his own wish to see her, was why he invited her to his mother's garden whenever his schedule allowed an impromptu meeting. In his eyes, the bond between them continued to steadily develop to the point where spending even a few minutes alone became his favorite moments of the week.

Throughout the years, he shared what he could with Marcus. His closest friend had always been supportive about the subject, though recently he found the enthusiasm more annoying than appreciated.

"Come on, Aaron! I'll be gone tomorrow for who knows how long, and if you can't be brave enough to see how she feels, then I have to wait even longer."

"You've become no better than a chattering old woman," he responded with a hint of bitterness. Still, he prayed for the courage to do more than simply hold her hand or pull her close when they were alone. The mixture of his nerves and responsibilities as a royal figure held him back from attempting to be intimate.

Across the space, he caught a glimpse of Coura speaking with a lady he recognized as Katrina, the merchant Donovan Neneme's wife. Both master mages seemed familiar with her, and the woman had never bothered either of Aaron's parents in the past. In his eyes, that made her someone favorable.

At her side stood Marcy Kilguire, a person he came to know well because of the problems her presence in Verona caused for the capital and the city of Dala. The woman's husband proved to be a wealthy but manipulative tradesman whose jobs included purchasing fish and meat from other areas, arranging for the products to be shipped to Dala, and dividing the produce between the local tavern and inn kitchens. The career often remained within the families who grew up among the system.

No trouble plagued that particular family until Marcy ran away and hid in Verona. She stayed with Lady Katrina, who, according to Emilea, doted on the guest like an older sister. Word got around, as it always did, and the tradesman named Ronald hired a handful of men to bring her back, which resulted in a public scene involving the city's guards. After the incident, she voiced the abuse she endured in the past and her wish to end their marriage.

Meanwhile, her husband already paid off the priest who performed the ceremony over a decade ago, making it a challenge for anyone aside from the new high priest to intervene. For the time being, though, the lord and lady protected her in their home.

The two women separated from Coura to join a party exiting the hall, and Aaron watched as she stood and turned away from the dancing. His friend appeared to be distracted by the artwork until a

Yeluthian appeared at her side. Nothing distinguishable came to mind to remind Aaron of his name while the two conversed.

"You lost your chance," Marcus chimed from his seat and picked at his fingernails.

Aaron scowled at the assistant general but said nothing. The stranger led Coura to the center of the room where they danced in a casual enough fashion to reassure Aaron the invite couldn't have been more than a friendly gesture.

Unfortunately, some of the younger ladies noticed him staring in their direction, and one pranced over to request he be her partner. He managed not to sigh or show his displeasure as he rose, extended his hand with a smile, then guided her farther into the room.

If he became proficient at any part of being royalty, it was proper dance etiquette. Like a carriage picking up passengers for a limited voyage, Aaron switched between women until they broke away. He never ended a pairing because his partners understood they would be hated by their peers for spending more or less time bragging about themselves or complimenting him. In reality, he often let the music drown out their voices and responded based on their inflection at a question or the tone of their words. That game always occupied his mind, keeping him sane while he entertained dozens of people at events throughout his life.

When the musicians paused to readjust themselves and Aaron bid his partner farewell, Marcus startled him with a firm hand on the shoulder.

"I have an idea," his friend began. "You need to ask Grace to dance."

"What are you talking about?"

The answer to his question slipped away as the assistant general crossed to the opposite side of the room. Although he believed he should be wary, Aaron moved to where Grace sat before anyone else could distract him.

The Yeluthian girl had matured into a young woman projecting confidence and beauty, and her eyes drifted to him as he approached to offer his hand.

"Would you care for a dance?"

She smiled, bobbed her head, then jumped to her feet before he led her into the crowd.

In the past, their movements seemed formal, so it surprised him when she wrapped her arms around his neck in place of keeping one on his shoulder and the other in his hand.

Grace's eager expression faltered at his reaction. "I am sorry. Is this too uncomfortable?"

"No, not at all," he replied before instinctively holding her hips and swaying in time with the song.

At first, she tried to converse about dinner, the Yeluthians who just arrived, and a variety of topics relating to the summer until they fell silent. Those few minutes allowed him to enjoy the peacefulness of the evening.

That sensation ended when Aaron noticed Marcus off to the side with Coura in the same position he and Grace were in. The Yeluthian ambassador noticed his attention elsewhere and followed his gaze; the upward curve of her lips straightened when the two came closer.

What happened next would have made him laugh if he hadn't been duped by Marcus' scheming already. The assistant general stumbled on an invisible object and bent forward to clutch his right ankle after releasing Coura, bumping into Aaron in the process.

"What's wrong?" his clueless partner asked.

Marcus rubbed his calf for a moment as Grace withdrew her hands. Those around them also observed the commotion before returning to their business.

"I think I pulled a muscle in my leg," came the fabricated excuse. "Sorry, but I need to sit down."

Coura crossed her arms with a frown. "Seriously?"

Instead of responding to her, Marcus reached for Grace. "I hate to spoil the fun, but would you mind taking a look?"

Their younger friend accepted his outstretched hand without reluctance, though Aaron hated separating on such a sour note. He and Coura could only look on as the two went to the nearest empty seats, then he faced her without hiding his disbelief.

"I hope it's nothing serious," she mumbled, though she raised an eyebrow at him after.

"Don't look to me for medical advice," he started with a head shake. In the back of his mind, Aaron understood Marcus' intentions, though he wanted to strangle his friend for being so frank about putting the two together. "Can I offer you a dance since he's out of commission?"

"I suppose so," she replied with a shrug while they turned away from Marcus and Grace.

After his first experience with Coura's skills, Aaron always feared for his feet and initiated any movements. Her steps became more accurate since then, yet he hoped to avoid the pain, as well as embarrassing her by wincing, when she made a mistake. They began with enough room in between for her to glance down often, yet he carefully brought her closer over time. With each advance, he worried he would go beyond his limited boundary, resulting in an immediate rejection, so he focused on being patient.

He also tried to hold a conversation, which didn't help as much as he imagined it would considering she seemed to be actively listening to every word. For one of the few times in his life, Aaron felt insecure when speaking to someone; however, when she stayed with him in between songs and talked more, he relaxed until they fell silent to simply enjoy each other's company.

"I'm glad you asked me to dance," she began without prompting and raised her eyes to meet his. "This is nice."

"You're welcome. I guess it sort of distracts from Marcus' behavior." Her resulting laugh made him want to pull her in tighter.

"You better never let him live it down! After all, he vouches for his athleticism. That was also inconsiderate of him, dragging Grace away. I'd be upset too if I were in her position."

This time, Aaron chuckled at her response. "Don't worry about it. You can count on me to chew him out. For now, let's just forget about him."

She smiled in confirmation, yet he thought he said too much when she removed her hands from his neck. An apology formed on his tongue until she wrapped her arms around his waist. At that, Aaron caved into his heart's desire without consideration for the dozens of eyes in the space and returned the embrace, holding her head to his chest while the pair swayed along with the music.

Every memory of when he wished he could have been able to help her, from the hardships she endured in the palace to battles with demons and demonic creatures, came to mind. Still, he took comfort in knowing she was there, safe in his arms. They remained together for three more pieces, savoring each other's presence.

What must you be thinking? he wondered absentmindedly. *Is this fine with you? Was requesting a dance in the middle of such an event too forward?*

Despite any internal doubt, Coura wore a content smile.

Part of him wished the moment would last the entire evening, but he understood it would be foolish to expect her to remain his partner. When the song concluded, the arms around his waist dropped to separate the pair. He released her as well, letting her roll her shoulders and address him as regularly as if they just noticed each other across the room.

"I forgot how much that bothers my neck," she commented without glancing away from him. "That was enough of a break from the ladies, right? At least I gave you a few minutes of peace."

Aaron frowned at her words. "That's not why I-"

"Anyway, I'm beat," Coura interrupted. "Now's your chance to escape, unless you plan to be up mingling even later."

Before he had an opportunity to reply, she moved to exit the dining hall while he looked on.

*

"What am I supposed to do? Why can't I act the right way around her?" Aaron begged no one in particular. He lied on the edge of his bed and extended a hand for the wine jug Marcus hugged as the two began their analysis of the night's main incident.

"Calm down! I haven't even opened the bottle," his friend snapped before a popping sound signaled the beginning of their final conversation for a few weeks. "Besides, whoever claims there's a right way to act around women probably never knew any."

"Well, I would take their advice after tonight." He sighed, accepted the wine after Marcus took a swig, and drank his share before handing it back. "I just can't read what she says or does."

"Are you two happy when you're together?"

"I am; she seems so too."

Marcus passed over the jug. "Then leave it at that."

Aaron's frown deepened, but he decided to ignore what uncertainty plagued his mind in favor of focusing on his closest friend.

They moved on to discuss other topics, primarily General Tont so Marcus could complain. His father had dismissed the idea of making Marcus an equal in status, which surprised all but the remaining generals. In Aaron's opinion, he had no business meddling with their system because the foundation of the army relied upon its experienced leaders deciding who would be successful in each position. Their relationships were based on a mutual understanding of the demands of the job, so he would essentially be overthrowing their authority by going against their conclusions unless the issue proved to be serious.

On the other hand, he sought justice for his friend. Marcus served him and the generals with an unwavering sense of dedication, often putting aside his own feelings for their requests. Although it made him a loyal assistant, that attitude didn't showcase his independence or leadership abilities, so Aaron never fought against General Tont's choice not to recommend his son. If Marcus knew the reason for his silence and put some of the blame on him, his friend never showed it.

When they thoroughly dissected that subject, they conversed about random ideas until the wine was long gone.

"Don't you think you should go to bed?" Aaron asked before raising his hand to cover a yawn.

Marcus had moved from his chair to the floor where he lied flat on his back with both arms and legs outstretched. "Are you kicking me out already? I'll sleep on the horse."

"Good luck with that," Aaron countered and tossed one of his pillows onto his friend's stomach, causing Marcus to jump into a sitting position.

"You should act more like a king," he countered as he tossed the pillow on the opposite side of the bed.

Aaron laughed and, in his slightly inebriated mindset, crossed his legs while sitting straighter. "What do you believe is proper of a king? Should I stick my nose higher? Perhaps if I invite the ladies to the palace for tea and desserts every day they'll appreciate my royalty. *You* would appreciate it if you stay in Verona."

That had Marcus grinning. "Right. You can barely keep Coura's attention without my intervening, let alone the dozens of nobility who would visit. I'm afraid unless you marry soon you'll earn a reputation for stringing women along."

"I would, you know. I'd marry her in a heartbeat if it meant I didn't need to interact with the noblewomen I hardly know well enough to hold a conversation with."

He chuckled at the vision of disappointment on the ladies' faces, though he remembered his father dealing with unwanted advances behind his mother's back. How people could intentionally act to break apart a legally acknowledged relationship for their own lust, greed, or envy never sat right with him.

While he became fixated on the aspect of freedom, Marcus stared in astonishment.

"You want to marry Coura?"

Only then did Aaron backtrack to his previous statement and consider what he had thoughtlessly admitted. "I guess."

His friend's eyes narrowed. "That is not something you should *guess*."

"I meant I would prefer her to the alternative."

A pause stretched between the two as Marcus continued studying him. Without a word, the assistant general stood, stretched, and put both hands on his hips while shaking his head.

"You of all people should never settle for someone just because you don't like the other options. That's selfish and unfair, and if you care about Coura as much as you let on, then you shouldn't behave so insincerely."

"I'm sorry," Aaron apologized with what he hoped appeared to be a considerate expression while Marcus moved to the door, spun around, and pointed a finger at him.

"Make it up to me by behaving. I expect to return to more news too, so don't be shy. Maybe play around with compliments or invite her to the garden for some personal time together."

The door promptly closed on his final word as Aaron's pillow flew across the room and plopped against the wood.

***

Departing from Verona to head north before sunrise allowed General Casner and the rest of his troops to avoid the blazing summer sun that would eventually catch up to them later in the morning. Marcus appreciated how his position allowed him to ride one of the dozen or so horses they were permitted to bring along. According to the spies under Aaron and the generals, the rocky terrain near the border would be dangerous for a mount to traverse, which meant a majority of the animals needed to be stabled at the city named Parnic closest to their destination.

According to Captain Harvey, the Nim-Valan commander who sent the request for aid, their group didn't need to hurry and could assume a leisurely pace during the week of travel. General Casner made sure to organize plenty of provisions, mark specific break and camping locations for each day, and arrange hand-picked soldiers up ahead in case of danger, such as an ambush or a block in the road. This eased most of Marcus' concern after he had been asked to accompany the general. The council thoroughly considered the journey and destination before sending a response to the northerners.

"Any hint of deception or a threat to break their word and we're hauling ourselves back to the capital," General Casner explained once Aaron finalized the decision.

At the moment, Marcus stood next to his mare and waited for his superior to start the march farther ahead. His duty focused on managing the rear side, which allowed him time to himself. He found there was a lot on his mind he needed to process during the first part of the trip, particularly what he would do once they completed this mission.

A familiar voice nearby drew his attention, and he glanced around until he spotted the source. A trio stood off to his left, consisting of a light mage in a white robe, a dark mage in blue, and Will in between shouldering an oversized bag. The herbalist seemed to be actively explaining something involving the land to the north of Verona, but he paused to greet Marcus when the latter approached with the horse.

"I wondered when you would notice us." Will's following laugh and those of the two mages he recognized from the training ground didn't sound fitting given the rest of the tired, quieter soldiers surrounding them.

Marcus couldn't recall reading his friend's name on the report of their assigned troops. "What are you doing here?" he inquired without hiding his suspicion.

Will's cheerful persona settled into a casual expression as he gestured to his companions. "I never had a chance to explore the area near the border. Once Clara and Jean told me they intended to go, I decided to join."

"This isn't a vacation."

"I know that," Will replied confidently. "I've trained with the soldiers for a while now, so I'm prepared to be a part of the squad."

"Even so, you need permission."

"I submitted my request on the grounds that I'm conducting research, primarily on the unexplored vegetation and terrain. General Casner approved it a couple days ago. It sounds like you just don't want me here."

When Marcus fell silent, Will shot him a nasty, irritated look, prompting the mages to excuse themselves.

Once the two were alone, he admitted the truth. "I have enough to worry about without needing to guard you too."

"Why would you assume I need you to be my guard?" Will countered while placing a hand on the sword at his waist. "I never asked you to act on my behalf. How about you do your job, and you let me do mine."

Marcus released a drawn-out sigh and turned this new information over in his mind. "Fine. I'm sorry I sounded so harsh."

"It's okay," his friend responded in a more sympathetic manner. "Clara already said she'll watch my back, and Jean threatened to kill me himself if I do something stupid. I wouldn't come unless I knew I could handle the journey. Besides, General Casner ordered me to guard the camp. Unless the situation changes, I won't be involved in any combat."

Marcus relaxed after as voices at the front of the group signaled the beginning of their march. He climbed into the saddle before addressing Will again.

"I'm still keeping an eye on you. I've seen firsthand how clueless you can be when you're conducting research in the field," he concluded with a slight smile.

Once the rear began moving, they merged with the flow and talked for most of the morning. Whatever nerves plagued Marcus steadily calmed, mainly because the heat started sucking away his energy like a famished leech. Because the majority of his concern stemmed from his father anyway, the leash tethering him to those emotions steadily grew thinner the farther they trekked from the palace.

I shouldn't continue to beat myself up for my past failures, Marcus thought after raising a hand above his eyes to block the sunlight. *Right now, I'm nothing but a disappointment to my father and the other generals. Have I neglected my responsibilities that much? The last time I remember having an opportunity to act on my own was with Calin and General Tio when the Dalans ventured to the capital. Ever since then, I've been weighed down by paperwork and training sessions under Father's instruction; however, he appeared upset when he informed me I would stay his assistant.*

He gripped the reins tighter when the notion spurred the question he often found himself asking. *If he pushes me to prove my worth in order to be a general, why has he been holding me back?* Despite her years living in the palace, Grace regretted not building her stamina beyond climbing three flights of stairs so she wouldn't be panting once she reached the top floor; however, her enthusiasm provided her with enough energy to do so without stopping and enough positivity to avoid complaining.

I cannot believe they are actually here, she thought and smiled as she ascended. *It has been too long indeed!*

For the first time since the alliance's reforging, her parents were in Asteom, and she would see them after years of being apart. Her position, along with the unforeseen problems, prevented her from returning to Yeluthia, though she wondered if her uncle would have issued for her return if she had given up hope when the former high priest kidnapped her. Still, Grace had stood against the man, assisted in ending the conflict he caused, and helped the humans in their time of need.

She felt proud of herself for becoming a person of authority with enough trained light magic to be of use if more trouble arose. The kingdoms steadily grew closer in the following months, allowing ordinary Yeluthian citizens to venture down into Asteom as welcomed allies. This included her parents.

Their letters will never compare to their physical presence. I cannot wait to show them around the palace and the rest of Verona!

Unlike King Arval, his commanders, and various other officials, Grace's mother and father departed with a separate group, so they only arrived that afternoon while she had been attending a social gathering in the city. In fact, she didn't find out until dinner when she greeted her uncle, who mentioned they would be resting from their journey. This led her to exit and rush to the room on the fourth floor where the king directed her.

Her eyes darted down the hall for the Yeluthian soldiers posted to supervise the area. Once she spotted their bronze armor and greeted the pair, she inquired about the king's quarters and worked from there. At last, she stood in front of what she believed to be her destination.

She couldn't hear any voices beyond to indicate if the room was occupied, but as soon as she knocked, the sound of footsteps came through the door.

"Yes?" came a baritone voice as the knob turned.

Grace didn't answer. A second later, the door opened wide, revealing the face of her father. Behind him sitting on the bed was her mother, who glanced over to see their visitor.

Despite the passing years, their appearances hadn't changed from what she remembered, and neither seemed to have aged a day. Her father, Nullan, towered over her, and just about everyone else she knew. Like most of the Yeluthians, his sapphire eyes pierced through whatever he studied, and his golden hair had been tied in a braid reaching the middle of his back. His brother and father shared a square face, though only her father never grew facial hair. This, along with his skinnier frame, reflected his position as a scholar and political leader in the kingdom.

Her mother held a similar position as a planner for the layout of Yeluthia and its few crops. This required her to sit on plenty of councils and complete paperwork, which Grace always recalled her mother doing at their home. Elenor Zelnar hardly smiled to show her pleasure due to her business sense, but she beamed upon catching her daughter in the doorway.

"Darling, move aside," she ordered her husband as she rose to step closer.

However, Nullan already had Grace wrapped in his arms. Their embrace lasted until Elenor came to interrupt and offer a hug and kiss on the cheek.

"Mother, it is wonderful to see you both again," Grace began while blinking to clear the rising tears from her eyes. "How was your trip to Asteom?"

"Fine," her father commented while ushering her inside so he could close the door. "Different, but nothing as tedious as some people made it out to be."

"I am relieved to hear that."

Before she could ask about Yeluthia's current state, her mother questioned her about the palace, Verona, and Asteom's culture as a whole. The pair listened while she shared her insight as the ambassador and what the role required of her. Their smiles relaxed but never faded the entire time she spoke, motivating her to continue until she ran out of topics to discuss.

"My, our daughter has established quite a life among the humans," Elenor chimed when the conversation seemed to end. Her hands remained folded on her lap until that moment when she placed them on Grace's shoulders. "No wonder their people hold us in such high regard. I am so proud of you!"

Her final comment caught Grace off guard. *I cannot remember a time when Mother said those words. Her expectations were always so great, yet I wished to meet them, if only to feel validated in my dedication to their faith that I would be successful one day. The pressure I dealt with growing up doubled when I left Yeluthia, then it steadily decreased during my time here.*

In the end, her hard work paid off, and her parents recognized it.

"I must admit, I had my doubts about sending you to Asteom," Nullan added to counter her previous thought. "You were young and had potential to follow in my footsteps."

"Instead, she forged the position for the next ambassadors," Elenor pointed out while glancing at her husband. "Everything fell into place, and now we can look forward to the future together."

Nullan nodded before addressing Grace. "When will you be returning to Yeluthia?"

She tiled her head with a slight smile. "Actually, I would like to stay in Asteom. I plan to-"

"Stay? Why do they still need you with the alliance in place?" her mother interrupted.

"I act as a representative when King Arval is not present, especially in the city."

Elenor eyed her curiously. "Yes, I suppose. I would think someone else could fill the role."

"For the time being, I am the primary contact, and changing that so suddenly would cause confusion."

For the first time that evening, both her parents frowned, causing Grace to grow warm. In actuality, no one had spoken with her about having somebody else become the ambassador for Yeluthia because of the other projects in place. She never considered an alternative due to her love for the humans, specifically her friends and the master mages. Lastly, she had no idea what she would do otherwise if she didn't live in the palace.

"We may need to have a word with His Highness about this," her mother muttered to catch her attention again.

Grace attempted a reassuring smile. "Please, that is not necessary. I really am content with my life. Everything I mentioned earlier is true."

"You do not need to settle for this position," Nullan added and crossed his arms. "What did we always teach you about reaching higher? My brother should know better than to restrict your growth."

Before Grace could reply, her mother scoffed. "Not to mention your suitors…"

"My what?" she asked quietly when the room fell silent.

Elenor placed the back of her hand on her forehead in a dramatic fashion. "It was supposed to be a surprise, but I guess I spoiled the news."

The smiles returned once the two looked at Grace.

"We narrowed down the selection for your suitor."

"But why-"

"Of course, the list was already long due to our connection to the royal family," her mother continued, as if she didn't hear her daughter. "Only a full-blooded Yeluthian in good standing with the king will do. More people became interested once they heard of your work in Asteom, and we had trouble choosing the best options."

She laughed at that, and Nullan joined in while visibly relaxing. Meanwhile, Grace's mind went blank.

"I can tell you are concerned, but do not fret," her father added. "We will discuss the matter with His Highness so you should not need to stay here to act as the ambassador. This may not happen for three or four years because of the recent developments you mentioned, but once that is arranged, you can return home to us and begin a new role in the kingdom."

As the two explored the idea in their usual, sophisticated manner, Grace stopped listening to assess her own feelings on the matter. She expected she would be sliding into the life they mentioned by marrying for status and filling a position in politics to please her parents; however, that had been when she lived in Yeluthia. Now, she tasted freedom and developed meaningful relationships in Asteom. She felt valued by her friends and many others in the capital because of her involvement in various projects, leading her to reach a decision.

With this in mind, she cleared her throat. "Thank you, but I would prefer to remain in my current position here."

The resulting pause that stretched for a few seconds became deafening. Then, her mother chuckled.

"Grace, I understand you are concerned, but please trust us. Your father should be able to relieve you of your position; you do not need to worry about getting in trouble or being forced to stay here as the ambassador."

"I know no one is keeping me in Asteom, but I enjoy working with the kingdom's leaders, and my friends-"

"What are you talking about?" Elenor interjected again, though this time with a hint of bitterness mixed into her confusion. "There are plenty of opportunities in Yeluthia. Why are you so fixated on staying?"

Grace opened her mouth to finish her explanation when her father picked up where his wife left off.

"We fought to have you sent here to grow your potential and open more doors back home. The humans warred with each other mere years ago. Did you forget that? You were kidnapped and then dragged into *their* conflict!"

"Father, I agreed to help them."

"Because of the alliance, no doubt. They seem to be taking advantage of you."

"No!" Grace cried before shaking her head. The last thing she ever intended was to spark an argument with her parents, yet she didn't understand their narrowmindedness.

I am happy in Verona with my friends. Why is that not good enough for them?

"Enough of this," Elenor said with a glare at both Grace and Nullan. "It is late, so I should like to retire for the evening. If you two wish to continue this discussion, please leave, but our decision is final."

The last words had been intended for Grace, who avoided the urge to drop her jaw in disbelief. When her father began rummaging through their belongings, she caught the dismissal and bid them a pleasant evening before trudging to her own quarters to process the news.

Overdue Lessons

Around mid-morning, Aaron, King Arval, the Yeluthian commanders, both master mages, and the recently appointed members of the council, including High Priest Jurek and the new generals named Terrell and Garvish, set off on a scheduled tour of the additions to the palace's south side.

Because of his familiarity with the MAA's grounds, Byron's input had been essential for the development of another training space, which would be utilized by the mages and Yeluthian soldiers. That area neared completion, save for the brick perimeter to mark its boundaries.

The beginning of a three-story structure loomed beside the open area. For the moment, it remained nameless, but the building would soon possess additional troops. This gave the Yeluthians privacy, as well as acted as extra housing for the soldiers and mages.

General Tont explained this while he led the party in that direction. "The architects tell me they expect construction to be complete by next summer, depending on the changing weather," he concluded with a sweep of his arm. "The first floor is already outlined, and the inside will be a reflection of the palace. We'll have staircases to the north and south, just as we discussed."

The Yeluthian king raised his hand to speak before asking a couple questions regarding the placement of its residents.

"For the most part, we want your people to feel welcome and included yet still able to avoid the burdens of living in the palace," Aaron added after General Tont finished answering. "Not only that, but this clearing provides the most open air space inside the city's limits."

"How considerate," King Arval commented with a smile before thanking the younger royal.

Byron noticed how pleased the Yeluthians appeared and figured he would appreciate being properly represented in Asteom if he were in their shoes. Furthermore, the current project would only expand in the future as the alliance strengthened.

Beads of sweat began showing up on their faces as the day went on, so they moved inside to the welcoming coolness of the meeting chamber. At noon, Byron, Emilea, and Commander Detrix were dismissed, and half a dozen well-known merchants and lords poured in for an afternoon discussion with the kings. The three chatted briefly before breaking apart for separate lunches. Byron requested a servant bring food to his room so he could read and ate in peace, then he napped until the sun dropped below the tree line. When he could tolerate the less humid air, he exited the palace to return to the new training ground.

His former student and most reliable assistant named Lydia waited at the farthest point of the clearing past the other mages scattered around the area. For a moment, the activity reminded him of his years at the academy, back when life seemed simpler. They greeted one another as he approached, then they dove into a discussion on sensing various levels of energy, an ability she had difficulty with. After, he drilled her on releasing elemental spells across various targets in the distance. He made sure to leave plenty of time before the sun set so she could ask questions and they could review her weekly assignments.

Lydia had been the first private student he took on as an instructor, though he did so because of her outgoing personality, which motivated her to try and hone new magical skills beyond her initial capabilities. That personality more than made up for her lack of a feminine figure or muscle, meaning she wasn't capable of much physically; however, from what he knew, no one had anything negative to say about her.

Although she had been a nearly perfect student showcasing an enthusiasm to learn, in the back of his mind Byron could never stop comparing her to Coura. This was due to the fact that Coura had originally been his choice for a successor until she lost her dark energy.

Even after all this time, the wound still pains me, he reflected while Lydia paused to drink from her waterskin. *Coura was always gifted at wielding both magic and a weapon. She's talented at assessing and following the flow of combat, as well as training others, which made her an ideal choice to take my place when I'm occupied with other business. I'm afraid poor Lydia will be in that shadow forever. She can listen, share input, and think critically when an issue arises, but her magical energy is far less than mine. I suppose I should just be grateful for the time we have to spend together and the independent work we started on ever since King Hernan reassigned me to Dala; otherwise, we would be making up those years of experience.*

The unmistakable sound of wooden weapons whacking together in a sparring session caught his attention, reminding him of the time. One pair usually worked in the new training ground during the busy dinner hour when the field grew empty, and they could only meet when King Arval and his company returned to Verona.

"Is there anything else you would like to go over today?" Byron asked his assistant with a tilt of his head.

Lydia's wavy, brunette hair swayed as she shook her head.

"Why don't we pick this up tomorrow then."

The nearby noise stopped abruptly, silencing the field.

"Are you planning on watching them again?" the young woman inquired before her lips curved upward into a knowing smile.

He crossed his arms and glanced over to where the combat started again. His eyes went straight to the familiar, female figure, who had her back to them. If Byron didn't recognize Coura already, he would have deduced it was her since she stood opposite her father, Commander Evern, who wore an emotionless expression.

The two readied their practice swords before diving into another fight. Coura took the offensive by lunging at the Yeluthian soldier from multiple directions as she circled around him. Meanwhile, the stationary commander blocked each attempt. After a minute, a swing at her left thigh connected, sending her stumbling backward to pause the session.

During the break, Byron turned to answer Lydia. "I think I'll stay for a bit."

"Then I would like to as well," she startled him by replying.

Although he wondered about her reasoning, he decided not to overstep his boundaries by prying. Together, they looked on as the combat began again; while they did so, his nerves and frustration steadily rose.

The previous year, Commander Evern assumed responsibility of Coura's training in weapons work and magic without consulting Byron, Emilea, or Marcus, who all assisted her in the past. This drove a rift between the master mages and Yeluthian for a time while Coura remained caught in the middle. Her former teachers not only felt hurt by her distancing them but also offended that her father believed his skills were the better option, despite her being raised as an ordinary human. Because of their familial relationship, though, Coura seemed obligated to participate; at least, that was Byron's explanation.

She never brought up the exercises, or resulting injuries, with him, so he tried to observe her progress when he and Lydia finished meeting. Over the past four evenings, nothing changed between lessons. First, Commander Evern had them spar, then he tested Coura's magic. From what he could tell, the session already wore on both participants' emotions.

He's expecting her to fight like a seasoned, Yeluthian soldier, Byron concluded after noticing how uncomfortable Coura's movements appeared.

Instead of striking with confidence, she would twist away when the commander blocked or switched to the offensive. This eliminated the need for what would normally be killing stabs or hindering wounds with metal blades, though it became apparent how much time it would take for her to perfect such actions.

"What are they doing? Is that the correct way to fight?" Lydia asked in a tone reflecting her confusion.

Byron scratched his chin and grunted as Evern struck Coura on the right side of her head, prompting another break for a lecture. "Technically speaking, there is no correct style for combat, just various options. Coura used to be my student, so she's accustomed to what I teach, which is to stay grounded in one area and aim to disable. Most soldiers prefer this approach since it allows a person to become familiar with the space available to them. My other philosophy involves targeting an opponent's limbs because most instances don't need to end with death.

From what I observed, the Yeluthians prefer a freer outlook with no mental limitations and sharp but less powerful motions. This allows them to weaken their opponent while adapting to the environment. They also aren't relying on the ground either."

Lydia remained silent, and the commander continued their session.

What Byron neglected to mention in his explanation was what Coura's past had done to her outlook on fighting. *The demon's energy residing within her for part of her life could heal any wound. Such an ability meant, as long as she could tolerate the pain, Coura had no reason not to welcome blows if doing so created an opportunity for a counterstrike. I'm sure she's having trouble adjusting to drawing out a match. Angels prefer to wear down their opponents, and that requires more patience than I think she will ever possess.*

As if to confirm his assessment, Evern retreated at a leisurely pace in order to lure Coura closer only for her to stay planted. When she refused to move, the Yeluthian shouted instructions with obvious displeasure. The following spar stretched longer than any of the others, but it soon became apparent Coura was reverting to her preferred method. The commander blocked or parried her lunges and swings with ease, yet she never backed off, even after Evern struck her in several spots on each limb.

"She's too impatient," Lydia commented from his side.

Byron glanced over to see her hands folded together in front of her mouth as her emerald eyes lingered on the two combatants. "That would fit Coura's character," he mumbled in response.

"How can she still be going after all that? I'm exhausted just watching them!"

He held his tongue after remembering what Coura had endured since living in Verona.

A few seconds later, the commander visibly lost his patience and swung horizontally to catch his daughter in the ribs. Byron winced when the wooden sword connected, and he heard Lydia's sharp gasp; however, Coura's blade pressed against the side of her father's throat at the same time, freezing the two in place.

"What just happened?" Lydia wondered aloud in a whisper.

Byron didn't notice until Evern's attack landed, but Coura had utilized her free hand in order to seize the weapon while simultaneously raising the other to corner her opponent and prevent him from retaliating. He shared this with his assistant as the commander collected the practice weapons, tossed them away, then began healing Coura's bruises and potentially broken ribs.

"That's an awful thing to do," Lydia muttered while crossing her arms. "Using serious attacks instead of addressing the issue. If she falls back into an old habit, he should stop to try again."

"It wouldn't have worked," Byron responded automatically. "Commander Evern's final actions were unnecessary, sure, but Coura consciously disobeyed what he instructed her to do. When the style didn't succeed, her next instinct was to adapt for success, which happened to lead her to what she grew up learning."

The empathetic, emerald eyes studied him with a bit of doubt. "You saw that all along?"

Byron's lips tugged into a smile. "Of course. Who better to understand how someone behaves in combat than the one who trained them."

Lydia hesitantly returned the gesture before mentioning dinner and excusing herself in favor of eating before the evening grew late. Already several, glimmering stars decorated the sky, yet Byron ignored his own hunger by mentally preparing for the magic to come.

While he waited, Coura's father strolled across the field, leaving her to stand alone and unarmed. If he couldn't catch the commander's frustrated expression earlier, it became unmistakable from this new distance. His insides twisted at that because the elemental spells used during the previous sessions left much more than bruises.

After the mess with Hendal and the demon had been cleaned up and some sort of normality returned to the capital, Commander Evern and Emilea each insisted on assessing the newly discovered, Yeluthian energy within Coura. The latter expressed her amazement that any power could become active after being sealed for the majority of an individual's life and offered instruction and guidance for the transition.

On the other hand, the reveal of her goddess gift, a rare ability even among the Yeluthians, shocked everyone. She explained why she dismissed it as another, foreign spell and demonstrated how it created portals between two locations in front of a select few who would be able to keep it secret for the time being. As impressive as it was, Byron and those present sensed the trepidation behind her casting, reminding them of the event that nearly took her life.

He hadn't heard of her using the goddess gift again.

Emilea also shared how Coura quit their lessons once Evern began training her. If she practiced between the sessions Byron observed, it didn't show.

The commander started by launching a blast of fire in her direction, prompting Coura to throw both hands up, as was standard for a shielding response, and craft a spell resembling a circular wall of glass. It appeared thin and shattered noiselessly when the flames connected with its surface, then the pieces floated to the ground where they faded away.

Evern repeated this tactic twice with the same result. By that point, the commander began shouting incoherent instructions, telling her to keep the spell steady instead of releasing it so often and that she needed to create a sturdier structure. Meanwhile, Byron bit the inside of his cheek until it bled as he seethed at the Yeluthian's incomprehension.

Doesn't he understand? Coura isn't abandoning the shield or crafting it so frail on purpose. Unlike with her combat skills, she doesn't fully understand what she's doing or how to change the release of energy. If she worked with Emilea longer, she would know dark and light magical energies are manipulated in opposite ways to cast spells.

My magic, and the way Coura learned, is based on shaping dark energy into the desired spell before it's released, meaning the output can't be altered once it's let loose. On the other hand, light magic is cast outright and adjusted while it's still tied to the mage after the energy is released. I'm assuming the Yeluthians don't understand how dark magic operates. That's the only excuse for an experienced wielder like Evern to be acting so crudely about this, unless he believes her incompetence is intentional.

When Coura failed to accomplish what her father asked a fourth time, he decided to switch tactics. Instead of fire, he launched three, dagger-like ice shards consecutively with a couple seconds between each. This meant they would reach their target over a duration of time unless her shield stayed up. Byron hadn't seen this during their previous sessions and could witness the event play out about as he expected.

Coura summoned the glittering shield once more to block the first icicle, but the spell collapsed immediately after contact. As if expecting the remaining projectiles, she managed to evade the second by pivoting to the left and attempted to do the same for the third. Unfortunately, either her timing was off or the glistening remains of the light energy clouded her sight, for the final shard struck true. It sank into the upper left portion of her chest, just below the shoulder, bringing Coura to her knees as she gripped the icicle.

Byron found himself too stunned by the commander's attack to react right away. His control slipped at some point during the next minute or so when Evern merely explained what he needed from her once more. Before he realized it, Byron's feet drove him in that direction.

"Commander," he nearly growled as the Yeluthian turned to face him.

"Good evening, Master Byron. I thought I spotted you nearby. Is there an issue?"

Any trace of the unforgiving teacher had been replaced by a polite, if not slightly concerned, soldier. The abrupt change in behavior caused Byron to hesitate before he could blow up at the commander in Coura's defense.

"I've been observing you two when I get the chance," he began, yet he fumbled for the best approach to help the situation. The main problem seemed to be that Evern always behaved respectfully after their initial meeting, holding Byron in high regard and acting as equals. Even as their eyes met, the Yeluthian's reflected sincerity in every word, movement, and look.

If I were to foolishly insult his skills or knowledge, he might consider it a challenge. Coura chose to do this, so I need to avoid sounding too opposing.

Before he could form the thought into an appropriate comment, the commander flashed him a genuinely pleased smile.

"I am honored to know you are interested in our training," Evern started. "It would be beneficial to hear a master mage's impression. Although, I suppose there might be a limit to what you can sense, considering you possess dark energy."

"Actually, I'm…"

"Just a moment." The Yeluthian glanced over his shoulder to where his daughter stood alone. "Coura, come over here."

"That's not necessary," Byron interjected. "I really needed to speak with you about these lessons." He shared his conclusions in a passive manner in order to convey the truth without stepping on the other's toes; however, he soon realized how little the commander accepted as advice.

"Your insight is as invaluable as always," Evern responded with a chuckle. "I believe you know my daughter's abilities better than I do. If you feel comfortable, it would benefit her to hear your take on light magic and how she can learn to wield it without considering the dark energy she used before. Once she understands, she should show more promise as a mage."

Byron repressed a groan but nodded. It dawned on him that perhaps he needed to speak with Coura first about what she wanted to do instead of indirectly influencing Commander Evern's approach to teaching her.

As he contemplated this, she appeared at her father's side with a hand on the bloody portion of her chest.

"Master Byron was kind enough to watch our lesson and has some thoughts to offer," the Yeluthian explained. "I suggest you listen and prepare for tomorrow. Until then, you are dismissed for the evening. Go see the medical station for your injury once you finish here."

He faced Byron again and flashed another, friendly smile when she didn't respond.

"Now, if you will excuse me, I am late for my king's dinner."

As Evern strolled across the field to enter the palace, Byron was reminded of his own hunger and sighed.

"Why don't we get you looked at," he began only to find Coura glaring at him.

"What are you doing here?"

She bit off the question in a voice tight with repressed vexation. Byron's experience with that temper prepared him for the imminent outburst.

"Lydia and I were training nearby, and I happened to notice you two."

"You had no reason to interrupt!" she yelled while pointing a finger at him, causing fresh blood to drip down from the wound.

"If I didn't, he might have continued in that misguided way. Hopefully, some of what I said might resonate with him, especially since he isn't familiar with your past training."

Coura pursed her lips and somehow managed to narrow her eyes even more. "I never asked for your help. This is between Evern and I."

Byron opened his mouth to argue, to remind her no one should expect a productive turn around for their physical or magical skills within a few months, yet she cut him off.

"Don't you think I know what he's doing? I understand what needs to happen in order for me to become like one of his soldiers. At least I'm trying."

"That's fine for the combat, but what about your light magic? Why not go to Emilea for assistance?"

"There's a lot you don't see; being able to train me makes him happy. I can handle getting beaten around until my magic falls into place. No one else needs to waste their time on me."

Byron frowned at her final remark. "The only person who sounds compelled to draw this out is you. If your father isn't the best teacher, you should seek someone who can lead you in the right direction, or at least prepare you for his tests. You're insulting Emilea and her underlings by assuming they have better things to do than what is a part of their responsibilities. I also suggest you inquire about a Yeluthian soldier stationed here who can work with you on their fighting techniques. At least then you'll learn how to defend and attack against the commander's movements if it isn't a style you can master."

When Coura didn't offer a rebuttal, he couldn't refrain from crossing his arms with a prideful expression. Her temper faltered until she spun around to trudge toward the palace.

"Go be nosy somewhere else," he heard her mutter as she did so.

Only when she slipped inside did his heart soften and stomach start to rumble. Byron tried to comprehend why she acted so stubborn about the new direction of her training, yet he couldn't come up with a clear answer.

Regrettably, he could do nothing more than influence her direction; the final choices Coura made were her decision, and had always been hers alone.

***

Most of the regular attendants in the medical station became familiar with Coura because of her frequent visits over the previous months. They initially grew concerned and inquired about the training sessions, including the participants and her personal feelings regarding them. She soon realized they might be afraid someone targeted her, so she explained how she worked with a Yeluthian commander and their relationship. Those who heard spread the news before her next appearance because no one brought it up again.

She entered the station without drawing attention to herself and sat on the edge of the nearest, empty cot. One light mage named Hannah always seemed to be on duty and usually tended to her when she entered the station. Within seconds, the healer came to her side.

Hannah proved to be younger than Coura by at least a couple years, for she once mentioned she was still in her second year of service according to the Mage Service Law. Her dazzling, gray eyes scanned the bloody mess, though without any indication of worry.

"Would you like numbing medication?" she asked.

Coura shook her head before shifting to lie on her back, turn her head in the opposite direction, and gaze out the window. A second later, the healer's hands gently touched the open wound.

"The icicle hasn't fully melted, so I need to remove it in order to continue."

"Go ahead."

A warmth of fresh blood trickling down her shoulder followed the inevitable sting, then a wave of soothing magic diluted the pain.

While she worked, Hannah attempted to converse. "If this happens again, you should have someone send for a healer instead of moving around. Not only can excessive movement tear the muscles and tissues even more, but you tracked blood in all the way from the training ground."

Coura had shut her mind away after leaving Byron alone, so the comment surprised her. After glancing toward the door and spotting a servant on his hands and knees wiping at the scarlet liquid, she felt a twinge of guilt.

"Maybe I should just send for you before the lesson begins," she mumbled and returned to staring at the night sky.

Whether she intended for the comment to be serious or sarcastic, she didn't know, but Hannah took it as the latter.

"If I were there, I'd be attempting to prevent an injury like this. Although, I must admit the burns from last time gave me some valuable experience."

A comfortable silence stretched between them for a while. When she didn't feel any more pain, Coura realized how hungry and tired she'd grown. Given the hour, it would be far too late to meet the rest of the guests in the private dining hall, not that she intended to attend with Byron and her father present.

"Do I need to stay overnight?" she asked when the hands lifted from her torso.

"I would recommend it as a precaution, but you never care about that," Hannah answered with a helpless smile.

Coura returned it before nodding. "Thank you, again."

The light mage pulled a rag out of her pocket and began to wipe the blood from her hands as she continued. "If you really appreciate it, you should talk to your teacher about limiting the amount of visits."

Coura sat up, inspected the clean skin beneath the punctured clothing, and promised to try.

Instead of moving to her room for the evening after changing clothes and grabbing dinner in the mess hall, she decided a walk through the queen's garden might provide a more suitable setting for contemplating the past couple days. The lack of people in the regularly populated area surprised her given the desirably warm weather, but she took advantage of it by finding her preferred seat located on the northern end, which happened to be one of the sights she admired during her first, unexpected journey into the space.

The stone bench she occupied had been positioned in front of the statue of an angel, and water flowed from the tilted pitcher in the figure's hand to pool at its feet. The other arm raised to showcase a sword, emphasizing its proud stance. She would often relax in its presence, letting the trickling sound lull her into a sense of peace; however, nothing quelled the emotions stirring within as Coura rested both elbows on her knees and dropped her chin into her hands.

I don't know what to do, she admitted to no one in particular after some time passed. *Byron's right about Evern's training, yet whenever either of them suggests I use my Yeluthian energy, I want to abandon the subject. I'm not meant to be a light mage. I was never supposed to be any better than an ordinary soldier after I lost the demonic power, and I can't even do that right!*

Although her father and former teachers hinted at studying Yeluthian combat, they never spoke outright about what she had been doing for a portion of her life.

What I remember most are the moments when I was in danger. The demon, or at least part of it, had always been present, and I relied on its energy, along with that experience, to survive. I don't think Evern has ever needed to worry about being too weak to win. How can he expect me to change when he doesn't understand that? Can I even adjust to match his soldiers? It's been months since I flew anything other than a leisurely route, so I suppose I need to worry about my skills in the air soon too.

She turned her face upward, as if scanning the twinkling stars far above for answers. Her concerns lingered until a pair of footsteps swept close enough to alert her of company.

Coura craned her head around and recognized Aaron approaching. He still wore his formal attire from dinner, including the crown nearly as golden as his hair, and he held a mug in each hand.

"I hoped to surprise you," he commented with a disappointed frown before halting behind the bench. "May I join you?"

She slid to the left and gestured to the available space in confirmation. In response, he handed Coura one of the drinks and sat beside her to sip at his own cup. A taste revealed it to be a sweet wine usually served during dessert at the private dinners.

"I considered bringing the whole bottle, but it would look pretty suspicious if someone notices their king sneaking away like that," he shared and observed the fountain.

She followed his gaze and agreed. "I take it you couldn't wait to escape the dining hall."

"It's less entertaining without certain people."

For a moment, Coura's heart fluttered at his reply before she reigned in the stray emotions, as she always had. "You miss him that much?"

Aaron's eyes shifted to her while his expression reflected his confusion. "Who?"

"Marcus. Unless you mean Will, but I didn't know if you heard he planned on leaving too."

"I wasn't talking about either of them."

The only sound between them for a few minutes consisted of the natural, nighttime insects and running water. When she finished her drink, Coura contemplated returning to her quarters but couldn't muster a need to go elsewhere. The idea of being alone with her thoughts troubled her, especially after two days of stolen sleep from nightmares. A part of her felt she should make conversation, yet the quiet mood held a calm air about it. When Aaron's next question came out of the silence, she wondered if the relaxed sensation had been one-sided.

"Can I ask you something?"

"What is it?"

"What's bothering you?"

Coura turned to stare at the king, prompting him to do the same so their eyes could meet.

"What do you mean?" she asked, even though his words were clear. He even narrowed his eyes a bit at her hesitation.

"I pay more attention to the gossip than you realize, more so within my council than anywhere else."

"You mean through Byron and Emilea," she added without hiding her annoyance.

"I can also sense it as your friend," he threw in to ease her negativity. "Do you not trust me?"

She shook her head before releasing a sigh in resignation. "I do, but…I'm embarrassed to burden you with my problems. They're nothing serious."

"How can I judge that if you won't share them with me?"

After a few seconds, Coura caved into his request and dove into the laundry list of issues involving her lack of restful sleep, Evern's training, Byron's meddling, and her fears about the future as a half-Yeluthian citizen of Asteom. She spoke through the rising dryness of her throat and hardly looked at Aaron the entire time; however, the inner tension began to ease once she finally confessed her problems aloud.

"I don't know what I'm supposed to be doing," she concluded, bringing her doubts full circle.

Aaron stared down into his empty mug for so long she worried he fell asleep.

At last, he sat straighter to stretch his back and chuckled. "I really should've grabbed more wine. Then again, I prepared for less."

"I'm sorry."

"Don't be," he interrupted before she could berate herself.

The royal figure next to her paused to slide closer, pluck her cup away, and set them both to the side.

"Listening is one of my strong suits after all the years I spent being patient with others. Do you remember when we spoke for the first time after returning from Dala?"

Coura prepared to rack her brain for the moment until she caught the pain behind his sapphire eyes and immediately recalled how she comforted him in the garden after his parents' deaths.

"When I felt afraid of the world, I longed to reverse what took place and return to what I grew up with," he went on, as if sensing her understanding. "I desired the stable life where I didn't carry the responsibilities of a king and where Mother and Father were there when I needed them. I couldn't focus on what to do next, yet you showed up and forced me to see the world as it was. You told me wishing for the past is useless, but accepting it helps us grow. When life changes, we adapt to move forward."

"Byron once told me that," Coura admitted.

"Then, he was right. Change is unavoidable. We'll have our ups and downs throughout our lives, so the best way to cope with the difficulties is to accept what's new before figuring out how to keep going."

She pondered his advice and found her spirits rising. *I became so preoccupied with what I lost that I couldn't see what's right in front of me. My family is alive and here in the palace, I have friends to rely on, Asteom and Yeluthia reestablished their alliance, and, most importantly, the demon is sealed away. My body and soul are my own again. Although I only possess light energy now, I suppose putting in an effort to learn how to wield it can help adjust my mind to the changes. At least I won't be sent to the medical station for a lecture from Hannah or another healer as often.*

"Thank you," Coura said aloud while meeting Aaron's eyes again to emphasize her sincerity.

He offered a pleased smile, reached over to place a hand on top of hers, and squeezed it gently. "Technically speaking, those were your words to me. Or rather, Byron's."

"Well, I appreciate you coming here to repeat them," she replied with a grin.

As they stared at one another, Coura wondered what compelled him to seek her out in the garden in the first place. It was no secret he'd been going out of his way to be with her lately, whether through his own actions or by enlisting someone's, usually Marcus', assistance. Whenever they could be together, she enjoyed their conversations. Based on his behavior and expressions, Aaron seemed to feel the same; however, he had no reason to show her special treatment or lead her to believe their relationship could develop beyond two friends.

Still, she wondered.

"Are you planning on staying here all night?" he asked suddenly while removing his hand.

Coura shook her head before a yawn crept up on her, reminding them of how late the evening had grown. Part of her longed to return to the warmth and safety of the palace walls, yet the other, impulsive side knew their time alone was a prime opportunity to learn about his true feelings. A mixture of nerves and excitement invigorated her in response. Before she could shy away from them, she tentatively leaned closer, drawing her friend's full attention.

At his resulting, slightly startled gaze, she hesitated. Her eyes instinctively darted to his mouth before returning to the familiar eyes, and she kicked herself for making the attempt so obvious.

Despite her blush, he finished closing the space between them until he gently pressed his lips against hers, sending a jolt throughout her body. Coura closed her eyes to savor the intimate moment even after he rested a hand against her cheek.

They broke apart seconds later, leaving her heart pounding with a desire for more. Still, something about his resulting, innocent smile reminded her of his position, the late hour, and his previous support during her internal struggle and settled her emotions. She hopped to her feet and glanced at the stone walls nearby.

"Maybe we should head inside before we end up sleeping on the grass," she added as casually as she could manage.

"Sure."

Coura heard him stand and walk behind her as they moved to the entrance where his guards waited. Then, he wished her a pleasant evening. Only before they parted did she muster the courage to face Aaron again. He smiled, bowed a bit, and went on his way, yet she caught a new light shining in his eyes. To her, that restrained joy was a welcome surprise.

***

Once King Arval settled into his quarters located between Isan and Detrix's rooms on the top floor of the palace, Evern dragged himself to the room he and Paulina shared, entered, and found his wife in bed with candles lit on both end tables. On either side of her sat Odell and Jackie, and all three appeared deeply invested in their books until he cleared his throat.

"Children," he began, causing all three to look up with tired expressions. "I hope you are not comfortable."

At that, his youngest daughter opened her mouth wide to yawn as his son rubbed his eyes with the back of one hand. Both seemed to slump into their mother, and, as he expected, Paulina draped an arm around each of them in a nestling embrace. Evern knew it would be useless to try and rouse the trio then, so he shrugged off his concerns from the day to settle into bed next to Jackie.

For a while, he took pleasure in that moment of peace.

His wife was the one to shake them awake before ordering the children to their own beds in the next room over. Odell, being the more responsible of the two, took his sister's hand and one of the candles and left without a word.

"They are too old to be sleeping with us," Evern commented as he readjusted himself and blew out the remaining flame. Once comfortably on his side, he wrapped both arms around his wife and pulled her in close.

"You will miss it when they become independent," Paulina said before pressing her lips to his.

"I will, however, always appreciate when we are alone," he responded at a lower volume and squeezed her waist, savoring the warmth she provided.

This caused her to giggle before she changed the subject. "How was dinner?"

"The same as usual. I would rather not have to go every evening, but it is only for a few days at a time anyway."

"You know I would go if I could."

He did, yet her reasoning did not end at spending time with him. His wife had grown fond of the palace and its master mages, who were becoming close friends of theirs. Evern felt an especially close bond with Master Byron after their shared experiences and the man's paternal relationship with Coura. Unfortunately, the private dinners proved to be for show, not so much for socializing, so anyone not deemed important or decorated enough to sit in both kings' presence was excluded from the event.

"What's wrong?" Paulina inquired during the pause.

He realized how tense his body became when he considered the extravagant dinner, including the lack of his daughter whose appearance never seemed consistent.

"Coura," he started while repressing a groan. "I hoped to speak with her at dinner, but she did not show up."

"What do you need to talk to her about?"

Evern felt uncertain about revealing the results of the day's training session, especially because Paulina disliked the people she cared about getting hurt, but he caved in when she continued to wait for an answer. He shared the issues with their daughter's abilities, both relating to combat and magic, and ultimately confessed what he bottled up until that point.

"At this rate, she is going to be living here instead of joining us in Yeluthia. Without the proper skills to become a soldier, Isan and Detrix will not welcome her into their companies, and I would hate to single her out for her weaknesses in mine. She might never be free of the past, of what she lived through in Asteom."

An unreadable silence filled the space. Evern feared his wife drifted to sleep during that time, but her voice appeared with as much reassurance as the sunrise on a clear morning.

"I worry too. All I desire is to keep our family together, even if she struggles. If Coura is safe, and those nightmares from when we were absent do not haunt her, then I see no reason for her to not be welcome in Yeluthia. She is already a citizen by King Arval's decree."

"What then?" he nearly interrupted. "I doubt she would want anything less than to be useful. What kind of life can she lead without that opportunity?"

Again, his wife didn't respond right away.

"I am not sure," she admitted. "I think you should discuss this with her. See what it is she wants to do and how you can assist her. Perhaps take some time off from the training sessions too."

"I suppose I could try that."

"Go into the city, or fly to somewhere secluded where you two can talk in private. She might experience less pressure once it is only you listening."

Evern considered this. Against his better judgement about waiting for flight once her wings lost their dark color and she learned proper combat skills, he decided it might relax his daughter more than anything else. He vowed he would make an effort to reach her through a different tactic tomorrow afternoon.

For the moment, he returned to hugging Paulina as a means of showing his gratitude for her wisdom.

A New Threat

The morning following her impromptu meeting with Aaron, Coura was shocked to find she slept until well after the sun rose and hurried to get dressed so she could grab a late breakfast. No training sessions took place that day, which meant the area would be mostly unoccupied as the soldiers and mages favored going into town or spending some time on their own indoors. In preparation for her father's lesson, she intended to practice without the burden of onlookers.

If I'm going to change my technique, I need as little distractions as possible so I can focus on what Evern is looking for, she told herself while procuring a wooden sword and arranging a practice dummy constructed from straw.

The warm-up motions became routine, and by the early afternoon, she fell into a steady rhythm of movements targeting limbs to mimic the angels' fighting style, or at least what she could understand from observing them.

After a break to bathe and change clothes before lunch, Coura decided to use the newer training ground to experiment with her magic. Handfuls of mages also roamed the area in pairs or trios all around, but she found an empty spot and began to attempt casting a consistent shielding spell. For some reason, the energy she poured into the structure refused to shape the way she imagined, then it would disappear when she manifested a partial wall of energy instead of remaining in place.

I'm doing a step wrong, she admitted at last while glancing at her palms. *The magic is unstable on its own. I need to keep it tethered to me or else it breaks apart. It's not a matter of how much energy I pour into it, but how it's controlled. Does that mean...*

"I thought I would find you here already, though our training is not for another couple hours or so."

Coura spun around upon hearing her father's voice and saw Evern standing nearby with his arms crossed in a casual manner. "How long have you been there?"

"Only a minute or so," he answered in an amused tone, which sounded like the complete opposite of their previous interactions. "I did not wish to interrupt, but it appears you are still having difficulty with your light magic manifesting a spell. Perhaps I did not notice it before, but you have had no direction with it, correct?"

Although the truth stung her pride, Coura nodded, then she raised an eyebrow. It took her a moment to realize why his behavior seemed so odd; he acted as a separate person from the Yeluthian commander, as the father figure she had sometimes caught glimpses of over the weeks when he visited Asteom. His carefree chuckle while he closed the distance between them confirmed he arrived with a less intense mentality.

"I had a talk with your mother last night," he continued while placing a hand on her shoulder and looking toward the empty clearing beyond that side of the palace. "I often forget you are not one of my troops, pushing me to berate you for not understanding the concepts that came naturally to me and others raised to wield light magic. We should explore a new approach to your problem, or possibly speak with a human mage, but those options can wait. For now, a scouting trip might help us both loosen up."

"You want us to fly?"

Evern tilted his head at her. "Is there something wrong with that?"

Coura shook her head as a wave of excitement washed over her. "No, it's just... Never mind."

"Then let us be off."

He stepped away from her before calling forth his snowy wings without any hint of hesitation. On the backs of the flying Yeluthians' clothing, two slits had been designed for the purpose of saving the pieces of fabric from being shredded by the energy during their spell. In the past, Coura avoided this problem by slashing through her training shirts, though at one point, she learned the magic would pierce through cloth anyway.

She recalled this as she summoned the Yeluthian power in her center, called it forth, and felt the familiar weight settle on her shoulder blades. Her father's eyes darted from the wings and back to her face in such a way that she knew their appearance still bothered him.

"We are going to monitor the treetops of the forest to the south. By the time that is complete, it should be just before dark."

He said no more and began to jog away, allowing his wings to extend in preparation for the leap into the air. Coura watched him steadily climb higher until the urge to join compelled her to do the same. Soon, the two were soaring with Verona at their backs.

*

While Coura swept above the clouds and dove into the cooling pleasure of water droplets clinging to her exposed skin and hair, her father kept to a steady line below her. She didn't care, though, since her entire body filled with a rush of delight that had her feeling like a child.

Whenever she attempted to discuss aerial combat training, Evern dismissed the idea until she completed her maneuvering on the ground, leaving her to settle for the casual flights. Aaron nor the council restricted the Yeluthians from flying, so many showed off their skills during the day to the awestruck citizens below. She only did so outside Verona where no one could see. This protected her from the wandering eyes of potentially dangerous individuals, as well as a pit of doubt haunting her damaged soul.

Both her inner voice and the Mintelian man at the Harvest Festival who gifted her with her most cherished possession warned of the impact of willingly playing host for a demon. Even if she could return to her soul space, which evaded her during the various attempts at meditation, she feared she would find it in a worse condition than before.

Coura shut her eyes before inhaling the crisp, thin air in order to take her mind off such negative thoughts. Then, she swooped down next to her father until they found a matching pace. When he glanced over, she found him beaming with what she believed to be a similar sense of elation. They turned their attention to the woods below consisting of multiple shades of greens breaking for grassy fields, open clearings, rivers sparkling in the sunlight, and the occasional lake every so often.

During that time, she didn't expect to land until they returned to the palace. In fact, she began to assume her father fully intended their time together to be nothing more than a bonding experience; however, Evern spotted something worth investigating and snapped his wings open to halt, forcing Coura to do the same a moment later.

"What's wrong?" she yelled over the beating of their wings.

His eyes scanned the area of trees the pair most recently passed before he waved for them to descend, against her wishes. Since the canopy possessed no opening straight to the ground, she watched as her father pulled his wings in and dropped feet-first below the uppermost leaves in a rehearsed manner. Her fingers and feather tips twitched after remembering the list of injuries she experienced when she last plummeted through branches, so she waited until shouting from below forced her to brave the meticulous landing.

Once she slipped under the first layer of leaves and twigs, Coura understood why Evern chose to enter at that particular spot. Thick branches jutted from all directions as she climbed toward the ground, yet her wings had enough room from above to remain partially open, preventing her from losing her balance and falling. She pressed them against her body until her feet touched one of the stable branches. Then, she released the manifestation spell and steadied herself.

By that point, Evern called to her from where he waited at the bottom.

"Coming!" she responded as she descended. Within the next minute, she jumped off the final branch onto the bright green grass.

Where the two entered appeared to be an uninhabited part of the forest containing no paths or any indication of human interference. Coura remained attentive despite the sense of normality and warily approached where her father knelt next to a sapling.

"What is it?"

He let out a low hum and remained frozen in place to study a patch of exposed dirt for long enough to worry her. Finally, he sighed, returned to his feet, and let his eyes wander over their location.

"I noticed a pair of shadows moving under the trees, but whatever it was left no sign of their presence."

"Wouldn't an animal create a trail to use for tracking?"

"Yes, my thoughts exactly. I saw familiar prints, and the birds fled because of us, but two shapes as wide as a horse caught my eye. A creature that size would not be able to move with haste in these woods without an open path."

Coura fidgeted once he finished his explanation. Because the two chose to depart from the training ground without a serious intent to scout for trouble, they didn't adequately prepare themselves for a fight. The two would be at the mercy of an attacker, and an escape could be hazardous given their current location.

Still, her sense of responsibility as a soldier urged her to confirm if a threat lurked around without anyone's knowledge. Even a clue or sighting would benefit the nearby towns and connecting roads while providing a reason to investigate further, depending on the danger.

"Why don't we split up and search the area?" she suggested when Evern appeared uncertain about their next steps. "I trust your sight. Also, I'd bet you'll feel bothered later for not trying now, even if we aren't able to find anything."

He took a moment to consider this. "The shadows moved south, so we can hike in that direction until we find an opening to return to the air. The day has grown late already, and I would hate to be here when no sunlight remains."

Coura agreed to his decision and monitored their left side as they moved through the brush, believing in her father's intuition.

Evern seemed to relax once the pair reached a wider break in the trees after what felt like hours of exploring the woods. They soon heard an active river to the right above the sounds of birds, insects, and other wildlife, and she stared up at a patch of sky peeking beyond the canopy and reflecting the sunset's vibrant colors.

Once her father concluded his final examination of the space, he mirrored her upward glance. "I suppose this is as open a space to take off in as we will get. You go first."

He stepped away to provide more room for her to manifest her wings, which she did on instinct, and promised to follow once she rose above the canopy. The ebony feathers bristled with anticipation as she extended her wings, crouched in preparation for a leap, and plotted where she needed to go and how to manage her body to successfully reach the spacious air.

As she stayed in that position, Coura realized the forest fell silent, except for the running water. She released the spell on her wings in order to spin around and scan the trees for the source of such an immediate lack of noise. Her father also noticed the unnatural hush since his eyes darted to where hers didn't look.

"Go," he ordered in a controlled voice. "Get to the sky."

Whether Coura intended to leave him alone or not didn't matter, for a rumble of growls surrounded them before she could respond. Evern hurried to her side in a heartbeat, seized her arm, and pulled her behind him before raising his hands in preparation for a shielding spell as the creatures emerged.

Three feline-like animals possessing all too familiar features that gave away their identity crept forward from the brush. The slimy looking, dark fur and violet eyes were straight out of a nightmare, one Coura had lived through more often than she cared to remember.

Demonic creatures…

"Get away from here," her father instructed while crafting a golden wall around them, stopping the three from coming closer.

"I'm not abandoning you," she started, though she projected bravery she wasn't certain she could maintain.

"This is not the time to argue. When I have the opportunity, I will leave too. You are vulnerable to-"

A bright blast slammed against his shield, producing a boom that sent the creatures crying with unmistakable bloodlust.

"What was that?" Coura asked before another, unknown force connected with the shield.

Instead of answering, Evern looked up, returned his gaze forward, and addressed her using his usual, commanding tone. "I need you to trust me. These beasts will not break through my spell, and neither will whatever is behind them. I am going to remove most of the shield in order to protect the front so you can escape."

Another blast smashed into the magical wall, and they could spot tiny flames fading into the grass.

There must be a mage behind this, she thought against the stubbornness. *I'm useless without a weapon and am only going to distract Father from fleeing, or fighting. For some reason, something doesn't seem right about this.*

Against her doubt, Coura backed away from Evern, manifested her wings, and prepared to leap into the air once again. Instead of assessing her direction, she would need to scramble through the mass of leaves and wood without getting caught in the thicket or hit by the stranger's spell.

"Ready!" she announced before holding her breath.

Her father removed the shield, just as he explained, while shouting for her to go.

Without considering the creatures or their potential master farther behind, she jumped and pumped her wings to get past the bottom branches. The orange and gray sky above remained her focal point until a force struck her left wing. Based on the burning sensation, Coura assumed the mage had circled around to the opposite side of the shield and aimed a fire spell at her.

She opened her mouth to warn Evern while pushing her wings through the pain in order to continue her escape; however, a shadow from below grabbed her ankles and dropped down, pulling her along as its weight brought them to the ground with more force than she expected.

Wings, arms, and legs all connected with several branches during the fall, but one hit to her head had her seeing stars before the pain could register.

*

Based on the demonic creatures' scuffling and growling nearby, Coura believed not that much time had passed since she lost consciousness. The left side of her head throbbed when she woke to find her body being dragged through the dirt by one arm. Without considering who her attempted kidnapper might be, she grunted and tried to free herself.

"Awake already?" came a baritone voice before the hold on her wrist released.

She rolled onto her stomach and pushed herself to her hands and knees while struggling to breathe.

How badly did I fall? she wondered as she evaluated her situation. *Where's Evern? Is he still dealing with those creatures? If I can run, I might be able to locate another opening. Will he realize where I am? Did he see I didn't break through to the sky?*

"Who are you?" she asked to stall for time.

Just to be safe, she released the spell on her wings to make it easier to flee; however, when the stranger turned around and Coura's breath caught, she knew there would be no way to outrun him.

The pair of intelligent, violet eyes confirmed his identity more than the fur-like patches covering all except his pale arms, face, and neck. Although his abnormally tall, burly body could be mistaken as human, two, spiked horns no longer than her fingers poked upward from behind his ears, and many of the front teeth had been filed into a sharp grin, distinguishing him from anybody else in Asteom.

"You're a demon," she mumbled as her voice withered away at the sight. Both body and mind went numb then.

"How perceptive," the dark figure responded in a condescending manner before offering a mock bow. "You're a smart human. Why don't we get started."

Coura stared helplessly as a black sword, the same sort *she* used to wield, appeared in his hand by magic.

Run! she screamed at herself while her mind began working again.

Unfortunately, her body trembled and refused to cooperate, and she sensed the energy in her center buzzing like a hive of bees. When the demon approached to stand over her, she managed to raise her arms in a feeble attempt for protection. He seized her wrist again before yanking her upward to eye level.

"Come on. Stand up!" he barked and kicked her shin.

Coura found her footing before she he released her and managed to not fall over. Still, she looked at him fearfully and without comprehension. This irritated the creature, who growled like an animal in response.

"Do it!" he yelled and plunged his blade into the ground. "Call upon your sword!"

"Why? I can't..."

The demon hissed. "I want a fight."

In the background, they could hear Evern's voice. Despite the unclear words and distance between them, his concern came across clearly.

I need to stall for time. That's my only option if I don't intend to die.

"Who are you?" Coura asked a second time in an attempt to stand her ground.

He retrieved the sword and stalked forward, causing her to step away. "I came here to challenge you, human. Are you not the one who assisted Soirée in claiming this country as her territory? Do you not share her power even as she rots in the demonic realm?"

Coura's legs froze. "Soirée? Territory? What are you talking about?"

"I really hate questions."

The creature lunged to shove her onto her backside and poised his sword at the side of her throat but did not strike. Coura swore his expression radiated disappointment as he towered over her.

"Your pathetic face says it all," he continued with less enthusiasm. "Finding you here was plain luck, though I would hate to discard such an interesting toy of Soirée's. My name is Terran. I suppose you could say Soirée and I competed for this land decades ago when we climbed to the surface together. She always won, so eventually I left to wander in the mountains and the desert beyond until a mutual acquaintance of ours filled me in on the fun that took place. I suppose now that she's sealed away, I am the only demon left to rule you humans."

The blade at her throat pressed harder, piercing though the uppermost layer of skin, yet Coura ignored the trickle of blood. What he revealed threw her mind into disarray.

"What do you want with me?" she continued as the once-lost memories of her first interaction with Soirée came to mind.

His following, sadistic smile sent a shiver throughout her body.

"While Soirée became entertained by exploiting manipulation, I enjoy earning my throne by slashing down those who oppose me. Since you belong to her, I thought you would be a sort of last line of defense, someone I can use to rightfully claim this country. Begrudgingly, I must admit I grew overzealous when I sensed her energy, but my rival did have her talents when it came to enacting her pets. That's why I'm going to leave you with that gift instead of killing you right away. Just make sure to remember my mercy the next time we meet."

At first, Coura had no idea what to think. The demon's unexpected appearance, threats, then information giving made him unpredictable.

That realization should have prepared her for what happened next. His sword raised and lowered in a long slice across her left shoulder before disappearing into the air. She cried out in shock and pain while placing a hand over the wound as it bled profusely.

"That was for wasting my time," the creature said to dismiss their conversation.

Coura stared at the injury until he spoke, yet when she glanced up, he had vanished.

*

It took a while for Evern to find her hunched forward and hugging the wound. The words he spoke as he knelt beside her, noticed the blood, and began healing were nothing but mumbles in her broken state of mind. The safe, stable life she promised herself had been thrown into chaos in a matter of minutes; the world of peace was disrupted by another demon, one who recognized her past with Soirée.

I haven't heard or thought about her name in months, yet that creature…Terran, he knew…

"Coura, answer me," her father ordered and shook her shoulders aggressively enough to rouse her out of her isolated mentality. "What happened? Who did this to you?"

As he brushed aside the locks of hair that slid over her face, she raised her wide eyes to meet his. "You…didn't see him?"

He frowned and resumed the healing spell on her head. "I noticed someone attack you from behind, but that is all. After eliminating the three creatures, I hurried to you as soon as I could. Tell me, what did they want from us?"

Not us…

The memory caused her entire body to tremble, which increased her heartbeat and, for some reason, reminded her of the restless, Yeluthian energy lashing out from her center.

"I did not notice any sort of venom on your skin," Evern went on, oblivious to her emotional state.

That was when she decided he needed to hear about her interaction with the demon, if only so he would take her condition seriously. Coura tried to be brief with her explanation, yet not much sunlight remained once her father pulled her to her feet after he completed the healing. Her body could move without much pain, but he never entirely fixed her injuries or paid attention to the bruises and lesser cuts during their lessons.

Instead of wasting the time, he paced around her while studying the forest and treetops in silence. She knew this meant he was contemplating their situation and safety alone, at night, and with a potential threat lurking in the woods.

"We need to return to the palace," he stated and halted before hesitantly selecting a direction. "Normally, I am against the idea of taking a blind leap into the air, but I cannot tell where we planned to exit earlier. Are you still able to summon your wings?"

Coura didn't reply and continued hugging herself in an attempt to ease the shaking.

"Can you fly?" he asked again, letting his frustration seep into the question.

Even so, she didn't feel certain about traversing through the branches without proper lighting. Their situation would become much worse if one of them got hurt during the attempt.

With that notion in mind, she decided to reach into the pool of light energy resting in her center and summon the spell she hadn't cast since Soirée's defeat. The power jumped as soon as she provided a destination and gave permission for it to act, then she raised a hand to create a glimmering portal. The image the spell reflected showcased little visually considering the hour, but Coura trusted it to be the training ground they departed from earlier in the day.

"You go first," she ordered without bothering to look at her father since his stillness revealed his surprise.

He approached cautiously yet stepped through without issue, leaving her to do the same immediately after. It amazed her how the effects were not as harsh as they had been during her first couple passings, even though she hadn't used her goddess gift in years.

Evern kept on his feet and showed no signs of disorientation as they stood side by side in the open space. Plenty of lamps outlined the fortified, stone structure nearby to confirm their new location. As she dismissed the portal, a phantom fist punched her in the gut to remind her of the toll such a power took on her center.

"Who goes there?" someone shouted from closer to the palace. A group of soldiers audibly drew their weapons before stalking toward the pair.

While Coura repressed her discomfort in order to walk toward the lights, her father jogged ahead to meet the guards. The exchange sounded like nothing more than introductions, then he returned to her, took her by the arm, and led her inside.

Neither spoke until they reached the medical station. Then, Evern requested a potion to calm her mind or stop her trembling. One glance at Coura's bloodied hands and chest beneath the ripped shirt had them fussing over her until her father repeated himself a bit forcefully. This prompted a woman to hand him two bottles and start explaining their doses, yet he interrupted to thank them for their time before guiding Coura into the hallway.

The two proceeded to climb the flights of stairs and cross the building to her room while ignoring various, alarmed stares and murmurs echoing after them. Only when they stepped inside did he release his grip, pass along the vials of medicine, and physically force her to sit on the bed.

"Drink them," he instructed while standing by the door.

Already, she figured his mind wandered elsewhere and it would be a waste of time and effort to pester him about revealing his thoughts. The first potion she opened consisted of a concoction she recognized from many sleepless nights, but the second tasted unfamiliar and bitter. Once she emptied the bottles and set them on her nightstand, Evern moved to leave.

"What are you going to do?" she inquired before he turned the doorknob.

"I will alert my king of what you told me, as well as the demonic creatures' presence in that section of the forest."

"And then what?"

He stared at her from over his shoulder with none of the fondness from when they first met nor the euphoria during their flight together. The Yeluthian in front of her returned to his position, the commanding, authoritative person she came to regularly interact with.

"You should stay in here until I send someone for you, or visit myself. Leave this information to me; do not speak a word of it to anyone."

The sleeping potion started to tire her senses, or else she would have protested. Evern accepted that as the end of their conversation.

***

What happened to Coura troubled Evern for multiple reasons, yet showing his daughter his weakness would only make her hysterical. He could see the negative emotions reflected in her eyes and knew from experience how leaving them unchecked would come back to bite him. For the moment, keeping her out of the picture would be better.

Since the evening meal took place around that hour, he figured King Arval should be in the dining hall guarded by Isan and Detrix. All three surely noticed his absence, which in turn would lead them to be cautious. He entered the private space while servants slipped around him to exit with platters and plates in hand. The scent of fresh food taunted the hunger pang in his stomach, yet the alarm and shock from earlier still suppressed his appetite.

Isan spotted Evern approaching first and adjusted his position to stand between the newcomer and their king. Detrix did the same while enjoying a glass of wine.

"Your poor daughter," the latter mused into his cup with a sly look. "You run her into the ground before dinner every afternoon. It is no wonder why she rarely shows up to spend time with you afterward."

"I need to speak with His Highness," Evern informed the two without hinting at the issue.

Still, they caught the urgency he projected and stepped aside.

King Arval appeared to be engaged in a discussion with the human king, so Evern gently laid a hand on his superior's shoulder to wordlessly announce his presence. Without drawing attention to the group, he leaned in close to speak quietly enough not to be overheard.

"I discovered danger to the south, Your Highness, and I wish to share this news with you as soon as possible."

The Yeluthian king dipped his chin in confirmation before continuing to converse, as if nothing changed. Only when their current topic concluded did he excuse himself for the evening and retreat to his quarters. Evern, Isan, and Detrix trailed behind and only spoke openly once they were together in private.

"King Aaron finally shared his father's implementation of mages around Asteom," their ruler began as he sat on the edge of his bed. "I found this information useful, though I will now need to bring the subject up again."

"Forgive me," Evern responded as he stood between his fellow commanders. Without further prompting, he revealed his scouting report, beginning from when he spotted the demonic creatures below the canopy. He never omitted the details of his work considering that would be a betrayal of the trio's trust with each other and their leader, so he only concluded after he described his unexpected, unconventional return using Coura's goddess gift.

"You are saying your daughter interacted with this demon?" Isan asked without attempting to hide his suspicion.

"Where is she now?" Detrix continued once Evern nodded.

"I escorted her to her room and made sure she drank a sleeping potion."

"So, she will be out of the way tonight," their king finished. He remained silent until that point, yet his commanders could tell the event bothered him.

Isan spit out a curse in frustration while Detrix paced near the door. None of them expected another demon to challenge the humans so soon.

"Commander Evern, did you sense these creatures before diving to the ground and searching the forest?" King Arval startled him by asking.

"I did not pick up on demonic energy, even when the creatures attacked."

An uncomfortable pause followed his response, and his king refused to remove his eyes from a particular section of the stone wall.

"Are you sure Coura was telling the truth?"

Evern felt a rush of anger at the unexpected doubt. Not only were his words being called into question but his daughter's account as well. "Is the blood on my hands not proof enough?"

"Do not misunderstand me," King Arval added and finally adjusted his gaze to meet Evern's eyes. "I believe in your abilities more than the memory of a scared, injured young woman. I trust in your senses. Why were you not able to feel a demon's power if it used magic? Why did it leave without killing either of you?"

Isan spoke before anyone else. "If what it said is true and it only sought your daughter to confirm the previous demon's sealing, it left her alive because of her connection to their kind. How do we know it is not manipulating her?"

"You can ask Coura tomorrow," Evern countered.

Isan narrowed his eyes but didn't offer a rebuttal. Thankfully, Detrix stepped in to ease the tension with his trademark, lax behavior.

"Your Highness, we were already suspicious of activity to the south. How can we overlook their encounter with that in mind?"

"You are right," their king responded and sat a bit straighter. "Our scouts have been investigating strange sightings of the creatures, but no one reported any attacks or deaths until now, and the reason being that Coura was present. I would like to continue to keep this between our kind so as not to worry the humans."

"Your Highness," Evern started; however, his king waved a hand to cut him off.

"Enough. Without reliable evidence to support the demon's appearance, I order this to remain a private matter. We will continue to send scouts on patrol throughout the day and night, and I will alert King Aaron of my decision. If no one reports another incident, we can assume the demon and its creatures are hiding. The best course of action is to find and eliminate them without drawing the humans into our conflict."

"Allow me to take the lead in the search," Evern proposed.

"No. Your daughter's involvement concerns me as well. Besides, your family lives in Yeluthia. Commander Detrix, you will head this mission. I want you to remain here until I am assured the creatures are no more. Commanders Evern and Isan will return with me to Yeluthia, along with those not staying under your orders. We will take the time to organize troops to join you before my next visit. Is that clear?"

The three voiced their confirmation in unison while placing two fingers on their brow in a salute. Isan hurried out of the room with an unreadable expression as Detrix bowed, promised their king a draft of the soldiers he would station in Asteom, and left. Evern turned to take his leave when he heard King Arval speak again.

"I expect you to keep a closer eye on your daughter in the future. Not merely because of her history, but also because her life may be at risk if the demon spoke true."

He swallowed and found his throat dry. "I understand, Your Highness."

That evening, Evern shared what little he could with Paulina about their departure the following day. No clear regulations had been established for the Yeluthians who would be leaving Verona, but because of his experience, he didn't plan on taking any chances by leaving them alone at any time during their travels.

As always, his wife listened patiently and agreed, though with some disappointment. She asked about Coura after in an attempt to change subjects, and he reassured her he would speak with their daughter in the morning. Although he intended to remind Coura she could join them, he had an inkling she would remain behind.

*

The morning following King Arval's meeting, Paulina offered to inform Jackie and Odell of their departure and help them prepare for the unexpected return while he would approach their eldest child. Both foresaw conflict, especially since Evern had more to explain, yet he already understood Coura's persistence.

Because of this, he wasn't as surprised as Paulina to see their daughter when she knocked and entered their quarters. Already, her expression displayed her annoyance, and she emphasized the emotion by crossing her arms and taking a firm stance.

"I need to talk to you," she told Evern.

"Coura, we have to tell you something too," Paulina began with a reassuring smile.

Evern let his wife share their intentions to depart for Yeluthia with those not assigned to stay on duty as soon as they packed and ate. Coura's seriousness softened when her mother approached to hold her hands.

"You are always welcome to join us. It is not that far of a flight, and you could come and go as you please. Your father will be doing the same under King Arval's orders."

"Mother," Coura replied after a melancholy sigh. "Perhaps in the future I can visit more often so you don't need to make the journey to Verona, but my life is here."

Evern noticed his wife squeeze the hands in hers before dropping them. "I understand. As long as I can see you enough to know you are doing well, I am content. Now then, I must get your brother and sister up and ready to go. Take care of yourself."

Paulina wrapped her arms around Coura in a tender embrace, kissed her daughter's cheek, and left Evern alone to finish the rest of the explanation.

"She speaks the truth," he added. "You are an honorary citizen of Yeluthia, which means you will be welcome should you wish to make it your home."

"I know that," Coura responded while watching the door. Her previous vexation returned when she faced him again. "What did King Arval say about yesterday?"

Repeating his king's orders would cause her to lash out against him; however, it went against his nature to lie, especially to someone he considered a fellow soldier with the same enemy. So, he summarized the conversation and waited for the explosion.

"What do you mean we can't tell anyone about it?" she demanded in reference to the demon.

"It is as I explained. King Arval desires peace for Asteom and its people. If anyone finds out about the creature aside from us, there could be panic. Not only does information get twisted over many tellings, but a negative reaction might encourage the demon to act. The best option is for our scouts to continue observing the forests around the country. With the extra support, other incidents, destruction, or damage to the people will shed light on the creature's intentions."

"What if it's planning on building its forces under the cover we provide? Did you forget how Soirée…I mean, the first demon hid in the palace with her pawns until they became fleshed out?"

"If all goes according to plan, we will be doing more within the next few weeks. Because we expect that, there is no need to raise an alarm for the creature or disturb the citizens of Asteom."

Coura frowned but must have caught on that arguing with him meant nothing as long as he obeyed his king. She crossed her arms again and leaned against the nearest wall where she rubbed the previously wounded shoulder.

"I suppose you're going to tell me I need to keep quiet."

Evern nodded. "I plan to escort your mother and siblings, along with the others who cannot fly, to Yeluthia. Commander Detrix and his chosen soldiers will remain behind for the time being in order to investigate."

"Are you going to order me to stay away from them?"

"Not yet. They may request your help with identifying the demonic creatures. I might not be here to protect you again, so I just ask that you consider your actions carefully."

Her eyes steadily wandered around the room, hinting at more on his daughter's mind. Finally, when they returned to him, the corners of her lips lifted into a slight smile.

"I can do that," she answered, to his relief.

The two moved next door to join the rest of their family, and the group offered their parting wishes. Coura walked with them to the front of the palace where dozens of other Yeluthians waited and lingered until the departure began.

Ambush

General Casner stopped his troops on the seventh morning of their march. It took exactly one week to reach the designated area outside the northernmost town named Parnic at their pace and without any inclement weather to hinder their progress. The clearing was magnificent to behold as pine trees taller than the palace's highest floor surrounded all sides except the entrance. This left a wide hole in the canopy, so the troops could monitor the sky directly above them. Of course, the downside would be their vulnerability to rain, but based on what a man in town explained to the general, the summer proved to be dry so far and would remain that way for the rest of the year.

Will made sure to document this, like he did with just about every piece of information Marcus shared with him, while they strolled beside the soldiers and mages chosen to explore the area. From years of reading and reorganizing records in the library, he learned there were few accounts of the northern woods due to the dangers of the terrain, as well as the ongoing suspicion of the Nim-Valans. That, coupled with how he remained in the palace for years longer than he ever intended to, led him to seek out General Casner and request an opportunity to research in the field.

When Marcus inevitably inquired about what could be studied on the border, Will shared all of this with his friend.

"It's rather ridiculous, in my opinion," he concluded. "For years, people lived in stations around here or in Parnic, and no one ever bothered to keep a journal of their observations, except in a military report. I already picked up several species of plants I want to sample on the way home, along with documenting the weather patterns from General Casner."

"Are you going to document what happens with Nim-Vala too?" Marcus asked while the pair stopped near the dirt path so his horse could nibble on a patch of dry grass. He chose to travel beside Will on foot during the end of their expedition instead because of the leisurely pace, reassuring, natural sounds within the woods, and to avoid the many, scattered rocks occupying half the path.

"That's one of the main reasons I'm here, you know."

His friend frowned but didn't ask any other questions. It became apparent he still felt bitter about Will's addition to what he deemed a dangerous assignment.

I already told him I'll be guarding the camp and what mages stay there. The Nim-Valans would be committing treason by crossing the border without permission. Besides, I'm more worried about him and the others willingly going to join the fighting on their side.

On the route back to the camp, the assistant general moved to the front and dismissed the party once they returned. By that time, the evening meals were already being prepared over several open fires. The lack of any potentially threatening weather and the seclusion of the clearing made Will feel safe as he slid next to Clara and Jean in the grass. Although, the one downside became a lack of extra breathing room.

Considering the hundred or so men and women sharing sleeping spaces, their bodies lined up in assigned positions meant to fit everyone together without them rolling on top of each other. The first night, he grew cramped and confined, but after the second, he appreciated the lack of concern about a threat creeping from the shadows, as he sometimes used to when traveling alone.

Early on the third morning of the troops' arrival, Will rose before most of the other people and decided to scribble notes on the fungi and fauna hiding around the nearby trees. The guards on watch during that time nodded to him, as if giving their permission, so he tried to keep within their line of sight; however, they rotated shifts at some point, for when he glanced over again, two, new soldiers stood at attention with weary eyes. Neither paid him any attention while he slipped under a chosen branch to document an unusual species of mushroom underneath.

That was when he caught them conversing at a hushed volume.

"Did Jeremiah mention if the scouts from last night returned yet?" the first asked.

"Not that I heard," the second replied in a gruff manner.

A pause followed the response.

"They should be here by now," the first man added without concealing his concern.

"So, they're running a little late. No need to get upset over it. I'm sure we'll catch them on their way in."

"What if we don't? What if a part of the plan went wrong? They left to meet the Nim-Valan general for-"

The dismissive guard must have nudged the first since Will heard a light clang of armor before the duo fell silent.

"Listen, I don't need to know what you're thinking," the second practically growled as the sounds of people stirring alerted them of the awakening camp. "The general already said we'd be packing up and heading home if an unexpected issue arises. I'm sure he already has an idea of what to do, so quit panicking and keep an eye out."

After a grunt in confirmation from the first guard, Will composed himself, finished his notes, and returned to his bedroll. He managed not to hint at the possible trouble, though Clara commented on his lack of enthusiasm throughout the day, and heard no more from any of the other soldiers, including Marcus.

As nighttime approached and everyone prepared to sleep, the camp remained in place without showing any signs of a retreat.

*

Despite what he overheard, Will tried not to let his distress slip into his words or expression when speaking with Marcus during the next three days. His friend seemed preoccupied when they had time to chat between their individual assignments, making him wonder if the missing soldiers occupied the assistant general's mind too. Everyone assumed the troops would keep to the camp while waiting for the Nim-Valan general, who explained how he planned to cross the border to meet with General Casner in a previous letter.

The entire situation seemed odd and unorganized to Will, though somehow Clara became his saving grace throughout the assignment. When he ventured from the site, she appeared at his side with an eagerness to explore the surrounding area. She listened to his explanations more attentively than anyone else he knew and asked questions selflessly. Many people in the camp, particularly the soldiers, either saw no use for his studies or expected him to perform miracles with the discoveries. In reality, the findings sounded lackluster, often consisting of taking samples, writing notes, or crudely drawing the observations.

Clara never minded, even going so far as to state her enjoyment of his passion for what others consider irrelevant to their positions. The two conversed during their walks and ate meals together while steadily growing closer until Will was startled to find her sleeping bundle next to his that evening. For the first time in his life, he didn't feel completely against the idea of having a partner.

The following morning, as Clara passed around their bowls of breakfast and Jean slipped over to sit beside Will, noise from across the camp caught their attention. The guards posted at the entrance drew their weapons when a man dressed in a muddy, black outfit similar to the soldiers' approached. Will and those around him remained seated but listened as the stranger began speaking. His voice sounded naturally deep and rough; that, mixed with his obvious lack of a fluent tongue in their language, gave the impression of a wild beast.

A handful of soldiers escorted him to the general's tent while the rest of the troops watched without voicing their curiosity until the figure disappeared inside.

"What do you think that was about?" Jean asked after the heavy silence.

Will shrugged. "My guess is the Nim-Valan general finally arrived."

"Are you sure? I didn't remember his hair being so dark."

"They all look the same to me," a mage from across their circle mumbled loudly enough for their entire group to hear.

A few grunts in agreement met his comment before everyone fell silent again.

The meeting between the Nim-Valan and General Casner lasted beyond breakfast, which added to the already inquisitive camp's suspicions. Will intended to return to a river farther south that he discovered at the end of his expedition the previous day; however, with his comrades on alert, he figured it would be safer where the rest of the troops remained. The general emerged from the centermost tent once he reached that conclusion.

"Gather around!"

At the order, the soldiers and mages scrambled to their feet and pressed together in front of General Casner, Marcus, and the stranger, who each wore a sour expression.

"Listen up," their leader began once the crowd quieted. "This is Ren, a Nim-Valan soldier second-in-command to General Harvey. As some of you may have noticed, the scouts sent ahead to monitor the border went missing after our arrival. Ren claims the barbarians we've been sent to deal with managed to assume control of the nearest fort and are preventing people on both sides from crossing."

A wave of murmurs erupted from the troops upon hearing the news.

"He was able to manage; we need to as well. General Harvey is requesting our assistance in freeing that fort in order to secure the border again. Soldiers and dark mages, prepare for combat. The light mages assigned to the field are coming too. Everyone else will stay behind under Assistant General Jeremiah's supervision until we're able to send a scout to report our advancement. Then, if the situation turns out the way we expect, we can begin the next phase by moving the camp into the base where Ren and General Harvey will be stationed. Does everyone understand?"

The following nods and salutes confirmed this.

"We'll head out after the noon meal. Consider our mission a necessity to protect Asteom, as well as contribute to the alliance with Nim-Vala."

With that, the general dismissed them, leaving the camp to buzz about the latest update. Will sensed excitement more than nerves throughout the group, which didn't shock him considering their pent-up energy after the journey.

"I can't wait to show them my magic," Jean commented in a wicked manner and rubbed his hands together. "They don't have it up here. I bet we'll be their prime source for entertainment!"

"You shouldn't say things like that," Clara scolded him with a frown.

Will voiced his agreement, yet the two became drowned out as the men and women around them discussed what was to come. Part of him found it odd to interact with the northerners who had been his enemies in the past. Still, he remained interested in their culture, especially as a member of the first generation to learn about their country.

No one sounded like this before, he realized while reflecting on the most recent conflict he had been involved with two years ago. *The inexperienced mages were overwhelmed physically and drained magically; however, after the battle, most took pride in their work. As much as I try to be indifferent toward my participation, I sometimes feel that way too.*

Every so often, he considered the fight against the demon-possessed Nim-Valans and how desperation and uncertainty nearly wore the Dalans away until the Yeluthians showed up. Using a weapon became so natural to him ever since then that he no longer shied away from harming another person in defense of himself or others. The sensation gave him an inner strength, as well as a sense of fulfillment in his own abilities, and he wondered if the same notion influenced those around him.

No one could take their mind off the news and orders, and eventually the cooks began serving the noon meal. Some didn't eat while most shoveled the food down in order to prepare for the upcoming trek into the northern country. Will was one of the last to finish and helped collect the dishes. Once the general shouted for those departing to line up, he looked on with mixed emotions. From near the back end of the camp, he caught Marcus rushing to issue commands and assist individuals with various tasks, such as strapping on armor or baggage.

Many found the assistant general's consideration for the men and women under his authority invaluable, or at least that was what Will heard through the cracks. Rarely did a general do more than necessary, which seemed to be expected in order for people not to rely too heavily on them. On the other hand, being personable and approachable assisted in developing trust between positions. It sounded like a tricky balance he became content observing from outside the army.

At the moment, he needed to see his friend off. Will hurried over to grab the assistant general by the arm before someone could catch his attention.

Marcus grew so focused on everything else that he stared at Will without comprehension until he scrunched his eyebrows together. "I thought you said you were assigned to the camp."

"I am," Will replied to defuse any suspicion. "Can't I say goodbye and wish you luck?"

Marcus' eyebrows rose to rest above where they normally sat to show his surprise. "Goodbye? We're going to be back here soon enough. This really shouldn't be dangerous, except if we face some untrained barbarians at the fort."

"Still, it feels like the right thing to say." Will rubbed the back of his neck in an awkward manner, causing his friend to laugh and place a hand on his shoulder.

"I appreciate it, but there's no need to be so concerned. The same rules apply out there as they do here. If there's a hint of trickery or lies from the Nim-Valans on our side, General Casner is going to return us across the border to guard it instead. He made as much clear to the soldier Ren."

That eased a part of the tension Will built up over the course of the morning. Marcus' hand dropped off his shoulder when those around them began moving with haste.

"Well, make sure not to trip on the rocks," was all Will could offer once his concern ebbed.

The assistant general grinned, rolled his eyes, and marched forward with the rest of the troops.

*

The remainder of the day and the morning following the soldiers' leave wound up being more exciting than before their departure. Aside from Will, five guards assumed shifts posted at the single opening while more rotated around the camp, allowing them to have eyes everywhere. According to Assistant General Jeremiah, who supervised for the moment, their presence kept the mages from misbehaving or acting out to harm his reputation. That indirect accusation struck a nerve with the twenty light mages left in the clearing, causing them to shun the soldiers, except for Will because of their familiarity with him. In retrospect, it was childish; however, it kept him going when the current leader forbade him from exiting the camp to pursue his research.

During lunchtime, Clara and two other female mages named Bryn and Zelma strolled by where he stood facing the trees, as he had been instructed to do.

"Is it time for a break yet?" Zelma asked, her lower-pitched voice filled with humor.

Will closed his eyes and dropped his head to feign sleeping at his post, prompting the three to giggle.

"Come on," Clara began. "You haven't eaten yet, right? We saved some leftovers for you."

"I should ask Jeremiah," he started once she looped her arm around his. Internally, he hardly cared about the man's permission, but he hated the idea of an extended shift due to what the assistant general deemed inadequate behavior.

Despite his half-hearted consideration, he found himself up against the three women who shoved him toward their circle of mages.

"Who cares what he thinks," Bryn chimed in as they let him sit.

Someone placed a bowl of the oatmeal-filled gruel in his hands, and the group chatted about various topics while he ate. At the meal's conclusion, their aforementioned supervisor stomped over, crossed his arms, and demanded they fetch water as something to do. No one argued, though many grumbled about the extra work, and everyone except Will moved to exit the clearing.

As expected, he received a lecture about his responsibilities as a guard on this assignment followed by the punishment of a double shift until dark. He spent that time organizing his thoughts for his journal and talking with Clara, who kept him company. The soldiers already adjusted to the evening watch resumed their duty soon after, leaving Will to rest in peace.

At least, that was what he expected until nudging from his right roused him.

"Are you awake?" came Clara's whispering. Her tone suggested nothing more than curiosity.

"I am now," he grumbled before yawning.

"Would you…like to go for a walk?"

"Right now? What time is it?"

"I don't know. The moon isn't out tonight."

Will repressed a sigh at the idea of rising from his comfortable position, yet Clara already got to her feet.

"Hurry and grab your cloak," she urged. "We can sneak under the brush near the general's tent."

"Why?" he wondered aloud; however, she tiptoed in that direction without responding, leaving him to reluctantly grab his glasses and follow.

The guards frequently circled the camp's perimeter while everyone slept, which meant the chance of the pair being caught remained high. Will kept this in mind as he crept nearer to Clara's silhouette in front of the rear line of trees. The insects' chirping concealed any noise from the two as they shuffled through the needle-covered branches and into the forest beyond.

Still, the light mage kept going without giving him an explanation for the sudden hike. It wasn't until he picked up on the sound of a nearby river that he learned they went south to a somewhat familiar area, though the figure in the lead halted before they saw the water.

"Do you think this is far enough?" she asked at a normal volume.

"Absolutely," Will muttered and rubbed his eyes. Some of his weariness wore away during the brief expedition, yet he believed it to be closer to evening than a new morning.

Clara giggled and hugged herself in a bashful manner. "I can relax now."

Why would she make an effort to ensure we aren't overheard? Will wondered before ignoring the urge to ask. He knew her well enough to predict she would willingly share the reason eventually, and in another moment, his patience was rewarded.

"I've been having difficulty falling asleep ever since we arrived here," she started with a serious expression. "This is the first time I left the capital ever since the original move from East Hoover, so I thought that might be why. I'm not so sure anymore."

"Why is that?"

Clara shook her head helplessly and stepped closer. "I don't know. Inside, I experience a suffocating sensation sometimes, like a new presence is hiding behind the trees surrounding the camp. I needed to go to a place where those invisible eyes wouldn't follow us."

Will felt himself sympathizing with her, compelling him to offer words of comfort. "It's scary being out in the open world like this. Inside the palace or another building, we'd have walls to keep the shadows out. Here, we become vulnerable, though we aren't alone. We all have each other to rely on, which is why it's important we stick together. Besides, if the situation goes according to plan, we're going to be living in the Nim-Valan fort soon enough."

His insight visibly calmed her. When he finished, she bit her lower lip, continued to hold herself, and lowered her gaze to stare at the ground.

"Would you…still stay by me? That is, when we move again…"

It took Will a moment to realize she referred to their sleeping bags. The idea amused him, and he chuckled until he noticed her body language reflected her embarrassment.

"That sounds fine with me."

At that, Clara glanced up with wide, emotion-filled eyes and threw her arms around him in an unexpected embrace. "Thank you!" she exclaimed with a smile.

Her appreciation took Will back, yet he returned the hug, savoring the developing connection between the two. For a while, he waited, selfishly not wanting to release her first.

Then, her body grew tense.

"It's back. There's…" Her words abruptly stopped as she pushed away from him to stand rigid.

"What's the matter?"

"That presence… It returned much more menacing than before! There has to be something causing it."

Clara darted away from the river, and he scrambled behind a few seconds later while calling out to her. Although he hadn't considered it when she initially explained the issue, a memory came to him involving demonic creatures after her final sentence.

What she's sensing is probably dark magic, but if we rush in, we'll lose the element of surprise. He reached for his sword and remembered he forgot to bring it, prompting him to swear through his teeth. *We don't even understand what it is, or if there is anything at all! I need to catch up before she passes through the trees and alerts the guards.*

A second later, a woman's shriek silenced the woods before the noise grew.

Both the screams and shouting, along with an eerie, red glow from above the treetops, told Will the camp was under attack. Whether they faced a demonic creature or not, the mages and soldiers could only hold off so much; he made it his first priority to observe the situation before joining in the fight.

Despite his best effort, Clara threw herself through the branches to enter the clearing. Will slid to a stop, observed the spot where she disappeared, then carefully slipped under the branches while attempting to stir them as little as possible.

The beginning of a massacre met him on the other side.

Based on what he could count from his hiding spot, fifteen bodies had been scattered on the ground, including the entrance's guards, who lied unmoving at their posts. The remaining soldiers and mages huddled in a circle at the center of the camp with magical shields forming a dome around them.

Their attackers frightened him the most. Unlike his expectations, they were not demonic creatures but men identical to the Nim-Valan soldier with long, unkempt hair and beards and the same type of uniform. A dozen surrounded the magical shield and took turns slamming at it with broadswords, shields, and maces. Will also noticed five others and one cloaked figure looming in front of the general's tent, which had been lit on fire.

From where he crouched behind a thin layer of foliage, the back of the tent stretched in front of him. Meanwhile, Clara crawled to hide there before poking her head around to look on. She glanced at him after, and her eyes reflected the gripping fear he felt.

We can't stay here, he realized, causing his heart to ache. *We would be no match for trained fighters, especially without a weapon. If either of us gets caught, we'll be killed too, so our best option is to wait for the strangers to lose interest and leave. Without magic, they won't be able to break the shield protecting the remaining mages. Clara should be able to confirm this, then we can see what to do.*

With something of a plan in mind, Will gestured for the light mage to return to his position only to find her shaking her head. He ground his teeth and tried again, but her attention became fixated on the tent. The pounding on the shield continued, accompanied by growls from the attackers in their own language, yet he was forced to watch Clara attempt to pull one of the stakes keeping the tent upright out of its position.

What is she doing? he asked himself with a mixture of frustration and confusion when it proved unsuccessful.

She turned and waved for him to join her.

This time, Will shook his head and repeated the question in his mind.

The stake came loose after another attempt. Clara set the wood down, lifted the bottom of the flap as far as it could go, and snuck under, to Will's disbelief.

Whatever she intended to do, he didn't expect her to actively close the distance between herself and the fighting, mainly because there would be no way to disable one of the bulky men without alerting the others. He waited until the cluster by the tent stepped forward to approach the dome and converse in their own tongue; only then did he shuffle to where Clara had been moments ago and copy her entrance under the fabric.

Once he could process his surroundings inside, Will understood why the light mage refused to flee. Bryn, Zelma, and two other young women huddled together in the farthest corner. They wore their loose clothes for sleeping, had messy, unbound hair, and held him with their wide, tear-filled eyes as he crawled over.

Before he could even prepare to discuss the situation, Clara leaned close to whisper in his ear.

"They don't know much. One of the guards screamed loud enough to wake most everyone when the Nim-Valans came. These four hurried here while everyone else was either killed or joined together for the shield, then they were surrounded."

This is bad, Will thought as all eyes continued to stare at him. He swallowed and found a lump in his throat. *This is really bad. The six of us in the tent can get away through the opening Clara made in the back, but we would be abandoning the others. None of the mages are experienced fighters, let alone possess the strength to take on a single one of those men, and my sword is out there in the open. Even if we could distract them, they outnumber those of us left from the camp.*

Ideas continued pouring forth without a plausible path for success. When a gruff voice spoke closer to their hiding position, he realized they needed to make a decision.

"There's nothing we can do to help," he whispered to Clara. "We should get them out and hide farther from the camp before the enemy finds us."

The light mage pulled away. Her horror-stricken expression told him she had not grasped the notion they would have to leave their comrades in order to survive.

Will took both her hands in his and met her eyes. *We need to go,* he tried to convey.

The petrified look melted into one of despair as tears fell silently from Clara's eyes, yet she pressed her lips together to keep from protesting.

The voice from outside spoke again, and a pair of silhouettes hovered in front of the entrance.

Again, Will leaned over to offer his friend instructions. "Lead these mages to the river through the back. I'll stay until they all escape and make sure we aren't followed. You should hurry."

She removed her hands, nodded, and gestured for the other girls to follow. At first, none of the four broke from their positions; however, once Clara ducked under the flap, they steadily snuck closer to do the same.

Meanwhile, Will felt around the unfamiliar area for an object that might act as a weapon should one of the strangers investigate their hiding spot. Many blankets, cushions, and clothes had been scattered in piles, and he discovered an extra set of boots, as well as a box of quill pens. Eventually, he settled on an unlit torch near the entrance. Once he procured it, he sat at the front where he could peek through the opening slit with his heart beating like a Sie-Kie musician's drum.

The hooded figure went up to the shield and spoke in a low voice while the men around him mumbled, to Will's frustration.

How can I figure out what they want if I don't understand what they're saying?

A sudden flash brightened the area for a heartbeat before fading, along with the mages' spell. After, a delayed shock struck him when he observed the glowing wall of magical energy crumble as horrified gasps and shrieks from the people behind it rose.

His remaining hope vanished once the barbarians could force their way into the previously protected circle at the center of the camp. Will jerked his head away from the scene, unable to handle the merciless slaughter; however, the cries of those he had shared meals with mere hours earlier rang in his ears, freezing him in place. No thoughts could form to free him from that immobility.

In the seconds of silence after the finishing strike, the two men standing just outside the tent shifted in place while holding their positions, forcing Will to consider his limited options. A startled, high-pitched squeak sounded from behind to remind him of the fleeing light mages.

He spun around while shifting into a crouch and found the rest of the space empty. Upon further inspection, one of the girl's ankles had gotten caught on a coil of rope at the rear side. Even as he moved to free her, a pair of deep voices from the opening told him the sound had not gone unnoticed by the enemy.

Against the screams replaying in his mind, Will abandoned his caution to hurry over, grab and unwind the rope from the mage, and shove her leg under in an attempt to warn the final escapee.

No matter what happens to me, I can't let them be followed!

At that moment, as the first of the strangers warily entered the tent, he acted purely on instinct.

The man spotted him charging forward, shouted an unintelligible warning, and drew a short sword as Will raised the blunt, unlit torch in his hands. He chanced a forceful swing, which connected with his opponent's left shoulder, then leapt backward.

The Nim-Valan was either well-protected or more muscular than he appeared, for the strike did nothing to hinder a diagonal slash. The blade grazed Will's wooden weapon when he held it up to defend himself, and the man repeated the move on the opposite side.

Because of his experience training under the palace's soldiers, Will became accustomed to finding an opponent's offensive pattern, adjusting to best protect his body, and retaliating by utilizing an opening. It didn't take long for him to figure out that the Nim-Valan was not an experienced swordsman based on the multiple opportunities to counterattack.

The sword fell again in the same, straight motion with plenty of weight behind it, so Will sidestepped to dodge and swung horizontally in order to catch the man across the skull. This caused the taller figure to drop with a loud thump. By that point, the next Nim-Valan entered, noticed his unconscious companion, and drew his sword while growling.

Will decided then that fighting would be too risky and waste his precious time. *Clara should have led the others far enough away by now. If I can break through the back of the tent and trees beyond, the enemy won't be able to pursue without fumbling to find our trail.*

The stranger stepped closer when the thought concluded. Will prepared for his next opponent to strike, yet the two stared each other down in the darkness, proving the man wouldn't be as reckless as the first. His hands gripped the impromptu weapon tighter while the additional enemies spoke nearby.

With nothing left to keep him in the tent, he raised his arms and threw the unlit torch at the figure's head. Whether the projectile landed or not, Will didn't see. He spun on his heel to sprint for the back, drop to the dirt, then crawl underneath the loose flap. Heavy footsteps sounded behind, but he scrambled to his feet before the man could capture him and dove face-first into the needles of the pine trees surrounding the clearing.

Move, body! I'll die if I don't keep going!

Many, veiled branches scratched his arms and cheeks while shouts from behind terrified him enough to not look back. Twice, he tripped and fell forcefully enough to rattle his teeth, yet he let his fear motivate him to rise.

By the time he heard the river, he had two distractions to worry about. Not only did the Nim-Valans' yelling and stomping come within earshot, but a slim silhouette off to his right caught his eye. Will recognized it as one of the light mages and changed direction.

She instantly shrieked while raising her arms in preparation for a spell until he verbally identified himself and slowed to a walk. Before she could respond, he took her hand, pulled her along, and followed the sound of the running water.

"We need to get to the river," he shared, both for her awareness and his need to focus.

The danger at their backs prevented him from concentrating on anything else, though the frantic beating of his heart threatened to suffocate him. Both became so prevalent, the pair nearly jogged straight into the river when its edge dipped sharply. Will dug his heels into the mud to stop before they could accidentally fall in.

"What do we do?" the panicked mage at his side asked with eyes fixated on the rushing water below.

He glanced ahead, then behind as several voices made his head spin. "We have to get across."

"What? We can't-"

"Can you swim?" Will interrupted. When the girl stared at him without comprehension, he clutched her shoulders and shook them a bit. "There's no other way to escape their pursuit. Clara was supposed to guide everyone else here, so I'd bet they went to the opposite shore. Can you swim?"

Her head bobbed up and down, though the uncertain expression she wore said otherwise.

By that point, Will saw the Nim-Valans charging with weapons poised. He wished to guide the mage across, yet both their lives would be at a greater risk the slower they moved. All he could do was remove his glasses, take a wild leap into the water, and aim for the direction he set as the opposite end of the river.

Several times, he lifted his head for air, though most of the attempts resulted in a mouthful of water; however, during those brief moments, the male voices grew fainter and another, feminine set could be heard. Will's body numbed and ached from the plunge to the point where he only knew he'd reached land when his arms and legs collided with the solid rocks and ground.

Someone took hold of his right arm then and hauled him onto the shore where he coughed until his lungs burned. After a few breaths, he realized someone called his name.

"Will! They're coming after you. We can't stop!"

The hands on his arm trembled while the individual brought him to his feet and shoved him onward. The sights blurred into nonsense, reminding him of the spectacles he still gripped, until the group slowed.

Again, whoever dragged his body out of the river addressed him.

Will lifted his head and blinked without listening. His limbs shivered, though he felt nothing. In another moment, he collapsed onto his hands and knees before passing out.

***

Given the terrain Marcus explored around their campsite during the previous days, he expected the journey to the border to take a physical toll on their company. There were points where the trail disappeared entirely or became blocked by boulders, forcing the general and Nim-Valan soldier accompanying the group to chart out the simplest path around the obstruction. The horses they brought along also acted fidgety because of the route and seemed to sense everyone's discomfort.

After three nights, Ren assured them their goal would be within sight, so they'd reach it soon. To Marcus, the stranger acted nothing like the Asteom scouts. He used short words in their language but often growled and mumbled in this own tongue to no one in particular. In addition to his secluded behavior, the man studied the horses with a hawk's eye. It gave Marcus an unpleasant impression, yet he restrained from mentioning this to General Casner, who kept the Nim-Valan glued to his side.

If the general was being cautious, nobody needed to raise the tension by sharing their negative feelings, and Marcus trusted their leader's ability to discern between a mission and a dangerous situation.

That morning, the troops were told the border lied directly ahead and the fort sat somewhere beyond within a day's march, meaning they would have to prepare to fight the barbarians holding it in their possession. When someone inquired about Ren's fellow soldiers, all the stranger could say were words like "join ahead" or "waiting."

That was where General Casner drew the line.

"I will not cross over into another country without meeting your captain," he stated with arms crossed at the front of their makeshift camp.

Marcus stood at his superior's side and nodded in agreement, to the Nim-Valan's confusion.

The man gave a lengthy response without any words they recognized before repeating "join ahead" several times with growing annoyance.

"He doesn't understand," Marcus grumbled and rubbed his nose.

General Casner placed a hand on his chest, then he gestured to the soldiers. "Waiting. Stay here. Reinforcements. Other Nim-Valans."

Evidently, some sort of message got across, for the soldier lifted his eyebrows and dipped his chin, though not without a hint of concern.

"Wait here," he answered.

"Yes," General Casner replied and nodded.

The Nim-Valan held his hands up in a gesture to enforce the message. "Wait here."

Everyone looked on as the man turned to jog away from the camp, across the border, and into the trees beyond.

"I guess he finally got the idea," Marcus added before the troops broke apart for a cold breakfast.

Later that morning, Ren returned with another one of his people, and General Casner addressed the former in a displeased manner.

"Who is this?"

The Nim-Valans conversed in their language for a minute, then the newcomer addressed him.

"I am not a soldier but a merchant." Each vowel sounded drawn out, as if he wasn't certain of the correct pronunciation. "I am here to make words clear."

General Casner let out a groan. "Tell Ren we will not cross the border without being accompanied by his comrades."

Another moment of silence stretched between them until the translator shared the general's message. The soldier's response went from a normal volume to shouting with wild gestures as the two seemed to begin arguing.

Marcus caught the newcomer's fearfulness of the burlier Nim-Valan when the latter appeared ready to bring the issue to blows, leading him to grab the hilt of his sword and unsheathe the blade a bit. "Enough."

The glint of metal caught both strangers' attention, and they stepped away from one another.

"He insists the troops are at the fort," the translator began with an uncomfortable glance at Ren. "They are fighting and need you to help."

General Casner raised a hand for him to be quiet before pondering their situation.

During that time, Marcus decided to share his opinion before a conclusion could be reached. "Sir, I'm not sure we should believe this man. I dislike the idea of going into Nim-Vala blind. Even if that is our assignment, we were told the negotiations would be finalized prior to any combat."

"I agree; however, this was part of the plan to begin with," his superior responded. "Our troops, especially the mages, should be enough to quell trouble in a fort, which means their people will experience what we can do. We also have to keep the camp in mind. If we return, our supplies won't last considering we're meant to join the Nim-Valans on their land. Perhaps we can learn more about their people once we settle there. Besides, now that we've got a person to translate decently, my hope is that communicating will flow smoother."

"Yes, General."

"Prepare everybody to move. Once we observe the layout or procure a map of some sort, I'll discuss a strategy with you. For now, keep these two in between us at the front."

*

After an uneventful trek, the Asteom soldiers reached their goal by mid-afternoon the following day. The trees steadily parted as they progressed north, revealing the fort atop a barren plateau. The snow-covered peaks of the mountains rose above an evergreen forest beyond.

To Marcus' dismay, they didn't have time to spare on admiring the magnificent sight. Many upturned patches of earth and puddles of a dark liquid reminded him of the aforementioned battle for the structure, and they heard further activity, even at a distance.

When they met that morning, General Casner offered a simple strategy, despite their disadvantage at the lower position. "From what we can get out of Ren, the Nim-Valans are already fighting inside. With that distraction, I'll lead the soldiers first. Mages, keep to the rear and be prepared to launch projectiles on my signal. Until then, keep the shields up, and stay alert."

Marcus replayed the orders in his head as he organized the dozens of bodies into six lines before remaining at the end. The two Nim-Valan men drifted over to stand on either side of him, so he mentally planned a defense should one or both turn against him.

The uphill march felt unnerving simply because nobody inside acted like they noticed the approach until General Casner reached the front gate. Only then did a horn sound from above the wooden barrier.

"Get ready!" Marcus heard someone shout, causing everyone to physically prepare themselves. At his left, he caught the empty-handed translator stepping backward with both hands on his cheeks, as if in distress.

Could the situation be worse than it appears? This man isn't a warrior like any of the Nim-Valans I've encountered thus far, so I'm sure he isn't experienced in battle. I wonder if this fort is his home.

A creak from the gate stole his attention again, and within a couple minutes, the entirety of the Asteom troops marched inside without conflict. The square they invaded proved to be empty, except for an attempt at a barricade farther down the road. Behind those overturned carts, crates, and other assorted items were pikes sticking nearly six feet into the air; impaled at the top appeared to be the heads of three, unfortunate Nim-Valans. Their long, raven hair covered most of the faces beneath, making it difficult to determine their identities.

However unnerving the sight, Marcus shouted to those around him to keep their composure. "The enemy may still be hiding, so don't let your guard down!"

Anyone who heard nodded, and the troops huddled closer together. From out of the corner of his eye, Marcus caught the Nim-Valan translator stepping away with the obvious intent to escape from the soldiers.

"Wait," he ordered and seized the man's wrist with his free hand. "If you run, it'll draw the enemy's attention."

Thankfully, the stranger remained both weak in strength and too afraid to move after Marcus took hold of his arm, though the assistant general longed to say more for reassurance.

"Barbarians, here," the translator choked out after.

"Stay by me so I can protect you," Marcus answered without hesitation before putting his back to the man. Of course, the chances of the Nim-Valan possessing a hidden blade or the intent to harm him lingered, yet a sudden clashing of weapons farther ahead indicated their enemy already sprang upon the troops.

The barbarians who appeared wore plain, charcoal-colored clothing and kept their hair in an unbound mess, as one would expect from the lowest class of citizens. Their maneuvering with a weapon also seemed wild, though the wide swings were backed by a power from their hidden muscles.

Despite the circumstances, the conflict took less than a few minutes to resolve. Marcus disarmed three opponents with ease, and the rebels were gathered in the center where the mages cast a shield to surround the enemy in order to prevent them from fleeing. No one had been killed since those who were hurt possessed wounds the light mages could easily heal.

While some of the troops collected the dull, discarded weapons, the remaining soldiers huddled together once more, and Marcus joined General Casner near the front to question the captives. Their translator had kept to his side throughout the fighting and voluntarily agreed to repeat the general's words to the Nim-Valans only for them to answer with silence. This left their situation at a standstill.

"What are we supposed to do now?" Marcus asked and gazed upward while putting a hand above his eyes. The sun prepared to drop below the tree line, though the summer weather would keep them all warm until they could figure out their sleeping arrangements.

General Casner turned to the translator. "Where can we keep the weapons out of reach?"

The man bit his lip while considering this. "Tools are stored at the rear end of the fort closest to the farms."

"Where can we lock these men away?"

This time, it took a few minutes for the Nim-Valan to speak again, and he glanced around in a nervous manner before doing so. "The soldier would know; the man who brought you here. I will not answer for him."

Marcus heard the general swear under his breath as he spun to look over those nearby. At the back of the group near where a set of soldiers watched the horses stood Ren.

"Bring him to me," General Casner said to Marcus.

"Yes, sir."

"We're going to move outside the fort until the soldiers we were promised show up. I expect to return to the camp across the border tomorrow since it seems we stopped the barbarians at this location. Without a clear Nim-Valan to follow, we're traveling in their land unsupervised, which makes it difficult to hold them to their word. As far as I'm concerned, we served our assignment for the time being."

Marcus held his own suspicion in check. "What about rations at the camp?"

"If we don't hear from someone in this country who's in charge, we return to the palace. I can count half a dozen reasons why we shouldn't remain here anyway."

The rest of the evening proved to be a strange but uneventful experience. No northern soldiers showed up, and Ren claimed they should be holding off the majority of the barbarians farther east. Even though the likelihood of a trained group of Nim-Valans leaving the fort unsupervised sounded impossible, the man assured General Casner of the fort's safety due to that fact. The captured enemy troops, which numbered a measly fifty or so men, were stuffed in the base's jail without resisting. By that point, many inhabitants revealed themselves. Heads of mostly women and children poked out from behind curtains and around corners to watch with expressions of either awe, relief, or fear, depending on what was being done in the square.

Marcus relaxed as the sun set, stars filled the sky, and food began being served. The Nim-Valans approached with their own offerings before retreating into their homes, but the gesture eased any thoughts of the people rising against them. Even the translator smiled as he informed them of the night watch's intentions to return to their positions. As far as Marcus could tell, the only person who still acted uncomfortable with the situation was Ren, who hid himself away among his people.

Marcus assigned the camp's own guards before falling asleep to the murmuring surrounding him. In the morning, they set out for the border once more. The people of the fort looked on, and some brought more offerings, yet no one directly spoke to them as they marched through the gate leading south. Ren and the translator stayed with the troops, and they reached the border later that afternoon before continuing for the next three days.

During the march, General Casner spoke with Marcus freely about the journey and the people of Nim-Vala, explaining his thought processes when the situation took a different turn. It sounded like useful information, so Marcus silently noted it. He often found the general's insight intriguing, and an open conversation left the pair in higher spirits until they recognized the familiar land.

In the distance, their scout returned sooner than expected, cried several warnings, then collapsed.

"Prepare yourselves!" General Casner shouted in response while he and Marcus drew their swords at the same time.

From the trees beyond emerged dozens of Nim-Valan soldiers similar in appearance to the barbarians except for their clothing, which reflected those worn by the men who visited Verona under General Harvey. That was all anyone needed to see to understand they were being ambushed, and on their own land.

It seemed too late to plan a defensive formation, but Marcus had faith in the experienced soldiers and mages as the enemy charged from every direction. He remained at the general's side to slash through bodies much wider in build than himself but lacking in proper form and the desire to survive.

The ambush became a blur when the northerners continued to target the front half of Asteom troops; however, the mages knew to protect their leaders, prompting them to cast shields preventing additional attacks from behind. Someone slashed for Marcus' legs, so he stabbed the stranger through the stomach and shoved the bleeding body away. Another warily approached only to catch a ball of fire from a mage behind Marcus.

Soon, shouting erupted until the Nim-Valans seemed to realize their numbers began dwindling, and they retreated into the trees. The dark magic wielders launched spells to stop many from escaping, but no one could count those who got away.

Marcus went straight to General Casner, who breathed heavily and wiped blood from his forehead.

"Those were Nim-Valan soldiers," his superior spat without repressing his anger before pointing his sword in the direction of their goal. "They were waiting for us."

Marcus felt his heart drop at the implications of the ambush. "If they hid here, what about the camp?"

General Casner's lips tightened into a line as he remained silent.

A mage approached to inspect their conditions, but Marcus turned away the assistance in favor of jogging to the rear where he knew the horses had been kept. Most of their soldiers sat or lied on the ground while waiting to be healed, slowing his pace. White robes fluttered against the gray backdrop, and soon he spotted a pair of men staring down at the limp body of a Nim-Valan when he reached the opposite side.

"Where is my horse?" Marcus demanded.

The two gestured to the enemy soldier, which proved to be Ren.

"He startled them into fleeing as soon as the ambush began," one explained. "We can search for them if you'd like, Assistant General."

Marcus internally cursed at their carelessness but dismissed the request with a wave. "I would never ask you to risk your lives with the enemy hiding out there just for a horse. Keep watch in case any return until we stabilize enough to move on."

The men nodded in confirmation before he returned to the general to report the news. General Casner listened intently before observing the remains of the fighting, rubbing his bearded chin, and contemplating their situation.

"You know what their presence here means, right?" the man asked at a lower volume.

Marcus nodded and remained silent.

"Their troops expected us to leave our vulnerable mages alone before striking in Asteom's territory, both at the camp and here. There's a likely chance they will attack again before we return to the palace. This is treason and cause for King Aaron to send soldiers to the border, but at the moment, we're in danger."

"What are your orders?" Marcus responded while his body grew tense.

"The afternoon is drawing near, so we should reach our original position within a couple hours, though I fear what we'll find. Once everyone is healed enough to move, I'll have you stay to the back with the light mages while I keep the soldiers up front and the dark mages in the middle. We can determine our next steps when we see the condition of the camp."

*

Although nothing supported the notion that the camp would be spared from the Nim-Valans, Marcus held onto a sliver of hope for those left behind. Unfortunately, even from a distance, the troops could spot thin tendrils of smoke rising and understood the scene would not be pleasant. They cautiously approached through the single entrance before stumbling into the charred remains of the entire area, including its inhabitants. The stench of burned bodies became too much for some people to handle, yet the implications of that smell threw most into emotional disarray.

Marcus felt nothing. His mind stayed focused on analyzing the outcome, and his body remained too stunned to react right away. This allowed him to search through the remains of sleeping bags, clothing, and tents with a handful of others who could tolerate the task.

For a while, General Casner stood alone near where his tent once sat until Marcus joined him to report his findings.

"Nothing of value has been left behind, including any weapons or armor. We collected the bodies in a pile so one of the light mages could offer a prayer over the pyre once you're ready."

"What are the numbers?" the general asked in an expressionless tone.

Marcus stared at the ground; thinking of the faces of those they left behind, including Will's, nearly caused him to choke up. "Around twenty found, though some are in rough shape. Hardly anyone has been identified."

"I see."

"Sir?"

This time, General Casner looked at Marcus. "What is it?"

"Five or six bodies are unaccounted for. If they managed to escape, shouldn't we send someone to search the area?"

"Are you absolutely certain they fled without pursuit?"

"No, but…"

"Then we would risk the lives of those still with us by sending individuals into the unknown woods," the general concluded. "Without knowing where the Nim-Valans who escaped us went or whether or not any of our people are still alive, it would do us no good to linger in this area. Aside from the danger, our rations here were reduced to ash. Our best chance for survival is to continue to Parnic, warn their people, and hurry to the palace."

"Why shouldn't we-"

"Do you disagree with your commanding officer?"

Despite his determination to avoid abandoning possible survivors, Marcus kicked himself for letting his emotions take hold. "No. It's just, I had a close friend staying behind."

General Casner's tired eyes softened to show his sympathy. "I'm sorry. Truly I am."

Marcus accepted the man's words before considering what options would contribute to the group's situation. "Allow me to scout the area during the pyre burning. I did so before we moved to the border, so I'm familiar with the perimeter in the daylight. This way, we'll learn whether or not another ambush is in place or if anyone is still alive."

The general's resulting frown reflected his previous intent to supervise the troops as a single unit, yet when he spoke again, it sounded sincerely considerate. "Fine, but be careful. We'll post guards to watch the forest as well. Stay within their sight."

Marcus thanked his superior before walking to the entrance where he informed those nearby of his self-appointed assignment. One soldier circled the site to keep an eye on him as he inspected every part of the ground and nearby plants without success. All he discovered worth noting were dozens of footprints to the south, indicating the Nim-Valans' escape; however, they continued farther than he could see and appeared to be old. With no other clues, Marcus trudged back to the camp where General Casner reorganized the soldiers and mages for their march to Parnic, then Verona.

The Aftermath of Betrayal

The summer weather brought weeks lacking rain with the exception of an overnight storm, leaving the grass and plants in Verona dry, prickly, or wilted. Nobody spent more than an hour outside at one time of the day because the cloudless sky allowed the sun to beat down upon the land. Still, many individuals would relax in the shade of the palace to soak in the heat without endangering themselves out in the open.

Despite what most people thought of the season, Byron despised having his energy unwillingly drained and remained inside the cool, stone walls of the palace whenever possible. He only had his responsibility to Lydia, which brought him out during the latter part of the day when the other soldiers and mages emerged as well. That particular afternoon, the pair worked in the northern training area due to the high volume of mages in the new space, then they chatted until their stomachs growled. His apprentice thanked him before heading to supper, and Byron grew tempted to follow until he spotted Clearshot farther away near the outer perimeter.

How long has it been since we talked? he wondered before setting aside his hunger and moving toward his friend.

The former full-time archer loomed behind four, young soldiers who drew loaded bowstrings and fired at a single target no more than a few steps ahead of them. Even at that distance, only two of the arrows landed on opposite ends of the haystack; one missed completely, and the final arrow slipped from its knocked position to fall to the ground. The presentation was enough to show Clearshot started assisting those without much, or any, experience, though Byron soon learned their abilities would develop under the right instructor.

He studied the group as the four were guided through the process of pulling back the bowstring and releasing it first. After, they did so without an arrow in place on the weapon. The lesson concluded with each firing another shot and all managing to hit or graze the target.

"That'll do for today," Clearshot announced as he wiped away the beads of sweat swarming his brow. "I will see you here tomorrow at the same time. Practice the motions, and take it slow."

His current students split apart to return the weapons and haystack to their places in the stable while Byron approached with a smile.

"They weren't too bad," he commented and licked his lips when Clearshot drank from a waterskin.

"Most of the recruits are like that, except for those who know how to hunt for their own food. Even that seems to be rare nowadays."

"You make an admirable teacher," Byron added before proposing a question half-heartedly. "Is that what you're aiming for now?"

His friend frowned, briefly glanced over before taking another swig of water, then responded. "Ironically, Emilea said I should continue training newcomers to help take my mind *off* my shoulder."

"She's right, you know. Besides, you do have other options to consider." Byron fully expected the glare resulting from his words.

"Don't start with that again," Clearshot muttered in an exasperated manner. The two had been over this topic just about every time they were together, but it seemed both refused to accept the other's side.

Clearshot's nerve damage initially prevented him from putting any strain on his left shoulder, which would have doomed his career if the man had been less determined. With his wife's instruction, he exercised the muscles regularly to the point where he could draw his bow for longer durations multiple times a day. Byron found this out through Emilea, though, because to Clearshot, the injury made him useless despite the recovery.

It hurt and frustrated Byron to see the normally cheerful soldier acting hopeless, so he always tried to provide support. "You're a good teacher, and not just for the beginners, but you limit yourself. I can tell you're building your skill again. Everyone views you as a leader; nothing in the past changes that."

"If you want to help me feel better, you can start by not pitying me."

"Why would I pity you?" Byron countered. "Everything I say is true. Did you forgot what you've done for Asteom, specifically the palace? Would your name have been in the discussion for replacing the lost generals if you weren't capable?"

Clearshot chuckled with a bitterness that irritated Byron even more. "I wish you would stop bringing that up. They considered all soldiers at the level of an assistant general."

"Does their faith mean nothing to you then?"

The man just shook his head and started to stroll toward the palace.

"When are you going to stop feeling sorry for yourself?" Byron demanded, more out of desperation than frustration. His surge of emotion seemed to reach his friend, for Clearshot halted instead of continuing to escape from the conversation. "Even if you continue to maintain your physical condition, your mind is at risk if you think so poorly of yourself. That's what Emilea says."

"You sure have been talking to my wife a lot lately," his friend added nonchalantly.

Byron caught the underlying accusation and, whether or not Clearshot's comment had been used to end the berating, glared with enough venom to display his distaste. "Now I *am* concerned about your mentality. Emilea and I see each other on a regular basis for council meetings, so quit acting so belligerent. Besides, it's not my fault if she comes to me instead of you because of that dismissive attitude you like to display around us."

The last sentence slipped from his lips, yet Byron didn't regret revealing his thoughts. During their previous encounters, when he did bottle his feelings up, Clearshot could shift the conversation away from the main problem.

I'm tired of this game, he reflected bitterly while his friend kept silent. *Needless overreacting and self-loathing becomes drama that nobody wishes for themselves. I'm dealing with this too often, and I won't let him fall into a depression because of what happened two years ago, especially when he is repairing his shoulder damage.*

Byron planned to say exactly that when Clearshot turned his face upward and spoke in a calmer tone of voice.

"I'm sorry for insulting you. Emilea just worries too much and likes to drag others into our personal business. The truth is, I've been considering requesting a stationary position in Verona or East Hoover. She hates the idea of me separating myself from the palace, but being reminded of the past every day is taking its toll on me." As he spoke, Clearshot rubbed his left shoulder and refused to meet Byron's stare.

"What about Mace and Lexie?"

"With Mace already at the academy and Lexie starting there this fall, no one will be home too often. I'd like to downsize, maybe move out of the woods and closer to a city. I don't know…"

"I take it Emilea wants to stay here?"

A sense of relief washed over him when Clearshot's genuine laughter filled the space between them, easing the earlier tension.

"Of course! Her students and life's work are here. Besides, she would never abandon those who are relying on her magic; she's a lot like you in that regard."

Byron didn't know how to take the comparison, but his rumbling stomach interrupted to remind him of the late hour, to his friend's amusement. "We should head inside for dinner."

The pair turned toward the palace together and approached the entrance where others in the training ground began retiring for the evening as well; however, before they could reach the doorway, a servant appeared in front of Byron, stopping him mid-step.

"Master Byron, I've been sent to find you. The king has called an emergency council meeting."

He wasn't the only person to hear the message. Everyone around them paused to lean over and catch the servant's words with concern etched into their features as they cast uncertain glances his way. The news of an unexpected gathering would always be alarming since it usually meant something impactful took place and immediate action was necessary.

"Did you receive any details?" Byron pressed at a lower volume. He appreciated how the boy understood to speak quieter after that, for the answer would have made everybody panic.

"General Casner and his troops returned after they were attacked by the Nim-Valans."

"Across the border?"

"I'm not sure," the servant answered and shook his head helplessly.

He thanked the messenger as an obvious dismissal before rushing through the opening, down several corridors, and up to the meeting chamber's guarded entrance. Only then did he realize a second pair of footsteps echoed behind him.

"Do you plan on eavesdropping?" he asked over his shoulder.

As he expected, Clearshot stopped at his side a second later.

"I'm a patient person. I can wait here until you and Emilea are finished."

Byron dipped his chin to acknowledge his friend's decision and faced the guards, who then led him inside. Around the circular table in the meeting chamber sat Emilea, General Tont, and General Garvish. All three glanced over sets of papers spread around the latter's side. Although Byron was surprised to find only a fraction of the council present, he took a seat next to the master light mage and greeted her.

Next entered General Terrell, who timidly moved to an empty spot, followed by Aaron, High Priest Jurek, General Casner, and Marcus. Even without the explanation, Byron noticed how worn Casner and Marcus' faces appeared, causing his stomach to drop.

Both are experienced in combat, conflict, and death, but I can't imagine the physical toll of a week's travel while keeping one eye open for trouble; that's on top of the Nim-Valan's betrayal. Marcus especially looks deflated. I figure he hates returning to his father with news the general can't brag about.

Aaron spent no time on a formal opening, permitting General Casner to share everything relating to their assignment, which he did without allowing his weariness to distract from the news. Once he concluded his briefing, the room fell silent.

The Nim-Valans betrayed our relationship and made a show of dismissing any hope for an alliance, Byron reflected with a hand on his chin. *Not only that, but they deliberately crossed over into Asteom's territory to ambush the camp and returning troops after they succeeded in freeing the closest fort from the border.*

"Are you certain these were soldiers and not the barbarians we were warned about?" General Garvish asked to initiate a discussion.

"Those who attacked us wore the uniforms we're familiar with," General Casner answered, letting his fatigue slip through. "The citizens in the fort recognized our guide as well, and he betrayed our trust during the ambush. We locked those barbarians away before departing, so they would have needed to plan to risk their lives in order for us to succeed first."

A new voice belonging to General Terrell spoke up in a hesitant manner. "In any case, don't we need to post guards along the border again?"

"Well, that's a given," General Tont barked and followed his words by slamming his fist on the table. "Get your head on straight! What we can do now is retaliate for such disgrace."

While the shier general sank into his seat and the others began voicing their thoughts, Aaron called for silence.

"Calm down. We shouldn't act out of impulse."

"His Highness is correct," piped the high priest. The frail-looking man doted over Aaron even more than Hendal had, though Byron understood his caring nature stemmed from his disbelief at being chosen for the position and his gratitude for it. "There's no urgency to make a decision at this very moment…"

From the farthest end of the table, General Garvish cleared his throat to draw everyone's eyes. "Forgive me for interrupting, but one who is not a fighter should listen to those with experience before assuming the best course of action. I second General Tont's motion to send troops to the border and eliminate the threats before they come to us."

Byron avoided the urge to roll his eyes at the younger man's remark. Garvish belonged to a noble household that sent children into the army to elevate their family's status and give them a topic to brag about. For years, he studied under General Casner, who vouched for his strategic sense and combat skills, until he was chosen to replace one of the open positions on the council. Whether or not he could live up to his reputation, Byron didn't know. The only impression the nobleman made was he felt like the smartest person in the room; worst of all, he never acted modest about it.

"A letter should be sent to the Nim-Valan king before anything else," Emilea interjected to move the conversation along.

Aaron nodded and voiced his agreement. "We can draft this tomorrow and assign a messenger after. General Tont, General Garvish, I am putting you both in charge of organizing the soldiers and mages to watch the northern border. Most are still there or were expecting to return anyway after the alliance's establishment; however, I intend to double the protection in case the enemy crosses again."

"What about the people they killed on our land?" General Casner startled them by asking at a lower volume akin to a growl. "What kind of image does backing away from an attack present to the Nim-Valans?"

His questions threw the council into a heated debate about their available options and if they should retaliate. The room soon split between those who wished to march into Nim-Vala and claim a portion of their land as a declaration of war and those who felt satisfied with waiting for their king's response to Aaron's letter. When it became evident they wouldn't agree completely with any course of action, the generals bickered with one another about what should be included in the message to the northern country's ruler.

Byron sensed a headache approaching and eventually kept his mouth shut when nobody listened to one another. It took much longer than he thought for Aaron to bring the meeting under control.

"Are we all satisfied?" the young royal asked in a sarcastic manner that reminded Byron of the late King Hernan.

No one answered, though most glanced away to show their shame.

"Never has this council been distraught enough to behave like wild dogs fighting over a scrap of meat. We must respect one another and consider every side of the situation; otherwise, what's the point of bringing together men and women of various talents and strengths?"

The resulting pause stretched until Byron's stomach rumbled and he spoke to get the group's attention. "Your Highness, the hour grows late. Some of us need food and rest, especially General Casner and Assistant General Marcus. Allow me to recap what's been said so we can leave on the same ground and contemplate the information."

"Well said, Master Byron," Aaron answered with a grateful expression. "Go ahead with the summary."

"Tomorrow, we'll meet again to craft a letter for the Nim-Valan leaders explaining the seizing of the fort, as agreed upon, then the ambush and attack on Asteom territory. At that time, we can decide where we stand on the alliance. Generals Tont and Garvish will prepare the troops to be posted along the border for the time being, and they'll depart with our messenger. We need to decide if we should wait for the king's reply before acting or launch our own attack as a warning. Should we take any sort of action, it might be wise to establish a base to the north similar to what's in Dala."

"Are there any other thoughts to share before we're dismissed?" Aaron asked the room. When no one responded, he gestured to the guards stationed at the door, and the meeting concluded.

Byron was one of the last people to leave the chamber because he decided it would be worthwhile to glance over the general's report. He noted some additional details, such as what the northern troops stole from the campsite and their interactions with a translator, but he soon came across the deceased list and slowly skimmed it. Most of the names were unfamiliar, though General Casner explained how the light mages had been left behind the border, and he figured Emilea already knew about them. Then, he saw Will's name at the end after Assistant General Jeremiah's.

Not Will... He set the paper down, put a hand over his eyes, and took a moment to collect himself. *The worst cases are always the victims, innocent people who aren't involved in a fight. Everyone who remained behind at the camp didn't deserve such a brutal fate.*

The sentiment wouldn't be lost on Asteom's citizens and would result in a rise of emotion when they found out who was killed and why. In his eyes, the council could deal with that later, so he suppressed his own grief while rising. Aaron and Marcus conversed by the king's throne while the nearby guards waited to escort the former out. Neither young man paid attention to him as he left.

Poor boys. I know the feeling of losing friends and comrades, yet the initial pain never seems to strike any lighter.

Byron stopped farther down the empty hallway. The tightness in his stomach reminded him he needed to eat, yet he desired nothing more than to lie down. He decided to find a servant and request dinner be brought to his quarters before continuing toward his room. Then, he remembered the friend who was supposed to wait for him outside.

Clearshot probably left with Emilea, he realized. *I don't blame him for wanting to comfort his wife.*

For a moment, the stone walls projected a haunting chill as Byron stood alone. Very rarely did he acknowledge that sense of loneliness or let it permeate his mind.

Sometimes I wonder if it's easier to overcome the pain with a partner or if they become a distraction. Then again, I can understand how the idea of dying alone frightens individuals. Still, I never feel that way; I'm curious as to why, though. I hope I don't give off the impression I don't appreciate company.

As the unpleasant sensation dissipated, he moved on.

*

After a warm meal and change of clothes, Byron sat at his desk with only a single lamp to cast the space in a comforting light. He wished to write two documents before his eyes grew too heavy to keep open, so he began with what remained fresh in his mind from the council meeting.

He put together a list of items that, in his opinion, should be included in the letter to the Nim-Valan king without writing every sentence out. The goal was to have items to present tomorrow compiled from the information and suggestions they discussed. Mainly, he planned to emphasize how going to war should be a last-resort course of action, if only to spare their soldiers and mages over the morals and statistics.

Something related to what General Casner explained regarding the fort didn't seem right to him either. For a while, he pondered the man's account without finding a clear reason for his restless thoughts until he forced himself to end that list before he became consumed by stray theories.

The second document needed to be finished that night if it were to be sent out in the morning. Byron selected a clean sheet of paper, yet his pen hovered above the parchment as he considered what to write.

This letter would be a personal message for his childhood friend, Cintra. Why he experienced a desire to reach out after months of silence between the two, he didn't understand; however, recalling the earlier moment alone in the hall compelled him to act. Once he recognized and dismissed his natural instinct to sound professional, what he intended to say came out clearer.

My dearest Cintra, it really has been too long since we last spoke, both through these letters and in person. To be honest, I've become so preoccupied with my work, I haven't gotten an opportunity to escape the palace in over a year. Of course, I know you never find it hard to believe I wouldn't abandon my position, even during these times of peace in Asteom.

Byron went on to share the progress in the new training ground, the Yeluthians' consistent visits, and various topics that sounded menial to him until he reached the bottom of the third page. An inexplicable chagrin rose when he wrote the final lines.

As I find myself at a loss for more to tell you, I realized I never thanked you for what you've done over the years. I always worry I abuse your ability, and I'm sorry for that, but you should know I'm even more fond of the woman behind the magic. Please, make some time to visit so I can show you Verona and the palace.

Your friend, Byron

He stared at the words and wondered if he should erase or change them, for nothing seemed to express the reasoning behind his desire to reconnect with Cintra. When his eyelids began to droop, he closed them momentarily to ease their weariness. A gentle knock at the door prevented him from falling asleep right then and there.

"Come in," he called before shuffling the papers together.

The hinges let out a single squeak as the door opened, and Coura stepped inside as casually as ever.

"I'm surprised you're still awake," she said by way of greeting, then she closed the door and moved to the edge of his bed.

Byron rubbed his eyes and frowned. "Why? What time is it?"

"Nearly midnight. Everyone heard there was a council meeting going on this afternoon. I thought I would stop by when I felt certain it'd be over. I guess you're pretty exhausted, right?"

"A little," he answered reluctantly.

The corners of Byron's lips tugged upward when his former student pulled her feet up, boots and all, to sit cross-legged on the mattress while glancing around the room.

"Are you waiting for me to ask why you're here?" he pressed.

Coura stared at him with an unreadable expression before looking at the wall. He could tell something bothered her and she was figuring out how to best bring up the subject, so he gave her a few seconds to sort her thoughts.

"There are a couple reasons," she started after returning her gaze to him. "First, I'm sorry I yelled at you when Evern and I were working in the training ground. You were only trying to help, and I was frustrated with him."

Byron raised an eyebrow. "That happened over a week ago. Besides, I don't hold grudges when I'm right about something."

"You're always so modest," she replied with a hint of sarcasm.

"What compelled you to apologize now?"

"It's been on my mind is all. I met with Emilea since then and discussed choosing a sparring partner with my father. You're welcome for coming here to tell you that."

"And you claim *I'm* the modest one," he teased with a grin to show he meant no ill intent; however, she ignored the jab. That meant whatever remained on her mind was more important than apologizing to him. Instead of pushing for it, Byron waited at his desk until she finally continued.

"I also wanted to ask about the council meeting. Rumors are going around from those who returned claiming the Nim-Valans ambushed the troops and destroyed the camp, killing most of the light mages. Did Casner happen to mention if he noticed anything suspicious about the attack?"

Byron kept quiet as he wondered what she hinted at. Finally, when he couldn't come up with a possible reason, he shrugged. "Nothing out of the ordinary, aside from it being soldiers not barbarians who ambushed them. General Casner was under strict orders to return if he deemed the situation too dangerous."

"That's all? Did Aaron add more, or did he bring up King Arval?"

Those questions took Byron back. "Not that I heard. What are you getting at?"

Coura's blank expression showed she seemed as puzzled as him. "I guess I thought there would be another explanation for why the Nim-Valans would do that. Maybe the Yeluthians have some idea, but we'll need to wait until they return to Verona."

He sensed she kept more to herself but decided she would share if it were important enough and dismissed the conversation for the evening by standing to stretch his back. "All I can say is that tomorrow the council will send a message to the Nim-Valan king about his soldiers' betrayal along with troops to guard the border. Everything else is up in the air for the moment."

Coura stared at the floor as he spoke, seemingly distracted until Byron cleared his throat. Then, her head lifted, and she realized he planned to go to sleep.

"Thank you for entertaining me," she commented, leapt off the bed, and crossed the room. "I guess I can talk with Marcus or Will about it tomorrow, or maybe in a few days when they recover from the journey."

An invisible blow struck his heart once he remembered the deceased list in the general's report.

She hasn't heard about Will...

"Coura, there's something I need to tell you," he started only for her to wave the words away with one hand and open the door with the other.

She pointedly covered a yawn. "Not tonight. It's late enough as is, and you've been cooped up in the meeting chamber. You can find me tomorrow afternoon when your council business is over."

"Wait-"

Before he could continue, she shut the door, abruptly halting his chance to share the news.

***

The week following the troops' return from the northern border proved to be a nightmare for so many people in the palace, including Coura, who found her rising hopes for the near future stripped away. It all began to slide downhill after her visit with Byron on the evening of General Casner's return. Although dozens of rumors and exaggerated stories related to betrayal and war floated around every corner, she remained preoccupied with making sure the demon from the southern woods wasn't responsible.

If anyone besides Aaron knows for sure, it would be someone on the council, she figured, leading her to wait until Byron became free to talk.

He revealed no answers, which she didn't expect given what her father explained about King Arval sharing the demon's appearance with the leaders in Asteom. When Coura excused herself to return to her own room and pondered what information she gathered throughout the afternoon, only one conclusion occupied her mind.

Evern lied to me. He promised King Arval would tell Aaron about our encounter with Terran, yet Byron would've mentioned whether or not a demon had been involved with the events to the north. Besides, he obviously had no clue what I was hinting at when I asked.

She flopped onto her bed, pulled the covers over her head, and continued reflecting on the situation. The sincerity from both her father and her former mentor left her wondering if the conflict with Nim-Vala could be a separate issue entirely. That notion frightened her since it brought about the plausible chance Asteom would be involved in a war with the northern country soon *and* have to track down another demon.

I don't think Evern is to blame here. In fact, I bet he just repeated what was said to him. Would King Arval lie to his own commander like that? Perhaps when the immediate issue settles down a bit, I can make time to ask him, Byron, or Emilea directly. Although I hate the idea of breaking my promise to Father about staying silent, they might want to know before sending soldiers and mages away from the capital.

Considering the extent of their involvement, she could only wait until tomorrow.

*

Coura spent most of the next morning in the training ground working alone until the heat became too heavy to bear and sweat coated her hair and clothing. After bathing, dressing, and moving into the mess hall for lunch, she noticed a melancholy mood hanging in the air as dozens of people kept to their own groups. Nobody spoke as loudly as they normally did, and she sat by herself to eat in peace.

Something happened beyond the attack, that she felt certain of, leading her to recall how Byron tried to catch her before she took her leave the night prior. If Coura wasn't supposed to meet with Emilea that afternoon, she probably would have gone to see her old teacher immediately. Still, the master light mage didn't expect her outside for a while, so she figured she could stop by the woman's quarters to discuss the lingering concerns. Emilea might be busy or not in her room, but Clearshot would also be worth asking since she knew the master mage informed him of the council's discussions, if only to gather another, outside opinion.

She hurried to the third floor, knocked on the door, and restrained herself from releasing a sigh of relief when both Emilea and

117

Clearshot stood inside. As she greeted the pair, she couldn't ignore the lines of worry sketched across their faces.

"We aren't scheduled to meet for at least an hour," the light mage began after letting Coura in and closing the door.

"I know, but I need to talk with you about what took place along the border. I'm tired of hearing rumors about the attack, so…"

"You came to me because I directly listened to General Casner's account," Emilea concluded while folding her arms together. When Coura kept quiet in a silent confirmation, the master mage shook her head. "This doesn't concern you."

"Can you promise me that?" Coura asked forthright, startling the two and prompting them to share a glance.

"What do you mean?" Clearshot countered after the pause.

She trusted Byron, Emilea, and Clearshot would understand her desire to assist when needed and involve her in any matter related to demonic mischief, especially if she took the first step toward being included in the discussion. If they claimed the events to the north had nothing to do with her after all they've been through over the years, she could believe the demon wasn't to blame.

Based on the couple's similar reaction to Byron's, Coura gave up on bothering them for details. "I just wanted to hear the truth from a reliable source," she answered.

Neither spoke for long enough after that she accepted their silence as a dismissal and turned to leave. When her hand touched the doorknob, Emilea told her to wait.

"Aaron plans to address the public tomorrow morning about our decision to strengthen the border, but I would wager many people already know who didn't return with General Casner's company."

Coura pulled her hand away to face the master mage when the woman didn't continue and saw tears filling the other's sapphire eyes. A second later, her husband wrapped an arm around her shoulders in a comforting gesture before picking up the explanation.

"While the general and his troops crossed the border, Nim-Valan soldiers attacked and destroyed the camp. The light mages, except those accompanying the troops, were killed, along with the guards stationed there. When General Casner and the rest of the soldiers and mages returned to Asteom, the Nim-Valans ambushed them. That's why there's talk of a war. We helped their people at their king's request, and as a result, they betrayed our trust and shed blood on our land."

As he elaborated, his temper slipped into the words. Meanwhile, Emilea's eyes lowered to the floor, emphasizing her defeated expression. Coura hadn't heard about the casualties from the camp's destruction and sympathized with the master mage, as well as those who lost their friends and loved ones unjustly.

"I'm sorry," she told Emilea, then she glanced at Clearshot. "I appreciate you telling me this before tomorrow. I didn't mean to bring it up again."

Clearshot's shoulders dropped to display how the tension stemming from his frustration left his body. "Nothing like this has happened during our lifetime, so I can honestly admit I don't believe anyone is prepared for what's to come."

Coura nodded and caught Emilea's eyes raise to meet hers.

"The list of the victims will be addressed tomorrow," the master mage added in a strangely hesitant manner. "High Priest Jurek is preparing a ceremony for later in the week."

"I see," she responded when no other words came to mind.

"I thought you would like to know since…"

"Since what?"

The look the pair exchanged did not bode well.

"I wasn't certain if you knew this, but Will remained at the camp when the general and troops departed," Emilea explained with a strain in her voice. "He was killed with the other guards stationed there."

The words fell like a hammer to strike at Coura's head and heart as she stared at the master mage. She wanted to demand what Emilea meant, yet her body became stunned by the shock of the news.

Will is…dead? He can't be…

She caught Clearshot take a step forward, presumably to offer a gesture of comfort like he did for his wife, and stepped back. "Thank you for telling me," she replied despite her disbelief before spinning around to grab for the knob.

Clearshot called her name as she pulled the door open, moved into the hallway, and shut it. Then, she hurried to her own room where she locked the door and pressed her back against the wood with deep, shaky breaths.

He can't be dead. Will had enough experience to go along, and they wouldn't leave him at the camp without help. They didn't...

While her thoughts continued to race, tears began dropping from her eyes as she sank to the floor and hugged her knees. The doubt jumbled together with the rising memories of the first real friend she ever made, leaving her to bury her head in her arms and weep silently.

***

The heavy scent of smoke lingered outside the palace in the southern field where hundreds had died defending Asteom merely two years ago. The smell rose from herbs and various incense the high priest burned in plenty as he tossed them into a bonfire surrounded by soldiers, mages, and ordinary citizens who wished to pay their respects to the dead. Marcus tuned out the man's prayers, just as he did for Aaron's announcement to the public prior to the ceremony, and stood between his father and General Casner at what was considered the front section.

During the journey from Parnic to Verona, he forced himself to stay strong despite the fear, suspicion, and negativity looming over their squad. As far as he was concerned, those under his and General Casner's command needed leaders bearing brave faces to turn to and follow. So, he obliged by shutting away his mind and acting to represent his duties as an assistant general. Unfortunately, every once in a while a stray voice spoke from the back of his mind, and he heard it whispering beneath the high priest's words of reverence.

If Will hadn't come along, he would still be alive. What could I have said to General Casner to stop us from crossing the border? Are the Nim-Valans worth trusting at all, or would I quench my thirst for revenge by standing on the front line?

The internal scolding ceased soon after, partly through Marcus' will but mostly because of the answers his heart provided. *Will would never want me to pretend my hands are the ones soaked in his blood, or the blood of the guards and light mages at the camp. He'd be upset and call me a fool if I considered all Nim-Valans the same as well. I saw the faces of those in the fort. They needed help to free themselves from the barbarians and are likely still suffering, along with many across their country. If there's any hope for an alliance, I should remain level-headed, for Will and the other victims.*

That desire for peace and his need to honor those who were murdered under his authority drove Marcus forward for the time being. He could face whatever he kept bottled up eventually when he had a spare moment; however, another matter conflicted with his position.

What am I doing here anymore?

The question recently haunted his thoughts yet reassured him of the morals he held strongly.

I'm supposed to be gaining experience and wisdom from the generals, but why do that if I'm being restricted to their assistant without the chance of a promotion? What lessons should I be learning? The most I've ever witnessed from someone who truly leads came from General Tio and Calin when I lived with the Dalans. In Verona, I feel alone in believing soldiers should establish comradery and build trust with one another. How can I explain this to the generals in the palace without being dismissed?

Before he could begin to sink into that topic, the high priest concluded the ceremony, and people approached the dying embers to whisper over them since the smoke was said to carry the prayers away. Aaron, the high priest, and the generals moved inside during the process. Marcus remained with his superiors until the group reached the king's wing, then when they paused to chat quietly in the hallway, he stepped away to leave.

To his dismay, one person addressed him, and he avoided turning around until a hand grabbed his elbow. A glace over his shoulder revealed Aaron as the culprit, though his friend's eyes reflected only weariness and concern.

"Where are you going?"

"To my room." The hand on his arm dropped after he replied.

"I thought we could spend some time together this afternoon," Aaron continued. "It's been a rough day so far."

Marcus dipped his chin and pretended to consider the offer, yet he ultimately shook his head. "I have other work to do," he lied and walked away. This time, nothing attempted to convince him to remain except for a sliver of guilt poking at his insides.

As he turned a corner, he expected to proceed without issue until a heavy set of footsteps approached from behind, letting him know someone else intended to hinder his escape.

"Assistant General," called a deep voice belonging to his father.

Marcus halted, waited for the general to meet him, then addressed the man as had he been instructed to do ever since he was a child. "What is it, sir?"

The set of dark brown eyes scanned every inch of Marcus while the sturdy, log-like build proved without a doubt he remain a warrior through and through. "Come with me."

His order hung between them before the general sauntered past Marcus, who soon trailed behind out of curiosity. The pair moved across the first floor until they reached a familiar section where a descending set of stairs had been carved into the ground. There, they entered the basement through a set of metal doors and paused to adjust their eyes to the dim lamp lighting.

The weapons storage area, Marcus noted while he continued to follow his father. *Why would he bring me here?*

Despite the passing of time, the space still seemed barren compared to its once-admirable collection. Hardly anyone could find their personal belongings among the wreckage resulting from Hendal's attempt to overthrow the palace, especially since the ex-high priest gave those under his command permission to raid the storage area for whatever they desired. Weapons and armor kept for generations had been lost to damage and thieves. False claims to another's property became an issue the generals silenced with firm fists, though Marcus wasn't certain every item found its correct owner. Now, nobody felt fully confident in the security of their possessions, so most housed them elsewhere.

His father admirably stood up for the palace's defenses and continued using the space as a holding for their family's belongings; however, he never mentioned how he took and utilized his own armor and weapons while under the demon's influence. The private collection in front of Marcus consisting of at least a dozen swords looked the same as it always did because of the man's vigilance afterward.

"These blades were passed down by my father and his brothers," the general began in an oddly gentle voice while caressing the nearest sword's hilt with his free hand. "Eventually, mine will stay here, and these will all pass down to you. Do you understand why that is?"

In the pause that followed, Marcus waited for his father to go on instead of answering; this sort of lecture became familiar to him over the years.

"It's because of what it means to be a real soldier of Asteom. To some people, these are toys to swing wildly or use as a way to end lives, but to our line, it means much more than such nonsense. When you hold a sword of our family's past, you bear the weight of what prestige the individual brought to our name. Each man, from myself to my great grandfather and his father and so on, carried this lineage to greater heights so we could marvel in the honor our name radiates. That is what we stand for, to be a beacon of fortitude to those without faith in Asteom through our bravery and courage."

As his father spoke, Marcus could see the pride emanating from the square face and continued to listen.

Regrettably, when the general turned to observe his son, the emotion shifted to discontentment showcased by the twisting of his lips into a frown. "When I was your age, I already proved myself a candidate for promotion. I needed to wait years for my opportunity to arrive, and when it did, I seized it with an iron grasp. That's why it infuriates me to watch you let the same, if not a better, chance pass by! Do you hate our family so much as to throw this away? Do you realize what your failure will do to your position?"

So, that's why he brought me down here, Marcus realized while the final question echoed into the nothingness surrounding them beyond their circle of lamplight. *No one is around to hear him berate me.*

"I acted under General Casner's command along the border," he replied in a professional manner despite the headache threatening to let loose his tongue.

"General Casner," his father spat. "He will receive the worst of it, but to let that man make all the decisions shows weakness. If you had any backbone you would've taken care of such incompetence and avoided that entire situation. Because of your feeblemindedness, I see only a coward in front of me, one who isn't fit to become a leader. Imagine what I'm feeling!"

Before Marcus realized his temper snapped, he had already scoffed at the words and started a rebuttal. "You? You mean the general who focuses on nothing except himself and his name? The man who let his body be taken over by a high priest and manipulated into fighting his own soldiers? I consider that more of an embarrassment for a person expected to be one of the greatest leaders in this country. You're so focused on me that you don't even care about those who died!"

"How dare you belittle me," his father growled while towering higher. "Having the respect of those holding power means more than the doe-eyed admiration of subordinates who would revere you regardless. Becoming a general includes subverting those expectations by doing the job of a soldier and more; that is what you don't understand."

"I *do* understand," Marcus interjected. He knew the type of man his father was, and he had been insulted during similar conversations in the past, yet remembering the horrors he faced and the many people left injured or dead around him stirred the embers inside his heart. "You have every right to be angry with me, but not for the reasons you're screaming in my face. You should be upset I couldn't save our camp from the Nim-Valans, and you should be disappointed I wasn't able to stop their ambush on our troops. I'm already blaming myself, considering what I could have done to save those who were killed then and in the years before, but not because I'm building a reputation like you imagine."

"No, absolutely not. You're content with being King Aaron's friend and a helper for the soldiers beneath you. Perhaps you didn't realized it yet, but that is why you haven't been promoted. You accept the responsibilities associated with someone lacking your level of skill without showing a desire for more. Training soldiers, supervising events, acting as a guard… Those are tasks for many others possessing less."

"You assigned them to me!" Marcus protested.

The general just shook his head. "You never argue. Why should I ever bother with what's beneath me? That is the question you should ask yourself more often."

"What do you mean, what is beneath me? I was raised as a soldier to care for my comrades and build mutual relationships with them. What kind of a man shoves aside others for his own rise in status? If that makes me weak, then I claim that part of myself, unlike you."

This time, the general huffed a laugh before letting his emotions melt into a disappointed gaze. "My son, accepting the life of a failure instead of trying to be a foundation for the future of his name. After all I've done for you. I brought you into the palace, made sure *you* were a boy possessing the skill to teach the prince, and placed you at my side as an assistant general so you would turn out even better than me. Surely the universe must be cursing me!"

Marcus bit the inside of his lip so hard he began to taste the metallic tinge of blood. He heard the rumors of his father's manipulation in order to get his son into the right places at the right times, yet he ignored them in favor of proving himself to those who doubted his position. Hearing the general admit this after all they've been through, not to mention the disinterest in any actions aside from what would elevate their family's pride, made him go cold inside with hatred. Rarely did he ever desire to harm someone, but his father's misinterpretation and over-inflated ego brought out that antagonistic side. He would never allow himself to lose complete control and physically lash out, though, so he poured forth the words that came to mind without hesitation.

"You must be the most pig-headed man I've ever known. Is your mind too full of fantasies about yourself that you aren't able to hear what I've been saying? Well, let me try to speak as clearly as possible, like talking to a child.

I understand my faults, and I wish I could change what happened so people didn't die under my watch, but not for the reasons you believe I possess. In my eyes, you and the other generals were people to look up to because you had the ability to protect the innocent, direct hundreds, and bear the responsibilities of a leader. I *admired* you as my father, but now I've realized what a crook you are, pretending to care about the lives you swore to protect. I hate you for not representing that anymore. I never want to become someone like you, even if it means giving up my chance at being a general."

Marcus breathed heavily as he released the last of what spilled out of his mouth. His father looked dumbstruck at first by the outburst; then, he steadily recovered, and the rage rose again, causing the man's face to flush a bright red.

By that point, Marcus was finished with the conversation. He felt sick about what he said, even if it was the truth, and wanted nothing more than to get away from the damp cellar and the haunting echo of his words.

Neither would accept the other's perspective, which proved true when the general shouted at him again. Without bothering to continue listening, Marcus spun on his heel and trudged through the darkness. He stumbled twice on his way to the entrance while attempting to ignore the booming voice following him all the way upstairs until it faded once he stood on the first floor again.

People passed him in the hallways without more than the usual greetings as he focused on composing himself. Finally, he embraced the solitude of his room, locked the door, and fell onto his bed to hide his face in a pillow.

126

Departing Verona

Just like Emilea and Clearshot explained, the high priest lit a ceremonial pyre in honor of those killed by the Nim-Valans, drawing a sizable crowd consisting of a majority of residents in the palace, as well as dozens of Verona's citizens. The event took place in the field to the south beyond the new training ground in order to accommodate for the hundreds of bodies.

Meanwhile, Coura observed the somber service from her window since it faced that direction.

She hadn't left her room since returning there except to grab an early breakfast and dinner over the past couple days and kept the door locked. Several times, knocking accompanied by a voice on the other side sounded, but she ignored them, opting to remain quiet with the hope that they would think she wandered somewhere else.

Her heart continued to ache, even when memories ceased to flood her mind. Once the initial shock wore off, she'd grown emotional until sleep finally tore her away from the pain. The morning after and ever since shifted into a steady recovery from the numbness.

Nothing motivated her to do more than that; however, as she scanned the faces present at the ceremony, she noticed Marcus near the front. He had been Casner's assistant during their mission, and Coura wasn't certain he learned about Will joining the company before the march to the border.

No matter what I'm feeling, I can't imagine it compares to his guilt, she realized with an even heavier sense of despair. *I bet he blames himself for the murders, at least partly. Although from what*

I heard, there didn't sound like a way for the soldiers to help since they crossed over into Nim-Vala by that point. Perhaps I should visit him; my support could ease some of that negativity, and maybe my spirits will lighten too.

After deliberating until late afternoon, she finally left her room, followed the hallway around to the opposite side of the third floor, and knocked on his door. When she didn't receive an answer, she tried the knob and found it locked.

"Marcus, it's Coura," she announced halfheartedly before knocking again.

People passed by while she waited without a response. Once she began to contemplate whether to return to her quarters or head to the dining hall, a click indicated the unlocking of the door, and a voice on the other side addressed her.

"Come in."

Hesitantly, she entered. Marcus sat on the edge of his bed as casually as ever, yet Coura sensed he feigned a relaxed attitude.

"What do you need?" he inquired as she dropped into the chair at his desk.

"I watched the pyre this morning, so I just wondered…"

"Don't worry," he interrupted with a shake of his head. "I'm doing fine. I would hate to cause even more trouble, and those who are grieving should have someone to turn to for comfort. Unless, is that why you're here?"

He's bottling his emotions up instead of being honest with me. What does he mean he doesn't want to cause even more trouble? Whether or not he's willing to share much with me, I should let my guard down.

She paused to consider her next words and what drove her to visit him while staring at her hands, which she folded on her lap.

"I can tell you're lying to downplay what happened," she started without hiding her suspicion. Even if he planned to hide his emotions, she chose to refer to them anyway. "I didn't come here to bring that up again; I'm sure you've been through enough. I guess I needed to tell you I can listen if you want to talk about it, or anything else for that matter. I feel useless sitting around moping, so perhaps this can benefit us both. That must sound pretty silly, considering how long we've known each other."

Coura raised her eyes when Marcus pulled his feet onto the bed to lie on his back and stare at the ceiling. That position prevented her from seeing his face.

"I should say it doesn't, but you're right," came his response. "I trust you as a friend, as well as my comrade; however, I still needed to hear you explain it."

When he didn't continue, she sensed him becoming less reserved and pushed for more, allowing her concern for him to outweigh her own grief. "Well, go on then. I have a free evening."

Thankfully, her comment proved to be all the prompting he needed to dive into his problems. Marcus shared his perspective on the assignment, impression of the Nim-Valans, and details she hadn't heard.

Then, he revealed his personal account of an earlier conversation with his father. General Tont's dismissive behavior toward his own child always seemed to be an issue Marcus frequently brought up, but to hear about their verbal fight made Coura uncomfortable. It was difficult for her to imagine Evern making such hurtful remarks given his caring nature over Jackie, Odell, and even herself most of the time. Not only that, but what the general said about his view of the soldiers beneath him disgusted her and led Marcus to become fixated on his lack of understanding when it came to his father.

She listened until their stomachs growled loudly enough to interrupt the conversation, and after they returned from a late meal, the discussion continued. Once he settled into a comfortable silence, Coura considered returning to her room for the evening until his next words startled her into paying attention again.

"I considered asking for a reassignment, you know."

When her eyes widened and darted to meet his, he glanced away.

"Would you lose your position if you left the palace?" she asked next, uncertain of the answer.

All that she learned about the hierarchy of Asteom's army pieced together based on what she heard from other soldiers in passing. It embarrassed her to admit her lack of knowledge because it reminded her of the position King Hernan had assigned her to as an additional asset to the palace instead of a soldier or mage under a general's authority.

She didn't start out as a soldier among the various ranks, so she was excused from their basic training. On the other hand, she never graduated as a dark mage either, meaning she skipped their introductory orientation. Byron occasionally mentioned how he would catch her up since he always assigned her studies, but she rarely stayed in one place or had the mentality to return to the fundamental lessons. Where she belonged never came into question until she lost her dark magic and straddled the line between acting as an Asteom soldier and a Yeluthian one. The experienced generals threw her to a newer one, whose name she didn't bother to remember, his assistant general delivered the proper paperwork, and that was that.

Marcus must have recalled her limited knowledge because he began to scold her, paused, then adjusted his position. "Yes, I'm almost certain. A few notable titles are associated with particular positions, and if I forfeit mine…"

When he shrugged, Coura's lips curved into a frown. "You would accept abandoning years of work just like that?"

"No, but if I won't be getting anywhere where I'm at now, it might be better to start over."

It dawned on her then that what he admitted and the confidence beneath the words meant he already made up his mind. When she mentioned this, Marcus dipped his chin in confirmation.

"Where do you intend to go?" she asked next. Despite her agreement with his mindset, her heart ached at the idea of not interacting with him on a regular basis.

"I'd like to return to Dala and work under General Tio."

His decision didn't surprise Coura, though she spent a moment considering the implications. "Why Dala? Tio isn't exactly the most easy-going person, and I'm sure he won't be too pleased with monitoring your progress on top of his normal responsibilities."

She studied his thoughtful expression before noticing a smile tugging at his lips.

"My father's prideful mentality is a trait I despise, and not just because he presses it on me. He would rather protect it through achievements, along with my accomplishments, than those under his command or the virtues associated with a leader. The man I aim to be is not one like him but someone who cares more about the people they protect than themselves. General Tio earned the respect of his base, those in the city outside it, and probably the various towns around the south under Dala's protection. For a single person to manage that is inspiring on its own. When I fought alongside him and Calin, I experienced firsthand the soldiers' and mages' adoration. Their cooperation stemming from one leader who earns their trust and loyalty is what the title is meant to stand for."

Again, Coura noted the determination behind his explanation, raising her confidence in a drastic change that might help her friend. She stood and raised her arms to stretch while commending him for the message before she approached the door.

As she placed a hand on the knob, an idea sprouted in the back of her mind. *Would I benefit from leaving the palace for a while too?*

"What's wrong?" Marcus asked when she hesitated.

"Nothing. Keep me updated on your reassignment." Then, she wished him a nice evening and left.

*

Despite the late hour, Coura couldn't relax after hearing Marcus' comments. She lingered by her window to stare at the southern field for most of the night without feeling compelled to sleep.

Without any news about the demon or orders regarding the Nim-Valans, I wonder if I should try a new route. The worst that can happen is they deny my request for leave, and I would at least seem useful. Still, Terran's words bother me. What did he mean when he brought up Soirée? Could what she did to me be why he left me alive?

She instinctively reached over to place a hand on her left shoulder. An idea flickered to life as she did so. *All I know for certain is my center is damaged because of the demonic energy I stored inside. I have no way of inspecting to understand if it's grown better or worse. The only people who provided insight on this were*

131

the Sie-Kie witch and the Mintelian man, Steiner. He didn't host a booth at the past couple festivals, so I should assume he returned to his people in the mountains. The Western Woods are within a week's walk, though, and I haven't visited in years.

Ultimately, that notion became the deciding factor regarding what she should do about her soul space.

The following morning, Coura stopped by Marcus' room, dismissed his concern relating to how tired she appeared, and requested his guidance to craft an appeal for leave to her general. She anticipated his questioning, leading her to answer honestly. Then, she waited while he considered whether or not to help.

"I suppose it wouldn't hurt to show you," he decided and moved to file through the papers in the middle drawer of his desk. "There should be one in here from a while ago when I needed my father's approval. Who is your supervising general?"

"I don't know."

He sent a doubtful look over his shoulder at her. "What do you mean you don't know?"

Coura shrugged, to his amazement.

"I can't believe this," he muttered while pushing the drawer closed with a sigh.

"He's one of the newer generals," she added.

"Which one? Generals Terrell and Garvish are the most recent additions."

Coura didn't answer.

After Marcus rubbed his temples in an exasperated manner, the pair traveled to her room, found the official document stating her position as a foot soldier under General Terrell, and returned to Marcus' room where he began copying the letter. From what she could tell, he mirrored the wording so it sounded nearly identical to his own version before handing it over once the ink set. Lastly, he explained how the general would look over the document, deny or approve the request, sign the paper, then order a servant or his assistant to deliver it to her quarters.

A few days later, Coura received a response from General Terrell. He approved her request and allowed for a week and a half of leave, which was more than she expected. When she saw Marcus in the training ground that afternoon and mentioned the result, he didn't seem surprised. In fact, she thought he seemed bothered by the news.

"What's wrong?" she decided to ask when her friend cut the conversation short.

After a moment when nobody nearby paid them any attention, he shared his answer.

"I mentioned my desire for a reassignment to Aaron," he began, reminding Coura of his intent to leave Verona. "Before going further with the transfer, I need to hear his approval."

She understood he did so in order to get feedback from his friend, not the king, and didn't urge him to elaborate. "What did he say?"

"He denied it."

"What?" Coura stared at him while attempting not to scowl. "Why would he do that?"

Instead of the discontentment she expected given how he behaved up until that point in their conversation, Marcus offered a slight smile and gazed across the clearing. "He believes I spent too much of my life earning the position I hold now, so it would be an insult to everyone who guided me along the way to abandon my efforts. Of course, he didn't mention how my leaving would break us apart and force him to choose someone else to guard him all the time."

"Still, it's your decision to make, not his. The purpose of a reassignment would be to better yourself for future opportunities. For Aaron to deny you that right simply because he doesn't want you to go is selfish."

This time, Marcus' eyes drifted back to her while he wore an unreadable expression. "You think I don't need his permission?"

"As your friend, no. There's no doubt we'll miss you, but a real friend wouldn't prevent you from growing in your profession for their own gain."

"Thank you for that," he replied and flashed a genuine smile. His body visibly relaxed as he went on to tell her more. "Aaron also mentioned I would be able to maintain my position if the council assigned me to Dala, just like when we went there for the first time. There's a report for General Tio I can bring along, so I should remain in the base until he sends me away or the council requests my return. I assume the information has to do with Nim-Vala."

While Marcus paused to contemplate that, Coura wondered if it would also state the appearance of a demon hiding in the woods to the south of the palace; however, she kept the experience to herself. When the time was right, she believed Terran would reveal himself again.

The time approved for her leave began the following week, so she felt more than prepared to travel by that point. No news came from Commander Detrix or any of the Yeluthians in the capital, and the king's council started to move troops from Verona to the northern border because of a lack of response from the Nim-Valan ruler. Everybody had an assignment to occupy their time, allowing her to slip out into the city, through the northern road, and onto the trail leading to the Western Woods.

***

King Arval and the commanders who left for Yeluthia with others from their kingdom returned sooner than anyone expected and with news for Aaron and his council about a demon they claimed appeared in the woods to the south of the palace. When the angelic ruler explained the encounter, Byron sensed some doubt and waited for more details; however, the king shared nothing else. The generals and Emilea asked questions about its possible intentions only to receive incomplete responses.

"Due to the creatures, Commander Evern and the scout accompanying him had a limited interaction with the demon," King Arval repeated. "He dispatched the three without much trouble, but it fled after injuring his partner."

"Are there additional observations you can give us?" General Garvish asked before raising his hands into an annoyed shrug. "The creatures appeared and attacked. Commander Evern killed them. A scout interacted with the demon, was injured, then it ran away without saying anything useful. Forgive my skepticism, but why would a being that intelligent show itself to your kind?"

Byron leaned back in his chair and crossed his arms to contemplate the question as the chamber fell silent. Until that moment, he wasn't willing to bring Coura into the conversation.

I agree with how odd the confrontation sounds, yet I wonder if we're missing a key component from Commander Evern. When she visited me to inquire about General Casner's troops and the attack on their camp, I could tell she had a reason aside from genuine curiosity, not to mention her hesitation after I didn't reveal a lot. Could Commander Evern also wish to keep her uninvolved with a possible demon? Wait... If that's true, how would Coura know about the encounter in the first place?

"Commander, what's the name of the scout who accompanied you into the woods?" he decided to ask her father.

All eyes returned to the witness.

The Yeluthian's expressions and body language remained unreadable when he chose to hide his thoughts, but Byron caught the corner of his lip tighten. "My daughter flew with me."

"You don't mean Coura?" Emilea exclaimed as the others at the table shared a look. Most of them were aware of her past connection to demonic energy, and some still didn't trust her after the first demon hid in the palace right under their noses.

"Why didn't you say so?" Commander Tont growled. "This changes the problem!"

"This shouldn't change anything," Aaron stated from his throne. Despite his composure, Byron believed the young man didn't expect the Yeluthian's answer. "Coura is more familiar with demons and their behavior than anyone else. Perhaps we can gain some insight into where it could be hiding."

"I am afraid she learned too little to assist us," Commander Isan shared before informing the council of what she told Evern.

During the following discussion consisting of the generals' bickering, Evern drew and held Byron's gaze in a mutual understanding that made his heart sink. *This demon has to be aware of her relationship to the first. I would even venture to guess it appeared to see her rather than to attack an angel. That must be why it distracted Evern with the creatures...*

A set of questions Emilea raised brought his attention back to the conversation.

"Where is she now? Can we have her here to describe the encounter?"

Glances flew between Emilea, Evern, and Byron until the timid General Terrell cleared his throat.

"I'm afraid she's probably outside Verona. I approved her request for leave and granted her a week and a half. I'd need to look through my paperwork to see exactly when-"

"Are you mad?" General Casner interrupted, causing the newer general to jump in alarm.

Before the soldier could begin a rant, Aaron interjected in a calmer manner than earlier. "She planned to visit the Sie-Kie people in the Western Woods. If you'd like a second person to vouch for my words, Assistant General Marcus knows this as well."

No one questioned how he heard this; as the royal council, they remained well aware of those close to their king.

"We can wait until she returns," Byron added to move the discussion along. "What we can't ignore is the possibility of more demonic creatures being summoned and used to attack Asteom."

King Arval practically pounced on the new subject. "Our soldiers are already scouting the country for leads. Before this encounter, they only worked on regular routes in the nearby area and found nothing to suggest a demon's appearance."

"Perhaps this would be an opportune time to share what we've been planning," Aaron picked up with a tilt of his head.

The Yeluthian leader nodded. "That is an excellent idea."

*

What the duo explained sounded similar to what Aaron's father, the late King Hernan, organized years ago. Back then, Byron had been assigned to Dala under General Tio's authority, but they abandoned the plan due to the king and queen's assassination, which forced Aaron to take the throne.

Because of the Mage Service Law, more magic wielders were available to be stationed with soldiers across the country, allowing the less populated areas to possess healers and protection, in addition to trained fighters. It sounded like a solid start to fortifying Asteom, one showcasing much potential. This updated version would reevaluate the cities and towns again and place a Yeluthian soldier or two on a scheduled route, allowing their watch to spread over a certain distance. Not only would this bring the soldiers, mages, and angels closer in regard to the relationship between their positions, but it also allowed citizens around the country to become accustomed to people traveling through the sky. Lastly, the arrangement would show off Asteom and Yeluthia's alliance to those farther from the capital.

Byron wasn't alone in favoring the idea. The generals appreciated the gesture and the respect for King Hernan's original plan, Emilea didn't seem to mind, and High Priest Jurek grinned throughout the explanation.

"To experience such unity will truly promote peace," the holy man commented after the others added their own insight.

King Arval thanked them for the support as the meeting headed for a more positive outcome. "To begin, Commander Detrix agreed to take a company of both Yeluthian and human troops around the southern forests where the demon may be hiding. I believe the less who know about the creature's possible existence, the better."

No one argued with his decision to keep the issue private.

The aforementioned commander stepped forward. "My soldiers are already aware of the situation. Five will join me in this extended scouting venture while the rest continue to monitor the capital. I am hoping for twenty or so of your own and a mage or two. Again, I wish to remain as inconspicuous as possible."

Byron began to consider who to send along when Emilea startled him with her own, confident offering.

"I volunteer to represent the light mage you'll need. If there is demonic activity, I'm familiar with enough spells to protect and heal, and there will be others in the cities who can assist."

"Lady Emilea, are you sure?" General Garvish asked with some disbelief.

Byron figured the man wasn't used to nobility taking on more duties and risking their lives too often. *Without Coura, the discussion regarding the demon's appearance must be tabled. I suppose I would rather investigate its possible existence with my own senses instead of waiting.*

"I can go as well," he added.

Emilea shot him an uncertain expression, yet no one else minded his participation.

"Then, it's settled," Aaron concluded with a smile directed at the pair. "When we gather additional evidence, we'll meet again."

***

As the days stretched into weeks, Grace found herself slipping into a pessimistic mindset. Her parents departed with the rest of the Yeluthians and didn't mention returning before they left. Worst of all, they pretended their argument never happened, leaving Grace uncertain whether or not to bring up the subject. In her heart, she wished they would have, if only to acknowledge her feelings about the future.

I did want... I do want to stay in Asteom. My friends are here, I am valued by their people, and I can still serve my kingdom honorably. Why must I continue to climb mountains when I found a place I feel content to call my home?

That had been her mentality for the first few days; then, her doubts surfaced.

The Nim-Valans' decision to ambush the light mages on their enemy's soil brought about the issue of her safety, especially after hearing about her friend. Reading Will's name on the list of the deceased startled, angered, and distressed her all at the same time until she recalled her father's recent words. Even though the ambushed group should not have been in danger, both because of their positions and because they remained within their own territory, they were attacked.

Will offered to join General Casner's company, I remember that much beforehand; however, he was never supposed to be a combatant. Neither were the light mages for that matter. It reminds me of my kidnapping despite my initial lack of involvement in this kingdom's politics. Some humans do not care about hurting the innocent if it furthers their cause...

138

Whether or not this proved true of her own people, she did not wish to consider. Yeluthia avoided conflict by remaining hidden from the rest of the world under her uncle's reign, but they stayed safe. If she were to agree with that decision, she would be admitting helping Asteom is a mistake; that would also lead her to agree with her parents' view regarding her position as ambassador.

Even so, she came to understand the risks. If she remained in her current role and continued to live in the palace, she would forfeit her safety compared to if she chose to return to Yeluthia.

The thoughts rolled around in her mind until she longed to share them with someone who might be able to provide useful insight. Unfortunately, her circle of close friends began to crumble. Will was gone, and she soon learned Marcus transferred to the southern base. She couldn't find Coura anywhere, and even the master mages had seemingly disappeared. This left Aaron, who she came to believe would understand her situation the best and offer appropriate advice.

After all that took place, though, she worried he would be too busy to talk, so she waited for the right opportunity to visit him. The regular updates from the northern border steadily contained less and less information, and life returned to normal for the people like her who were not directly involved with defending the kingdom. It felt right to seek out her friend's company, so she decided to start her search where he had been for the past week and a half.

The people passing her by on her way to the council's meeting chamber bowed with a polite greeting as she nodded to acknowledge the gesture, but none followed her direction. Soon, she reached the final hallway and stopped to brush the wrinkles out of her dress, then she raised her hands to make sure no stray hairs ruined her updo.

I hope he is here, she thought while inhaling a deep breath to settle her nerves and approaching the guards on duty.

"Hello, Lady Zelnar," the man on her left began with a smile. "To what do we owe the pleasure?"

"I would like to see King Aaron," she answered while offering a polite curtsy.

"I'm sorry, but His Highness asked for no interruptions this morning."

Although the response annoyed her due to her patience over the last few days, she upheld her appearance by nodding. "I understand; however, King Arval sent me to deliver a message meant only for his ears."

The man scratched his chin and knit his brow. "What is it this time?"

She didn't believe his grumbled question needed a response, yet she considered a more lighthearted approach. "King Aaron and I are close friends, so I promise not to disrupt his business. If you require proof of my intentions, please accompany me inside."

"With your permission, my lady," he agreed and knocked before opening the door to lead her inside.

For being located at the center of the stone structure, the chamber proved well-lit thanks to multiple lamps around the space. The only table in the room held dozens of documents, which had been scattered into various piles, and standing over them with one hand on a stray page was Aaron. He faced the entrance and glanced up as Grace entered behind the guard, who started to introduce her until the king raised a hand to dismiss the formality.

"Grace, what are you doing here?" her friend inquired in a slightly concerned tone of voice. His expression matched his question, reminding her of how he probably started to suspect every random update to bring about a new issue.

She resisted the urge to walk past the guard and offer a friendly greeting until the two were alone and she could share her reasoning. On the other hand, she lied to the soldier in order to gain entry. If she began with that excuse, she would need to explain herself afterward.

To her relief, Aaron seemed to catch on to her desire to speak in private and excused his guard.

"Now, tell me you're not here to give me more work to do?" he began with a slight smile once the metal door slammed shut, confirming her previous theory.

"I am sorry to interrupt when you are so busy," she offered. "I can only imagine what you must be dealing with."

Grace avoided going into detail and moved to stand beside him. Instinctively, she stared down at the nearest paper, which seemed to be a report from someone reassigning troops at the northern border. Her eyes wandered to the numbers and comments until Aaron reached over to flip the page upside down, deliberately keeping her from reading more.

"It's fine," he replied as he did so. "I'm due for a break anyway."

Grace knew he paused to give her an opportunity to converse, yet a chill from the secluded room seeped into her skin to remind her of the last time she had been in that space. Her body shivered, so she hugged herself and averted his gaze.

"Sorry. I do not think I will ever be able to forget what took place in this room. The memory is harder to suppress than I imagined."

"That was a different time than now," he replied in a sympathetic manner. "I promise you're safe in here; it's just us."

After releasing a sigh, she decided to sit and figure out how to best approach her issues. Aaron joined her and purposefully shifted away from the table to give her his full attention.

Based on what I read, the conflict to the north has gotten worse. I tried not to disturb him, but I suppose it cannot be avoided.

With that in mind, she shared why she sought him out, starting with her parents' visit and their subsequent argument due to their misunderstanding. This led her to admit her desire to remain in Asteom instead of returning to her home to marry and assume a new position in the kingdom.

All the while, Aaron kept silent. He seemed surprised to hear she would rather continue to live with her current role; however, when she finished, his lips dipped into a frown.

"I know this is trivial compared to what you are dealing with, but I suppose I just needed to tell someone about it," she concluded to ease part of the tension in the chamber.

He shook his head. "Don't say that, Grace. You're my friend, so we should be able to reach out to each other when we need to talk about our problems. Unfortunately, I just haven't had the time to catch up with anyone lately."

The resulting pause revealed his attempt to hide his thoughts.

"What is it?" she pressed. When he still seemed uncertain, she crossed her arms. "I shared my troubles, so it is only fair you do the same."

Her stubbornness earned her a bashful smile from the king, who caved into her request a moment later.

"Fine, you win. I'm not sure how much you've heard, but let's just say I've been given enough to think about and do for a while. Sometimes being alone allows me to get more work done without worrying about others for a change. I don't get lonely until I find myself in a position like this, where you needed me and I wasn't available. I start reflecting on what more I can do, who I can delegate these tasks to, what I could have done better, and the impression I'm making on everybody. In a way, shutting myself in here distracts me from reality."

Grace found herself at a loss for words. It was inevitable the king of Asteom would constantly be focused on his country's needs, yet Aaron remained a kind, compassionate person in the midst of his responsibilities. He genuinely cared about his people and fought for their best interests, even if that meant sacrificing his time and weakening his relationships.

"Anyway, you came here to see me," he continued with his regular smile. "My parents had a similar attitude when it came to preparing me for the future, especially my mother, so I can sympathize with you there; however, you do have a choice in the matter. I'm not sure why they undervalue the role of an ambassador since you've been extremely helpful with providing input on Yeluthia's behalf. Also, I can arrange for a personal guard or two to escort you, if that will make you feel safer in the palace."

"Thank you," she replied without accepting the offer.

"I won't get too involved, but you can trust me to defend whatever decision you make going forward. Should you choose to stay, you'll always be welcome as the ambassador."

Hearing him state such a claim lifted a weight from her shoulders, and she expressed her gratitude once more.

"I'm afraid that may be all the assistance I can offer," he admitted next while rubbing his hands together and averting his eyes. "The last part about the arranged marriage might be a private discussion within your family. Actually, when you mentioned it I was reminded of my mother."

"Did she wish for you to marry a noblewoman?" Grace ventured with a slight wince. She never became close with the late queen, yet she recalled how the ladies in Verona made Aaron a popular topic of discussion.

He must be in a similar situation; I would be a fool to think otherwise. Still, it is a shame we are unable to decide for ourselves who and when we would like to wed. Although, his position is dependent on an heir in case anything should happen to him. I wonder if his council has been pushing that notion.

When he nodded, she avoided lingering on the subject. "My marriage will depend on where I am in the next year or two, so I am not too concerned; however, I appreciate your sympathy. If there is anything I can do to help you, please do not hesitate to reach out."

The pair rose together as he thanked her before she took her leave. Each guard bowed and bid her a good day, then she returned to her quarters to reflect on their conversation.

For now, all I can do is continue my duties and try to assist where I am needed. I must keep my friends in mind too; when the time comes for me to face my parents again, I know I will need their support.

***

When Will stirred from his unexpected slumber, he immediately took notice of three things.

The first and most problematic proved to be a fogginess clouding his mind. Every thought took time to come together, as if he'd been drugged, hindering the reliability of his senses. That led to his second observation: a thick, smokey smell forcing its way into his throat to invade his lungs and irritate them. Lastly, he heard hushed, female voices nearby. He understood some of the discussion, but most of the words sounded unfamiliar to him. Instead of attempting to push past his confusion and weariness in order to investigate, his body naturally relaxed, and falling asleep seemed like the best option.

This happened twice until he noticed a set of footsteps and the people fell silent. Then, a male voice spoke in that foreign language. One of the women replied, and Will noted the difference in their fluidity; while the man's dialogue sounded sure, allowing each word to fit in an ordinary cadence, the woman's became choppy, showcasing how she contemplated each syllable.

I remember running away from the camp. Images of fire and shadowy figures reminded him of the attack a second later, along with his reluctant plunge into the river south of their position.

That's right. I crossed the water with someone in order to put distance between us and the Nim-Valans. How many of the light mages made it to safety? What happened afterward? We should have traveled farther south in Asteom, so they must've found help. I don't understand why I passed out so suddenly. My body feels heavier than normal too...

Will pried one eye open, tried the other, then blinked in the near darkness. When his eyesight remained blurry after adjusting to the light, even without his glasses, it took him a moment to realize a haze lingered in the air from an indoor fire. He occupied one corner of a wooden building just wide enough to house several people with plenty of room to move freely. It also retained heat because the only openings seemed to be a door behind a group of huddled women and a hole at the top directly above the firepit where smoke struggled to escape. As for the individuals, he couldn't see their faces because of the poor lighting, but they wore dark-colored clothing and possessed black hair to match.

With a meager grunt, he pushed himself into a sitting position in order to evaluate his body, which seemed unharmed except for a thick set of bandages wrapped around his right thigh.

"Will, are you awake?" someone asked.

The people in the space noticed him rise and hurried to move to the opposite side where he had been placed. His instincts kicked in then, leading him to glance around for a weapon.

The Nim-Valans! Did they manage to capture me? I can't underestimate them just because they kept me alive...

One of the women knelt beside him to lay a hand on his shoulder, but he slapped it away before his mind could catch up to his body.

"Stop! It's me, Clara!"

At the mention of his friend's name, Will froze, glanced at the supposed stranger, and squinted in order to assess the round face. Beneath the hair, hollow cheekbones, and smudges of dirt and ash across the chin and forehead, a pair of glimmering, sapphire eyes met his.

She must have noticed his recognition in his following expression since she put her arms around his waist in a tight embrace. "I'm so glad you're awake! We've been worried about you."

"What are you talking about?" Will muttered while looking between each of the smiling, sympathetic faces. The man he heard earlier didn't appear within the group.

Clara pulled away, gestured for her fellow light mages to sit, and began explaining what took place after his most recent memory. Her tone sounded pained and weary, but she didn't stop until he was fully informed of the situation.

"As you might remember, the enemy ambushed our camp, and we were the only ones who escaped their slaughter. I led Bryn, Zelma, and Mary-Ann across the river thinking that would stop their pursuit. We saw you and Lissa jump in and swim to us, but some of the Nim-Valans trailed after you while most stood on the edge of the water with bows and arrows.

You two reached us, we started running until we felt certain they lost track of us, but you collapsed. That was when we noticed an arrow in the back of your leg carrying a new poison none of us have the skill to heal, though we tried. Bryn, Zelma, and I took turns carrying you. Soon, we heard the soldiers at our backs and began to panic. Then, a stranger suddenly appeared out of nowhere to help."

Clara glanced over her shoulder at the opening, referencing the man from earlier.

"He only claimed to be an ally and ordered us to lift you onto his back. When we did, he led us at a brisk pace for days, only stopping and sleeping in shifts when we could, until he said we didn't need to hurry anymore. We've been resting here, just outside a town's perimeter so he can bring us supplies."

Despite their luck, Will found it difficult to accept the explanation. He placed a hand on the bandaged wound only to discover the area numb. "How long has it been since…"

"I don't know," Clara answered with a dip of her chin. "I stopped counting after the first few days."

"I would say close to three weeks," Zelma added from her right.

Will was a bit surprised by how little the length of time bothered him. "How is my leg? I can't feel anything there now."

That seemed to be a more positive topic of discussion, for their faces lit up.

Clara's smile also returned. "Really? There's no pain?"

He shook his head.

"Whatever the Nim-Valans used was unlike any poison we've been trained to heal and worked fast. You had a fever, and your muscles began to seize, as if your body went into shock. Because we were escaping, though, the man who guided us refused to tend to the injury until we could do so at a safe distance. He rubbed medicine on it and treated it more when we arrived here. You drank water and broth, but nothing changed until yesterday when the fever broke."

"We thought you would die," the youngest-looking girl mumbled while hugging her elbows.

"Lissa!" the one next to her hissed with a glare.

Will's eyes wandered from person to person while they stared at him. *Their expressions seem tired but hopeful*, he noticed and rubbed his right thigh impulsively. *Whatever the stranger used, it must be counteracting the poison's effects. I doubt it amplified my body's natural healing ability. Also, I assume he didn't want them using their magic in case we were followed or the Nim-Valans have someone who can sense magical energy.*

That much thinking, as brief as it was, began to make his head ache and reminded him of his weakened state. As if sensing this, Clara put a hand on his shoulder again.

"Stay here," she ordered in a gentle manner. "We'll warm a light meal for you and bring water. Rest for tonight, then we can talk in the morning."

His impulse to ask the many questions forming in his mind became overshadowed by a weariness hindering his ability to process the information. He kept quiet for the time being, and soon his friend brought him a thin soup and a chunk of stale bread. After cleaning the wooden bowl, he finished the waterskin she left for him and fell asleep as soon as he lied down.

Mysterious Powers

Compared to her first, solo journey to the Western Woods, Coura found herself admiring the alterations to the path and behavior of the citizens in that area. Most prominently, dozens of people occupied the road, which always provided a sense of comfort and opportunities to socialize. The plains to the west projected an air of calmness compared to the hustling capital city, and now that the Sie-Kie were open to guiding visitors through their forest, more travelers used their assistance to move south instead of heading through Umbridge, Fester, and Dala to reach the less populated towns, such as Medina and Marinich. Over the past two years, the former recovered from the demonic creature's slaughter that left only a portion of its townsfolk alive, and Coura continued to hear positive updates here and there. In fact, she wanted to be certain of its recovery and chanced talking with others on the road.

A handful had been through Medina and readily shared what they knew, which happened to be accurate with her information, to her relief. Plenty of conversations followed in addition to the questions, though most of it proved similar and expected. Marcus reminded Coura before she left that, as an Asteom soldier, she was required to wear her uniform to showcase her status in case of an emergency or other situations requiring her intervention.

The travelers who noticed asked about news from the palace, the Yeluthians, and various topics she could readily discuss. Thankfully, no one pried into more personal matters, but almost all wished to hear about the northern border and Nim-Vala. She spoke about the topic lightly yet not in a misleading way, mentioning how little the soldiers were made aware of what their people did or the status of an alliance. It became apparent after a while she wasn't going to reveal critical news, something Marcus warned against, and the people left her alone for the time being.

The guard station closest to the Western Woods stood at the end of the road that split to the north and south. Coura trailed behind those moving left underneath the looming canopy and peeked at the station out of curiosity to see if she recognized the soldier posted there. It wasn't surprising to catch three men in the same uniform as hers standing idly inside with the window wide open to survey the road as they chatted. The sun hovered high in the sky when she passed under the enormous trees whose branches blocked the direct rays of light.

Unlike her first visit, nothing ominous threatened the people on the path, and the sight of a Sie-Kie man up ahead projected a sense of safety. Everyone moved on without fuss, though Coura noticed several individuals glancing at the strange, half-dressed warrior gazing over them with a spear in hand. Those she walked with continued until they reached the next Sie-Kie man, who looked as if he had just reached the age to be out on his own.

"A campsite lies ahead to the right," he explained and gestured with his own pike in a bored tone of voice. "I advise staying there as you will reach the edge of the woods during the daytime tomorrow. Otherwise, be careful if you traverse during the night since no light from the moon pierces through the treetops."

Coura waited for everybody to move on before speaking with the boy. "How far are we from the Sie-Kie village?"

The question seemed to be a common one for the guides, for he showed no sign of emotion when he answered. "My people's village is built within the trees on branches off this road. We are not unwelcome to visitors but ask they be respectful of our customs."

She debated whether or not to share her previous encounter with Barnelus, the witch, and the demonic creature, yet she decided against it. "I understand. Can you show me to the entrance?"

"Beyond those bushes is a trail." He pointed his spear in the direction he faced, which led through the foliage.

With nothing else to go on, Coura thanked him, adjusted the single pack over her shoulder, and pushed through the greenery. The trail proved to be hardly suitable for an unfit individual or someone carrying more than one or two bags due to its lack of a flat surface, jutting branches grabbing for loose clothing, and misleading openings, but she felt confident from her experiences that the village would reveal itself eventually. As the forest dimmed to signal the sunset outside its cover, she shoved her way into an open area no larger than her room at the palace where a rope dangled from above.

"Hello?" she called and glanced upward. Instead of climbing it immediately, Coura waited until voices sounded from above, and the line wavered as another man slid to the ground.

"State your business," he practically demanded while looking her over.

"My name is Coura Galdwin. I'm on leave from Verona to visit someone in your tribe."

"Who?"

"She's the woman who acts as your peoples' witch."

That took the Sie-Kie villager back. "You came to see the *shalma*?"

The title rang like an old, almost forgotten melody, and Coura nodded.

Again, the man stared at her before coming to a conclusion. "Wait here. When I drop the ladder, you may climb to meet us."

She watched as he pulled himself up the rope in a feat only someone raised with the practice could manage. A minute later, the promised ladder fell.

*

By the time Coura received a space to stay, bedding, and a meal, evening enveloped the forest, so the woman waiting on her promised to take her to their witch the next day. She provided a sleeping gown before disappearing through the opening curtain, leaving Coura to rest. In the morning, a tray of the interesting delicacies acting as her breakfast and a clean, tan dress to change into awaited her.

Her caretaker from the previous night returned just after she changed with the request that she remain close behind. Together, they crossed the uncomfortably exposed, wooden bridges between the trees with the dozens of citizens going about their business. Most lingered to observe and point the two out in their own language along the way. The huts of the chief, his family, and the witch were located at what Coura had always seen as the center of the raised village where a wide platform provided space for gatherings and celebrations.

When an elderly woman with striking, colorless hair stuck her head out from one of the hut's openings, Coura's guide halted.

"*Shalma*," the Sie-Kie villager muttered, as if startled by the sight, before glancing back at Coura. "You may go to her."

Coura voiced her gratitude for the assistance, noticed the white-haired head disappear behind the curtain, and went to enter the witch's dwelling. The inside remained a mess, though an ironically organized one, of mysterious oddities from floor to ceiling, distracting her enough that she couldn't help but gaze around for a minute before taking a seat on the flat cushion laid out at the center. Meanwhile, the old witch kept her back to the room as she studied the outside world through a short window at eye level.

"You decided to return," came the woman's harsh greeting.

Coura didn't expect the unfriendly tone and wondered if the woman felt ill or was simply displeased to see her again. Because of that uncertainty, she stayed quiet and waited until the elder turned to face her; however, this took a while to happen.

The *shalma* remained as still as a statue with her hands clasped behind her back, causing her to hunch forward. Slowly, she shifted away from the window. The wrinkled expression appeared to project warmth, complete with a gentle smile, yet behind the mask Coura immediately noticed a sadness radiating from the attentive eyes.

"I shouldn't be so insincere," the witch went on at last, confirming Coura's belief that the woman acted bitterly toward her. "The *shimla* and his sons will be glad to see your face again, as will those who remember your deeds for our people. You may have noticed already, but a wind of change passed through here after you left. Our leader sent warriors to the capital city, and soon those from around the country began wandering into these woods. Considering the danger brought on by the wicked power of a demon, the village is optimistic."

When she paused, Coura sensed she expected an additional comment and obliged. "If the chief will be pleased to see me, I suppose my meddling with the Sie-Kie led to changes for the better."

The *shalma* bobbed her head, then the old woman chuckled while placing a hand over her mouth in a bashful manner. "In the moment, we never appreciate the positives it brings about because it's so easy to focus on the negatives. Our lives may have been comfortable as we kept to the trees, but outside help was necessary. Now, we can learn about our friends and the dangers to the world around us. Mages came to visit me too, though I wish I could provide them with more than what this aged mind keeps together. My hope is for my apprentice to learn their ways and adapt for the future, but she is still too young to understand what that means."

For the rest of the morning, the two talked about the changes the village underwent over the months following Coura's last appearance. Although traditions with the *shalma* stayed the same so she remained the lone magic user among the Sie-Kie, the people welcomed light and dark mages, admired the strangers' power, and learned how to best use their skills both for and against such allies. They were also able to ask questions about the world outside the Western Woods, including what magical energies are, how they are utilized, and what the Yeluthians are like.

What the witch became most excited to share was that she had been permitted to alter the customary inheritance of the title she held. Instead of passing it along to a daughter, future magic users could choose their successor to train in protecting the village. Coura didn't know if the woman had children and felt asking would be insensitive, but she found herself smiling as the witch beamed with pride. Then, they shifted to a discussion on the woods' safety.

"I've heard nothing out of the ordinary about the creatures below," the *shalma* revealed.

A sense of relief washed over Coura after the woman's words, and she released a sigh to show it. "Most of Asteom is the same."

"Most?" The elder raised an eyebrow while the curve in her lips evened out.

"Unfortunately, I encountered a trio of demonic creatures recently. That's why I came to see you…"

She summarized the scouting mission without omitting the demon's presence or his words meant only for her. As she spoke, the witch's nature became less sympathetic until the woman practically scowled. Then, she remained silent until Coura begged for her help.

"What is it you want with me?" came the sharp response.

Coura paused to consider her center of power and the energy within. It had been months since she encountered hostility for what she was, but experience aided her in getting straight to the point. "I can't enter my soul space to learn what's wrong, no matter how often I try meditating. You could sense the demonic energy before at a distance and understand its behavior in a unique way. I was wondering if you can teach me to do that, to look inside myself-"

The *shalma* raised a hand abruptly to interrupt her request.

"What you are requesting takes years of practice to master, and one cannot peer into another's *chi alve*, or what you refer to as soul space. Besides, I already told you what would happen should you pursue that unnatural type of power."

"You mean with the creatures, like what happened when I first entered the woods."

The witch nodded. "I warned you against taking their power into yourself. The markings may be gone, but their effects still linger."

"My center is damaged because I accepted the demonic energy," Coura added as she recalled being scolded by Byron, Emilea, and others in the past for her decision. "I was able to hold it because of how my soul space adapted, and my body suffered every time too. I'm not surprised by what that did to both, but I need to understand what's happening in case more creatures appear."

"If all you need is information, allow me to share my observations with you," the woman said, echoing their first encounter. "I told you if you valued your life, you wouldn't traverse the path you inevitably did; that included your entire life after your encounters with the creatures. You may be familiar with how your body and *chi alve* adapted to contain such power, but what resulted was a broken soul. The damage is irreversible."

"How can I still wield magic if what you say is true?" Coura asked next.

For a moment, the *shalma* pondered the question.

"Allow me to clarify my previous words," the older woman began again while deliberately slowing her cadence. "By broken, I do not mean you should not be able to use the energy. You could say the walls are cracked, like a dropped, clay pot. Even if the pieces are reforming, as they mostly likely did when you were recovering, there are always going to be noticeable fractures that allow energy to pass in and out."

"Why would that prevent me from meditating?"

"That I do not know," the elder replied in a calmer manner. "The cause could be many aspects relating to your mentality or your *chi alve* itself. What you need to understand is beyond observing the space because the issue is with the power emanating from your body."

Coura gaped as the witch promptly glanced away. "What does that mean? What power is emanating?"

"If you consider the clay pot I used as a comparison, the cracks would still allow water to pass through, correct? Because of what you've done to accept the energy demons manipulate, your center will continue to absorb any. Likewise, it has a route for escaping thanks to the pathways that created those markings."

Coura laced her fingers together and placed them against her lips as she tried to process what the *shalma* revealed. "Were you able to see or sense this the whole time?"

"As I mentioned earlier, I don't believe we can peer into another's soul. I noticed by taking a moment to evaluate your body with my senses in order to detect what energy flows through you."

"That must be how Terran recognized me," Coura muttered to herself.

Still, the witch grunted in agreement. "The demonic power is not overwhelmingly noticeable, but if one were to try locating you nearby, they could do so right away."

How could this have happened? Coura wondered in the resulting silence. *I always accepted what Soirée did to me, but I suppose I assumed once she was gone my soul space would repair itself...*

A sudden chill slid down her spine as she remembered what took place in the demonic realm.

What if she isn't dead? I don't know if the ancestral weapon acted like a regular sword, but she should have bled out eventually. When the rogue angel stabbed me with the dagger, her presence and the demonic power were stripped away. What if our connection wasn't severed and she's sealed away instead?

"Is there anything else you can tell me?" she dared to press after.

"I'm afraid I'm at my limit of what knowledge I possess on the subject. What I claim stems from this interaction in relation to the previous and what you shared with me. At the moment, the only danger this poses is that the power within you attracts the demon or its creatures, who hunger for that energy. I'm at a loss for advice on resolving this issue."

Coura decided to free the woman of such a burden by taking her leave and voiced as much when she rose. "You've been more helpful than anyone else. Thank you for tolerating me."

The cold personality present throughout the majority of their conversation warmed into what she became familiar with. The *shalma* smiled and led her outside where the aromas of cooking dinners revealed the time.

When she returned to her hut, Coura found her caretaker standing outside with another tray of food in hand and accepted the meal before dismissing the woman for the evening. She ate her fill while contemplating what the witch shared and eventually drifted off; however, a nightmare shook her awake long before sunrise. Once she fell into sleep again, she woke late in the morning without any memory of what stirred her during the night.

*

With the original task at hand complete, Coura focused on using her time off to relax and catch up with the Sie-Kie. Barnelus proved to be available during the afternoon, so the two met up for a hike through the forest. As he guided her along a common trail their people wore down, they reminisced about his time in Verona, including the battle that killed his younger brother. Both earned plenty of honor from the village, along with their comrades, and the markings etched into the center of his exposed back showcased the event, as well as his status.

Coura had heard about his marriage to a childhood friend last year from Aaron after the king received an invite to the ceremony. There didn't seem to be an expectation for him to attend, though he extended the offer to her if he chose to accept, but the council replied with a set of gifts instead. Barnelus shared little about the wedding because it sounded like a traditional affair, yet he revealed he and his wife were expecting a child.

Although Coura congratulated him and he appeared pleased, the Sie-Kie warrior didn't linger on the subject. He went on to share how the birth would make him the new *shimla*, according to the village's customs. That was when she learned about the system of the chief's position, as she had with the witch's.

"The next in line for the name *shimla* is to be wed and assume his responsibilities when two conditions are met," he explained while they returned to the trees. "The current *shimla* must deem his successor worthy and be present when the marking is bestowed, and there must be another in line. My father voiced his permission months ago but needed to be patient. Now that I married and our child will arrive soon, I can take up the name and lead the people under his guidance."

"You already do that from what I've seen," Coura commented.

The conversation ended before he could respond as they climbed back into the canopy. Then, he invited her to the *shimla*'s hut where she greeted the current chief and his family again and met Barnelus' wife named Serena. They ate together, talked as well as they could between the gap in languages, and moved outside to enjoy the noise of the Western Woods with the many people who came to do the same.

The next day, Barnelus took her to meet the group of warriors under his command. They practiced sparring before slipping into raves about the past and bragging about their markings. Most, especially the younger men, shot her doubtful glances since she was the only female and an outsider, but they eased up when their leader reminisced about her first visit, the demonic creature, and how he traveled to the palace afterward to aid the kingdom. He even repeated the nickname Coura forgot about just to prove her inclusion and acceptance among the Sie-Kie. Once evening approached, she returned to her hut for dinner.

"Night-Cleaver," she mused to herself with a childish grin. "I wonder why that seemed so fitting."

The memory lingered until she began to contemplate what to do the next day.

If I return to Verona, that would leave me with at least a couple days to myself. I could also spend a day heading west to the coast since I've still never seen it. Maybe I can wander through the city when I return. The more ideas she put together, the better she felt about using every spare hour, leading her to develop a rough schedule.

In the blink of an eye, night brightened into morning. She didn't need to pack much, and her uniform had been cleaned by her caretaker the previous afternoon, so she threw it on after eating breakfast. The Sie-Kie woman led her to the ground via the same rope ladder she used to enter the village, through the untamed brush, and directly onto the path where a new guard monitored the area. Coura followed the dirt road north despite passing at least a dozen strangers heading in the opposite direction and emerged near the guard station just before noon.

The same trio of men still occupied the smaller building when she requested directions to the coast. Although they acted friendly and offered the information in detail, one eyed her up before asking about her business to the west. When she realized he referred to her uniform, which lacked the crimson coat due to the summer heat, she shared her name and position under the newer general.

The one who addressed her recognized the name, whether because of her father, her other relationships, or her involvement with the battle against Hendal, and showed a new interest in her. He appeared to be double her age, yet his excitement rivaled a child's when he questioned her about the angels. Then, he babbled to the other two about how she was the Asteom soldier with the ability to fly.

Coura remained patient while they discussed the past instead of involving her, thanked them afterward, and departed along the northern road.

It's been a while since someone behaved like that around me, she reflected and felt her cheeks blushing.

When the kingdom no longer dealt with the former high priest or Soirée and the remains of the battle outside the palace had been cleaned up, Aaron and his new council publicly praised a general list of the soldiers, mages, Yeluthians, and ordinary citizens who went out of their way to aid their country. The Dalans were present and celebrated for three days straight in the city, bringing plenty of business to the shops and taverns despite some annoyance at their rowdy personalities. Mainly, King Arval and his commanders, General Tio, Calin, Marcus, General Casner and his assistant, Byron, and Emilea were seen as the heroes who stopped Hendal, but anyone who fought or who knew her abilities recognized Coura as well.

She considered that in the past and tried not to linger on what it took to stop them. Rarely, even years later, people involved with the palace gossip recalled how her name became synonymous with the image of an angel possessing black wings, and they thanked her in their own way.

The grassland near the coast provided ample space for camping, which many locals did during the summertime, so Coura paused to rest, allowing the sound of the moving water nearby to lull her into a peaceful nap. When she woke, she hurried to the edge of the earth where ruthless waves slammed against the rock walls and boulders below. It was awe-inspiring to observe such natural power, and more so when gazing to the endless sea spanning as far as the eye could see.

Coura stayed much longer than she anticipated, making herself comfortable in the grass and continuing to stare beyond what she considered the edge of Asteom itself. It didn't seem possible to gauge how far the ocean stretched since nothing rested on the horizon. She thought flying might reveal land, yet the idea of hovering over nothing except blue water for hours without being certain of an end frightened her; it would either reveal a new world on the other side as a reward or become a suicidal endeavor. The imagery followed her as she took her leave of the magnificent, terrifying sight.

*

Most of the people following the road to the capital city kept to themselves, except for a cheery group of men Coura figured had to be merchants. They flirted with all the women, including her, as if it were a game and jostled the other men like they had been friends their entire lives. It might have been irritating if the weather hadn't cooled down to the perfect temperature, putting everyone in higher spirits. By the time they reached Verona and broke apart, the sun started to set, so Coura purchased dinner at a local tavern she favored before returning to her quarters for the night.

On her final day off, she slept in until her stomach growled enough to bother her, then she grabbed lunch from the mess hall with the dozens of other soldiers and mages. The plan she orchestrated for the day involved getting dressed, moving into the city to visit the shops, and ending with a meal at the inn where Aimes worked. Every step went as expected, though the older man from Clearwater looked pleasantly surprised to see her. The pair talked about nothing in particular aside from her visit out west, which intrigued him.

"Perhaps next time you can join me," she offered once she finished the last of her cooled wine.

Aimes laughed at her comment, a hearty sound in the otherwise dull space. "We'll see. For the time being, I'm happier here than I've ever been! All thanks to you, might I add."

"You mention that every time," she grumbled and rolled her eyes before rising to exit.

Her friend shrugged but ended the conversation there.

The two wished each other well as she left to stand alone in front of the building. Although she didn't acknowledge it often, she was proud of herself for guiding Aimes and Marcy to Verona instead of leaving them to scavenge for themselves near Dala. At the time, the hasty decision didn't seem like anything spectacular, but now she had the pleasure of watching them blossom in better environments.

I suppose I should get back since I start training again tomorrow, she thought with a yawn and shifted her eyes to study the road ahead.

Most of the inns were located at the outskirts of the city because of the space the area provided for travelers' horses and what livestock they brought to sell. Several lights illuminated the paths and alleyways, including one behind her, but most of the activity stemmed from farther into Verona. As Coura considered this, her eyes fell on a lone structure off the road and practically out of sight behind the other buildings. Only a stream of smoke and a lamp hanging by the entrance showed any signs of life.

That's the prison, she realized a minute later. *No wonder it's isolated from the rest of the capital. It doesn't just hold petty thieves but serious criminals too. Murderers, notorious swindlers, and…those who commit treason against the crown. I forgot Hendal is still alive in there.*

The ex-high priest proved to be nothing more than a weak man after Soirée's power had been stripped away and the rogue angels abandoned him. At the time of his judgement, Coura was one of many believing him to deserve a death sentence; however, it surprised her when both Aaron and Emilea, two individuals forced under his control, vouched that he be left alive.

The master light mage's reasoning proved to be sympathetically motivated, for she felt the situation put the people through enough and killing a high priest could be seen as a bad omen despite his actions. On the other hand, Aaron considered imprisonment a worse punishment than death. His maliciousness startled Coura until she realized his comment was most likely influenced by his personal experience acting as a mindless slave because of the demon's power. The ultimate decision hadn't been announced publicly, but many individuals within the palace learned of Hendal's fate and whispered it among one another.

As Coura remembered a conversation she had with Aaron, Marcus, Emilea, and Clearshot, who discussed the verdict one afternoon when they found themselves together, she began to wonder about the ex-high priest's connection to Soirée.

Nobody could sense demonic energy within him after the Yeluthian's spell, so the council assumed he wouldn't be dangerous enough to worry about...

At that reminder, an alarming suspicion froze her in place.

If no one sensed the power that attracted Terran's attention except the Sie-Kie witch, is it possible Hendal has been unwillingly obtaining demonic energy too? Could he still wield it without Soirée assisting him? Is he a potential threat like me? If Terran came after me, would he also be able to locate and free Hendal?

Before she realized it, Coura jogged across the area to reach the front of the prison; however, she hesitated to knock on the metal door. Her lack of experience utilizing her authority as a soldier led her to worry if the guards would turn her away, yet that proved to be the only option she could think of. With that in mind, she stripped her bag from her back, dug out the coat, and threw it on before pounding on the door.

After a moment, a creak sounded as the hinges worked. The man on the opposite side who opened it stood tall and puffed his muscular chest, which did bode well for the prison's security, but his expression projected curiosity instead of dismissiveness.

"What brings you here, young lady?" he inquired while leaning on the doorframe in a casual manner.

"I'm hoping you can tell me the regulations for visiting a prisoner here," she decided to say. The less she revealed, the better considering the slim chance he would recognize her just by her appearance.

Although she expected hostility, the guard scratched his chin as he looked her up and down without responding right away.

"They usually don't get visitors, but it is permitted under supervision for ten minutes per day."

"That's it?"

He grunted in confirmation and stood straight. "Having outsiders here is a risk because we can't vouch for your safety."

"I understand," Coura replied. Still, she was willing to push her luck before abandoning the effort. "Would I be able to see someone tonight?"

"That depends. Who is it you'd like to visit?"

When she mentioned Hendal's name, the guard's eyebrows flew up, then they furrowed while he frowned. "What business do you have with him?"

His less friendly demeanor was reason enough for her to share more about her intentions, though she didn't line the pieces up in order. "My name is Coura, and my father is one of the Yeluthian commanders, Evern Galdwin. They have reason to believe the former high priest might possess information relating to the appearance of creatures to the south posing a problem. He asked me to interrogate the man, with King Aaron's permission of course."

As she spoke, he appeared interested, doubtful, and curious all at the same time and paused to ponder the information.

If this works, I'll need to let Aaron and Evern in on what Hendal may be involved with.

"I can understand your reasoning," the guard began again. "Do you have the documentation?"

Coura shook her head and shrugged. "I returned from leave earlier today and decided to stop by to hear the visitation guidelines before picking up the paperwork. Asking to see the former high priest now is just a personal request so I don't have to come back tomorrow. I guess I'll need to bring the paperwork anyway…"

She turned around without finishing her comment. Part of her felt relieved, yet the rest hoped the man would be more understanding. When he called for her to wait, her heart jumped with anticipation.

"Listen," he grumbled and scratched the side of his head with a glance behind. "You've got the uniform and badge, and you informed me of your purpose. I'll head to my office to note your conversation for our records. Then, you can bring the paperwork later. You'll be assigned a guard with you at all times, though; not even soldiers are exempt from that policy."

"Thank you, and that's fine with me," Coura added.

The guard nodded before stepping aside and gesturing for her to enter.

The inside of the building was just about what she pictured a prison to look like. Rooms half the size of her own lined the walls with metal bars crossing horizontally and vertically as a barrier. Beyond them, the spaces held nothing more than a cot, a pair of buckets, and a basin for water. All the prisoners remained quiet, yet she felt their eyes lingering on her as they continued on, sending a shiver down her spine. At the end of the hallway, a split set of stairs led up to the next floor and down into a basement.

Her escort halted and pointed to the descending set. "Once you reach the bottom, you'll run into Irwin. He's on duty for the basement cells, so he'll be observing your interaction and lead you to the exit when you're done."

Coura nodded before moving downstairs through the slim corridor. She figured the layout would be similar to the main floor, which it proved to be; however, she only noticed two prisoners within the many spaces upon first glance.

The second guard named Irwin shut the book he was reading under the light of a dim lamp at his desk and glared at her as she approached to introduce herself. With an incomprehensible grumble, he stuffed the thick novel under one arm before walking across the hall. He didn't speak until they reached the last set of bars, and before that, he grabbed his book and slammed it against the metal, sending a loud ring echoing through the underground area.

"Wake up!" the guard shouted. "You got a visitor."

The closest lamp provided enough light to see the entire cell, so she stepped forward to peer in. On the side of the bed sat the ex-high priest, who wore a dirt-colored shirt and loose, matching pants. He folded his hands together and bent his body so his forehead touched the fingers in a prayerful position. Despite the noise, he didn't stir.

"The man's a loon," Irwin leaned over to mutter. "Aside from sleeping, eating, and using the bucket, he stays like that all the time."

Coura didn't respond. She had to remind herself why she chose to go there in order to calm a stirring anger directed at the person who hurt so many of her friends and the kingdom she served.

The guard snorted a laugh and strolled to the nearest wall where he leaned against it to pick up his reading. "Good luck getting him to talk, or even acknowledge you."

For a few minutes, she contemplated what to discuss and how to address the man concerning demonic energy. Her gaze dropped to the floor as she did so until a voice broke through the silence.

"To what do I owe the pleasure of seeing you?"

It was a disturbing sound, not because of its hoarseness or the cracking of vowels, but because of the strength pushing the words through to the end of the sentence. It proved to be the voice of someone who, despite not speaking as an authoritative figure, still prepared to.

Irwin growled and responded before Coura could answer.

"You still talk so formal for a criminal!" he yelled and stormed over to slam his book against the bars once more. "We can cut out your tongue, you know. Maybe I should let you out so we can recapture you and restart your life sentence."

"That's enough," Coura snapped as she looked at the guard. "I don't care how he speaks to me. At least I know he'll listen."

Irwin didn't seem offended, but he backed away, opened his book, and spat in the cage's direction before focusing on the pages. She returned her eyes forward and found Hendal sitting straighter to watch her with an expressionless gaze reminiscent of their initial encounter when she first arrived in the palace with Byron.

"I need information from you," she started, only to be interrupted by the former high priest.

"To see you here, Coura, must mean a matter is on your mind relating to our mutual acquaintance. I doubt this has to do with anything else given the past."

Hearing him speak carefully in the presence of another person surprised Coura, especially since that meant he wasn't prepared to reveal their shared knowledge of demonic power and Soirée.

It would cause a lot less trouble, and less explaining, to leave Irwin and the other guards out of the loop, at least for now. Depending on what Hendal shares, it might not mean much.

"How have you been feeling?" she chose to ask next. If he planned to dance around with words, he would understand some of what she hinted at.

Unfortunately, he kept quiet, providing an opportunity for the third person to bud in again.

Irwin let out an irritated groan and waltzed over to peer through the bars. "So much for listening. I told you, he's not sane. Being cooped up in here does that to a person. I've seen it with everybody. All his properness a moment ago is nothing but a sham. Inside, I bet he's trying to figure out what you just said."

Coura considered telling the guard to shut his mouth and leave them alone, yet she held her tongue after recalling the prison's policy. If she needed to be supervised around the former high priest, it would be better not to aggravate the man more than Hendal.

With a final jeer, Irwin spun around and marched even farther away to begin reading again. Her eyes followed him until the space fell silent, then they returned to the cell where its prisoner continued to study her carefully.

"Are you going to answer my questions or not?" she finally demanded and crossed her arms.

Hendal smiled to show he found the question amusing.

Meanwhile, Coura waited, kept her attention on him, and prayed Irwin would stay out of their business.

"I suppose the best place to start is at the beginning," the prisoner responded. He shifted to face her and folded his hands on his lap, as if the two were chatting over tea.

What does he mean by that?

"I was born and raised in Kercher as the second son of the head messenger, which put me in a binding position. Are you familiar with the structure of Kercher's society?"

The question seemingly came out of nowhere, causing Coura to pause and contemplate the eastern town she knew little about.

Apparently, Irwin did. He produced a chortle to intervene once more. "They were supposed to bring messages all over the country, then they up and disappear. Who hasn't heard about that lousy village?"

"I never did," Coura replied firmly enough to hint at her temper. "What about Kercher's society and the messengers?"

Ignoring the guard's outbursts proved to be best since his voice trailed off into nothing when neither addressed him, allowing Hendal educate her on his hometown.

She learned how it became famous for serving the angels and a pair of deities because the people acted as messengers between Yeluthia and Asteom. Even before he mentioned the town's dwindling numbers and isolation from the rest of the country, she figured Yeluthia's own seclusion hurt their society. The former high priest didn't hear if Kercher improved with the reintroduction of the old alliance, and Coura couldn't remember any updates about the town either, but he stopped there just when his voice grew too worn to speak.

"What else?" she pushed during the pause.

"There is far too much to explain in one night," he answered before turning to face the wall, like he'd been doing when she first arrived.

"You didn't tell me anything."

"Come see me in a few days."

This time, Coura's eyes narrowed into a glare while she stepped forward. "I need to know about your connection with her!"

The shout fell on deaf ears. Hendal didn't speak again, no matter what she tried, and she kicked the bars in defeat. Irwin, who tuned out their conversation to read, jumped at the metal bang and hurried to close his book when Coura stormed by.

"I told you, he's not sane," he repeated and returned to his desk chair as she climbed the stairs to the ground floor.

When the first guard inquired about her visit, she half-heartedly mentioned another sometime soon before returning to the palace.

Kercher

Kercher

Becoming a priest had never been a choice. Many people thought it required an incredible amount of magic; even more believed there to be some sort of connection to one or more deities. With a variety of religions, it was easy to assume much. Hendal stopped caring about such notions by the age of nine. If the gods couldn't answer his prayers, were they really worth his time? If he was forced to revere them, couldn't they at least free him from his life of servitude?

Even though he had been born in Kercher, he never considered the town to be his home nor felt any connection to its people. At some point in his lineage, the Yeluthians apparently blessed his family during Kercher's founding as a necessary means of communicating between the humans and angels. Only in their family did the eldest child carry the expectation to produce many offspring. All but the second child of the previous generation's first born were trained as messengers to travel across the country on Yeluthia's behalf and would raise their own families to grow the system. It became their responsibility to connect the two kingdoms, a task meant for no other household.

Meanwhile, the second child, the one considered a special gift, was given to the town's priest or priestess as soon as they could be separated from their mother. The church then accepted them as their mentor's replacement. Since a servant of the gods wasn't allowed to create a family, this ensured there would always be someone to honor Kercher's founding faith. The tradition continued for generations, even when the angels stopped visiting and the townsfolk began to leave and never return.

Hendal's mother had been the eldest of three to his grandparents and bore a daughter at a young age. She loved the child dearly and spent much longer than normal training her. With a lack of news to spread, his mother felt less pressure to produce any more offspring. In fact, as far as he understood, the only person who harped about the tradition had been his uncle and the town's priest, Verdic. By the time Hendal came into the world, his mother nearly reached the age to no longer conceive and readily gave him away as soon as he could walk to silence her devoted brother. When Hendal turned three years of age, his sister, who was over two decades older, welcomed a second son. As per tradition, she passed off the boy when he seemed at the proper stage to join the priest.

At first, the lessons Verdic taught emanated a sense of wonder and left Hendal in awe. He and his nephew, Wesley, learned about the angels and demons, the power of light and dark energies, the history of their town, and the god Summa and goddess Izina, who were said to be all-knowing life-bringers. The foundation of their town's church reflected the principles of Summa and Izina, stating all life is precious, the energies of the world are meant to be balanced, and tradition is necessary to honor the ancestors of Kercher. Since Hendal developed a better memory for studying the texts passed down by the priests, he helped Wesley along, and the two grew close enough to consider each other brothers.

Eventually, the reading and memorizing became tedious. Hendal often stared out the church's window to watch the other children skip around and enjoy their freedom. The next day, when his uncle brought them in front to repaint the wooden building, he decided to bring up the subject.

"Why aren't we allowed to play outside?" he asked Verdic after a pause to wipe away the beads of sweat trailing down his face. No matter the season, the priest still required them to wear gray, woolen robes at all times.

"We were born different from the others in Kercher," his uncle answered without looking away from his work. "While they have their duties that allow for such activity, we must continue on with ours."

"But why?"

Verdic's lips scrunched up, as if he'd eaten a tart piece of fruit, then he glared down at his pupils. "What does Izina say about questioning one's life?"

Immediately, Wesley attempted a guess. "She says to live as though each day is a gift that will only last for-"

Hendal watched in horror as his nephew's sentence cut short when the flat paint brush in their teacher's hand struck Wesley across the face.

"The destiny of one's life is predetermined by the gods! As it is written in Nedian's journal seventy years ago, "…for the goddess herself cast upon me a vision of paradise and promised eternal bliss for those loyal to their human lives. One cannot hope to escape unless they wish to spoil the future of their people, and thus, end the line of Annonely, who spoke with Summa's ancestor…"

Wesley put a hand to his cheek, and Hendal could see his shoulders begin to shake. As the smeared paint began to dry, the two boys continued listening to the crazed priest spew verses and quotes from their studies. Verdic only stopped when he ran out of breath, but Hendal caught half a dozen sets of eyes on them from the children and adults nearby.

After the first incident, he never mentioned anything like that to his teacher again. He and Wesley worked diligently to avoid sparking the priest's wrath; however, Hendal would share his feelings with his only friend late in the night when the thoughts kept him awake.

"Why would Verdic get so upset?" he whispered to his nephew while shifting positions on the wide cot they shared in the attic.

"I don't want to bring it up again," came the soft reply. Wesley usually acted sensitive about the experience, yet Hendal grew more confused and frustrated by the unexpected outburst.

"All I wonder is why we have to be priests? Why is it necessary to keep the tradition going? Would something bad happen to the town if we didn't?"

"I don't like when you talk like that."

Hendal rolled over to turn his face toward Wesley. Even in the darkness, he caught the other's eyes on him. "I'm sorry," he offered in a sincere manner, "but do you ever consider what life outside is like? What could we do if we were not forced to be priests?"

"We would be messengers."

Hendal ended the conversation there since it became obvious his nephew didn't understand what he meant.

*

During the next couple months, not a day went by that the boys didn't fear stepping out of line until a sickness spread throughout the area in early spring, causing Verdic to be bedridden. The man would only comment on how the gods destined their circumstances against a fever clouding his mind. Hendal's mother visited to give him medicine; otherwise, the two boys had been left alone. At first, all they could think to do with their new freedom was go outside and join the other children in their games until their uncle recovered. Wesley felt too concerned with being punished, though, so Hendal crafted a plan.

"We can take turns. I'll leave in the morning, and you can go after lunch."

"Won't someone tell the priest?"

"Not if we claim he let us outside in order to keep us from getting sick. We'll still study when we're here and at night together."

After some more persuading, Wesley nodded, albeit hesitantly.

The next morning, Hendal snuck through the kitchen's back door and, for the first time in his life, sprinted through town until he reached the fields beyond. His lungs burned once he slowed to a stop, then he spun around and walked back through Kercher. The few people tending to the fields and opening their shops gave curious glances, but no one spoke to him.

The sun's light shined bright and warmed his skin, prompting him to pause, close his eyes, and savor the sensation as much as he could. *Why would a priest not be allowed to enjoy this simple pleasure?* he wondered.

When he stumbled upon the children his age participating in a game requiring one person to chase and tag the others, he asked to join. Most of them mumbled their uncertainty while the rest remained silent.

"Aren't you living in the priest's household?" one of the youngest girls inquired without displaying more than genuine curiosity.

"Just because I stay inside to study doesn't mean I can't be here with you," he replied to reassure both the children and himself.

After accepting his explanation, they taught him their game and eased up enough for Hendal to have fun during the rest of the morning. Around noon, they scattered for lunch after he informed them Wesley would be there in the afternoon. He returned to his nephew and enthusiastically described what the town was like and the game he learned. Although Wesley remained uncertain, Hendal sensed excitement underneath the nerves. The other boy scurried away, leaving him to relax in the church's library with no small amount of envy.

Once alone, and for the first time in many months, Hendal put his hands together and prayed. Whenever his uncle led the action, Hendal knew Verdic could not control what he thought, so he often let his mind and imagination wander. He never believed Summa or Izina were listening because he hadn't experienced a moment in his life that he considered spiritual. This time, he tried to focus.

Please, he begged without addressing a particular deity. *I don't want the life of a priest. I desire to have choices, not people relying on me to stay here, study the scripture, and teach information I'm not sure I trust. Grant me this one request, and I will do whatever it is you need of me.*

Never before had he felt a desire to ask for more than his simple, methodical lifestyle. The game allowed him to express himself, and the children provided an opportunity to interact with other people. That taste for the world beyond his duties, beyond what he began to see as chains, stirred a restlessness previously sleeping within.

*

A week passed until Verdic recovered. Hendal and Wesley resumed their daily routine in the church, except their chores and lessons became tiresome. The priest noticed them fidgeting in their seats, glancing longingly out the windows, or slacking on their work and would yell or scold them into submission before they outgrew his vocal reprimanding. Then, he resorted to physical disciplinary actions. One morning, he started carrying around a thin branch as long as his arm and used it to strike their hands, or faces in severe instances.

Wesley ceased his misbehavior since pain influenced his mentality; Hendal reacted in practically the opposite manner.

Week by week, he hated his teacher and the life lined up for him more and would often bring about the punishments by questioning the material they were being taught. Verdic's denial about why they might not be needed as priests, along with his unwillingness to address any information other than Summa and Izina, led Hendal to consider the possibility of other religions and beliefs that did not align with his uncle's. Instead of following the assigned readings, he sought new sources, and what he found infuriated him. Dozens of books mentioned differing ideas from what Verdic preached regarding their gods and history while a few contradicted their ancestors' writings.

The next day, he approached his uncle at the priest's desk in the library, threw down the materials, and demanded answers. Hendal raised his voice without fear, asking the man before him what went on outside of Kercher's church and when they planned to lecture from the pieces in front of him. He expected Verdic to unleash his fury once the room quieted, but the silence stretched for an uncomfortable amount of time. While their eyes remained locked, Hendal could sense the rage seething within Verdic, and even Wesley's terror nearby, until the priest finally lowered his hands from where they had been folded in front of his nose.

"One chosen to worship the deities who blessed their people with life should never question the existence of secondary gods or goddesses who mind their own peoples. We were given our assignments by those before us as a way to be thankful for what we have and who we are, lest we forget the sacrifices, obstacles, and acts leading us to be the people we are today."

"A people who's dying away?" Hendal countered and avoided wincing when his voice cracked on the final word. At the lack of a complete, credible answer, he dipped his chin to stare at the ground.

"Changing, perhaps, but not dying," Verdic continued while showing more patience than Hendal expected. "You will understand in time. For now, Kercher needs someone to give them hope, to keep their faith strong, and to teach them how to live as Summa and Izina instructed the founders of our town."

Hendal refrained from letting out a long sigh in defeat and glanced up; however, the priest's eyes no longer rested on him but gazed over his shoulder. He glanced around to see Wesley sitting at the table behind him, watching their argument without expression. Then, Verdic stood, picked up the items containing writings from the line of priests before him, and spoke once more.

"I'll take a look at what you brought me. It is possible they were disregarded for false or inaccurate information by those who lacked the comprehensive knowledge of our beliefs."

Hendal held his tongue as his teacher exited the room.

He never saw those books, journals, or papers again.

*

For a time, Hendal abandoned his fight against the position fate demanded he accept. He and Wesley, who grew into a handsome man and adequate scholar, only left the church on Verdic's orders, which frequented as the priest's health declined. When Hendal was twenty-five years old, Verdic passed away in his sleep with Wesley holding his left hand and Hendal his right. They chanted prayers through the tears in their eyes and looked at one another helplessly before releasing the lifeless, limp hands. The man had requested he remain in his room during his final days, so announcing his death to the public fell to his successor.

"Hendal," Wesley muttered when neither moved.

"What is it?"

"You're the new priest."

"Yes, and?"

174

"You should go tell everyone what happened."

"I suppose I should, shouldn't I?"

"I will accompany you."

Hendal didn't answer but stood and wiped the tears away. Although he hated his uncle and always would for such narrow-minded actions and opinions as their caretaker, as a man, Verdic acted wholly faithful to the people of Kercher and their other relatives.

"Is that all it takes to be a priest?" he voiced aloud to nobody in particular.

"What do you mean?" Wesley asked in a soft, empathetic manner.

Hendal clenched his fists when a surge of old emotions welled. "He was a rotten teacher. He never listened to us or anyone who believed something different. We've been sheltered because it's tradition. We couldn't raise families or build friendships because it's tradition. There's so much to learn about the world, but he…"

Wesley rose to stand by his side and made a sound to interrupt, but Hendal continued.

"We never had a chance to live our lives. I want to blame him for that. Deep down, though, I know it wasn't his fault."

"Of course not," his nephew responded while sliding to stand in front of him in order to put both hands on his shoulders. "You're right. Our lives have been predetermined according to Kercher's religion and its god and goddess. We were not allowed to do much, yet you're still responsible for leading us forward. At least, unlike Verdic, we have each other."

Wesley let his arms fall to his sides before returning to their teacher to drape the blanket over the peaceful, gray face. After a moment, Hendal left his uncle and nephew alone.

*

The first month of heading the church began as a strange experience. Hendal and Wesley spent at least three days clearing out their old mentor's belongings, sorting through his writings, and moving Hendal into the priest's quarters. Although he missed the company, having a personal space to relax and think in private felt invigorating, and it inspired him to make additional changes to their routine. Once a week, he opened all the windows in the building and, along with his nephew, thoroughly cleaned the inside.

"I don't remember Verdic ever ordering us to dust and scrub so well," Wesley mentioned before he plopped down on a bench next to Hendal, who frowned at the memory of the previous priest.

"That's because he didn't care for much besides his duties as a holy man."

Wesley didn't comment. Soon after, he left for the kitchen and returned with two glasses of water. They enjoyed the peace for a while longer, allowing Hendal to consider what his nephew thought of their current situation and what he should do.

I'm in charge of how the church functions now. If I wanted to, I could introduce new ideas or traditions. Who would question me, aside from Wesley? He's technically my student anyway.

Despite his cynicism, the idea of abandoning the church's customs disturbed him. *No, I could never turn my back on what the people of Kercher consider sacred, even if I don't truly believe in Summa or Izina.*

"Do you think there's more we can do?" Hendal asked after scanning over the old yet somewhat brighter chapel.

His nephew gave him a sidelong glance. "What do you mean?"

Hendal couldn't help himself from running a hand through his thinning hair. He knew how Wesley felt about priesthood, how his nephew could embrace the writings and teachings, take them to heart, and discuss the lessons with the townsfolk whenever Hendal was busy. The young man at his side fit into the position and displayed more empathy and understanding than Verdic had.

"I guess I'm wondering is if there's anything else you can think of to improve this place. Could we encourage the townsfolk to join us here for moments of prayer? Can we find a way to help them see us as approachable instead of…of…"

"Instead of those who would verbally condemn them? Instead of speakers of the gods possessing some ability that makes us seem different than them?"

The accuracy of the guess startled Hendal, causing him to snap his head over to meet Wesley's understanding look.

"You forget I've known you my entire life," his nephew continued while raising his eyes to the church's ceiling. "I can tell what you're trying to do and agree our people should feel more welcome in our presence."

When Wesley stopped speaking, Hendal could tell the younger man began contemplating the request, so he pushed for more. "I won't judge you for new ideas. We're a team in this life. We might as well bounce our thoughts off each other. In fact, we'll probably be reigning ourselves in from getting too eccentric!"

His nephew chuckled and eased up enough to speak what was on his mind. To Hendal's amusement, the most daring suggestion involved creating a garden in the unused space behind their building. Neither of them could remember noticing life beneath the tall, wild grass filled with weed patches, and it seemed possible to do. Their other ideas branched off their current duties, such as re-categorizing the library and mending the worn or broken prayer books available by the entrance. They agreed to start the following morning since their conversation lasted until it became time to prepare supper.

*

Spring rolled over into summer, making the fall season quite pleasant. By that point, they accomplished their original goals and more. Wesley took a personal liking to the garden they established, even going so far as to use it as a space for outdoor worship. Plenty of the townsfolk would poke their heads around to see what was happening and accept his offer to pray together. Since the land proved less fertile than they expected, the two only successfully grew flowers during the first summer. Of course, Wesley expressed his optimism about continuing the following spring, and they savored the floral scent that found its way into the church.

While his nephew spent extra time in the garden, Hendal became invested in the library project. Seeing many loose papers gutted him because their bindings had been torn, poorly crafted, or worn down so the yellow pages crumbled between his fingers. He, and Wesley once winter showed itself, worked diligently to copy the writings

177

onto fresh parchment, tie them together, and organize the completed pieces. At the end of the season, they burned the older papers at once while praying over the flames. To Hendal's amazement, several of the townsfolk who appeared here and there around the church and garden joined in. Wesley made sure to explain what took place afterward, then he learned their names and thanked them for participating in the process. Hendal kept smiling and greeted them when addressed, but for the most part, he remained behind his nephew.

That evening after lying in bed, he reflected on what took place and how the experience made him feel. It seemed as though he should be upset by Wesley's outgoing behavior because Hendal acted as the lone priest of Kercher. He saw no reason for his nephew to remember details, such as names and faces, greet the townsfolk in such a casual manner, or try to be liked.

Still, the negativity backfired immediately. He loved Wesley and would never shy away from how proud he was of the man his nephew had become. To criticize him for acting in an opposite manner as Verdic would be like admitting the former priest's methods should be tolerated, and Hendal could never do that. The more he considered what he believed a priest should stand for and what purpose they serve, the less he felt any sense of self.

Over the next few weeks, he stepped away from the church, often without announcing his departure to Wesley. Unlike when Verdic acted as the priest, Hendal had no qualms about moving through the town or allowing his nephew out as well. There were those who bowed or appeared shocked to catch them walking nearby, but more faces appeared friendly and gracious. Almost every time they ventured around, someone offered them a piece of fruit, baked goods, or spare change as a donation. At first, Hendal had his suspicion about the people hoping to bribe their priest for positive favor with Summa or Izina, so he would refuse in a polite manner; however, his efforts proved futile because those individuals became persistent, in a humble, kindly way.

"They didn't beg for acceptance, mercy, or forgiveness," he later shared with Wesley when his emotions grew complicated enough that he needed to vent. "I think they just wanted to offer those gifts to be nice. It doesn't make sense why they would do so when they spot us in town instead of stopping by to see us here."

His nephew laughed at his lack of understanding. "People can act out of the goodness in their hearts and souls because it helps them feel fulfilled. Isn't this what we preach about all the time?"

Hendal had mumbled his agreement yet did not fully comprehend the notion.

At the moment, plenty of people roamed about Kercher to bask in one of the first warm days of spring. He passed a trio of women around his age who smiled and greeted him. Although his heart fluttered upon catching their natural beauty, years of celibacy under his former teacher kept a wall between them. An older lady stopped him to chat, which turned into her complaining about her grandchildren spending too long away from the town. As he usually did in these instances, Hendal stayed quiet. In most cases, the person would request his opinion or a prayer to ease their minds and hearts, but the older woman sounded as if she just needed an ear to babble to.

Once that lengthy session ended and he wished her well, he moved to the empty fields beyond where he meditated until his legs grew stiff and evening approached. He and Wesley prepared supper when he returned, and his nephew questioned his whereabouts until Hendal refused to discuss what he had been doing. Every day after, he repeated this routine. The townsfolk came to expect him down the road, and his nephew became less dependent on him.

*

Eleven months after he began leading the church, he learned of the birth of Wesley's niece, the eldest brother's second child. The news didn't affect Hendal since he knew it would be at least a couple of years until they would be expected to raise the child, but Wesley acted distraught. His mother, the sister Hendal rarely spoke to, visited the church to announce the news with eyes red and swollen from weeping. The baby arrived too early and was underweight. Its skin turned a sickly, pale color, and it never cried, according to its mother. Based on the impression Hendal received after hearing this, they expected the child to die any day.

Despite the odds, Wesley would go to the family's home every morning to pray and ask for Summa and Izina's blessing. Hendal remained in the church until his nephew returned, then he left for his daily meditation. A sense of guilt hindered his otherwise emotionless reflection, though.

I'm the priest here, not Wesley. He doesn't bear the responsibility to care for Kercher yet, so why does he insist on serving with more dedication than me? Could he actually care about the family he never got the chance to know? Does he wish for the child to live so he possesses a pupil to look after?

The next day, his thoughts expanded on those questions. *What will happen if the baby lives? It would be Wesley's duty to raise her, not mine. I've been spending more time away from the church so he has a chance to experience the lonely life of a priest and what one's tasks entail. Perhaps I went about this all wrong...*

That evening, Hendal sat with his nephew and shared his reasoning for being so distant.

"Wesley," he began after the lengthy explanation, "you understand I didn't want this life. When Verdic died, I felt too uncertain to abandon the church, and I would never leave you behind. So, I took up the position."

"Why have you abandoned your duties here then?" his nephew asked without placing any sort of blame.

Hendal swallowed around the lump in his throat. "I hoped you would experience this life for yourself. That way, you're justified should you wish to leave. If you're lonely or you hate it here and asked me to go, I would let you."

He couldn't stand to look at his nephew after Wesley's lips pressed together and the blue eyes watered, forcing him to stare down at his hands. Despite the stir of emotion, he spoke his remaining thoughts aloud in a gentler tone of voice.

"You are so unlike our teacher that my impression of a priest has changed. Where he was abusive and impatient, you're kindhearted and always willing to listen. Verdic would never hear anything having to do with another god's beliefs, or he would dismiss the writings I found containing blasphemous information. I've seen how you approach prayer with the townsfolk. You answer their questions after taking every detail into consideration and never shy away from what is new. You care about them, Wesley; that's the difference between us."

"Thank you, Hendal," he heard his nephew whisper.

For some reason, admitting his feelings lifted an unfamiliar weight from his shoulders. He tilted his head back and smiled at the dark ceiling. *Not only do I not understand his way of thinking, but I fear it is a process I simply can't comprehend. No matter how much work I do, I already set my mind on a life outside of the church. In my heart, I know I don't deserve this position.*

He took Wesley's closest hand in both of his and bowed his head as a warm energy filled his body. "Let us pray for the child," he ordered and dove straight into a chant asking the gods for healing.

*

Due to her daughter's weakened state, Wesley's sister didn't bring his niece to the church until the girl reached the age of four when she could act on her own, at least physically. Mentally, she spent more time learning words and behaviors and managing what she needed to in order to get by within her family. Her emotional state proved to be the worst hinderance, though. The child severely relied on her mother for everything and, at the mention of living somewhere new with two strangers, broke down in tears when Hendal and Wesley went to meet her. Although Hendal tried his best to coax the girl named Lyla into coming along, Wesley surprised him by arranging an agreement.

"If you visit me at the church every day, even for a minute, I won't make you live there unless you want to," he explained in a calm manner and without any trace of frustration or urgency.

Lyla nodded while her mother glanced at Hendal.

That's right. I'm the official representative of the church, he reminded himself and smiled as reassuringly as possible before adding a comment in support of the compromise.

As they left the home, Wesley lost his composure, blurted out an apology, and attempted to justify his words.

Hendal interrupted his nephew mid-sentence. "Every child is unique, and if you believe this is the best way for her to become accustomed to this life, then I trust your judgement."

"Doesn't this go against tradition?"

Hendal paused to consider his personal feelings on the matter, then he shrugged. "In some cases, traditions need to change for the times. How I see it, we're not going against any rules relating to Summa or Izina. Updating our duties doesn't necessarily mean shunning the prayers or teachings. For example, you tend the garden space and invite others to join in the experience."

"I see. That sounds a lot like what Verdic used to say," Wesley mumbled just loud enough for Hendal to hear. They spent the rest of the walk contemplating this in silence.

The next morning, Lyla, accompanied by her mother, poked her head around the building's wall to where Hendal worked with Wesley to plant the bulbs and seeds from their garden last fall. Although he longed to become involved in kindling a relationship between the girl and his nephew, he allowed Wesley to act without his influence, which the man did regardless. They stayed for less than an hour to silently observe before taking their leave. The next day passed in an identical fashion, except Wesley convinced Lyla to bury the final bulb in the garden while he said a prayer over the space.

Every morning after remained similar. Lyla and her mother would stop by, the girl assisted with whatever project they were doing, the pair listened to the priests' chanting, then they left. Before long, Wesley's niece arrived at the church on her own and for growing periods of time. Hendal hardly spoke, but his nephew asked sincere questions to get the child to open up to them. He seemed patient, warm, and approachable without expecting Lyla to linger after every visit. Only when the two became fairly comfortable with one another did Hendal begin his treks outside of the building to meditate once more.

As the weeks turned into months and Lyla finally felt comfortable enough to accept her role as Wesley's apprentice by moving into the church, Hendal wondered about the world beyond Kercher again. He often sparked up conversations with messengers when they returned, using the excuse of offering a prayer of thanksgiving for their safe return. His few relatives delighted in the honor while Hendal learned about the cities to the south, those hidden in the woods, and the grand capital city. Just to keep the information coming, he would offer simple updates on Kercher and include bits and pieces of rumors about the angels, or rather the magically gifted beings from the mysterious place known as Yeluthia, before sending the messengers away. He figured no one ever questioned a priest when it came to religious intentions; no one except his younger self, then his nephew.

Once Wesley caught wind of what went on, he confronted Hendal at his desk in the library.

"I know what you're doing," his nephew began and stood frowning with arms crossed.

The years had been kinder to Wesley than Hendal. His chestnut hair trailed down his back in a neat braid while a strong jawline accentuated his stern expression. Not a wrinkle or blemish marred his fair skin either, though they were still in their thirties.

Meanwhile, Hendal already lost most of the thinning hair on top of his head and dealt with crow's feet. He tried not to think about those physical aspects as he pretended to read the papers in front of him.

"What are you talking about?" he asked, willing his voice to mirror innocence. On the inside, he had been dreading this conversation ever since he started sending the messengers out of Kercher. His nephew didn't speak again until Hendal raised his eyes.

"Lyla's mother stopped in to see her and mentioned you were giving the messengers news about Yeluthia. Why are you saying such things?"

Hendal licked his lips and contemplated an answer. It would be all too easy to avoid admitting the truth. Wesley would believe him if he claimed his meditating brought about a vision of the angels, especially if he acted passionate enough to defend the notion. Still, he could never forgive himself for lying to his nephew.

I spent days preparing for this moment, contemplating how to approach my decision. Even if I deviate from the reason, my actions and the outcome will probably be the same no matter how I respond.

"Come with me," Hendal ordered and rose from his seat. Together, they walked to the main chapel used for prayer and procured a bench in the front row.

"Do you remember why I make my daily route through town and leave you alone?"

The audible gulp before Wesley's reply showed his nephew became aware of what their talk was going to be about. "I do," came the quiet answer.

"You're not like me," Hendal started. "What I mean is, you're a better priest than I could ever be. That's because we both know my heart isn't in this. I never desired a life trapped in one place, forced into a position requiring me to believe in inexplicable deities. Actually, it's not so much Summa or Izina. I'm curious about the world. The more I hear from the messengers of our family, the more I long to learn what is out there. How many gods do the people pray to? What kinds of lives do they live?"

Wesley didn't speak during the following pause, though Hendal wished his nephew would.

"If I had a choice, I wouldn't have been a priest," he continued. "At least by sending the messengers, I'll hear their stories and enjoy what I can without leaving." With his explanation complete, he released a long sigh, leaned forward, and rubbed the back of his neck.

"Is there anything I can do for you, uncle?" Wesley asked.

Hendal clasped his hands together on his lap. Although he felt he shouldn't, he turned to glance over at his nephew, who stared with what he could only describe as incomprehension. *No, this is an issue I don't believe anyone in Kercher understands how to help with. A community rooted in tradition that involves appointed assignments should long to feel the freedom of making decisions regarding their lives. Still, no one expresses their disdain for Kercher's outdated positions, except for me. Maybe those who did are the ones who abandoned their homes for what's beyond the fields.*

Hendal wanted to tell Wesley this, to pour out his heart to the one person who would listen and not judge him for the way he felt; however, hope reflected in his nephew's pleading eyes. Not a hope for the new, though, but a wish for what had already been established. Silently, he begged Hendal to remain at the church.

After their brief discussion, which abruptly ended when Lyla entered the space to inquire about supper, the two dropped the subject.

*

Hendal continued his business despite a rising apprehension as he sensed some inexplicable force stirring. Soon, they learned about a sickness spreading in the northern cities, which did not bode well because of the approaching winter. The messengers refused to risk their lives, leaving him frustrated with their fearfulness.

Meanwhile, Wesley did his best to introduce subtle changes to their daily routine in an obvious attempt to make the life of a priest more tolerable. Dinner options rotated every week and often involved guests bringing their own, delicious offerings. It succeeded in cultivating more relationships during the usually basic meal, as well as require Lyla to interact with others in Kercher. His nephew also invited the townsfolk to prayer sessions or to join in chants. When that happened, they sometimes ended up with a large choir whose unified voice breathed life into the building.

If Hendal had not set his sights on life beyond the church, he might've been able to tolerate those changes and others they tried out. The most unavoidable one seemed to be Wesley's push for Lyla to spend more time with Hendal. Her mentor certainly influenced her behavior over the months; she always observed the world with wide, bright eyes and obeyed his requests. Despite that, she shared Hendal's sense of curiosity. Whenever the two sat alone, usually during his reading hours in the library, Lyla would ask several questions at once regarding a variety of topics in a gentle yet confident manner.

At first, he grew eager to converse. *If she is as interested in the world around us as I am, perhaps we do have something in common. Who knows what we could discuss and how I can help her cope with what I feel,* he originally thought.

Over the cold, snowy weeks, his excitement subsided. Lyla liked to hear information but was either not at the age or did not possess the ability to consider what she wanted for herself. She couldn't understand Hendal, and that fact put him in a sour mood. He soon gave up on replying to her questions with such encouragement.

In the months following spring, the sickness plaguing the rest of the country subsided enough for the messengers of Kercher to obey Hendal again. Life returned to normal while they were away, but each returned wearing the same, exhausted expression and announced a somber message. The king of Asteom fell ill during the winter and died, along with the palace's high priest and hundreds of citizens in the capital alone. A mourning ceremony and funeral took place before the next king had been crowned.

Hendal didn't recognize much from what they described about the events or people, yet the updates brought him a sense of comfort. Outside of Kercher, life continued on despite the circumstances.

The evening after hearing the news, while sleep evaded him, he thought about the piece of information that had piqued his interest the most. *The palace's priest is gone. They must have another to replace him, as we do here, but would they be willing to let me study there? Would one's death allow me to take a student's spot? As much as I hate the idea of spending my life as a priest, it would allow me to learn more than I ever could here.*

Even in his dreams, the idea persisted until he acted upon it. He called forth the eldest of the messengers, who happened to be Wesley's younger brother, and gave him a letter with the church's seal.

"Bring this to the palace and request it be presented before their new priest," Hendal instructed while showing what composure he could muster. "Tell them the priest of Summa and Izina in Kercher wishes to aid them during a time of loss, as instructed by the god and goddess."

The man's eyes lit up from some unspoken emotion, then he nodded and hurried off with the letter. Nearly a month later, the man returned with a notice.

Priest Hendal of Kercher,

> *Your letter has not been read by blind eyes nor heard by deaf ears for now is the time to start anew. A message from your gods cannot go unnoticed after the losses Asteom has faced, especially with many taking advantage of the uncertainty following those of us who were recently appointed. Because of this, I request your presence. It is imperative we find a high priest worthy of acting as a member of my council, and your letter reflects this. Show the king's seal to the guards at the palace's front gate. You shall be escorted to the proper person. Best wishes for a safe journey to Verona.*

King Hernan

Hendal brushed a thumb over the golden wax stamped into a crest at the bottom of the page. He became too stunned to process the request and dismissed the curious messenger.

For three days, he spent every waking hour alone to reread the words and consider what to do. As the time passed, his initial shock faded to reveal apprehension, fear, and regret for his poor decision. To proclaim the gods spoke to him would surely backfire when those in the capital realized how clueless he was about the rest of the country. Still, Hendal remembered no one would believe he lied unless he acted suspicious.

No deity bothered to assist me throughout my life so far. I already renounced their existence, but no one knows that, not even Wesley, he reflected as his lips twisted into a frown. A minute later, they curved upward to form a wicked smile. *This is my chance to leave Kercher! Even if it only lasts for a few weeks, I must try to convince them to allow me to live among their people.*

For the rest of the day, he repeated the thought often and soon grew excited for the change. Wesley caught on to Hendal's secrecy after his brother's return, so Hendal showed him the message and explained the situation in order to avoid any arguments later on.

"My meddling led to an opportunity to help the people in the palace," he finished, letting his passion slip into his tone of voice. "I've been so selfish by sending the messengers. Perhaps this is a chance to atone. I'll never make up for my mistakes until I go there."

To his amazement, Wesley agreed, though with no shortage of mixed emotions spread across his face.

The following morning, Hendal prepared to depart. He summoned his younger nephew, informed the messenger of the king's request, and assigned the man as an escort. As soon as they were both ready, they left the church. Many lingering eyes forced Hendal to hold his head high and smile despite his nerves. He didn't expect to see Wesley that day since his nephew had not appeared throughout the morning; however, he spotted a figure wearing the gray robe against an overcast sky on the road farther ahead outside of town. Lyla stood at his side, though she looked clueless about what was taking place.

"Wesley," Hendal began before realizing he hadn't planned how to say goodbye.

His escort continued on to give them some privacy, and Lyla stepped forward.

"Have a safe journey, Priest Hendal," she offered in a rehearsed manner, bowed, then glanced at her teacher, who dipped his chin. At his dismissal, the girl left them to jog into town. Hendal watched her go while his nephew spoke.

"She really does admire you. I believe she noticed your interest in learning and tries to absorb as much as she can."

"I couldn't think of a better teacher than you for such an innocent child," Hendal admitted. He turned his back to the buildings while Wesley watched him with watery eyes. "I guess this is goodbye."

"You don't have to leave."

Hendal looked over to see the man, the *new* priest, squeezing his eyes shut and balling his hands into fists.

"Wesley…"

"You're in charge, and there's nothing else… We *need* you here! I can't…"

This time, Hendal's eyes welled with tears he refused to shed lest he give up his opportunity for a free life. He stepped closer to his nephew, laid both hands on the sturdy shoulders, and spoke his truth in a wavering voice. "You don't need me. For years now, you never needed me. Sure, you *want* me to stay, yet who would that truly benefit? I envy your commitment to this life; you're destined for it, and I can't imagine you doing anything else. Not only do you care about the people of Kercher, but you also bring about positive change for the present and the future of this town. You and Lyla will continue to do good here."

The tears Wesley repressed slid down his cheeks, though he didn't make a sound until after Hendal spoke. "Please…"

The whispered plea tugged at Hendal's heart. He inhaled through his nostrils and pulled his nephew in for a final embrace.

Although he kept still, Wesley's shoulders trembled as he tightened his hold. They remained shaking when Hendal broke away to walk toward the awaiting messenger without another glance at what he left behind.

*

Hendal had some idea of what the capital city would be like, though he never expected to pass through it on their way to the palace. Even with a sickness that killed hundreds, according to the messengers, people crowded the streets of Verona, moving in all directions on their own business. As daunting as it became, he forced himself to act as though he belonged while keeping close to his nephew, who led them straight to the tallest stone structure.

Once they hailed a guard and showed the letter's seal, the soldier guided the pair up a set of stairs and around the building's winding halls until a metal door appeared. Then, the stranger dismissed Hendal's escort before knocking. The idea of being in a tight, unknown space petrified him, but he pretended not to mind when his nephew thanked the man before disappearing down a different passage. Someone shouted for them to enter, yet he went alone while the guard remained at attention in the hallway.

The inside of the room elevated his discomfort. A circular table with several chairs rested at the center, and the only sources of light came from lamps hanging along the stone walls. To his right, a portion of the flooring had been raised so a throne could be positioned above everyone else.

"Priest Hendal, I presume?" someone asked to get his attention.

Hendal cleared his throat and stepped farther in. He took a moment to study each person's face as five sat at the table and one on the throne. He addressed the latter after swallowing his nerves. "I am Hendal, priest of the church in Kercher. His Highness summoned me, so I came as soon as I could."

"I believe we sent for you over a week ago with the expectation you would arrive sooner," the young man wearing the gold band on his head responded without allowing a pause. His attitude seemed to consist of annoyance, impatience, and an odd amusement.

The response startled Hendal, causing his mind to go blank. "F-Forgive me," he managed to bumble while keeping eye contact with the new king. "I wasn't prepared for your request." Only after he spoke did Hendal consider he might be disrespecting the group by making such casual remarks and glances.

In any case, the young man on the throne scratched his chin, which already displayed a full beard, and addressed those at the table. "We can pick up our previous discussion another time. Califer, would you explain to Priest Hendal what it is we are doing in regard to the high priest's position?"

Hendal watched as one of the older men rose in a slow, careful manner. His white hair had been trimmed to his shoulders, and he wore a similarly colored robe embroidered with golden thread only visible when he moved due to the lighting.

"Allow me to introduce myself," the man began with a hoarse voice. "I am Califer, the master mage of the palace. Our previous high priest named Ronaldo came from Clearwater and served the kingdom for forty-seven years before his death this past winter. We invited you, along with several other religious men and women who wish to take up the position, in the hope of finding someone worthy to fulfill this role, join our council, and assist King Hernan."

After each word the mage spoke, Hendal felt himself starting to sweat more. *This isn't what I expected*, he thought while fighting the urge to wipe his forehead with his sleeve. *They didn't already have a replacement chosen? Isn't their faith based on a religion requiring more than one leader of the church? Did he say other priests are here too? I'm not-*

"Well? Is this a job you believe you can handle?" the king asked, interrupting the mental concerns.

Hendal closed his eyes for a moment to consider what he planned to do, yet an answer poured forth without him fully understanding the offer. "I would be honored to receive an opportunity to serve in the palace and learn more about Asteom's religious cultures."

When he opened his eyes and bowed, he noticed the people at the table glancing at one another while the young man on the throne tilted his head a bit with what Hendal assumed was interest.

After the panic-inducing encounter, a servant led him to an empty bedroom and left him there. Just when he began to wonder about meals, another person entered bearing a tray of miniature, savory pies, fruits, roasted root vegetables, and a sweet pastry he never tasted before. Hendal cleared the platter, then he fell into a deep, comfortable sleep.

The next morning, a servant presented an invitation to tour the palace with the other candidates. No one spoke the entire time except for their guide, though another man around his age and a woman at least a decade older smiled warmly whenever he caught them staring. Otherwise, they kept to themselves. In the afternoon, the group reunited in the same meeting space Hendal had first gone to the day before. There, a guard stationed by the door instructed them to sit around the table, and they found Califer waiting inside.

The mage's presence made Hendal feel odd, mainly because he wasn't familiar with magic wielders since none lived in Kercher or visited, as far as he knew. Such a foreign topic intrigued and terrified him considering how dangerous such power could be in the wrong hands. Not only did he worry about that, but many questions surrounded the spellcasters. One thought related to the angels in their legendary city in the clouds and how they were said to use a different type of magic from a human's. He never considered the subject, yet he believed it would be necessary to understand should he remain in the capital city.

"It's a pleasure to see you all again," the older man started while offering a slight smile. "Our kingdom is fortunate to possess so many leaders of various religions to guide people to more fulfilling lives. Each one of you comes from a sect separate from those seated around this table. The representation from across the country is marvelous! With that in mind, I would like to take the time to inform you of what being the high priest entails."

Hendal expected a list similar to his duties in Kercher; this priest or priestess would need to participate in ceremonies, daily prayers and chants, visit the sick or whoever requests their blessing, and such tasks. In that case, he had little to worry about aside from studying their main deities and rituals. Instead, the description Califer gave wound up shocking him.

"The high priest was established as a figure of faith to stand beside the royal family because Asteom doesn't follow a single religion. Citizens are able to choose what gods or goddesses to worship, so the country is diverse. The high priest must be a representative of the churches across Asteom, no matter the religion."

During the pause after his statement, Hendal sat stunned, though not against the notion. The idea of requiring everyone to serve the same deities just because of the royal family's beliefs would not be tolerated by the established churches. Whoever suggested the palace host a single person to speak on behalf of both the rulers and the faithful had been taking precautions. Essentially, they avoid the kings and queens favoring one religion over another when making decisions, donations, or judgements and keep the leaders grounded.

Many in the room did not comprehend this, or they thought it to be unacceptable. The man to Hendal's right jumped to his feet, slammed his hands on the table, and announced his view.

"A priest's duties are to his church! If the king does not follow a religion, why is it necessary aside from keeping an image with the people? That's blasphemy!"

"I agree," the woman who smiled at Hendal during their tour added. She had been frowning ever since they entered the space. "You misuse the title so it seems as though the position pleases a religion when it just serves your needs."

"Not necessarily," Califer replied, surprising Hendal with his calm demeanor. Based on his behavior, the man had prepared for backlash against the explanation. "I cannot speak for the previously appointed high priests, so I shouldn't assume the motivations behind their decision to accept the position. Perhaps it is better to say this in plain terms. We're seeking someone who can keep their minds and hearts away from one particular religion or church in order to understand the rest spanning across the country. Whatever you choose to personally follow is your business, but the high priest must not be biased lest they betray the peace and freedom of religious beliefs established in Asteom. It is their sacrifice in order to assist the king. We also require the high priest to be an active member of the king's council because their knowledge could contribute to various efforts. Is that clear?"

A couple of people at the table grunted a response while the rest remained silent, so the mage dismissed them for the evening meal. When the candidates reconvened the next morning, only Hendal and three other men were present.

*

For four days, the remaining priests met with numerous people, both in groups and individually. He couldn't remember most of their names or faces and often wondered why he bothered to leave the safety of Kercher. The questions he faced focused more on his daily routine and how he felt about taking on extra responsibilities. Hendal made sure to give honest answers, even admitting his hope to learn about the world and how he thought the capital city would be the best way to serve the country. Only once did he mention something he later regretted, which had been when the master mage of all people asked about a city to the south and their religious affiliations. Hendal didn't understand the topic or what they wanted from him. Ultimately, he shared that he would not return to Kercher because of his interest in the world outside of the town, whether they chose him for the position or not.

Two more days passed, and he didn't hear from anyone. A knock at his door in the evening seemed to signal an update, especially when he saw Califer enter. The man greeted him with a wider smile than normal before cutting right to business. A decision had been reached, and the council selected Hendal as the new high priest.

He stopped listening once the realization dawned on him.

Califer noticed, shut the door for some privacy, and ushered him to the bed where they both dropped down. "I must admit, I expected this reaction," the man added and chuckled.

Meanwhile, Hendal instinctively brushed his hair down. "I can't believe it," he mumbled.

"This is why I come to you now, before the announcement is made by King Hernan in the meeting tomorrow morning. After that, preparations will be arranged for your appointment."

Hendal kept silent.

"I also wish to explain the reasoning behind our decision," Califer went on. "You see, our two main qualifications involved someone familiar with the religious life who could also willingly set aside their own faith in order to study others for the purposes I've mentioned. Those not a part of any system of belief would never be able to understand its necessity regarding the royal family. On the opposite side, like many religious leaders, if the person is too stubborn to accept different faith systems in Asteom and why it is permissible, they will no doubt show preference to their community of followers."

"Yes, I figured," Hendal commented with a little more energy.

"Exactly! You comprehend the entire assignment and can leave Kercher in your nephew's care. Also, you expressed your interest in learning about our country."

So, my honesty worked in my favor. What luck!

"Out of all the priests and priestesses invited to the palace, you showed the least bias for your own gods too," Califer added, reminding Hendal of the outcome. "I want to prepare you for the council's presentation. Should you accept, we'll begin the transition immediately."

The two talked for a bit longer on the matter before the mage exited. Although Hendal contemplated what this would mean, he knew the offer was one he shouldn't refuse.

I spent my whole life trapped in Kercher as their priest, desiring nothing more than to escape. If acting as the king's servant means access to freedom, I think I can manage. Besides, I won't need to uphold my previous responsibilities and traditions anymore. This might be better for me after all.

From the Shadows

Over the next fifteen years, Hendal watched the world around him change from inside the palace where he fulfilled his duties as Asteom's high priest. Hernan developed into a man with an iron will, married a nobleman's daughter the year after Hendal's appointment, and they welcomed a son, who shared much of his appearance with the king. Califer acted as Hendal's mentor until the master mage's health declined, forcing the older man to retire to his home out west after naming a successor. During the following months, Hendal grew fond of Califer and wrote to him often, though this led him to neglect his nephew. Wesley's letters arrived frequently for a while, then they tapered off before stopping altogether. He assumed Kercher's priest understood they both had more important matters to attend to.

The days flew by, especially since Hendal spent most of his free time reading about Asteom's geography, history, and various religions. Once he lost interest in what the palace's library held, he sought knowledge elsewhere, but his position prevented him from leaving the capital unless King Hernan approved the trip. The world he had seen as limitless steadily narrowed, preventing him from obtaining knowledge outside of books.

My escape from Kercher only ensnared me in another trap, he reflected one evening as he paced around his room. *This position is nothing more than a puppet for the king and his council. I possess no authority, yet I must attend their meetings and be present to the citizens. Those people are human too; the lone difference is what families we were born into. It reminds me of the system of priests in Kercher. Without an opportunity to speak for myself, I remained sheltered. Now, I see the country for what it is, and what it could be.*

The following afternoon, he received a message from Califer. The former master mage's health took a turn for the worst, and he requested a final blessing from Hendal. His message moved Hernan enough to permit the high priest to leave without a fuss.

Two guards accompanied Hendal toward the northwestern region to a town called Wailon, which proved to be nearly half the size of Kercher, and its people brought him before the frail, bedridden man. Califer greeted the visitors, then they were left alone. Because of his profession, Hendal grew accustomed to acting as a friend during a person's last moments in life; however, seeing the master mage so weak after all the man had done for him hurt.

"I was beginning to think King Hernan wouldn't let you come," Califer commented while lifting his head a bit.

Hendal smiled, sat in the lone chair placed by the bedside, and took the former master mage's hands in both of his. "The news of your condition troubled us," he responded before changing to a lighter subject.

They talked about what went on in the palace, especially surrounding the people Califer would know, until they wound up discussing the additional defenses along the northern border. Hendal didn't mind doing most of the speaking, though he understood less about the military's business because of the generals' secrecy.

"Rumors of conflict make their way into the council meetings, but that's all they seem to be," he concluded.

Califer paused to cough and shook his head. "I'm thankful I don't deal with the politics and troops anymore. It's too much to keep up with when you're older. You start to realize what is most important."

"I can understand how you feel."

The man's eyes drifted around the room until they fell on Hendal again. His next words carried an oddly serious weight. "Have you any regrets in life?"

Over the course of their friendship, Hendal revealed his distaste for his position in Kercher as its priest and his aspiration to learn.

He recalled how Califer never judged him for his opinions, yet the question made him uneasy. "What do you mean?"

"I remember you mentioning your desire to explore the country. Although the high priest is provided for, as is the master mage, they're confined to the king's side. Sometimes, I wonder if I could have had a family here to the west. What about you?"

Hendal shook his head. "I never considered such a path in life."

"Interesting," the older man muttered. His attention seemed to go elsewhere. "Once the time comes for a person to stare death in the face, they can reflect on who they are, or their true self. Were their goals fulfilled? Did they leave behind a legacy worthy of their name? Will their regrets tie them to this world after they pass on?"

Hendal didn't know how to respond, so he remained silent.

The former master mage coughed again, wheezed for a moment, then continued with less enthusiasm. "I suppose I'm saying you shouldn't waste what time you have left. Even if you're not living your ideal life, you can still get fulfillment out of it."

"You should relax," Hendal felt the need to recommend.

Califer smiled in his ordinary, gentle manner while squeezing the hand in his. "If only you could've been able to study magic with me. Despite the circumstances being out of my control, it will forever be one of my greatest regrets."

The mention of magic caught Hendal's interest, in addition to the older man's indirectness. "What?"

"I sensed your potential during our first encounter. Perhaps that explains why I favored you above the others."

"I can't wield magic."

"Not anymore. At least-"

"No one in my family has ever been able to," Hendal interrupted after remembering Califer's explanation of how light and dark mages inherit their abilities.

"Are you that familiar with your family's lineage?"

Hendal pressed his lips together and couldn't defend his previous statement. Because he had been separated from his parents when he was young, he never knew most of his other relatives. Verdic also considered the topic of magic irrelevant to their duties, thus dismissing it.

"A mage at the master level must possess the power to sense energy within others," the older man went on, straining his voice until it grew hoarse. "I noticed a spark in you, but your body already developed, making it too late to start working on it. You would've been a wonderful healer, full of compassion. I'm just glad…I could form one…worthwhile connection and help…those I did."

"Wait," Hendal practically shouted when Califer's eyes closed and his breathing became shallow. "I was supposed to be a mage like you?"

The pale man cracked open one eye after the other. "You had the potential," he whispered. "If that power doesn't act on its own, or if it's not trained, the energy seals itself away. I believed you'd found your calling as the high priest, so I left it alone."

Hendal's chest ached until he realized he'd been holding his breath. *I would have had another life…a better life, without Verdic trapping me in their cycle…*

"Please," Califer begged before falling into a coughing fit. "Give me your final blessing. Give…me hope for…the afterlife…"

Seeing the man so weak and helpless brought out an uncharacteristic, primal sensation from within Hendal. *He possesses the power to heal yet is unable to fight off this sickness. We're not so different, and we'll both die when our time comes. Doesn't this prove how equal human lives truly are? At least, they are when we're given a fair chance.*

The older man watched him with a hopeful gaze and tear-filled eyes.

"You asked me if I have any regrets," Hendal managed to say against his mixed emotions. "I had the opportunity to live another life, but it was stolen from me by those who believe their worth enables them to manipulate others' freedom. In a way, you held me back by never mentioning my potential or bothering to train me."

Califer mumbled what sounded like an apology before his hand went limp and dropped out of Hendal's.

The high priest turned away without pity or sympathy. "If we're all meant to die, why must we be restricted by those with more authority? Why should they claim the innocent civilians' futures by neglecting their potential and limiting their opportunities?"

He received no answer, not that he expected one. With nothing else to say, he rose and exited the room.

I might be forced to act as the high priest until my death, but my eyes have been opened. Califer, I shall use you as an example. My loyalties will lie with my own heart and mind, not someone else's, especially people who were gifted a position of power. I vow to change this kingdom so it is possible for everyone to choose the life they want to lead.

*

Califer's death, as painful as it was, solidified Hendal's goal to help Asteom and support the people who wish to escape a predestined fate. If ever his faith in the idea faltered, he would simply remember his late uncle, Kercher's traditions, and his lost future.

Even if his resolve held, he needed to understand what actions he could take. He considered this while staring through the window of the fourth floor's outer hallway where he often came to think without disruption.

How can I possibly convince other people that the leaders they follow might not be the most qualified or the best suited for the position? Can I use my limited authority as a priest somehow? If I do, they might consider me a hypocrite for acting as high priest and staying in the palace. I suppose I would need to make them aware of my past, in addition to how I earned this role over several priests chosen by the king and his council. I'm discovering too many moving parts and conflicts right now.

Hendal released a weary sigh, stood straighter to stretch his back, and slipped inside using the nearest doorway. A meeting had been arranged for that afternoon to organize the kingdom's next steps regarding the northern country's actions near the border, and for some reason they needed him present. His frustration with his unnecessary involvement quelled suddenly when a servant stumbled into him in an intersecting hallway.

The boy didn't appear older than thirteen, but he blurted out an apology and bowed upon realizing his rude behavior. "My apologies, high priest!"

"Where are you going?" Hendal asked without attempting to hide his annoyance.

"To find His Highness. A messenger from Kercher arrived with news from the city in the clouds."

Hendal frowned. "City in the clouds? Do you mean Yeluthia?"

Evidently, the servant didn't know the proper title of the kingdom said to house the angels of legend. He tilted his head from one side to the other while tapping a foot. "The messenger claims the news is from the city in the clouds and requested an audience with King Hernan. That's all I know."

When the boy bowed again and attempted to hurry by, Hendal reached over to grab the servant's shoulder. An itching sensation compelled him to not let this opportunity go to waste, so he intended to take on this task instead of involving the king and his council unless they were needed.

"We mustn't bother His Highness right now. You see, he's leading a rather important meeting. Allow me to speak with this messenger. I am from Kercher after all; perhaps I know them." In reality, Hendal had not returned to his hometown since he departed fifteen years ago.

In any case, his poorly contrived excuse succeeded. The servant's eyes widened, he bobbed his head twice, then he spun around to escort Hendal to the grand hall at the front of the palace.

Soldiers, servants, and well-regarded civilians scurried about on their own business when they entered, though one man stood alone. As they neared, Hendal admired the stranger's blond hair and toned physique but hesitated to approach when he caught the odd sense of urgency behind the man's blue eyes. His guide didn't stop, so he continued.

The boy introduced the messenger as Jaspire before considering his duty complete and leaving. Hendal stared at the stranger until the other spoke once they were given some privacy.

"I believe I requested the king's presence, not another one of his servants."

Hendal raised his eyebrows to emphasize his surprise at the disrespect. His mind filled with replies, both polite and equally rude, yet he grew curious about the messenger's identity since he doubted Jaspire was really from Kercher. Because of the town's tradition, he assumed no one trained to present information at the palace would speak so unkind, let alone not recognize his position.

"King Hernan is in a council session and sent me to inquire about your arrival," he lied. "After all, you wouldn't give details to a servant or myself. We don't know if you're a spy or an assassin."

"I am neither," the stranger snapped in response.

"How interesting. I offered to speak with you first as the palace's high priest, a trusted source in Verona, and because I was born and raised in Kercher. Whose household do you belong to?"

Hendal decided to suggest a few names to demonstrate his knowledge of the town's residents. If the man really came from Kercher, he could have easily corrected or added more information given how Hendal spoke based on the experience from over a decade ago.

The stranger kept quiet, though he did lower his gaze slightly.

"Is there anything you *can* tell me?" Hendal pushed while taking advantage of his title. "People come to me all the time to share their secrets, sorrows, and regrets in confidence. It's my duty as the high priest of Asteom."

Nothing in the man's facial expression or body showed what he thought, but he did raise his eyes to meet Hendal's before clearing his throat. "You may call me Jaspire. I traveled from Yeluthia to pledge my service to your king."

Growing up in the town connected to the angels' home provided plenty of fodder for Hendal's imagination as a child. He learned about the Yeluthians through his studies, including how they wielded a unique type of light magic and could manifest wings, and he fanaticized about meeting one someday. Over the years, that dream faded.

"I don't believe you," Hendal responded to cover his shock. "No one has heard from Yeluthia in nearly a century, yet you expect me to accept your claim? Somebody would send a *real* messenger ahead to inform King Hernan. He doesn't meet with just anyone wandering in from the street."

Jaspire inhaled through his nose and opened his mouth, as if to retort, but he paused. His eyes darted around the hall where people continued walking or conversing nearby, revealing his intent to keep his presence a secret to the public.

Hendal took advantage of that behavior to establish his authority within the palace. "Why don't we find a better place to discuss what brought you here."

He motioned for the Yeluthian to follow as he crossed the hall. They passed through one of the doors lining the wall, and he purposefully used an extended route in order to avoid giving his guest an opportunity to memorize the floor's layout. After a few minutes, they entered a decorated room used by the royal family for their social gatherings, which remained unguarded when not in use.

"Now, let's talk," Hendal began when they were both seated in two of the cushioned chairs. "Why are you actually here?"

Jaspire still appeared displeased since he kept dealing with someone besides the king, yet he caved into the request to discuss his business. "It is as I said. I wish to serve Asteom's ruler."

"Why?"

"Are you humans familiar with the class system in Yeluthia?"

The question startled Hendal, and he shook his head.

"One's birth determines if they will be given the chance to lead, or if they must follow," Jaspire responded. "I am from one of the upper families you might consider nobility."

When he didn't go on, Hendal sensed the Yeluthian contemplating his next words and ventured a guess. "So, you would pledge your loyalty to the king of Asteom in order to give your family's name more value?"

"Yes, that is correct."

His eyes narrowed at the immediate response. "Why did your people not send any prior messages?" he countered. "Surely they would bother to communicate beforehand."

Again, Jaspire fell silent.

Hendal took advantage of the pause to share his own opinion. "If I were to guess based on your behavior alone, I would say you haven't mentioned your departure to the Yeluthian leaders."

The sapphire eyes darted to the door and back. "In a way, you are right."

"What's that supposed to mean?"

Jaspire slid a hand into his pocket to remove a knife no longer than those found in an ordinary kitchen. Its dull blade didn't shine at all but displayed patches of rust. Still, the Yeluthian admired it as though it were a prized weapon.

Meanwhile, Hendal squirmed in his seat. He had a feeling his guest lied about pledging his service to Asteom's ruler, yet he hoped to utilize Jaspire as a resource if he was connected to the city in the clouds.

"Explain yourself," he demanded with more courage than he felt.

"I did not intend to interact with anyone other than your king," Jaspire began, his voice threateningly calm. "I believe I can make an exception."

"You're wrong."

The Yeluthian tilted his head, giving Hendal time to continue saying whatever came to mind.

"If you kill me, my body would be discovered before you reach King Hernan. Also, you wouldn't be allowed near him without someone like me escorting you."

"Clever, human. I am pretty adept at cleaning up after myself, though." Jaspire leaned forward yet made no attempt to attack.

Wait a moment, Hendal thought once his mind caught up to the situation. *If he came here to murder the king, his goals might align with my own. He hasn't tried to strike, so he must be providing an opportunity for me to apologize, leave him alone, or do something to provoke him into killing me too.*

The notion provided a sense of strength, and he cleared his throat while forcing his body to relax. "Perhaps we can help each other."

"What can you possibly offer me? My people do not value coin, property, or possessions except for sentimentality."

"I have a presence in the palace, one established over the last fifteen years. The people here trust me, and rightly so. Your actions are a means to a finite result, which makes sense, unless you want more." As he expected, his words proved alluring enough to tempt the Yeluthian.

"What are you saying?" Jaspire asked next.

Hendal held his chin high, smiled, then leaned back in a position reflecting his confidence. "Why don't we start over? Tell me, why do you wish to eliminate the king of Asteom?"

The resulting silence lasted longer than the previous, yet he dared not interrupt because he knew his guest used the time to debate revealing the reasoning. In the end, it paid off.

"I mentioned my family's status," the Yeluthian began, showing less intensity. "Our lives and responsibilities involve serving the citizens. Since most assignments are decided at birth, promotions are few and far between unless someone dedicates their entire being to another, but demotions are enforced easily. Those of us who fail expectations, even accidentally, even if it is *one* incident in twenty years, find ourselves branded as less than deserving of better. When I learned this, I sought vengeance."

"Why give up what you had to travel through Asteom?"

"From my understanding, violence in my country results in a similar punishment to what happens in yours."

A shiver went down Hendal's spine at the icy reply, and he attempted to hide his discomfort. "So, you hurt one of your people, and they tossed you out."

Jaspire scoffed at the assumption. "I left of my own volition."

"Then, murder here will redeem you? Is that what Yeluthians believe?"

"No, quite the opposite. My sacrifice shall be our revenge."

In that instant, Hendal understood why Jaspire targeted King Hernan. "By killing the leader of Asteom, you hope to place the blame on Yeluthia."

He received a sly, disturbing smile in answer.

It's not a horrible idea, yet he can't do this alone. Firstly, even if he claimed to be from Yeluthia, I doubt the generals would go to war over a stray dog. His reputation in his home country would vouch for his insanity and thirst for blood, succeeding in uniting us instead of dividing the races. That is, unless others support his cause.

"I have one final question," he continued once the situation became clear. "What change are you trying to bring about?"

The question seemed to confuse Jaspire, who narrowed his eyes and frowned. "A war between humans and angels is not enough?"

"No one will fall for such an obvious trap. You may have friends to take more lives, but Asteom would label your rebel group as the problem, especially if they contact Yeluthia to confirm their lack of knowledge about what goes on below their kingdom. In this scenario, murdering the king won't do much."

Jaspire's eyes widened, as though the honest criticism offended him. Instead of lashing out, which Hendal expected, he returned the knife to his pocket before folding his hands together and speaking at a lower volume.

"What I do is for the people praying for better. The blind citizens revere their leaders while remaining stagnant, accepting their lives because it does not bring about conflict. I desire change and redemption, even if it means resorting to violence."

Hendal stared at the Yeluthian and recalled his final conversation with Califer. The reminder of the future he envisioned, where opportunities would be available to all regardless of their status, education, talent, or other classification, lit a flame under him.

"The king, his council members, and the nobility behave similarly to those you describe as stagnant. Most stand above the weak because they formed connections with those in powerful positions or were born into their roles. They base their status on who they know possessing riches and influence over the capital city and other locations around the country, denying those beneath them the chance to learn and develop their potential. All of that is to hold onto their comfortable, peaceful lives. My goal is to end such delusions. As a victim of their carelessness, I claim it as my right." Hendal went on to summarize his childhood, duties in Kercher, and eventual transition to high priest before sharing Califer's betrayal.

"Our ideals can converge here," he concluded. "Once Asteom is liberated, then we'll possess the means to do the same in Yeluthia. We need each other, Jaspire. Join me, and let us fulfill our destiny."

The Yeluthian's expression shifted from suspicious to dubious before appearing uncertain. Then, he pressed his lips together and nodded.

*

The others Jaspire referred to consisted of Yeluthians who had also been shamed for their beliefs, according to him. Hendal didn't care who assisted them, but he insisted they gather followers before attempting to go into action.

"It won't happen right away," he warned the newcomer. "It might take years. As long as we remain steadfast, though, we can succeed." After, Hendal sent his assistant out to collect the Yeluthians exiled from their home.

A little over a year later, he heard from the angel again.

Jaspire communicated with a letter addressed to the high priest, describing the location of a meeting space in the capital city. During his next period of free time, Hendal snuck through Verona until he found the seemingly abandoned, one-story building that looked to be about as large as his quarters in the palace. He knocked and waited.

Not a moment later, Jaspire opened the door. He hadn't aged at all; if anything, he appeared younger and wore a robe similar to a priest's. "Please, come in," he said by way of greeting while gesturing Hendal inside. "This home may be cramped for twelve people, but it is cheap enough. The owner does not ask questions either. Allow me to introduce you to everyone."

Seven males, who looked physically stronger and meaner than Jaspire, and three, beautiful females in dresses stood around. None of them paid Hendal any attention while they were introduced.

"We make up a wide range of skills," Jaspire added once the group assembled. "Four among us can wield magic, including myself and my goddess gift, and the rest are trained warriors. I think you will find this suitable for our purposes."

"What have you told them?" Hendal asked, ignoring his curiosity stemming from what Jaspire referred to as a "goddess gift." Those present had to know the angel's plan to go against Yeluthia's rulers.

Their leader confirmed this.

Before Hendal could consider more, one of the males stepped forward with a scowl. "Let us get started already. You gathered us here, so tell us what to do."

Jaspire opened his mouth in preparation to scold him for the outburst, but Hendal spoke first.

Over the months, he spent the evenings alone to plot where his personal scouts would be placed based only on the mentality and skills best suited for each area. Now that he could do so, he explained this, leaving the group to figure out who would fit at these locations. Essentially, the major cities needed to be under their watch since they'd provide precious information. Then, when the time felt right, they could strike.

Hendal kept an eye on Asteom through the group planted across the country. Those in the south sent updates to Jaspire, who remained the lone member in Verona in order to avoid any direct connections with the palace. Three took cycles in and around the Dalan base, which proved to be the second most guarded area. The others scattered east as nothing worth the trouble would be to the west.

He didn't receive news from Jaspire for a while until someone near Kercher reported seeing another Yeluthian flying high above. In their report, the messenger carried a letter addressed to King Hernan regarding an arrangement to reestablish the old alliance. Hendal could hardly believe the news and ordered future disruptions, both from Yeluthia and Kercher, to be silenced.

Either the first attempt hadn't been serious or their people were cautious because Hendal didn't hear about the alliance again for many months.

*

At long last, their patience was rewarded. After four years of studying the country from the comfort of the palace, the council dragged Hendal into a discussion about their military. Normally, he had no interest in such matters because the king never requested his opinion, yet that day proved to be the exception. The temperamental generals shouted over one another when he entered the space, giving him some idea of what took place. Their concern arose from the number of troops available if most were to be sent away from Verona, especially the mages. They debated how to solve this, even going so far as to invite the nobility Hendal distasted for their greed and prideful nature.

Fortunately, their presence didn't seem useless that day. Someone familiar with the Magical Arts Academy in East Hoover knew about the opportunities offered after a mage graduates and suggested King Hernan take advantage of the system.

"If most of the trainees request to be stationed somewhere around Asteom, why not ask them to serve their country first?" the nobleman threw out with a foxlike grin.

"Would this make them more or less fearful of the army?" another added. This one appeared much younger and acted oblivious to the others' interests.

"What do you even know about the army?" the first sneered, causing the second to cower.

Everyone else in the room ignored their behavior.

"I like it," General Tont continued and tugged on his beard. "I doubt they do much physical activity anyway, so this'll help them prepare for the world outside of their academy."

Evidently, King Hernan sided with that rationality after more input. "I will send for a representative to collect their thoughts and opinions on the idea," he concluded, ending the matter for the time being.

A mage instructor named Byron Rinod arrived a few days later and traveled back and forth from Verona to East Hoover under the king's orders. From their first encounter, it became obvious the man was capable of speaking in a professional manner on behalf of the academy's headmaster and faculty. He proved intelligent enough to hold his ground without lying, instead countering points the council made in favor of what King Hernan deemed the Mage Service Law.

Hendal soon grew envious of the master mage's ability to manipulate the flow of a conversation. In fact, it prevented the proposed law from taking place for months. Still, the council's frustration entertained him, especially their king who couldn't do much with words alone.

With the tension building, Hendal privately recommended they use a more direct tactic. During one of the mage's visits, he arranged for a breakfast with the nobility and announced the future plan to enact the service law. While they flocked into the grand hall, Hendal took pleasure in seeing Byron attempt to keep his composure. The lords and ladies worked perfectly, believing their king's proposal as fact and spreading the news throughout the city. Further word on how excited the people were to have the prospect of mages to keep them safe sealed the deal. The academy could not turn away such a request without appearing selfish and inconsiderate. Instead of severing their relationship with the palace, Byron agreed to return to the academy with his tail between his legs.

The evening the master mage was scheduled to leave, a sudden concern about the magic users living in Verona struck Hendal, so he hurried to see Jaspire. Three others from the group were present and glanced at him after he barged into their building.

"Can a mage sense your power?" he asked just after the Yeluthian spoke a greeting.

Jaspire pointed to the opening in a silent request for privacy. "What do you mean?" he countered once the door closed.

Hendal proceeded to explain the service law, finishing with the idea that brought him to their abode. "I heard mages can sense another's power. If dozens more are wandering through the city, what are the chances they'll figure out you're here?"

Jaspire didn't reply right away. One of the two females in the room stared at him with an expression Hendal couldn't read while the other male threw in his opinion.

"Is there not a master light mage in the palace already? If they have not felt our energy by now, I doubt anyone else will."

"Unless we cast a spell near them," Jaspire added after nodding to himself. "The only power we expended for some time has been for our wings, and that is beyond the city. Perhaps it is similar enough to a human's light magic, so anyone who senses it thinks nothing of it."

Hendal still wasn't convinced. "Perhaps, but be careful. I want an update sent to your companions as well to inform them of this new law."

"It shall be done."

"Good." Hendal self-consciously brushed down his tattered cloak and prepared to leave; however, a feminine voice filled the space before he reached the door.

"Did you say the law *will be* passed without issue?"

Hendal glanced behind and noticed the others staring at the female beside Jaspire. She seemed frail and physically harmless, but her eyes glowed with a mischievous interest.

"Once Byron, the mage I mentioned earlier, brings the documents to the academy's headmaster to sign, they'll begin the transfer."

"So, the law is not complete," she added with a sly grin rivaling any nobleman's.

"What are you getting at, Elsa?" Jaspire asked.

She stuck her chin up. "This could be our chance! If these mages are a necessity to the palace, would it not be suspicious if the master mage is killed and the important documents disappear?"

"We want to avoid any involvement with the humans' business," the other male replied in an annoyed manner.

Elsa merely shook her head, opened her hands in front of her, and chuckled. "Drake, if no one knows about our presence here, what would they assume if they catch one of us flying away?"

Hendal heard himself gasp as the idea clicked into his mind. "Yeluthia!"

She snapped her fingers so abruptly that Hendal jumped. "Exactly! Not only do we weaken the defenses in the palace by delaying this law, and possibly causing conflict between the two human cities, but we can also frame Yeluthia for intervening."

"We would need to leave the master mage alive in order for it to work. Then, he will be the first to report," Jaspire added.

The angels' willingness to accept the plan right away startled Hendal, but he found he liked the idea. *Not only will this initiate distrust between Asteom and Yeluthia, but I will also rid the palace of Byron and prevent him from interfering anymore. I do recall two students with him. General Tont's son is also acting as a guard for their return.* He shared this with the others in the room.

"I guess we will only need one alive," Elsa finished with a chilling calmness.

The other female rolled her eyes. "I think you just keep talking because you want to get out of here."

Elsa flashed her a smile and stood. "Would you like to accompany me?"

"No," Jaspire interrupted. "Thelma is a magic wielder, not a fighter. Devan, I am sending you along. Keep an eye on your sister."

The other male grunted his confirmation. Hendal remained with the group until well after midnight when the assigned pair left to hide in the woods before Byron departed in the morning.

"That Elsa is one scary woman," he mumbled to Jaspire and Thelma when the three were alone.

"I have known Elsa my whole life. She enjoys the freedom Asteom provides," Thelma shared.

"Was she always…like that?" Hendal felt compelled to ask, even against his better judgement.

The female tilted her head. "Yes, I suppose so; however, it grew worse when we were banished. Elsa, Devan, and I found pleasure in killing animals for sport across Yeluthia and the mountain range. Every so often, a Mintelian or a farmer ended up in the wrong place at the wrong time. That gave her a thrill. I am sure you can imagine the rest."

Hendal had not cared to hear about any of the former Yeluthians' histories for that reason. Some, like Jaspire, had been cast aside for their beliefs while others were demented.

Instead of continuing the conversation, he brought up various ideas, such as luring the Yeluthian king to Asteom for an assassination and blaming it on King Hernan, or something less drastic to sever the alliance between the two kingdoms. After, he would be able to help Jaspire and his companions without being a threat to his own country. It seemed the details were falling into place, and Hendal rested well that evening.

*

"We have a problem."

Hendal frowned at Jaspire's words as the angel stood in the high priest's quarters. He knew some part had gone wrong not only by the tone of the statement, but also because of the fact that the Yeluthian snuck in to visit him. "What is it?"

"Our attempt to kill the master mage and those accompanying him failed. They will probably reach East Hoover within the next two days."

At first, the update shocked Hendal, and his face paled. He prepared to demand an explanation for their failure before voicing his regret for not learning the angels' skills. Jaspire's glare suggested more, though, so he pressed his lips together to avoid blowing up until he could handle the rest.

"What else?"

This time, Jaspire let his internal hatred seep through, biting off each word as he spoke. "A demon became involved. It possessed the young woman traveling with the master mage, killed Elsa, and took Devan's right foot."

Any emotion heating Hendal drained from his body, leaving him shivering. "A d-demon?" he stuttered, unable to pull himself together at the thought.

Demons were a subject no one wished to venture into. Thankfully, the topic of possessions and rituals had been constituted as a magical matter for the master mage in the palace and their assistants to handle. Sometimes, though, people requested him to exercise spirits believed to be influencing a person into committing crimes or catching an incurable sickness. Matters relating to the creatures, even bringing up the word in most places, became taboo.

213

"Devan is frantic," Jaspire went on, too caught up in his fury to consider Hendal. "He will not sit still long enough for the wound to heal and demands we avenge his sister."

"We can't do that…"

"I said the same, but he does not listen! Besides, Thelma and I are in Verona. No one else will be returning unless I call for them."

"Yes!" Hendal yelled from the fear creeping up on him. "Inform the others. Fill them in on the situation, and I'll stop by after. We can decide our next steps then."

"What about *it*?" Jaspire growled through his teeth while narrowing his eyes into a glare.

Hendal held his breath. *I don't understand his reaction. Something else is creating these deeper emotions, and it's going on beneath our scheming. This will distract his group and thwart my plans if I don't handle it properly.*

"Whatever your feelings are on demons, you must put them aside for now," he replied. "Its meddling has led to the end of our opportunity to use the Mage Service Law. If Byron is still alive, he'll see his duties through and most likely notice the connection between Devan and us if we do more. Gather the rest of your companions, then send for me."

Jaspire tried burning a hole through Hendal's head with a furious glare but never attempted to interrupt or deny what needed to be done. The Yeluthian left without so much as a nod to let Hendal know he would follow orders.

*

The hectic days after their meeting passed in a blur. Even before he saw Jaspire and the other angels again, Hendal learned of Devan's fate and cursed their rotten luck. The injured angel acted on his own without consideration for what his actions would do to his companions. He got himself killed, confirmed the presence of his race in Asteom, and still couldn't kill the master mage or demon. The law passed, but that news had been swept under the rug when General Tont received a letter from his son, which he flaunted to the council and his men. Apparently, he claimed a rogue angel wounded the young man, though his son had been aided by what the assistant general referred to as an individual with unique, powerful magic being kept at the academy.

As Hendal listened to the general read the letter word for word, he began to put the pieces together. *The demon possessed Byron's student, but it hasn't completely taken over her mind or body. Worst of all, she can manifest wings now and fight someone like Devan while remaining sane.*

Once he finished, General Tont laughed in a condescending manner. "Who here scolded me for appointing my son as an assistant general? Now you heard it! He's done some sneaking around, and we can bring their weapon here for us to use."

"You would want such a creature in the palace?" the master light mage named Emilea asked without hiding her disbelief. "Demons are terrible beings that cause nothing except pain and destruction. There *is* a reason why any involvement with them is against the law."

Hendal nodded and voiced his agreement, noting this moment as the first the two ever spoke in favor of the other's stance. "I concur. Lady Emilea has worked with conflicts regarding demonic possession, so it would be ignorant to push aside her experience. We should end it while we have the chance."

Somehow, he knew his words didn't hold much weight when it came to discussions relating to military power. General Casner, the harsh-looking man who always sat directly across from the king's throne, pounced on that notion.

"Easy for someone uninvolved with the soldiers to say. We organized just enough in Verona to get by, but our worry is for the future, more specifically, for the worst scenarios."

"It's only the north we're focusing on, though," General Dillon offered. He proved to be the least explosive commander, emphasized by his soft demeanor and clean-shaven face. "I highly doubt we'll see any armies climb over the Ghurun mountain range or cross the western or southern seas. Besides, we're welcoming dozens of mages from the Magical Arts Academy."

"They'll need training too," General Tont countered. "I'm not saying we need a possessed mage in order to survive. We should just be making moves to see if it's willing to fight on *our* side before killing the person."

Hendal caught Emilea sitting up straighter. "That's insane!" she exclaimed with hands balled into fists. "You don't understand how unpredictable the creatures manipulated by demons can be. Everyone's life is at risk, as well as the sanity of the mages. Demonic energy puts us in a state of unease because of the opposite nature. Even the dark mages would find it unsettling."

General Tont frowned while General Casner huffed a laugh. Hendal half-expected the master mage to slap the soldier for his disrespect if he didn't sit out of reach. He glanced at King Hernan, who typically watched the meetings while processing what the council said. Only when the man felt a sufficient amount of information had been presented did he state his conclusion. It drove Hendal crazy at times like these when the king would not share his opinion aside from asking a question or two.

When the space fell silent, Hendal chanced a peek into what their leader thought.

"Your Highness, do you feel the risk of keeping one possessed by a demon is worth the reward of another, skilled combatant?" he asked in his gentle manner to suggest concern. Underneath the facade, Hendal hoped the young woman responsible for losing him two angels would be executed. Without her around, Jaspire and the others under his command could focus on starting another plan.

Unfortunately, King Hernan typically sided with the generals.

"I don't care for sharing the same roof as one touched by a demon," the man began in a firm tone of voice. "I trust the concern of the mages as well as the direction of my military leaders; however, I also have a strong feeling the renowned academy would take measures to eliminate anyone who poses a threat to our kingdom, lest they be punished for their negligence. I will leave it up to them, then. Should they leave her alive, we can assume they relinquish the demon's power to us." King Hernan finished that sentence by nodding to General Tont.

The news disgusted Hendal, yet his disappointment continued to grow when the man went on.

"Lady Emilea, keep watch and handle any disruptions if the mage becomes a threat. I expect the academy will send Byron Rinod as their representative since he is most familiar with Verona and the palace. He's also capable of holding himself accountable, especially when his students and reputation are on the line."

Hendal managed to resist the urge to groan and sensed the light mage doing the same. The king dismissed everyone, and Hendal saved the information to share with Jaspire whenever the Yeluthian sent for him.

*

If the situation with Elsa and Devan did something for Hendal, it solidified their companions' resolve to stand behind Jaspire, and thus behind the high priest. They all managed to gather together just after the Harvest Festival took place, which had been much later than Hendal preferred.

By then, a Yeluthian child acting as the ambassador for their country slipped past their patrol because she didn't fly, though the letters their group confiscated and another messenger from Kercher mentioned her arrival beforehand. Jaspire confirmed her position, adding how she was the king's niece and used a goddess gift for mind-to-mind communication. That had been when Hendal learned what the term meant, as well as his assistant's ability to heal another's injury from a distance. The high priest soon acted as a guide for the young Yeluthian named Grace. She would remain in his sights, but more importantly, she would not see him as a threat or connect him with Jaspire's group.

Meanwhile, the demon-possessed mage named Coura worked closely with Byron, who became the second master mage in the palace, and did little aside from make everyone uncomfortable. Hendal wished she would slip up and lose control of her magic just so King Hernan had an excuse to get rid of her. During their council meetings, he, along with Emilea, questioned her progress and behavior. Byron always eased the tension with his smooth explanations, providing plenty of detail as he admitted his own concerns. Eventually, he managed to get Emilea to trust him, forcing the high priest to intervene.

When the opportunity presented itself, Hendal approached King Hernan with the idea to inquire if Coura could demonstrate the demonic magic. Byron danced around the subject again during their council meeting, but after more pushing, their ruler caught on to the master mage's avoidance. Hendal pounced on the king's doubt.

"If it distresses the people here, why not send her away?" he suggested when he got a moment alone with the man. "An area with less mages could allow her to practice the magic. Besides, if she does lose control of herself, there will be less people around to harm."

King Hernan raised an eyebrow at that, so Hendal pretended to babble an apology for being so insincere. Despite that, after a moment to contemplate the idea, he caved in. "That would be a feasible way to rein her in. I've been meaning to send someone to Dala for months now too. General Tio heard about the service law and requested we bring mages south for their base. I would guess you heard the shadow creatures are roaming the country."

Hendal nodded. Whispers here and there came from soldiers and citizens traveling outside of Verona, yet he actively tried to stay away from what could hinder his work, specifically an issue that would distract Jaspire again. He needed the angels to focus on the rest of his plan.

"I can spare those with adequate physical skill," the king went on. "After all, we underestimated the combat training offered in East Hoover."

"Yes, Your Highness. How were we supposed to know without a means of communicating between the capital and academy?" Hendal added before noticing the man hesitate to speak, which was a rare feat. "Is there anything else?"

"You're right. I feel like I've been neglecting the citizens outside the capital city. Several people propose I do some readjustments to how soldiers and mages are placed in the cities and towns across Asteom. I believe now might be the best time to do it."

"Who would you send? One of the generals or their assistants?"

The king contemplated this just as they reached his quarters. "Aaron might enjoy leaving the palace for a while. I won't risk those necessary here or in Dala."

Hendal's mouth fell open to reflect an inner sense of disbelief that the man voiced his willingness to send his only heir away from the safety of the palace. He understood what this meant for his cause and composed himself before replying with fervor.

"That is an excellent idea! Prince Aaron is of the age to explore on his own, though with a few guards of course. I'm sure as long as only a handful of people know he's gone, and he doesn't flaunt his position, the matter should turn out fine."

Despite the enthusiasm he projected, King Hernan frowned. "As a ruler, I concur. As a father, I'm not sure about it. I haven't even told Freya yet, but I can hear her harping at me."

Hendal involuntarily winced. The queen proved to be a woman with little capability for deep thought, so sending her only child away would not go over well. He patted the man's shoulder to express his genuine sympathy before moving on.

On the evening of the prince's departure, Hendal kept a close eye on the young man before he and his guards set out. The web of his plotting steadily weaved together, which shouldn't have put down his spirits; however, it felt as though a foreign presence lurked around every corner. The unknown eyes on his back were enough to make him anxious and quick-tempered. During the night, he called Jaspire and the remaining angels to a private space in the palace for fear of wandering through the city alone. He knew the evening meal took place at that time, so the least amount of people would be roaming the halls.

The meeting went according to plan, even with their sour attitudes. He sent the four possessing the greatest speed and ability to blend into their surroundings to Kercher, Clearwater, and the northern border in order to patrol the country's perimeter. They had all agreed it would be dangerous to stay grouped together and lead to suspicion if any were caught. That consideration seemed important once Jaspire, Thelma, and three others named Drake, Hector, and Urvin flew to Dala. Hendal would still utilize those whose faces would not be exposed to the southern base. Once away from the city, he entrusted the assignment to Jaspire. All their group needed to do was take down the troops and its general, then capture the prince.

"The backlash on Yeluthia for his kidnapping will bring about the end of that petty alliance," Hendal concluded with a glance at the nine sitting around him. "We can kill him later once the hostility is strong."

"What about the demon?" the bulkiest of the bunch asked.

"What about it?"

All eyes slid to Jaspire, who reached into the satchel at his side and removed a bundle. With a wide, wicked smile, he unwrapped a dagger seemingly made of gold. Hendal wasn't familiar with weaponry, yet he couldn't mistake the glorious craftsmanship humming with an unseen power.

"This is an ancestral weapon," the angel explained and held up the dagger, which glistened even without a direct light source nearby. "Our ancestors crafted these weapons as gifts for the humans once they rid the land of demons. It amplifies light magic, allowing one of our people to use several spells compared to one or magnify a single casting. Yrian brought it from Umbrich's underground market. With this, we can get our revenge."

Hendal frowned despite the malicious smiles of the others in the room; worrying about a demon gave him a headache.

"We should leave now before the sun sets," Thelma suggested. "Then, we can catch that group on the road."

Silently, most of the table moved to rise.

I can't let them ruin this, Hendal realized. *There's no chance of hiding their wings, and they'll reveal themselves to Byron and those with him by attacking his student. We'll lose our element of surprise on the Dalan base.*

"I tell you when to go!" he blurted out in a rage before slamming his fist on the table, causing the angels to freeze. "This is our final opportunity to make progress on our plan to frame Yeluthia and spark tension between your people and Asteom. We need to organize this business, or else they'll catch us. I think it's best you leave tonight, under the cover of darkness."

Those standing returned to their seats.

"You are certain he will leave tonight?" the outspoken Drake asked, referring to the prince.

"Do you question my sources?" Hendal snapped to emphasize his rising temper.

The shortest person in the room named Hector put a calming hand on Drake's arm. Hendal knew the two were related, yet their facial shape hardly suggested it. "What about the royal family?"

Hendal brought his fist down on the table once more. "Your main concern for now is the base! You have your orders and a leader." He expected someone to continue the questioning, but thankfully they didn't.

"We understand," Hector ventured to speak on the others' behalf.

"Good. Now, get out of my sight."

Jaspire took over the meeting then, leaving Hendal to put his throbbing head in his hands. The four monitoring the perimeter would travel on foot to their destinations while the remaining party headed south for the woods near Dala. He offered to stay behind and arrange the kidnapping with Hendal.

"It would be too obvious we know more than we should about matters in the palace if we attack right away," the angel explained. "Not only that, but it would be smarter to focus on both goals once the prince arrives in Dala."

Hendal could not find any reasoning against this decision, so the discussion concluded there. They all left, except his assistant.

"High Priest, is there something wrong? You appear distressed." The question wasn't as sympathetic as it sounded, instead reflecting Jaspire's annoyance with Hendal's behavior.

"It's nothing. I'm just nervous because we're acting again."

Jaspire raised an eyebrow before carefully removing the golden dagger and running a finger back and forth across the edges to caress the metal. "We hate being in this palace too," he startled Hendal by saying. His voice remained soft yet still full of venom. "It is irritating to say the least. That is why I am going to seal it away with this ancestral dagger. The creator placed an old spell on it to keep the energy inside the demon's physical body, essentially killing it. As I mentioned earlier, the essence it holds also amplifies the power in my people's blood. I already feel my energy swelling. The lone drawback is it really can only be used once, for if the blade is removed, the seal is broken. Who knows how disastrous that could be. Demonic energy latches on to a host for more power. They are truly disgusting creatures."

He hid the dagger in its wrapping before returning it to the satchel. Jaspire's fierce attention relaxed as he turned to leave the room. "I want to be near here for a while, probably until spring. Then, you can expect us to return."

Hendal couldn't think of a response. His eyes followed the angel out of the space before he decided that returning to his quarters seemed like a better idea than lingering alone in empty places.

Days later, he recalled the conversation when Jaspire returned and a demon appeared to them to offer its assistance.

Tracking the Demon

I must admit, I'm amazed to see you again."

For the second time, Coura stood opposite Hendal as he calmly sat and stared without revealing his true emotions. She spent a week deciding whether or not visiting the man would be worth it, but when General Terrell called her into a meeting with Aaron and the other generals, she needed any information she could get about Soirée's power.

They learned about Terran through the Yeluthians while she was on leave and pressed for details. No one proposed a worthwhile solution to the issue after the questioning, though they shared nothing with her about how they expected to combat it. Aaron simply ordered her to remain in Verona until they discussed the matter with Commander Detrix, Byron, and Emilea, who weren't present for her interrogation.

Coura crossed her arms to display her rising annoyance with the situation and eyed the cell. Irwin didn't bother to harass Hendal this time and seemed just as surprised by her second visit. "Are you going to tell me what I need to know?"

"Maybe, maybe not. I can discuss my experiences, and if that provides the information you desire, then the answer is yes."

After a brief glance over her shoulder at Irwin, who appeared enraptured by whatever novel he had this time, she released a long sigh. *I hope being here is worth it. This place feels so unpleasant...*

"Well, where did we end our conversation?" Hendal began with a bit more energy than before.

Despite the feigned forgetfulness, he picked up with the families of Kercher. Coura listened as he revealed his appointment as the next priest, his uncle and nephew's personalities, and some of what their daily routine had been like. Then, he dismissed her for the day.

She didn't hide her frustration, yet two ideas kept her returning every week after.

Hendal is an intelligent man, she reminded herself when she considered what she knew about the former high priest. *Someone who was able to do what he did in the palace wouldn't play dumb without a reason, and I'm sure he's sane no matter what Irwin believes. I wonder why he feels the need to drag this out, though. Perhaps he really is toying with me.*

The second notion proved more difficult to swallow. *Does he plan on humanizing himself by telling me about his childhood and early life as a priest? I suppose I'm gaining insight into Kercher and the town's relationships across Asteom, but it's still tough to view him as anyone other than the man who hurt many people. I think I'm actually interested in what influenced him to seek power through the use of demonic energy. What if that mentality had all been Soirée's doing? What does he plan on revealing through these stories?*

*

Every week or two after her initial visits to Verona's prison, Coura returned to question Hendal. At first, the man's life story sounded like an excuse to cover up what she hoped to hear about Soirée, which bored Irwin enough for him to begin staying at his desk instead of listening nearby. Of course, the ex-high priest wouldn't skip ahead when they were alone.

Still, her hatred quelled significantly once she learned what drove him to live in Verona and especially how his magical potential had been dismissed. During that time of internal distress, he met Jaspire and the other, rogue angels, who encouraged him to pursue their twisted idea of justice. Soirée took advantage of their appearance in Dala to join Hendal after, manipulating the man's views on what was fair and how he could use her power to bring about his goals.

As much as it made her sick to acknowledge, the situation resonated with her more than she expected. *I accepted Soirée's deal because I had no other option except to become her puppet, or at least that's what I thought. She sealed my Yeluthian power away in order to force me to wield dark magic stemming from her demonic energy. When we were separated, she still kept some control over me by threatening innocent lives all to use me as a means of experimenting with her kind and the angels. Both Hendal and I are haunted by the memories of Soirée, not because she remained an outside threat, but because she wormed her way inside our minds.*

"As for the rest of my account, I'm sure you heard about it from Byron," the man went on as he recapped his time in the palace. Instead of a crazed or spiteful tone, he just sounded tired. "I lost and was captured, then they threw me in this cell to rot. Nothing new has happened since you arrived."

Coura shifted her weight to the other leg when the basement fell silent and observed the hunched figure slouching at the end of the bed. Nothing about him looked intimidating whatsoever. "You didn't tell me anything I haven't heard before or new information that's relevant to what I need to know."

"I warned you what I shared might not be helpful."

"You did," she replied without hiding her frustration. "Why couldn't you answer my questions instead of wasting my time then?"

To her surprise, he glanced upward with a natural, sincere smile. "We're all alone, aren't we? The rest of the guards rotate, but Irwin prefers to stay here where he doesn't work too hard. I figured when I bored him enough with Kercher and the palace life he would leave so no one would bother you if you continued to return just to hear me ramble."

So, I was right about that part.

"There is another reason," he continued in an even more defeated manner as he tore his eyes away from her. "You can see how I'm treated by the guards. Having company who listens instead of lashing out immediately is a blessing I've been fortunate enough to experience with you. Believe it or not, recounting my life's journey allowed me to reminisce about the better moments and put more thought behind the mistakes I made. Although I can't change the past, and I'm not sure if I would given all that has happened, I appreciate your visits. It is a bit humorous considering I don't recall us conversing in the past."

While he concluded with a dry chuckle, Coura found herself unable to remember speaking with Hendal anytime in the palace; mostly she would listen to someone else, like Byron, talking with him.

I'm sure Soirée intended to keep us apart to hide his identity as a traitor, she realized. The notion made her feel some pity for the ex-high priest. *Could I have helped him break away from her? Would I have even noticed he was the one commanding the rogue angels and working with her? I'm under the impression his mind became corrupted by Soirée and the power she gifted him. She encouraged the ideas of ruling Asteom and almost made it possible...*

Coura sensed the time they had left would be up shortly. After a brief glance over her shoulder to confirm Irwin still preoccupied himself with his book, she stepped right up to the bars and decided to interrogate him directly.

"Have you felt any hint of demonic energy around you or this building?" she asked at a lower volume without sacrificing her firm tone.

At the urgency of her words and movement to close the space between them, he leaned forward to listen and spoke quietly after. "None at all; however, you should know my connection with the demon never ran as deeply as yours. There were hints as to how much you were involved, and once she revealed your Yeluthian lineage the evening you escaped, I understood that better. Once her power left me, I never sensed it again, though I feel different than I did before."

Coura couldn't help herself from chewing on the inside of her cheek in thought and stepped away from the metal bars. *I didn't notice Terran's energy or the creatures' until they appeared, which means he may be able to suppress that power, like a mage. What Hendal said doesn't eliminate the possibility of damage to his soul space either, which can be picked up by a demon. After all, Terran targeted me.*

She had plenty to contemplate but still not enough solid information to raise her confidence and push her to bring the subject up to Aaron and his council or the Yeluthian leaders. For the moment, though, her discussion with Hendal was over, so she prepared to leave when he voiced a question.

"Why is it you came to visit me?"

"I needed answers."

"Your reaction to what I said makes me wonder if you were expecting to hear something different," the man countered and stood to approach the bars. "Why are you asking about demonic energy after all this time?"

Coura didn't reply. When he narrowed his eyes, she purposely avoided his glare.

"What's wrong outside these walls that drove you to come see me? Unless you can't reveal the reason with a prisoner, you shouldn't act so secretive. I would also venture to guess you're here on your own without anyone else knowing since you never mentioned your orders or permission to Irwin. Are there demons or their creatures wandering around Asteom? Is *she* roaming free from-"

Coura abruptly turned away, cutting off his next question, and hurried at a brisk walk toward the staircase as Hendal shouted for her. Irwin offered a snarky comment, but she already climbed halfway up to the ground floor to avoid a conversation. The guard posted at the entrance wished her a nice evening when she stepped outside and into the cooler, night air, which eased the heat on her face and limbs.

After returning to her room in the palace, a sudden weariness dropped onto her shoulders, prompting her to change clothes and lie down. Despite that, new thoughts surrounding the ex-high priest continued to surface as she focused on Soirée's involvement.

Hendal held crazed ideals, but what could have happened if he didn't become involved with her? Energy that unnatural and in such a great amount no doubt influenced his mental state, corrupting him, at least partially. I experienced her meddling firsthand and know how that kind of power can destroy a person's life. She tore me away from my family and my home; who knows how my life would have turned out.

He also mentioned his potential had been ignored for the sake of his family's traditions. I might never have trained as a mage without a teacher or been brought to the Magical Arts Academy. I can't deny how my life has changed for the better because of her. I studied under Byron, met Will, Marcus, Aaron, and Grace because of my assignment to Verona, and traveled the country. Demonic energy is meant to cause chaos, yet without it...

Coura couldn't finish the thought. She would never admit, not even to herself, that using such malicious, wicked power could be justified.

***

As the weeks Commander Detrix led his company around the centermost cities and towns of Asteom went on, Byron grew more curious about the presence of another demon. Not even a whisper from wandering folks on the streets or at the taverns revealed a hint of trouble outside the regular, mundane problems. While he became intrigued, though, everyone else with him doubted the assignment.

If Coura alone saw the creatures, I would be more skeptical; however, Commander Evern was there as well. This means the demon is hiding, but without confirmation from our group, we won't know why it appeared to her and not her father, or anyone else. I'm concerned we may be playing right into a trap if it expects us to pursue.

He reflected on their situation as the troops marched into Fester where they would stay to scout the area before returning to the palace. The lingering summer weather meant the sun didn't retreat below the horizon until later, so Byron forced his mind to focus on preparing camp, procuring a meal, and figuring out how to spend the evening. Of course, he remained familiar enough with the city to feel comfortable and planned to visit the tavern once their leader dismissed his troops.

Commander Detrix directed them across the city for everyone to gaze at with nothing more than a proud smile complimenting his character, as if he reveled in the attention his bronze armor drew. In an open area on the opposite side, they set up their sleeping bags, left the provisions and other packs, and split up to comb through the busy streets once the commander appointed the night watch.

As Byron turned to move onto the road, he heard the Yeluthian call for him and Emilea to wait.

"Would you both stay behind a moment?" Commander Detrix asked without any emotion in his voice that might hint at concern. Once the trio stood alone, he continued. "There is a matter I wish to share with you now that we are on the last leg of the mission. An air of doubt has been following us to spread through our ranks."

"So, you can sense it too," Byron muttered as he recalled his previous thoughts.

Emilea didn't appear startled either, so the commander went on.

"Their behavior indicates a lack of attention to detail in the search, but the three of us are enough to fill those blind spots, whether consciously or not. I believe it resulted from my briefing papers sent to each of them discussing the problem and need for secrecy. In them, I mentioned what my king explained at the council meeting with King Aaron and how there was not a confirmed sighting of a demon."

Byron frowned. "What do you mean by that?" Before he could go on to mention Coura's encounter, the commander raised a hand for him to pause and released a reluctant sigh.

"I understand there is a plausible chance one appeared to Evern's daughter, but without her account to solidify the facts, we need to tailor our orders based on what we do know, which is that there may not be a demon per say but someone using demonic energy."

"That makes sense," Emilea commented with a thoughtful expression. "Our soldiers aren't slacking off, yet the more drawn out our search grows, the less they believe the cause to be an actual demon. If you confirmed this, or had proof, that would lead to a suffocating sensation considering we haven't found any leads. Granted, there has to be someone who summoned the demonic creatures anyway, but we can hold our own against a human using illegal magic."

Detrix nodded.

Byron wasn't entirely comfortable with the approach despite King Arval's transparency with the council, and the commander with his company. "Why tell us this now? Why not wait until we're back at the palace?"

"To be honest, I forgot you two did not receive a briefing."

His following laugh startled the pair of mages before they recalled his laidback personality.

"You must forgive me," the Yeluthian picked up. "I am getting used to how organizing a group like this works in your capital city. Once I remembered, I felt as though it would be best to wait until we could talk in Fester instead of telling you on the road in front of the others."

Byron caught Emilea rolling her eyes and avoided the urge to do the same. Ultimately, the search would continue either way, and the news wouldn't hinder their assignment dramatically. He mentioned as much before the commander voiced his appreciation.

"We will discuss our findings from tonight as usual, spread out to scout the area tomorrow, and, depending on that, plan to move to Verona the day after."

"Yes, sir," Byron responded.

Emilea repeated the words but added more after. "Commander, I want you to know that no matter what turns up, or doesn't, I trust Coura and her experience. You may not believe there's a demon, but you've also never faced one, only someone possessing demonic power. The difference is staggering."

Although she spoke with no intended harshness, Detrix's grin faded and his eyes narrowed slightly. "Well then, I will be off to the skies for tonight."

Byron and Emilea stood together as the commander put his back to them, walked farther away from Fester, and manifested his white wings, which seemed to glow in the surrounding darkness.

While he leapt to soar above the nearby forest, the same one where Coura encountered the first duo of angels years ago, Byron faced his fellow master mage. "Thank you, Emilea," he said in reference to how she defended his former student.

The woman shook her head. "I didn't do that for you. I would think Coura has earned some trust from the council and the Yeluthians."

"I'm sure she has," he replied. As usual, he caught his mentality switching to see the opposite perspective. "When she's able to stand before us and tell her side of the encounter, they'll have no reason not to listen. For right now, we're doing our part in this."

"I guess you're right." The light mage ran a hand through her blonde hair. "Are you planning on visiting Cintra?"

Byron winced at the idea but didn't turn it away altogether. Aside from the search, the two talked a lot over the weeks; at one point, he revealed his attempts to contact his childhood friend. To his dismay, his letters received no response, leading him to wonder if he took advantage of her ability enough for her to harbor negative feelings toward him.

"You'll never learn the truth if you don't see her," Emilea continued. "I'm going to stay here tonight and catch up on lost sleep. I expect to hear more from you in the morning." With that, the light mage abandoned Byron for her belongings nearby.

Eventually, he chanced a drink at the famous Wilken's Tavern and mustered the courage to inquire about Cintra only to be told she left the business a couple months ago and hasn't been back since.

*

Before the sun rose on the second day, Byron stirred after a jolt stemmed from his center, one he hadn't felt in years yet would never be forgotten. *Demonic energy!*

A surge of the foreign power vibrated in his veins and caused his own energy to flare, like a bristling cat or growling dog at the first sign of danger. From across the snoozing bodies littered around the open area, he spotted Emilea scrambling to stand and someone he presumed to be Commander Detrix jogging toward the woods.

Byron began to shake those around him, resulting in grunts and complaints until they realized who bothered them and the likeliest reason why. When they took to rousing everyone else, he threw on his boots and hurried to the commander.

"What should we do?" he asked, cutting ahead of explanations. Already, the invisible trail steadily grew fainter as the surge faded.

A pause followed his question before Detrix answered. "I will go on ahead to find the source's location."

"You shouldn't abandon the rest of us."

"You can sense the presence dying too, right? I will make sure it does not evade us while you and the troops catch up. Believe me, I would not risk running headlong into a fight with an unknown enemy, but it would be foolish to let this opportunity go to waste."

Byron bit back any further protests and nodded. "We'll be there as soon as we can."

The commander flashed a brief, somewhat strained smile, reminding Byron of how demonic energy bothered the Yeluthians, before sprinting into the trees. As soon as the angel disappeared, those standing around looked to the master mages for information and their next orders.

"Gather around," he called at a louder volume while facing the wide-eyed soldiers. Emilea also ushered people toward him as he spoke. "Magical traces of our target just appeared in these woods. Commander Detrix went to investigate and make sure it doesn't move or vanish, so we are going to meet him. Be ready within the next couple minutes, tread quietly, and watch my light."

An apple-sized flame appeared in the palm of his open hand at that. Its brightness would lose them the element of surprise, but wandering in the pitch-black forest would also cost precious time and most likely create more noise to alert the enemy.

I just hope Detrix understands what we're up against, Byron thought as he observed the men and women throwing on their armor, grabbing for weapons, and standing at attention.

*

The trek through the trees revealed a worn trail that was by no means easy to maneuver through, causing the metal bodies to clang as the troops shifted and bumped into every stray branch or kicked rocks scattered on the ground. At each sound, Byron ground his teeth and attempted to stay focused on the thin trace of demonic energy lingering farther into the woods.

At this rate, we'll end up lost and make ourselves known to the demon and its creatures. There's no way to bring everyone there while covering our backs, and Detrix is hiding his presence to keep himself invisible. Unless... Are we meant to act as bait to draw the target out? Would he risk our lives to capture the enemy?

Byron halted after considering the plausibility of that idea. This led to the people behind him audibly stumbling into one another.

"Are we close?" someone asked above the worried or irritated mumbles.

We'd waste time if I paused to explain right now. Besides, I don't know the truth. Our best option is to-

A rustle from the bushes to his left had everyone jumping to draw their swords until a familiar voice told them to calm down and be quiet. From the shadows emerged Commander Detrix, who stood as tall and proud as ever while projecting an air of reassurance, at least to Byron.

"I located our target," he explained for those nearby to hear. "They established a shelter in a cave to the west off this path. I counted four demonic creatures guarding the outside, but there is a chance more are inside by their master."

"Did you see it?" one of the soldiers pressed.

Detrix shook his head. "I only spotted a hooded figure looming at the entrance; however, I believe we should avoid approaching them with the creatures present."

Byron caught the commander's resulting glance, which proved to be all he needed to comprehend the situation. *I was right to assume he needs us to act as a diversion for the enemy's guard dogs. Once we lead them away, he can go straight to whoever is in charge. I suppose I'll manage the troops since my magic is dangerous in close quarters, and having over two dozen people crowding such a space will make the enemy more of a threat.*

"Let us handle the creatures," came a deep voice from within the group.

The commander, Byron, and those circling the pair stared as a barrel-chested soldier with cropped hair stepped forward to speak.

"This armor's been creating enough noise. If we quit being careful with each step, we should be able to get their attention so you mages can go in and cut off the serpent's head."

"It's too dangerous," Byron began. "No matter what you may have heard about the creatures, they're unpredictable."

To his amazement, that doubt seemingly encouraged the soldiers to accept the task. One after the other, they placed a fist over their hearts to display their loyalty without a word.

An amused chuckle from the Yeluthian commander brought the conversation back to strategizing. "If that is the way you want it, I cannot argue with you. The cave is still a distance away to the west. I will guide you nearer before Byron, Lady Emilea, and I split apart."

With the plan outlined, the troops followed Detrix as noiselessly as they could manage until he stopped them to issue orders.

"Wait five minutes for us to sneak to the opposite side before moving forward," he said and pointed ahead. "A small clearing lies to the south where the creatures wander outside the opening. This should provide plenty of room for you to hold your ground. Focus on distracting them until you notice Byron's shield sealing the entrance. Then, do what is necessary in order to defeat the creatures and stay safe. Remember, once their master is apprehended, they might defect or flee. Remain alert."

A soft chorus of words expressing the group's confirmation assured the magic users they weren't sending their comrades into a fight the soldiers couldn't handle.

We must trust in our allies, Byron told himself as the trio moved through the trees again. *Sometimes the most difficult part of a mission is ignoring the desire to be in every position at once, especially when you're powerful enough to contribute a significant amount of assistance. Then again, that strength and skill can't be replaced or replicated. No one else can take on my assignment, even though I can do theirs. I'll never forget how General Tio scolded me for dismissing my worth when I expected to remain in the Dalan base. All I need to do is fulfill my role.*

Emilea had a difficult time keeping her footing along the unlit trail, slowing their pace tremendously. Byron sensed Detrix's impatience as the Yeluthian attempted to wait until the clashing of weapons sounded in the distance, like rumbling thunder. They continued to move with more urgency until the three finally reached a unique break in the wooden trunks that overlooked the mouth of the cave.

Through this opening, they saw the aforementioned demonic creatures stalking away from their direction toward the metal-clad group, who yelled and banged their weapons together as a distraction. When the trio seized the opportunity to hurry into the cave, Byron would craft a shield to seal them inside and prevent the creatures from returning to their master. What the commander intended to do once they encountered that individual, he had no idea.

"Go, now!" came Detrix's fierce whisper as the angel burst through the brush, leaving the pair of humans to catch up.

All the while, Byron kept his eyes on the shadowy beasts. He predicted it would be a mere matter of seconds for the creatures to catch the intruders if they noticed the three.

Together, he and Emilea slipped beyond the rock, pressed themselves against the damp walls, and glanced between the tunnel and the fight commencing close by. Once he confirmed their safety, Byron threw up his hands to create a wall of shimmering, violet energy encompassing the entirety of the opening. As he did so, he suppressed his power to prevent their target from sensing their arrival.

"Admirable work," the commander commented without the normal humor in his voice. "Emilea, you are with me now. We must assess our enemy first, though I expect to use a prism spell, at the very least."

"Right," she answered with a glance farther into the cave, which stretched deeper to prevent them from looking ahead.

"Master Byron," Detrix went on. "I request you remain here for the time being."

"I got it!"

Byron already faced his shield with both hands outstretched in order to continue the spell and heard the pattering of hurried footsteps behind him as the Yeluthian and Emilea ran to meet their target. He figured the light mages would rather keep him between both ends of the chaotic attack as a precaution, especially since his specialty was offensive magic. This left him alone yet in the best position to aid each side.

Hardly any of the action could be deciphered beyond his shield, though the clanging metal and snarling seemed to grow even louder. Byron thought he heard murmuring from within the tunnel echoing off the stone walls and wondered if he started to lose his mind until a male voice began shouting incoherently. Then, the pulsing of demonic power tainted the air.

The creatures must have been alerted by this change, for they charged back to the cave only to find the entrance blocked. It became impossible to count how many powerful sets of claws began scraping the shield after. Between the creatures' growls, the hisses of their scratching, and the shouting, which morphed into screams, from behind, Byron focused on retaining his sanity. He figured none of the soldiers would get too close or be able to draw the beasts' attention away again, so it was up to Detrix and Emilea; he just needed to be patient.

After what felt like an hour, the strikes on the magical wall diminished to the point where he could clearly spot two of the demonic creatures, leading him to consider bringing down the shield and using a timed lightning spell to subdue them. The noise from behind faded as well until that point. He allowed himself a moment to breathe, but a high-pitched shrill that sent shivers along Byron's spine had him glancing over his shoulder. The sound prompted the image of a tortured soul crying out for vengeance while in pain.

As abruptly as it started, it disappeared.

The clawing ended too. When he turned his attention forward again, the shadows beyond his spell vanished. Byron kept the shield in place, though, and only dismissed it when the group of soldiers approached.

"The remaining creatures fled into the woods," one explained before sharing how a handful of the troops had been injured after they managed to bring a creature down and wound two more.

Still, Byron expected worse news farther in the cave. He ordered them to begin the recovery process and monitor the area in case the creatures returned before he moved to join the light mages.

As he expected, the scene he stumbled upon wasn't pleasant, and the demonic presence lingered enough to irritate his senses. The end of the tunnel opened into a wide, circular den where dozens of items, such as piles of clean bones, scattered papers, patches of black fur, and knives, revealed the situation to be one dealing with a case of demonic possession caused by some sort of ritual. A meager fire at the center of the room cast the area in a dim light.

He expected the Yeluthian to be involved in the investigation, yet at Byron's arrival, Detrix passed by to abandon the mess.

"I could use your help," Emilea called to him from the other side of the space where she knelt next to a body lying face down in its own puddle of crimson blood.

"What happened?" he inquired while walking around the fire to stand over her.

"If you can't tell already, this was a case of possession. Probably the worst I've ever seen."

"Are either of you hurt?" he asked next as he observed the body.

The stranger's skin appeared to be a sickly, pale color, and he was naked except for an ebony pelt around his shoulders and one tied around his waist. Black, unkempt hair trailed in a mat down his back, but oddly enough, every exposed part of his body had been wiped clean.

Emilea interrupted his inspection by reaching for his hand, which he offered. When she stood beside him, he noticed drying blood splattered on her outfit.

"Neither of us was physically harmed," she added after following his gaze. "It took most of my magic for the prism spell. I believe this foul energy left the commander in a sour mood."

"So, it came down to the purification spell."

She gestured toward the body. "This man's mind was gone. We tried using words to elicit a response, but he babbled nonsense and lashed out with uncontrolled spells until Detrix knocked him off balance with a physical attack. When I began to perform the prism spell, he panicked, shrieked loudly enough to make my ears ring, and grabbed for a knife."

"He stabbed himself then?"

"Several times," she answered while wiping her forehead. "I kept the spell going for as long as I could. I think the commander figured it would be a mercy to let the man end his life."

Byron had no additional comments. They collected and reviewed what papers were available as they threw everything else into the dwindling fire. The pages proved to possess undiscernible stray lines and shapes drawn with a charred stick, so they burned those as well. Emilea took her leave when the pair completed their analysis, forcing Byron to finish cleaning up the remains of the man with his magic.

*

The following day was spent surveying the land surrounding Fester until the commander seemed satisfied. Byron led one group through the trees to the west and found nothing out of the ordinary, though the wildlife sounded far more active than it had been before. He accepted that as a positive omen and shared the update with Detrix and the rest of the troops, who noted the same change in the remaining directions. After collecting everyone's observations, their leader dismissed them after mentioning they would be starting the trek back to Verona the next day.

By then, evening steadily approached. Although Byron wondered about the possibility of unexpected danger, the evidence thus far proved the possessed man had been what they were after, not a demon. Still, it would be foolish for the king's council and the Yeluthians to assume no other threats lingered after Coura's experience; he planned to say as much once they gathered again.

With the matter put to rest for the time being, he debated exploring what buildings remained open in the city that could pull his mind away from their potential issues for a while. He noticed most of the soldiers heading to Wilken's Tavern, yet without Cintra, he'd only have the company of the celebrating men and women he'd dealt with for weeks.

Emilea felt the same when he asked what she was going to do, so they strolled down the main road, chatted about the journey, and began searching for a place to acquire dinner when their stomachs growled.

The pair decided on a smaller tavern sitting at the opposite end from their camp where an older-looking yet tough woman welcomed them. Once they had mugs of cider in hand, Byron began reminiscing about his history with the city, including his childhood and visits over the years; however, he paused when he reached the part where he led Coura, Will, and Marcus into the city. He didn't believe Emilea heard the details of their arduous return to East Hoover.

When she expressed interest in the subject, he decided to tell her about Will's unfortunate encounter with the first angels seen in decades, how Coura went to save him and somehow triggered the demonic power within her center, and when Byron and Marcus caught on to the trouble. He only omitted the part where he had to be dragged away from Cintra and the delicious wine she continued to sneak into her room, but that would stay between him, his friend, and his former student.

The light mage remained silent as she listened to him vocally connect the events from that night to what they learned about Coura years later. All the while, Byron glanced around the dimly lit space while he spoke.

"Who could have thought one assignment from the academy would cause such an impact on the future of the country."

Emilea chuckled and raised her mug to drink.

Byron did the same yet found his cider gone. He craned his head in all directions to locate a server for a refill and caught a familiar face at the far end. The woman's blonde hair flowed over one shoulder as she casually talked with a customer. Even at a distance, he recognized her facial features and hourglass figure in the modest dress.

Cintra, he realized with a start and practically jumped to his feet.

"What's wrong?" Emilea asked at his sudden movement.

He set his empty mug on the table before flashing her a reassuring smile. "I'll be right back."

Whatever motivated him to rise seconds ago dwindled with each step as he crossed the room to speak with his old friend. The doubt piled into an inexplicable sense of nervousness, yet his feet continued pushing him forward until she noticed.

She didn't respond to my recent letters. If she doesn't wish to see me, what right do I have to interrupt her evening and barge into her life?

"Byron?" he heard her squeak in surprise while taking a step backward.

At that, he came to a jarring halt. "It's been a while, hasn't it?" he commented and offered a genuine smile.

To his surprise, she didn't react how she normally would by hurrying to throw her arms around his neck in an energetic embrace. Instead, she apologized to the man seated in front of her, approached Byron, and hugged herself in a shy manner.

"What brings you here?"

He heard no joy beneath her words, simply intrigue behind her striking, blue eyes, and his smile faded.

"I'm in Fester on an assignment. My comrade and I walked farther away from our camp to get some space from the soldiers, but I wasn't expecting to see you." He purposefully left the comment open-ended to allow her to share any input.

Her eyes lowered to the floor, leading him to wonder if she realized he sought her out.

Cintra's next words confirmed it. "I didn't want you to look for me."

Byron expected the resulting sting of rejection as he recalled worrying she would feel this way and contemplated leaving her alone then. Still, the need for closure between the two before he departed outweighed his desire to be respectful of her dismissiveness.

"Can we talk in private?" he decided to ask in a more sympathetic tone of voice. "I owe you an apology, and I could never forgive myself for ignoring that fact."

Cintra's eyes darted upward to meet his while her mouth parted a bit to reflect her shock before she promptly closed it. He sensed her hesitation as she considered his question and glanced around the busy tavern, but she gave him a hopeful answer.

"Meet me outside in five minutes. I'll be waiting in the front."

With that, the woman headed toward the back through an opening leading into the kitchen. Byron stood alone, looking on and composing his mixed emotions.

He returned to Emilea after and explained what took place without sounding too hopeful. As they rose to depart from the building, she grinned, wished him luck, then strolled down the main road, presumably to return to the camp.

Not a minute later, he heard the sound of footsteps approaching from around the nearby corner, and Cintra appeared with a cloak draped over her arm.

"You may walk me home," was all she offered before turning to move west without waiting for him.

If it hadn't been obvious by that point, Byron knew she held some resentment toward him. *Whatever our relationship has become, I promised myself I would try to mend it. If she doesn't accept an apology, then I must respect her wish to be left alone.*

"What is it you planned to say?" she inquired when he caught up, though he continued his attempt to put the words together.

"Well, I suppose I should start with this," he began. "I'm sorry, Cintra. I left you behind in Fester while utilizing your ability. Recently, it dawned on me how often I neglected to thank you for your help in saving the kingdom. You never did hear what happened?"

"I picked up some pieces here and there. Of course, it always seems like more is added or embellished with each retelling."

"In any case, you hid here to protect yourself from being used by people like me who hold power in the palace. I apologize for abusing you in that way."

The silence between them hung in the air after Byron's words, stirring the guilt, shame, and anxiousness he attempted to repress until she spoke again without the chilling dismissiveness.

"Is that really all you needed to tell me? You were bothered so much by that you needed to apologize?"

Byron opened and closed his mouth while considering a defense. "I owe it to you," was all he managed to reply.

Cintra slowed her steps to guide him to a stop and faced him with compassion radiating behind her softened expression. "You keep saying that. What do you mean you owe it to me? I offered my foresight because I knew it would help. If I didn't want to, I wouldn't have."

"I thought you were upset with me," he added as her honesty left him uncertain of what he needed to respond with next.

She bit her bottom lip before dipping her chin. It became evident in that moment she didn't expect what he admitted.

"No, I just..."

Byron moved to close the distance between them and placed his hands on her shoulders, forcing her to gaze into his face. If he intended on using the truth to get through to her, he would have to commit, no matter how uncomfortable it made him feel on the inside.

"Cintra, what's bothering you? You're my dearest friend, and I've always loved you. You know that, right?"

As tears welled in her eyes, no other emotions broke through her concerned expression, meaning she did understand.

"Just as you offer your magic to others in Asteom because you want to help, I'm not abandoning you when I can see there's a problem."

"Byron..."

"Why did you leave Wilken's Tavern?" he decided to ask as a starting point.

Their eyes remained locked until she sighed and glanced away. "We're not as young as we used to be. Why keep a woman with half her life left when you could get someone more attractive to fill the position."

He shook her shoulders a bit to grab her full attention. "Is that the truth? You didn't quit because something happened?"

"No. At least, not yet…" The words trailed off into nothing.

"Please," he began in one, last attempt to mend their relationship. If he was at fault somehow and she refused to reveal more, that burden would remain with him forever.

Thankfully, his plea didn't fall on deaf ears.

"I left two months ago."

"Why? That's been your home for years."

Her golden hair draped over her shoulders when she shook her head and let the tears fall. "It was, but you could find me there. You weren't supposed to come looking for me!"

A lump formed in Byron's throat while he listened, and he wondered why she avoided him. Then, she started to weep into her hands, leading him to remember what usually caused her to become so emotional. "It's your foresight, isn't it? What did you see in your visions?"

"I can't say!"

"You must, Cintra," he demanded.

When it seemed she'd be reduced to sobs for the time being, he pulled her into his chest, wrapped his arms around her, and waited. It took patience, and the moon rose to illuminate the sky, but the description soon revealed itself.

"You and I are together in Verona, celebrating in a square, dancing and eating, and that's all there is for a while," she offered timidly. "The image vanishes, then I'm standing alone all dressed up for a formal event. I can hear others mumbling in the room. Soon, I'm covered in blood, they start screaming, and after I collapse to the ground, that's the end. A disaster is going to take place following our time together, Byron! People are going to get hurt; I think that might be when I-"

"Enough," he interrupted at a hushed volume.

Cintra's voice wavered while she spoke, and utter helplessness mixed with borderline hysteria was written across her face.

I've never seen her like this before, he thought. The scene shook him to his core, though he repressed the paranoia. *It's too late for us to be standing out in the open. I also refuse to leave her after such a horrific conversation. It would be best to get her to bed; then, we can worry about the vision once she calms down.*

*

Ever since her mother's death, Cintra took up residency in the attic space above one of the local butcher shops not too far from where they paused on the road. No one appeared to be inside as she wrestled a key from her pocket to unlock the back door, and she didn't protest when Byron followed her up the three flights of stairs. Overall, the floor seemed spacious for a single person yet warm enough to feel comfortable, even during the days leading to fall.

They sat on her bed in silence, leaning into the other while simply relaxing and letting their minds creep closer to sleep.

"Do you have extra blankets?" Byron asked after accepting the fact he would be spending the night with her. He knew Emilea would trust him to return before the troops left, or she would explain his disappearance to Commander Detrix.

Cintra rose to open a closet, removed a couple quilts bundled inside, and instead of spreading them on the floor like he expected, she threw them onto the bed.

"It's going to be a little snug with two people," she commented while offering a sympathetic smile.

That openness she expressed before they lied together reminded Byron of the type of love they shared. He didn't hear about it from her often or bring it up because it blossomed over the course of their longtime friendship. They had always cared for each other, but until that point, he hadn't considered a need for their relationship to go any deeper. Once it did, it proved to be one of the easiest changes to accept.

Byron slept better than he had on the ground at the various campsites, even though he still woke to the near darkness just before sunrise. When he moved to sit up and stretch, he found Cintra watching him; an amused smile danced on her lips.

"I wasn't expecting a sleepover," she admitted and chuckled as they rose.

"Did you really believe I would leave you alone?"

"I hoped you wouldn't," she answered with a somberness to remind them of the previous night's conversation.

Byron looked away while she slipped into a new dress and decided to address her fears before returning to his duties. "About your vision, I can understand if you stay away from me, but I don't think you should."

"What do you mean?"

"Your foresight can't be ignored. I won't tell you to forget about what you saw, but the future does change. Outside of us, you can always tell me if you pick up more because it could save lives in the capital. If you run away from me, the one factor you identify in the images, you'll disregard what could be the best years of your life."

Before Byron realized the additional meaning of his final sentence, Cintra already began laughing. Then, she threw her arms around his neck in a familiar manner.

"That sounds like a poor proposal, you know. Either I stay with you, or my life will be worse."

"I wasn't proposing," he added despite his cheeks heating into a blush. "What I said is true. You can't spend the rest of your life in fear of death."

"I understand, and I do have a solution."

"You do?"

She nodded, leaned in close, and whispered into his ear. "Stay with me. Let's live together here in Fester."

Byron closed his eyes as his chest ached. "I can't."

"Why not?"

"I'm here on an assignment."

"Come back once you're finished."

"I have other responsibilities right now."

"I can wait."

"It's not that simple."

"Why not?"

When he didn't answer, Cintra removed her arms in order to step back. Everything about her in that moment looked entirely vulnerable while she stared at him with a sense of optimism. She was giving him more time to reconsider, yet Byron couldn't tell her he didn't want to abandon his life and the people who needed him elsewhere.

He bowed his head without a word, unable to place his personal feelings over his sense of loyalty to the kingdom.

"I'm sorry," he heard her respond in a wavering voice. "It's unfair of me to ask that you throw away what you work so tirelessly to protect."

After a pause, Byron straightened and took her hands in his. "Come with me. We'll find a home in Verona where I can keep you safe!"

Although he squeezed the delicate hands to emphasize his commitment, they sat limp until he released them.

"I'm sorry," she repeated and moved to the door. "I just can't."

With heavy hearts, the two descended to the ground floor where Cintra left him to wander back to the campsite and rejoin the commander and his company.

Suspicion

Byron hardly recalled the trip from Fester to Verona and shoved the stray thoughts regarding the possessed man and demonic creatures, as well as what took place with Cintra, to the back of his mind until the next morning when the king's council was summoned. Usually, he prepared some sort of written account with notes and suggestions to discuss, yet he felt no motivation to do so ever since his return due to what occurred, leaving him to enter the meeting with an open mind.

The rest of the members filed in when he approached the chamber, and Byron joined them to sit around the table in front of Aaron. King Arval and his commanders didn't appear comfortable until the session began and the Yeluthian leader ordered Commander Detrix to recap the investigation around Asteom.

Since Byron lived through the experience, he spent the time observing everyone else's reactions, which steadily morphed into stoic expressions once they heard about the scene in the cave. That was when Emilea picked up the explanation due to Detrix's hasty exit once their target died.

After the conclusion, Aaron informed the trio who were away from the palace of how they questioned Coura. General Terrell, as her supervisor, recalled her interaction with the demon then. Most of her account sounded similar to her father's, except for minor details Byron noticed based on his own memories of the previous demon, such as the new creature possessing short horns behind its ears and both being able to manifest a blade out of thin air.

"Should we call her here again now that we found more demonic creatures and their master?" the general asked at the end.

Byron hesitated to make the decision because he wasn't fully convinced they caught their true enemy.

"I see no reason to waste time on another interrogation," General Casner answered before anyone else could comment. "She told us what she knew, so someone can fill her in later."

King Arval spoke next. His voice rang deep but in an uplifting manner filled with optimism. "Let it be understood, if only between those gathered in this room, that it was not a demon the search party discovered but a human breaking the law and summoning one's power. The man controlled the same beasts described by Commander Evern and his daughter, appeared as they witnessed with pale skin and dark fur, and hid near the original location."

The chamber echoed with murmuring from the council members, and their nods signaled their agreement.

Despite the authority of such a frighteningly radiant king, Byron voiced his doubt. "I believe we should pursue this."

"Are you serious?" General Tont blurted out before Byron could elaborate. "We've got more to deal with, especially to the north. You were there, and you saw the man's corpse. Isn't that enough?"

"I concur," General Garvish added. "At least, I don't agree this warrants a full council to discuss or should include bothering the Yeluthians if they think the matter is put to rest."

Byron noticed Emilea, Aaron, and General Casner staring at him to show they weren't willing to drop such a risky topic so easily either. "Allow me to offer my observations based on my own experience with demonic energy. Firstly, let me reiterate that Coura's description of her encounter is our best piece of information to go from. Whether you trust her or think she wasn't mentally stable, she would have mentioned any uncertainties to this council. If you don't trust my claim, we can call her in and ask her directly. With that in mind, she mentioned the demon possessed short horns behind its ears and manifested a black blade, which it used to wound her shoulder. I only noticed a disheveled mat of hair."

"If I may comment, a tuft of hair stuck up from behind each of the man's ears," Detrix interjected. "Perhaps she mistook those to be horns."

"Even if that's the case, what about the sword? Did you or Emilea see it?"

Both shook their heads.

"His hair could have been mistaken for horns, but why wouldn't the man summon a weapon to defend himself?"

"Did the situation call for close combat?" General Garvish countered.

Emilea and the Yeluthian commander shared a look before the former replied.

"It's never certain what could or could not happen, but I cast my light magic as soon as we entered while Commander Detrix moved to immobilize the target."

"Would a demon hesitate to fight one of your kind?" Aaron asked the Yeluthians at the table despite the obvious answer.

"You raise a fair point," King Arval replied without acknowledging the question.

Still, Byron didn't feel satisfied with their lack of caution. "In addition to those notes, the creature spoke to Coura in a clear voice and with a sane mind. What Emilea and Detrix found seemed to be quite the opposite."

"That's right," the master light mage added after. "However, one could argue the demonic power corrupted the man, rendering him unable to communicate properly by the time we cornered him."

A gruff voice belonging to the Yeluthian commander named Isan joined the conversation for the first time during the morning discussion. "Perhaps that is why he kept himself away between the first and second encounters."

Byron remained quiet while the rest of those gathered mused over the idea and formed their own conclusions.

"Do you have anything else you'd like to present?" Aaron asked as he turned to face Byron with an unreadable expression.

When he shook his head, the king moved on.

"As someone who understands part of what a demon is capable of when it comes to sharing power with humans, I will not let the matter rest until there is absolutely no proof of one's existence in Asteom. With that being said, I also agree this should be kept between us. Those who traveled under Commander Detrix already swore to secrecy when they were assigned to search for the source of the demonic creatures. I would like to move forward with the new team assignments for our soldiers, mages, and the Yeluthians."

He glanced at King Arval for approval, which the angel granted by dipping his chin. "General Tont, Master Byron, and Master Emilea, you three will discuss, choose, and place the soldiers and mages you wish to leave Verona. Please keep in mind that the hundreds of people relocated to the Nim-Valan border won't be returning anytime soon. King Arval, I request one of your commander's assistance to do the same with your troops, along with plotting specific routes for them to travel on."

"Commander Isan will assume responsibility for that task."

No hesitation came from the Yeluthian king, nor a hint of surprise from the older angel at his side, making Byron wonder if the assignment had already been arranged between the four. For the moment, it sounded as if a solid solution was in place to ebb the lingering doubt, which was why it seemed like a bit of a surprise when King Arval spoke again.

"I would prefer to continue to keep a scouting company of troops under Commander Detrix around the capital city. With this extra protection, I will permit my people to return here to train, as we originally planned before their living quarters are complete."

Aaron took a moment to consider the proposal. During that pause, General Terrell suggested an addition to the idea.

"Your Highnesses, would it be permissible to assign ground troops to scout the woods as well? Obviously, they cannot travel the same distance, but they would follow a similar route within a day's walking distance."

"This would also give them experience outside the training ground and away from combat," General Casner mused.

Aaron extended the offer to the Yeluthians since any human troops with this particular assignment fell under Detrix's authority as well.

"A permanent company consisting of both humans and Yeluthians sounds like an interesting idea." After a moment, King Arval's lips stretched into a broad smile. "What do you think, Commander Detrix? Would you be willing to organize and lead such a group?"

The youngest-looking commander straightened. "Yes, sir. I do have one request. I believe Coura would be a valuable asset right now with her skills and experience. If you allow it, I plan to add her to the scouting party."

Yeluthia's king rubbed his combed beard before addressing the council members. "We must ask her commanding officer. General Terrell, would you allow Commander Detrix to assign one of your soldiers to his company?"

At first, the request confused Byron until he caught Detrix glancing at Evern, then the pair shared a brief, serious look.

Because the demon showed itself to her specifically, I would venture to guess the company will benefit from keeping Coura around to lure it out of hiding, if it's even in Asteom. It would be dangerous as well, but I highly doubt the Yeluthians would ever leave her alone. Besides, her father didn't object or appear upset by Detrix's decision to include her. I wonder if they, or maybe just Evern, wanted a reason for her to remain in Verona.

General Terrell agreed to turn Coura over and inform her personally of the reassignment, but Aaron commented on the latter.

"If I may, I'll let her know this afternoon. She will need to hear about what Commander Detrix and Emilea found and our decisions regarding its search."

As the general offered a polite response, Byron noticed Aaron restraining a smirk, which revealed why the king felt he should talk with Coura.

Because a demon wasn't responsible for controlling the creatures outside Fester, she'll probably argue against everything the council discussed. If General Terrell explains this, she wouldn't blow up on him, but I'd bet she would come after me, Emilea, or her father. I agree with Aaron; it's better for her to learn the details from a close friend who will expect her to protest.

The generals made additional comments before the meeting ended. Byron, Emilea, General Tont, and Commander Isan stayed behind to converse about how they should restructure the stations and routes around the country.

***

After a few more days of recovering in the wooden building, Will felt like himself as his body healed. At least one of the light mages, usually Clara, lingered nearby in case he needed anything, and their regular conversations allowed him to better understand their situation.

He first asked for details on the stranger who rescued them. Unfortunately, the man hadn't shared his background seemingly giving him knowledge of the area, leading Will to believe their group either interacted with a Nim-Valan sympathizer or someone looking to earn a profit by turning them in. His suspicion grew once the light mages admitted they didn't recognize the land, only that they were moving north.

Next, he brought up their altered hair color. Bryn had been eavesdropping on his conversation with Clara and brought over a bottle half full of an inky substance while explaining how they were ordered to wash their hair in the river and apply the dye. This precaution prevented their lighter-colored hair from drawing attention if somebody spotted them.

"That man gives us more of it every time he returns to this cabin," she concluded with a shrug.

Although neither Bryn nor Clara seemed too concerned, Will believed the task was a clue as to who they were dealing with.

If the Nim-Valan intended to kidnap us to use for his own gain, why disguise us at all? he wondered afterward. *What this really means is he plans on relocating us to a populated area soon and doesn't want us to be recognized. I'm assuming that's why he instructed them to study the pages translating Asteom and Nim-Vala's languages.*

The rest of the mages mumbled to one another while glancing over the sheets nearby. For some reason, he thought he should be disgusted by the practice, as it stripped away their pride as Asteom citizens; however, the more he heard, the greater his interest piqued until he requested to see the transcriptions.

In the hours that followed and the days after, he studied the words, then he pieced together the sentences in which they were meant to be used until he caught on to the patterns. He practiced this with the others, though they had a difficult time understanding.

In addition to learning about their current situation, Will began plotting escape options in the back of his mind. *I figure the man keeping us here doesn't intend to haul me around, especially if we're supposed to blend in. We'll probably stay here until my leg heals completely then. I haven't tried to use it, but until we are able to get some answers, I'd prefer to make him believe it needs more time. Next, we should try talking with him before attacking or running away. If he ends up being a threat and is planning on turning us in, it would be better to know that sooner rather than later. We deserve to hear what his stance is on assisting us.*

The following morning when he woke, he noticed their supplies had been restocked and asked Lissa about it since she was the first to rise.

"He's been stopping by before the sun rises every three or four days," she explained. "As far as I know, the last time he addressed any of us was when you stirred."

Will filed the new piece of information away before deciding he needed to test his leg's strength. With Lissa's help, he managed to stand with only minimal pain in the right thigh, and after more practice, he could walk as long as he had someone beside him to act as his crutch.

That afternoon, he drew everyone's attention in order to share what he put together about their situation, including his prediction regarding the stranger, their views on being hidden in the log building, and their most plausible location near or across the northern border. The group didn't show much surprise while he spoke, but it appeared they feared the next steps.

From then on, Will began to tally the days by marking the floor next to his sleeping spot in order to remember how long they remained there. Confronting the man would need to wait until he fully healed and could use that strength to his advantage for an escape, if necessary.

The light mages were permitted to wander outside and gather water from a stream, so Zelma offered to show him its location while supporting him. It proved to be a long yet not so strenuous trek because it lacked a clear trail, but the foliage spaced out enough for them to move side by side easily. Will found himself admiring the landscape once they reached the water source, collected what they needed, and took their time returning. Plenty of hills varying in sizes became visible between the breaks in the needle-covered trees, and he thought he spotted a couple mountain peaks in the distance, which cut upward against the bright, blue sky. Every color looked vibrant, as if the harsh winters regularly expected in that area wiped every leaf away so spring could develop against a clear slate.

That moment of freedom in the wild reminded Will of his first months exploring the world and traveling to research its wildlife; every location seemed new, held potential and surprises, and practically begged to be noticed with leaves, petals, moss, thorns, and other, distinct features.

By the time Zelma led him though the open door and into the windowless room, he yearned to leave their confinement.

*

The Nim-Valan returned three days later, as expected, but Will didn't feel prepared enough to confront him. He feigned sleep, expecting the stranger to leave, yet the man stood around and spoke with the light mages in the foreign tongue to test their dedication to learning the language. Finally, when Will figured he pretended for too long, he rolled over and sat up gingerly.

At the slightest movement, the stranger came over to stand above him with arms crossed, as if analyzing Will's physical condition through sight alone. Nothing noteworthy stood out about his appearance to make him memorable to Will. His skin looked no fairer or tanner than anybody else's, and his light brown hair hadn't been cut too long or short; however, his chestnut-colored eyes projected a keen wit, but only during certain moments.

"Can you stand?" the Nim-Valan asked without the hint of an accent, which sounded a bit jarring to Will.

"I haven't tried," he lied but made no motion to do so.

The man remained silent and still to keep from revealing any indication of what he thought. That type of control over his body and facial expression put Will on edge. After a moment, he bent forward to grab Will's right arm with both hands and yanked upward, forcing Will to either stand or drop to the floor.

If he didn't consider what to do next, Will would have used both legs to catch himself. Instead, he reacted by placing all his weight on his left leg and grasping the nearest arm that hauled him to his feet. It felt awkward, though he counted on the lack of balance to support his false injury.

The Nim-Valan grunted when Will steadied himself. "Try to use your right leg," he ordered firmly yet without emotion.

Will hesitantly shifted the weight while keeping his hold on the man. The wounded thigh healed enough to where he didn't need someone's help anymore and stretching didn't hurt; anything more than that, he wasn't certain of. Still, he pretended to experience a sharp pain and returned to using only his left leg.

"I can't," he said after.

"Try again."

He repeated his actions with similar results. "If I put weight on it, the pain becomes too much."

"Lie down again," the man responded and helped lower Will onto the blankets. Then, he knelt while staring at the afflicted leg. Clara had insisted he keep bandages wrapped around it, even though a scab remained, and this managed to fool the Nim-Valan.

"Who are you?" Will decided to ask in the resulting silence; however, his words were ignored.

"We don't have time to stay here. I'll be back with a crutch to support you for the time being."

With that, the stranger left for another three days.

When he returned, Will could walk, run, stretch, and kick as normally as before the poisoned arrow struck. He continued to feign weakness when the Nim-Valan approached him after he stirred, though. This time, he didn't plan to let the man push their questions aside.

Clara stood behind to listen while the other light mages shuffled in front of the lone door to prevent their target from leaving. If it came down to it, they would use their magic to craft a shielding spell as a means of blocking the exit.

"Can you stand on your own?" the stranger asked with a wooden crutch in one hand.

Will debated starting his questioning then, yet waiting would present him with a makeshift weapon. Wordlessly, he pushed himself to his knees before rising using mainly his left leg and keeping off his right one entirely. The stranger handed the crutch to Will, so he placed its padded, topmost bar under his arm and leaned on it, as if he were actually injured.

"Try walking around the room," the man instructed next. His indifferent persona seemed stressed, and Will intended to take advantage of that impatience.

"I want you to answer my questions first."

"We don't have time for talking. Now, move."

Will shook his head. "I don't follow orders from a Nim-Valan."

That struck a nerve with the man, for his eyes narrowed. "Not even when one is attempting to help you?"

"How can we be certain of that? You may have carried medicine for the poison in my leg, but you stopped my friends from healing me and practically kidnapped us. Who's to say you don't plan on bringing us to your leader?"

By that point, Will felt as if his heart jumped into his throat. He never addressed anybody so deliberately in his entire life, yet he forced himself to maintain the facade; if not for his future, then for Clara and the others. What was worse, the stranger stood about a head taller than Will with a lean build, including tight limbs to show he could hold his own in a fight.

Will clenched the handle of the crutch to prevent his nerves from distracting him and breaking his hardened expression. To his dismay, nothing about the man appeared to change.

"If you are well enough to walk, we may go outside, and I will answer your questions."

"What about us?" Clara interrupted while placing her hands on her hips in an annoyed manner.

The stranger glanced over his shoulder to see the mages attempting to stare him down. Will swore the man's cheeks reddened slightly.

"You should remain in here."

"Why?"

A pause stretched between them before he responded. "You must understand, women are not treated the same in Nim-Vala as in Asteom. If I break that code now, it could become detrimental in the future."

"What you tell me, you tell them," Will stated once he noticed the majority of the women's chests puff in preparation to retaliate. He understood they felt appalled by the blatant segregation and knew they would blow up shortly.

"Not now," the man replied in the same tone of voice. "If you wish for my continued assistance, you will obey the laws of this country, or I shall leave you alone to fend for yourselves."

The seriousness with which he responded didn't bode well for the light mages, leading Will to believe the Nim-Valan would follow through with his words. He swallowed, turned to Clara, and held up his free hand in a reassuring manner. "Let me talk with him outside."

"You can't-"

"I need to if we're going to figure anything else out."

She appeared to want to argue, yet her lips pressed together to reflect her displeasure.

The other light mages followed suit and stepped away from the door as Will hobbled behind the stranger. Once outside, the two stepped around to the rear side of the cabin where they stopped to lean on the wooden exterior.

"What is it you wish to know?" the man began without meeting Will's curious stare.

"First, what's your name? Or, what do you expect us to call you?" It sounded like a simple question, but it resulted in a minute of contemplation before Will cleared his throat.

"Here, my name is Finnley. People refer to me as Finn, but you can call me whichever you prefer."

"Here? What do you mean by that?"

After another break in the conversation, Will shook his head before shrugging.

"If it takes an hour for you to answer every question, we're going to be here for days. My friends and I need to trust you, you made that clear, so why are you hiding so much from us? What danger are we in that you had to bring us to Nim-Vala?"

"The group who attacked your camp pursued."

"Why did you save us then? Aren't they your people?"

"Yes and no."

Will repressed the urge to groan at the indirect response. "Fine. If you're a Nim-Valan, why were you across the border in the middle of the woods at night?"

"I was on my own business."

"I can understand if you don't want to share more, but you shouldn't be surprised by my doubt. From my point of view, you're a man looking to use us as bargaining tools for your own benefit instead of an unexpected hero emerging to lead us to safety. If that's the case, tell me what it is you plan to do with us. My friends are capable of holding their own, so leaving you bound in this cabin while we return to Asteom won't be a problem."

For as much as Will provoked him, Finn retained a stoic expression and tilted his head at that comment. "What makes you so sure you will find friends beyond that border?"

Before Will could reply, the Nim-Valan pushed himself off the wall with swagger rivaling any nobleman and continued.

"A war is coming, and you and those women are in the middle of it now. I followed the so-called soldiers who attacked your camp because I received word they would be targeting troops across the border in order to send a message. Your escape and their intent pursuit made me curious about why they were trying to capture and kill your group."

"That doesn't fully explain why we should stay here or what your plans are."

"Perhaps, but it's an answer."

Will watched as Finn turned to move to the front side of the cabin, as if the motion would end their conversation.

This doesn't seem right, he thought while remaining where he stood. *Unless regulations on the border are weaker than I've been led to believe, he shouldn't be able to pass through whenever he pleases, and not just on Asteom's side. I imagine Nim-Vala has similar laws preventing people from wandering in and out of their country. General Casner and his company had permission to enter near the fort as long as they were accompanied by the Nim-Valan commander and vice versa, but that must have been a trap to lure our soldiers away.*

"We should get going," Finn said from where he stopped to wait.

However, Will began to piece together what happened those weeks ago. "How much do you know about us?" he asked and raised his eyes to the Nim-Valan, who shrugged off the question.

"You were pursued. I found you because I was following the soldiers. Shall I repeat myself again?"

"Because you trailed the enemy who attacked our campsite, you must've known what their intentions were," Will added.

Finn didn't comment on his statement.

"We traveled to the border with a company of soldiers and mages requested by a Nim-Valan general named Harvey in order to assist in recapturing a fort taken by those they claimed to be barbarians. When our combatants left, that was when we were attacked."

"Your camp became vulnerable," Finn muttered with a bit more interest. "The request from Nim-Vala had been a rouse to take away those who would protect the magic users with the ability to heal."

"I acted as a guard for the camp, not a mage," Will clarified. "The women inside are, though, and the rest of our company will note our disappearance."

The Nim-Valan appeared to stiffen as he contemplated what he just heard. Even if Finn would continue to keep secrets, Will felt more comfortable with him understanding what drove them away from Asteom and the situation surrounding their camp.

After what felt like the entire morning, the man seemed ready to speak again.

"What I am about to tell you remains between us," he prefaced in a serious manner. "I was ordered to scout the fort where the Asteom troops were expected to meet Captain Harvey because his superiors didn't receive a response to their summons. What I found consisted of slaughtered soldiers stripped of their uniforms, armor, and weapons by who you claim to be barbarians. In actuality, they are full-blooded Nim-Valans. I won't go into details, but these men desire the power to overthrow the capital city and its structure because of their positions along the outskirts of the country. Somehow, they united under a person possessing magic similar to what is used in Asteom."

"What?" Will whispered in disbelief. He suddenly recalled the robed mage among the Nim-Valans who brought down the light mages' shielding spell; it felt like a nightmare thrust upon him again.

"It is as I say," Finn went on without hesitation. "The hundreds, perhaps thousands, of men split apart before I learned more. Some stayed at that fort, others moved within the country, and one group trekked across the border in secret. I followed them, noticed you and the women fleeing, and made sure you were able to get away safely. Unfortunately, that was all I could manage without being caught."

"You decided to protect us instead of continuing to obey your orders?"

"Yes, though I was certain I would be found out eventually since they had their leader, the magic user, with them. This proved to be the better decision."

"So, you're a spy for Nim-Vala?"

Finn dipped his head in confirmation, yet revealing that secret appeared to have no effect on his composure. "I've been moving throughout this area to gather intel and supplies. From what I discovered, it won't be safe for much longer, which is why we're going to head north."

If we go south, there's a chance the enemy Nim-Valans hiding there will find and kill us. Finn rescued the mages and I because he could. Still, it's a little hard to believe he would go out of his way even now to bring us farther into the country instead of finding a way to return across the border. In fact, why does he care what happens to Asteom if the rest of Nim-Vala is in greater danger?

When Finn signaled for them to return inside, Will shook his head while the question settled in his mind. He vocalized those thoughts and kept a close eye on the Nim-Valan's reaction until one idea forced its way to the forefront.

"I wondered how you knew so much about Asteom, especially since you can speak the language fluently and cross the border without trouble. Not only are you a spy for the Nim-Valan leaders, but something tells me you have established ties within Asteom as well."

Silence stretched between the two before Finn physically responded. From some fold of his loose clothing came a knife he held as if he had been raised to wield the metal weapon. At the sudden movement, Will's instincts kicked in, and he forgot about his feigned injury to stand firm, swing the crutch up into both hands, and hold it out in front to create a defensive measure.

The Nim-Valan hadn't come after him, though. The two stared the other down; Will with a frantically beating heart and uncertainty, and Finn with nothing more than his regular sense of coolness. Steadily, the knife lowered and disappeared again as the man's deep brown eyes wandered to Will's left leg.

I gave up the ruse. Did he think I was faking the entire time?

"Remember my previous order," Finn warned. "Repeat what we discussed to no one."

This time, when he turned he committed to going inside, leaving Will to stand alone and compose himself. When he did rejoin the others, he carried the crutch into the tent and set it aside after.

*

That afternoon, Clara and Will went down to the stream so he could dye his hair the same, inky color as the others, then the group abandoned the cabin and hurried to a town as ordinary as those in Asteom before the sun set. Finn instructed them beforehand not to speak unless they felt comfortable replying in the people's language, which none of them did. Whoever sheltered them for the night obviously knew the situation, for they spoke to Finn, passed along a key, and left without acknowledging Will or the light mages. They slept in an unused barn that somehow contained plenty of hay and blankets for warmth and supplies prepared ahead of time.

The next morning, Finn gathered them together.

"I will be leaving again," he began in the Nim-Valan tongue slowly enough for them to comprehend. "The people here are not unkind to Asteom travelers, but avoid giving them any reason to form a connection. I've asked a few to take you in, in exchange for their services, that is. Be respectful, continue to learn the language, and I will return as soon as I can."

Will didn't expect to be working within a few hours after Finn's departure, yet a knock on the wooden, barn doors caused them to jump until a plump, gray-haired woman entered. Their group shifted uncomfortably while she looked them over before pointing at Mary-Ann and Bryn.

"You and you," she said curtly to announce her selection.

The same happened later for Clara, then Zelma. Will and Lissa were left wondering what would happen to them when none of the others returned that evening.

Early the next morning, another, loud knock startled the pair awake. The man who spoke with Finn and provided the key for the barn entered with fists on his hips and a sad but not unkind smile.

"Only two," he muttered and gestured for them to follow him outside.

They stopped at a nearby brick home pouring smoke from its chimney. The door had been left wide open, and the sweet aroma of baked goods revealed it to be a bakery. Their guide told Will to wait outside, which doubled his growing appetite to twist his stomach, but he listened intently as the man bargained with a middle-aged woman at the counter. Eventually, she agreed to accept Lissa, though it sounded like an ordeal to convince her, and the man exited while wiping his forehead.

"Tough as a mule, that one," he grumbled with a low chuckle before facing Will. "What about you?"

After learning he would be working in the town, Will prepared several words and phrases that would explain what he preferred doing. Mostly, he hoped to avoid physical labor, such as farming or butchery, in case he needed to conserve his energy.

"Medicine," he answered immediately. "I know herbs and plants and how to tend to wounds."

The man rubbed his chin in a thoughtful manner. Instead of replying, he led Will to the farthest end of the road and halted before a place similar to the log cabin where Finn hid them earlier. After knocking and waiting several minutes, the door creaked open to reveal a thin, almost sickly looking woman possessing a long, horse-like face and wispy hair tied on top of her head. To Will's surprise, her eyes were a startling green that glinted as they flashed between the two new faces.

After the man's explanation, she prepared to close the door until he mentioned Finn's name. She repeated it, surprised by his connection to them, then waved for Will to enter.

Part Two

Direction

Something about the air in Dala brought a sense of relief as it welcomed Marcus back. Two dozen soldiers and a pair of dark mages trudged behind him, though only three others rode on horseback while the rest remained on foot through the busy road leading to the southern base. The past six months had been the longest stretch of time his miniature company had been away from their home, and probably would be for some time. Marcus kept moving with his chin held high in order to act as an example to those at his back. Any wandering eyes would notice the faces of weary, concerned soldiers, and that gives their onlookers the impression danger took place outside the safety of Dala; even though it was true, the people didn't need to become worked up at the moment.

When the base came within sight and his troops emerged from the building-lined street and into the clearing beyond, Marcus raised a hand for them to halt. He circled his mount to face them after.

"As I mentioned this morning, you're dismissed once we reach the entrance. You would normally receive your notice for two weeks off duty, and I'm going to vouch for that, but rest in case we're called out again. I hate filing through the list of soldiers and mages for replacements."

More than one person groaned with displeasure at his order.

Marcus considered addressing the outbursts, yet he understood they had every right to protest since they had been traveling together on and off for the past year. Instead, he narrowed his eyes as a warning.

They're worn down, hungry, and in need of a decent bath, he reminded himself. *Not only that, but no one stationed to a base expects to be on the road for months at a time.*

Before he could start their march again, a man at the front raised a hand and addressed him. The soldier removed his silver helmet once Marcus nodded to grant permission for him to speak. Underneath the metal, he recognized the face as it mirrored his own, except for the beard he collected from months without shaving.

"If I may, we're supposed to be stationed at the base," came the man's comment. "The first couple trips around the south were fine, but what we're doing is work for those posted in the other towns who have soldiers, mages, and Yeluthians monitoring the area. Why are we-"

This time, Marcus raised his hand to interrupt the question he knew he wasn't permitted to answer before addressing the soldier directly. "Jason, we're not the only troops being sent around the south. As you should already understand, we patrol the southwest in shifts, and there are additional forces for the southeast and to the north of the base. This isn't a selective assignment; all of us must fulfill our duties."

"Yes, but why are we handling demonic beasts on our own?" someone else farther to the rear shouted. "Where are the angels?'

Several voices murmured their support for the individual's questions, prompting a frown from Marcus. Even though he agreed with their sentiments, it felt like too late in the day to begin arguing, especially out in the open.

"I don't know about the Yeluthians," he lied. "What I do know is there will be time for talking after we reach the base, eat our fill, wash away the grim, and enjoy a peaceful rest. Does that sound fair?"

No one continued the complaining, not that he expected them to given his relationship with the soldiers and mages, so he led them across the plain and into the southern entrance.

A debriefing was in order as soon as the group split apart despite Marcus' desire to make himself more presentable. He kept his gaze level and greeted the familiar faces passing him by on his way to the general's meeting chamber while reflecting on how to share his report. The double doors had been propped open, revealing General Tio and Calin huddled on the farthest end to glance over a wide map. Once he cleared his throat, both heads popped up.

"Well, it's about time," the general roared, though he offered a grin and gestured for Marcus to enter.

At his side, Calin smiled but said nothing. Neither appeared to have changed on the outside except for additional bags under their eyes. Marcus pulled the doors closed for some privacy before accepting a seat nearby.

"You must've missed me since you decided to copy my look," Tio joked and used the stub where he lost his hand to stroke his dark-haired beard.

The corners of Marcus' lips tugged upward at the general's carefree personality. "Six months will do that."

"Is that all it's been? You smell like you've been away in the wilderness for at least a year!"

While Calin snickered at the comment, Marcus rolled his eyes. He expected some variant of the jest upon debriefing each time he returned.

"If you prefer, I can clean up before my report. I'd hate to distract from it." Marcus' words projected the severity of his assignment, which pushed the meeting forward.

"What was it like this time?" Calin asked without hiding his interest.

"Worse than the summer," Marcus answered as he ran a hand through his hair. Before his company left at the beginning of fall, Calin had also been preparing a trek to Clearwater and the Valley Beyond lasting nearly as long. Both assistant generals were absent for most of the warmer months prior to that.

After a pause, General Tio broke the silence with a grumble. "Well, let's hear it."

Marcus had been at his reassignment in Dala for five months before trouble arose in the southern cities. The issue started with a letter from the soldiers in Medina, then one from Clearwater about demonic creatures killing livestock and attacking travelers on the road, though they didn't experience any human fatalities. He heard about Aaron and King Arval's restructuring of the soldiers, mages, and angels around Asteom because the transition had already been in progress, yet more requests for aid arrived at regular intervals. By then, it was summertime. General Tio sent Marcus to Medina while Calin led a company to Clearwater.

Neither of them interacted with the Yeluthians on their ventures, and when they asked people outside Dala, they learned the demonic creatures only attacked away from the posted angel's route. Although the general tried to keep that piece of information between the three of them, soon everyone seemed to have heard and grew frightened. The demonic creatures' appearances were calculated according to the Yeluthians' visits, meaning somebody planned the incidents.

The idea of another demon in Asteom conjured nightmares for those who survived the battle outside Verona, so General Tio decided to order his assistants to lead groups around the south to provide extra protection while he wrote back and forth with Aaron and the other generals and monitored the base.

Whatever the kingdom's leaders agreed on took place after Marcus and his company left for Umbridge. He defeated dozens of creatures firsthand and chose only the bravest soldiers with experience, as well as the pair of mages who fought alongside the Dalans for years. Together, they moved from town to town until reaching the Western Woods where the Sie-Kie greeted them. Their people also noticed more of the demonic beasts but didn't request additional aid.

For those six months, Marcus' company protected the towns until one of several angels returned. A few patrolling the wide area meant no place would always be watched, though nothing else could be done aside from preparing the residents. He recounted this with General Tio and Calin.

"We lost no troops this time and managed to kill twenty of the creatures," he concluded. "Some civilians were poisoned and healed by the light mages and Yeluthians, but nothing proved too difficult for us to handle."

"At least something positive came from your report," Tio picked up and stared down at the map once more.

When the general didn't continue, Marcus glanced at Calin, and the two shared a mutual look to reflect their concern.

"The townsfolk are asking questions," he decided to add. "My soldiers stopped me before reaching the entrance. I doubt we're fooling anyone by staying silent. How long until we can admit there's another demon, or at the very least someone controlling the creatures? Yeluthia is supposed to help us against such issues."

Still, Tio didn't respond. He appeared to be contemplating the information and analyzing the map further.

Marcus' eyes returned to Calin. His fellow assistant general knew their superior better than anyone, so he hoped to convey a sense of urgency.

"I concur," his comrade said with a brief nod directed at Marcus. "Hiding the most likely cause may prove to be dangerous, especially when the majority of citizens already suspect a demon."

At that, the general pointed a finger to a spot on the map. Marcus shifted to lean over and saw it hovering above the middle of a forest to the south of the palace. Calin raised an eyebrow in response to show his own interest.

"You see this area?" General Tio began while circling the finger around the forest before retracting it. "About two years ago, before these creatures began appearing, some around here attacked a pair of Yeluthian scouts. They believed a demon controlled the beasts, but after further investigation, a private squad found the source to be a possessed human summoning demonic power. That was that, and no one's heard anything else relating to demons or demonic creatures from the north."

Aaron never mentioned this to me when I lived in the palace, Marcus couldn't help from admitting with no small amount of alarm. *Why would he keep this a secret after what we've been through?*

General Tio leaned back in his chair with his arms crossed and eyes closed. "While you two were away, I ordered scouts to investigate the capital. None reported serious suspicions, and all returned safe. Then, I had them go to the palace and request aid. Mind you, I've been sending letters ever since Medina and Clearwater brought the creatures up and received responses every time, along with a chart of the angels' routes. The kings and commanders are still plotting out some of the details while moving forward with the newly established Yeluthian squad kept there. Additionally, I guess Nim-Valans are crossing the border to take control of the northern cities, meaning there's a limit to who can be sent south. For the time being, we wait until the soldiers and mages arrive."

Marcus frowned but didn't argue. He had been hearing whispers beneath the fear of demonic creatures about a war to the north. Too little arose to believe the rumor, so he trusted his superior's judgement, even though it meant he and Calin would most likely be on the road again soon.

After his report, Tio sent him away, claiming his smell muddled the general's mind. He decided to bathe first before changing clothes and did so by sundown. Calin found him on his way to the mess hall where a majority of the troops gathered, took him by the elbow, and spun him in another direction instead of joining him.

"Where are we going?" he asked with a bit of concern given the unexpected events.

Despite his worry, the other assistant general smiled as naturally as ever and released his arm.

"When was the last time you ate in the city?"

Marcus didn't answer, yet he continued to follow his comrade anyway. Aside from the meals he consumed while on duty at various inns, he couldn't remember eating or drinking for pleasure.

When the pair reached the city streets, he decided to pry. "Why do you want to avoid the mess hall?"

"Who says I'm avoiding anything?" Calin countered as he selected one of the busier taverns.

They were led to a table near the back where talk could be heard and drinks consumed at their leisure. A skinny barmaid delivered a steaming plate of buttered potatoes and cubed lamb for each of them, and they ate while observing the room. Only when they felt full and sipped on glasses of mead did Calin reveal his intentions.

"The general's worried about you."

"Me? Doesn't he think I can handle myself out there?" Marcus expected a joke given Tio's sense of humor, yet Calin shook his head in a sympathetic manner.

"Actually, it's sort of the opposite problem. You're *too* willing to accept work whenever it's available."

At that, Marcus set his mug down in order to cross his arms. "Is it wrong to look for something to occupy my time? Did you drag me here to see if I could relax?"

"Don't be so defensive," Calin warned with a knowing smile as he let his eyes wander around the space. "I just wanted to talk about you somewhere outside the base. After all, that's where you like to hide when you're not on route."

The comment sounded like an obvious attempt to encourage Marcus to initiate the conversation, and he took the bait willingly. "What do you mean?"

"What do you recall of your reassignment? What's your purpose for being stationed here?"

Marcus shrugged. "I needed a new environment where I'm able to learn without restrictions."

"Learn what?"

"Same as you."

Calin finished his drink and slammed the mug down dramatically while releasing a content sigh. "No, I've stayed in Dala my entire life. My logic is simple: I wish to take care of my home. You transferred for another reason."

The wording the assistant general used rubbed Marcus the wrong way until he realized why Calin wasn't being forward with him.

"General Tio told you," he said and narrowed his eyes. "He shared what happened on the border with General Casner."

"Not only that," Calin continued without missing a step. "I know about your father and how he dismisses the idea of promoting you because of his image."

"They informed General Tio?" Marcus asked without hiding his surprise. He didn't believe his father would waste time explaining the issue.

Calin shook his head to confirm this. "Of course not. You remember how much General Tio cares for the politics in the palace. That doesn't stop him from piecing an issue together, though. We've been wondering why you chose to live in Dala."

Marcus had an impulse to accuse the pair of placing bets on his decision but kept quiet. Months went by since he last considered the reassignment to General Casner's company or his father's words, so he became genuinely curious how the base's leaders perceived his behavior.

"All you do is work. When you're not training or supervising the training, you're sparring with the foot soldiers. When they stop, you find a way to continue alone. Aside from the adventures around the southwest, you hardly care what happens to you. Is that what you believe makes a person worthy of being a general?"

He had no answer.

"Listen, we don't know all the details about your life in Verona. To be honest, I don't care to be wrapped up in someone else's problems, but you're my friend. Friends give each other advice, right? Mine is to figure out what kind of person you're striving to be and go from there."

"What about becoming a general?" Marcus added while processing Calin's words.

"For the most part, generals uphold the same responsibilities wherever they are. What sets them apart is who they are underneath. You're a finer soldier than most; probably better than me. Is obedience the only quality you plan to showcase for the rest of your life?"

Marcus raised his eyes to the ceiling and contemplated a response. When he couldn't comprehend it well enough to give an honest reply, he faced his fellow assistant general again. Meanwhile, Calin waved the barmaid over to refill their glasses.

"Why do you think I chose to move to Dala?" Marcus decided to ask after the woman left them with their new drinks.

The question hung in the air for a moment until Calin cleared his throat. "That's a tough one. I guess it's because the people in Dala aren't distracted. We find solutions and a purpose without worrying about status, power, or politics unless we choose to waste our time with them."

"I see."

"Don't be afraid of those," Calin went on before raising his mug for a swig of mead. "You shouldn't hide in Dala because of what you don't wish to face in Verona. Your reassignment is still temporary."

Part of Marcus desired to hear more with a slim hope the answers he sought would reveal themselves. Unfortunately, a handful of men became violent at the opposite end of the tavern, causing the whole space to go up in a loud frenzy. It seemed like a usual scene and not one needing their intervention, at least not at the moment.

When the excitement died down, they moved through several topics until the hour grew late.

***

As Will entered the home sitting on the outskirts of the Nim-Valan village named Muld, he shouted his caretaker's name and closed the front door behind him. The older woman was nowhere to be found inside, which would have been difficult for anyone else to discern given the unkempt state of the place. Books, bottles, plants, and more littered every available surface, and even plenty of space on the floor, yet it proved to be an organized mess for the residents, allowing them to locate what they needed whenever necessary. Will couldn't help but smile to himself as he recognized how alike the two really were, then he moved into the kitchen to set down the items he picked up in town.

Muld seemed like every Asteom village he had ever visited, except it possessed a dual culture. In the twenty months since he and his friends were forced to hide across the northern border, he learned its history between conversations with the locals. Its population originally stemmed from an extended farming family who found success with the soil in the area, which became excellent for beans, corn, and potatoes, as well as herding cattle, sheep, and chickens; however, because of its location near Asteom, or rather the outer ring of Nim-Vala, they faced the danger of bandits and barbarians who stole their animals or burned their crops. Despite this, the family continued growing to the point where they could afford expending enough workers in order to create a defensive system, and their troubles stopped for a few years.

Because of that peace, the town took pity on refugees and welcomed them and their services, or so Will figured. Their capital never showed concern or interest with their business, so the area developed into one tolerating Asteom's traditions and language as long as the citizens remained respectful toward Nim-Vala. As for the rest of the country, nowhere else became as accepting of strangers; at least, that seemed to be the people's common knowledge.

"Geneva," he shouted again and decided to speak the new language instead of Asteom's. The older herbalist usually forced him to switch anyway despite understanding both. "Where are you?"

When he didn't hear a response, Will started to explore the home. The new setting had been much kinder than he expected, and he used that time to study as much as he could under the more experienced botanist. What her background was, she never revealed, yet something about her personality invited him to continue learning about the world. It truly proved to be a blessing for Will since he never could find a mentor, leading him to leave Clearwater and explore the world on his own.

His friends from Asteom weren't as fortunate. The young women trained as light mages, but using their magic became risky because it wasn't common in Nim-Vala. This left them to pent up their natural powers while taking on mundane tasks issued by their own caretakers. He frowned when he recalled his conversation with Clara that afternoon while the two shared lunch.

"I'm forced to hide a part of myself that was never viewed as frightening or different," she admitted in a dejected manner. "Now, I don't even know who I am anymore. I'm a servant to a farming household with no real freedom. We haven't heard about Asteom for months either. What should we do, Will?"

"Will?"

The feminine voice that croaked his name shook Will from his thoughts, and he recognized it as Geneva's. "I'm in here," he replied, unsure of the direction from which the call came.

"Come out to the yard for a moment."

He followed her words to the back door where a neat, well-maintained garden stretched beyond. In addition to the vegetables and fruit trees, each flower, herb, root, and weed had a purpose relating to some type of medicine; that had been Geneva's first lesson: Keep only what is necessary.

Will stepped out into the sunlight, raised a hand to shield his eyes, and scanned for the older woman. He figured she would be alone since no visitors stayed longer than a few minutes to collect their orders, but the silhouette of a person standing next to her hunched, kneeling position in the grass startled him.

"Who is that?" he asked hesitantly.

"Your tongue sounds more fluent," replied a male voice before Geneva shifted to sit cross-legged and gestured for Will to come closer.

"You remember Finn," she started in Asteom's language, which felt surprising considering she would only do so to make conversations easier for him to follow.

"Of course I do," Will replied with mixed emotions. "Why is he here?"

The two exchanged a look before Geneva waved a hand in the Nim-Valan man's direction. "Go on, tell the boy. *You* came to see me, after all."

A smile tugged at Finn's lips as he faced Will. He hadn't aged since he last visited half a year ago, but his embellished, leather clothing suggested he lived a finer life than anyone in Muld. "Little news from the capital ever reaches this part of Nim-Vala," he began while gazing around the garden. "Soon, the area will face a sickness, and I came to warn Geneva."

Will continued to stare at the man in disbelief. "You've been to the capital city? What about the fighting on the border?"

"I'm a spy, remember? I go wherever my master sends me."

"Why would they send you to us then?" Will asked next. Something about Finn's tone suggested an unfamiliar emotion, which perplexed him. "Surely it wasn't just to warn the town about a sickness to the north."

During the following pause, Geneva remained silent and inspected the nearby herbs with a keen, patient eye.

For once, the Nim-Valan hesitated to respond and even lowered his gaze for a heartbeat before the cool exterior returned. "I am familiar with Muld and needed to see if Geneva might be able to give advice on how to treat the symptoms of this new illness. The area is still unaffected, and winter will hinder travel later. My best option was to visit her first before trying elsewhere."

Will waited for more information, but as usual Finn only shared what he wanted others to hear instead of the entire truth. He turned his attention to the older woman next. "What did you suggest? Is this a case you're familiar with?"

"Partly. As you can imagine, without observing the victims and being present it's difficult to recommend medicines and treatments, especially when there is such a great distance between the capital and here. Even in a day's time, the lack of proper care could spell death."

After spending plenty of time with her, Will had grown accustomed to her honest, if not blunt, personality and nodded. She returned to her work while he glanced at Finn. To his amazement, the Nim-Valan paled, though nothing else suggested the herbalist's answer bothered the man.

"She's right," Will offered in a sympathetic tone of voice. "Without a healer present, the issue will just be drawn out."

Finn let out a breath through his nostrils. "I believe you both. That's why I requested Geneva accompany me on my return to the capital."

Will's eyes widened, but he didn't comment. *My knowledge is limited, but the town doesn't usually come up with problems I haven't learned how to handle. Most of the time, I'm the one dealing with people anyway so she can remain at home to prepare the medicine. That would explain why they're acting so cautiously; they might feel like it would be a burden to abandon me.*

He opened his mouth and prepared to reassure them he was capable while Geneva went away; however, the old woman spoke before he could.

"I told Finn he should ask you to accompany him instead."

Will's jaw dropped, then his mouth worked for a response. "Me?"

"Why not? You're mobile, far more tolerant and headstrong, and my home is here."

Her last reason resonated with Will the most as he considered the current state of his life. Without hiding his displeasure, he returned his eyes to Finn only to find the man glancing somewhere behind Will.

"Well?" the Nim-Valan pressed.

A burning sense of irritation twisted in Will's gut, prompting him to scoff. "*Well?* Is that all you can say?"

"It's about a week's travel on foot to the inner circle. We can pick up appropriate clothing along the way and-"

"No," Will interrupted. He let the tension hang in the air while his heartbeat sped up. He rarely became so upset, yet the Nim-Valan's lack of consideration grated his nerves. "Give me one reason why I should help your people? I'm from Asteom. Although you rescued me and my friends before, it's been the townsfolk who took us in and have been providing for us now. You disappeared when we were vulnerable, and we haven't heard any information about when we can return to our homes. We don't know what's happening across the border, but all you can think about is treating your own people. My answer is no!"

Again, the lone sign that the response reached Finn was the change of color in his face. His cheeks flushed slightly before returning to their grayish shade. For a moment, Will grew worried he pushed the man too far and a hidden knife would appear to threaten him.

It would make sense, he thought bitterly. *If we don't cooperate after he saves us, which is enough for us to assist him despite what I said, he'll plan to eliminate the Asteom refugees, thus protecting his people and his image.*

After a minute of silence, Geneva's voice cut through the tension in an uncharacteristically gentle tone that seemed to shake the two out of their frustration. "Finnley, wait inside. I would like to talk with Will alone."

As if waiting for such an excuse, the Nim-Valan man dipped his head and hurried at a brisk walk through the back door without making noticeable sound.

"He's too good at sneaking around," the woman commented.

Will stared at Geneva while she adjusted herself to face him with her complete attention and a tired but not displeased expression. Instinctively, he began to protest the request until she stopped him with a wave of her hand.

"Let me go first," she chided. "You don't seem surprised we know each other. You also never questioned how I can speak Asteom's language so fluently."

The thoughts hadn't crossed Will's mind and successfully drew him into what she prepared to share.

"Most of the people from Muld were brought across the border over the course of the decade thanks to Finn. He has a way of finding the most broken, most desperate individuals and sweeping them away to new opportunities. It might not seem like it, but he does care."

"So, he helped you into Nim-Vala then?"

Geneva nodded slowly. "I've lived as a medicine woman my entire life, and not everyone understands a healer isn't a god. People die under our watch; that's just life. A woman in my care passed from a suspicious poisoning, but when I tried to bring it up to her husband, I became the scapegoat. In summary, I went on the run for the supposed murder since he had been wealthy enough to hire mercenaries to come after me. I chose to go north, crossed the border, and soon found myself lost. When I spotted a young man in the woods, I thought I began hallucinating."

She paused to cough before continuing. "He suggested I hide my identity because I would be one of the first refugees to build a new life here. I hadn't left any possessions or family behind to warrant a return, so I became Geneva, the local herbalist. It's been six years since then."

Will waited for a proper conclusion, yet the old woman's eyes glazed over while she recalled the past.

"That's why you're attempting to convince me to go with him, because you owe him too."

"Absolutely not." Her resulting scowl seemed more like the woman Will had come to know. "Finnley isn't like other people. What he does isn't based on earning a reward or being able to call upon favors at a later time. This is the first instance I can remember him asking something of me, which says a lot when you've honed the skills I possess."

Although he valued her input, Will couldn't drop the idea of abandoning Clara and his other companions in Muld, as well as their desire to return to their home country. He said as much afterward.

"I suppose the decision is up to you," she replied and reached for a hand to pull her to her feet, which he provided. "Still, as someone who deals with mending the physical body, it's your responsibility to aid those in need, just as it is mine. My reasoning stands too. You possess more energy, are stronger, and will be less susceptible to this illness. I recommended you because I acknowledge your skills and ability make a decision, nothing more. Besides, you'll get an opportunity to talk with Finnley about crossing the border."

She began hobbling toward her home, leaving Will to stand by himself in the sunshine; however, when her hand rested on the wooden knob, Geneva turned to shoot him a serious look.

"Whatever your decision is, I want you to let me know before dinner. I'd prefer to have enough time to pack and rest, if necessary."

With that, the older woman disappeared inside. Finn didn't return to pester him, so Will wandered around the garden and focused on pulling the few weeds and picking up the tools Geneva left behind as he contemplated the best course of action.

In his heart, he felt the same about helping those in need. He also wasn't willing to abandon Clara or the other light mages, even if it would only be for a month or two. In the end, the sun began to set before he reached a decision, and Geneva called to him for dinner.

Finn had stayed but kept quiet while the three ignored what took place in the garden to eat in silence. Will cleared the table after, and when the old herbalist washed the dishes, he approached Finn, who moved to stand by an open window at the front of the house. He planned to bring up crossing the border or bargain on behalf of his friends in exchange for his services, yet he spoke before he finished considering exactly to say.

"When do we leave?"

His reward was a hint of a smile from the Nim-Valan.

***

Although seeing dozens of people rotating in and out of the new training ground became less of a shock as the weeks passed, Coura appreciated Evern's foresight for their session that afternoon.

Winter had been harsh and unkind to every living creature as snow fell in blankets, the bitter winds made being outdoors nearly unbearable, and a mild sickness spread to ensure the soldiers and mages dealt with coughs, stuffy noses, or both. However miserable the season was, spring arrived right on time to melt what froze and begin healing again.

Those who worked in the grounds also grew excited by the events of the past month. Before winter struck, the finishing touches were placed on the building south of the palace meant to house a majority of the soldiers, mages, and new Yeluthians, which became known as the dormitory. Most of its residents waited to transition into their prepared quarters due to the weather, so the first week of warm temperatures caused a stir in the capital city. The angels also arrived when traveling proved safe, including Evern and the rest of the soldiers not stationed in Verona under Commander Detrix's authority. Everyone seemed eager to be outdoors, burn their pent-up energy, and strengthen weakened muscles.

As for Coura, she agreed to act as a member of the area's scouting party despite her frustration regarding what took place after her encounter with the demon in the southern woods. She forced herself to remember Terran's name and face, if not for the kingdom's future than for her own sanity, though she heard no indication of demonic activity recently.

The questions ceased on the subject as Detrix organized his scouts' routes. No other incidents arose, so the focus shifted to Nim-Vala's attempt to settle across the border.

Perhaps that's why the troops are training so often, she reflected with a glance around the space from where she stood at its farthest end. *No one can talk about anything other than proving how capable they are with the dream of being reassigned to the northern company. I should remember to ask Evern if King Arval decided what his troops will do yet. Aaron's pretty anxious about that...*

"I see you beat the rush."

Coura smiled to greet Lavine when the Yeluthian approached and tucked the stray thoughts away. "Evern went to fetch the blades," she replied with a jerk of her chin toward the busy stable. "He's been out here for a few hours to supervise some of the mages, so he saved the space for us."

"Will the commander be observing our spar today?" he asked while raising an eyebrow.

Coura just shrugged before the pair listened to the noise filling the area.

Lavine had been one of the Yeluthian soldiers assigned to stay in Verona and almost immediately became somebody she grew comfortable enough with to approach for lessons on his combat style. Her request startled him, yet he accepted in a feigned prideful manner. Soon, they bonded over the experience. His friendship and the sessions managed to ease her into a solid relationship with the other angelic soldiers, who often volunteered to spar or critique Coura's efforts, both physically and magically.

Whatever their impression of her had been before then, they acted supportive now. The human soldiers and mages also learned to look beyond her previous association with demonic energy. Aside from the occasional visit to the prison to check on Hendal and the encounter with Terran two years ago, nothing reminded Coura of that dark past anymore.

Evern joined them after another minute when he procured a pair of authentic, steel blades. Lavine weighed one in his hands as Coura accepted the other.

"I suppose you don't want to try flips or retracting, do you?" she asked her partner with a smirk.

Her father shot Lavine a look reflecting his curiosity while the soldier laughed and shook his head.

"I began experimenting with our training," he hurried to explain to Evern. "Sometimes, we can shout a trigger word, and the opponent would need to switch their weapon to the opposite hand. Retracing is also based on a vocal cue where we must backtrack our steps in order to understand movement during combat."

The commander appeared to approve of the creative, if not outlandish, methods; however, his expression grew serious as he eyed Coura up. "Right now, all I need is for you behave normally. I expect to see your physical progress, as if it were a real fight."

Coura nodded while the smile disappeared from her lips. Lavine stood at attention, so she mimicked his position before her father stepped away.

"Ready?" the Yeluthian asked and slid into a fighting stance, just like he did on any other day.

Instead of a vocal response, Coura charged with sword raised to take a wide, easily blocked swipe at his throat. With the spar initiated, the pair fell into a familiar rhythm of stabs, parries, ducks, and dives as they circled the space while remaining completely aware of the surrounding observers. She became more comfortable with additional eyes judging her progress after the first time she bested Lavine, which boosted her confidence.

Byron always said I focus better when I'm in front of a crowd, she thought absently and lunged away from her opponent's blade when it came for her chest. *I know my body has adjusted to the fluidity of the Yeluthians' style too. I'd wager Evern is here to observe that specifically.*

Coura switched to the offensive in order to drive her opponent backward, then she sidestepped to circle around him and push in the opposite direction. Still, the most difficult aspect of working with Lavine was patience. Dozens of spars provided what appeared to be opportunities to end the fight prematurely, yet she found herself on the ground more often than not when she fell for these false openings.

"We use stamina to our advantage," he once explained early on in their training. "Power is important, but if you tire too soon, you risk more than if you carefully wear down an opponent. This also allows time to analyze and strategize."

The words echoed in Coura's head as she forced herself to ignore one of the Yeluthian's physical taunts and instead take a few steps back to break the combat up for a moment. In response, she noticed the corners of Lavine's mouth crawling upward to display his approval.

"Pauses are not always necessary, but they allow you time to assess your body," his piece of additional reasoning echoed in her mind. "Are there wounds you had not noticed in the heat of the fight? How is your breathing? These are the basic questions to ask yourself then."

Of course, Coura's instinct had always been to continue pushing in order to prevent such pauses for her opponent; however, she never considered doing so would allow *her* some reprieve. It sounded like such a simple concept, yet it took her the longest to put into practice. That, and the idea of moving around instead of standing her ground.

This time, Lavine charged to slash diagonally from below for her chest, leading her to block using a downward swing. With her sword pressed against his, she waited for him to let up in order to retreat again, but he held his blade there with what felt like all of his strength.

Coura matched the force, which prevented the weapons from moving toward her torso any farther, and wondered what he planned to do next. A sharp twist of his foot instantly revealed the answer.

It's a physical blow! Even as her mind shouted the words, her body responded, sending her right foot backward to brace for impact.

Lavine released the power in his arms so suddenly, her constant pressure pushed his blade away to follow through with the motion. This left both their bodies wide open, so he took the opportunity to shove his shoulder into Coura's chest.

If she hadn't prepared herself by moving her foot seconds ago, she would have been knocked off balance, probably enough to be unable to recover in time and keep the fight going. She caught herself as she stumbled in response, then she propelled herself forward, like a slingshot.

Her opponent wasn't expecting a strike so soon after his blow and tumbled to the side, just managing to escape her sword as it sliced through the air where his head had been. Instead of pursuing, she stayed in place to allow Lavine a moment to scramble to his feet.

A handful of the onlookers clapped or shouted cheers of approval for their performance during the pause; however, beneath the noise, Coura heard the prolonged hiss of a sword being unsheathed. The crowd's abrupt silence proved concerning enough to prompt her to spin around with her blade raised. What she didn't expect to see was Evern drawing his own weapon while approaching with an unreadable expression.

He doesn't think Lavine is finished already, does he? she wondered.

The urge to glance behind at her original opponent grew until she noticed Lavine's footsteps on the dry grass. That in and of itself explained what the pair had planned.

They're working together. This isn't an ordinary session for Evern to watch; it's a test he would join when the momentum shifted.

Coura expected the negative feelings spurred by the addition and frowned at her father to show her lack of enthusiasm toward the change, but she ultimately accepted the situation. A real fight could play out in such a fashion. She had the notion they knew she would understand that; after all, she lived through plenty of unpredictable battles in the past.

When Lavine's footsteps stopped, Coura gave them her full attention. The realization that she would be facing both Yeluthians at the same time finally dawned on her, and the nerves settled in. If she had a chance to succeed, she wouldn't do so by keeping herself between the two.

She adjusted her position to assess Lavine, who lingered nearby before charging with his sword pointed at the sky in preparation for a vertical slice. As he started to lower the blade, Coura noted the space under his weapon-bearing arm and took a risk on that opening. She practically dove for the right side of his body, reached with her free hand to grab the raised forearm, and stopped it from falling so she had enough room to slip underneath and behind him in one, swift motion. Then, she gifted them another break.

Lavine spun around wearing a baffled expression at her escape while Evern raised an eyebrow to show his interest. Meanwhile, Coura felt sweat building on her forehead as she put together something of a strategy.

I fought with Lavine before, so I can manage one-on-one combat against him. Evern is another story, depending on how seriously he tries to win. It's been months since I trained with him too. Then again, I've been getting stronger through these sessions. If I force Lavine in the middle, I should be able to focus on one at a time until they figure out what I'm doing. After that... Well, we'll just see how the first part goes.

Her father already moved forward to stand beside his underling, so Coura sidestepped to keep him at the farthest distance. She brought her sword up as a new idea came to mind.

Unless they're completely comfortable with each other, I doubt they would venture to fight close enough to risk a foolish injury. I'm the smallest of the three, which could allow me to be pretty personal if I want to be. Lavine seemed surprised by that before, so what if I try physical combat? If she chose to do so, Coura believed she would need to commit wholeheartedly since she was also the weakest of the three.

Before she could consider alternative tactics, Lavine leapt to meet her.

Similar to the start of their spar, the two traded blows without much effort while Evern hovered in the background. He tried to circle behind Coura several times, but she slipped away from Lavine for long enough to distance herself again. This led to accidental scratches on her arms and torso, which were necessary in order for her to manage each opponent's position. Only when she began panting from the effort did she decide to change her strategy and attack Lavine with the intent to finish him off.

Coura sidestepped once more to break the combat cycle and allowed the Yeluthian to charge at her. Instead of trying to actively avoid Evern, she focused on the person in front of her. Lavine started with a pair of horizontal slashes, one for her throat and the other for her midsection, and she blocked them by keeping her blade perpendicular to his. His intent to pressure her into backtracking became obvious based on the strength behind each strike. Coura made sure to hold her ground until he attempted another physical attack, just as he used earlier when she wouldn't budge.

After his shove, he wasn't expecting me to spring forward. If I can recreate the opportunity to knock him off his balance, I'll use that to stop him.

In order to cause Lavine to resort to such a maneuver, she needed to demonstrate consistency by showing how his regular moves wouldn't finish the fight. She also had to watch for Evern, though her initial assumption proved correct, as her father kept his distance from the close combat and only came closer when Coura pulled away.

Every muscle in her upper body sang from the strain of meeting each of the Yeluthian's attacks head-on without sacrificing her ground. Internally, she fought the urge to either retreat, accept defeat because of how unfair the situation became, or lose her building temper and strike without considering the circumstances.

Finally, the moment arrived when Coura noticed Lavine beginning to target her left shoulder; she somehow understood what he aimed to do then. Because protecting that side forced her to cross her prominent weapon-bearing arm over her chest, his attacks from the right would compromise her balance, as well as her body if she wasn't expecting it. His strategy supported the logic behind the angels' style of combat. Instead of circling or staying grounded to one location, which Byron and the weapons instructors taught at the academy, utilizing fluid motions would prevent an opponent from focusing on a specific part of the body.

Lavine wanted her to dance away, just like they practiced over the past year. The only problem was her father hiding in her blind spot.

I can't believe this, she thought with no shortage of wry humor. *Either I pass their challenge by proving I learned their technique and step right into Evern or I fail because I revert back to holding my ground to stay in one spot. I suppose they're assuming I wouldn't choose to disregard their style of combat. How would they react if I switch on purpose?*

It became too late to question whether her idea would succeed, for Lavine pulled his sword back and twisted at the waist to swipe at her left side. In a regular, one-on-one spar, she could chose to block his blade or dodge; however, he wouldn't expect a retaliation.

Coura pulled her weapon to the right without hesitation to mirror his strike and aim for his left side. If he didn't adjust to her decision, the blades would reach their targets, though she prayed he would move away instead in order to avoid being cut, for both their sakes.

A Test of Worth

Because of the previous issues regarding his eldest daughter's skills, Evern did not predict the fighting would last as long as it did. He trusted Lavine's abilities well enough, but Coura's former training with the humans, not to mention the manipulative methods of survival the demon brought out, meant she would essentially need to relearn how she moves on her feet, positions her blade and upper body, and processes her surroundings during combat. The last item concerned him the most based on his time working with her in the past.

Still, she did not balk when I approached to join, he reflected as he circled around Lavine. Of course, Coura attentively made sure to keep him as far from her as possible, and for good reason.

His subordinate had been fully aware Evern would be participating, though not why, and the two decided they should attack separately in order to prevent their single opponent from creating a moment's rest.

When he stood behind Coura at a safe distance while Lavine kept her attention, he hesitated to slip in and finish the lesson. *She is caught between two swords. I wonder what she will decide to do if given the time?*

Lavine probably figured he had a purpose for the delay and began hammering at Coura's weaker left side to draw out the match. When his daughter refused to back away and blocked the blows instead of dodging, Evern frowned.

She will tire before he stops. Not only that, but I can tell Lavine is planning a new attack based on how he is targeting a single part of her body. I hoped she could understand how using the steadfast method pins her to one place between two opponents and not abandon her efforts to return to that former way. Perhaps my presence or the onlookers intimidate her too much to continue.

A bit of disappointment poked at Evern's heart, yet he stepped forward when Lavine prepared his sword for a slice across the middle. If the blade in front of her did not land for any reason, he would be there to finish the fight; however, the last thing he expected Coura to do was bring her own weapon outward opposite Lavine's in a matching attack. For a second, he recalled their private sessions where she accepted injuries in order to counter his strikes, though Lavine would do more damage than Evern ever had. The imagery in his mind caused him to cringe, mostly because it seemed to be the worst possible action to display in front of their audience.

Then, she surprised him.

His subordinate either grew concerned about hurting a vulnerable opponent or wary of her movement, for he shifted to turn and knock Coura's sword aside instead of following through with the slice. This provided an opening for a physical strike. As precise as a viper, she stepped close enough to place her left foot behind his right leg and press their hips together. At the same time, she shot her free hand out to grab his throat before shoving him. The closer distance coupled with the sudden force managed to knock Lavine onto his backside.

Although Evern sprang into action before his partner's body hit the ground, Coura tapped her first opponent's chest to mimic a killing blow, thus effectively removing Lavine from the spar. She spun to face her next target a second later.

Evern did not wait to see what his daughter planned to do next. His immediate reaction to her physical attack allowed him to swing for her before she could get away, resulting in a deep cut across her left thigh as she leapt in the opposite direction. Instead of pursuing, he paused while she stumbled backward to put more space between them.

Lavine sat up during the break and rubbed his throat without attempting to rise or do more than sit and watch the remainder of the fight. Next, Evern noticed Coura put weight on the wounded leg before removing it when a concerning amount of blood poured forth; however, she raised her chin a bit, as if accepting the challenge.

That has to be causing plenty of pain, he noted. *If this continues for much longer, she will pass out from blood loss.*

This led him to consider attacking without restraint in order to end the spar on his terms so she could receive assistance. To his confusion, *she* was the one who charged with the same intent written across her face.

What followed proved to be an interesting combination of techniques Coura used against Lavine earlier at a speed he could manage with ease. Doing so left him without a moment to go on the offensive, but he marveled at her level of stamina, which rose far beyond where it had been a year or two ago. She also showcased an impressive amount of concentration to simply keep him occupied.

Evern continued to backtrack with his daughter pursuing until they reached the edge of their ring of onlookers, who scurried out of the way before the pair could harm them. Subconsciously, he recognized how their combat could be dangerous for those nearby while parrying one of Coura's swings and cutting her forearm.

In response, her eyes narrowed into a scowl as they focused on his right shoulder. She raised her sword after and brought it down with the intent of striking there, prompting Evern to block her attempt. Their blades pressed together when neither removed their weapon, so he put more pressure behind his sword in order to push her backward; however, she didn't budge.

Has she finally lost her temper? he wondered when she released a grunt. *I assume this is the remainder of her strength. So be it. I am not above displaying my own physical power, and I refuse to allow her to make a fool of herself by being hotheaded.*

In a battle of muscle, he would surely win. This proved true as he gradually forced his daughter's weapon toward her by using more strength.

Suddenly, the opposing force disappeared when she abandoned her effort and utilized her smaller build to sidestep his sword. Evern caught himself before he could lose his balance enough to fall, yet the energy he sacrificed to do so left him unable to prepare for Coura's next move. She switched her weapon to the opposite hand as soon as she could and tilted the blade upward to place the tip at his throat. By that point, he realized the trick had been what Lavine used on her earlier, though without such success.

A stunned silence from the surrounding onlookers stretched for several seconds while the two remained frozen except for the rising and dropping of their chests as they panted. Then, the audience erupted into claps and cheers.

At the sound, Coura's focused expression vanished as she appeared to process her victory, and she removed the blade from Evern's throat. He straightened afterward before sheathing his sword without hiding the genuine smile that crept up on him. It faded a moment later when she attempted to step back, winced, and kept her weight on her uninjured leg.

"Be still," he ordered and approached to kneel beside her. Although he felt he owed it to her to heal the damage he caused, he primarily needed a chance to suppress his immense pride and elation stemming from her hard-earned progress.

"You don't have to do that," he heard her say in between breaths; however, she didn't protest again when he started, so he proceeded to complete the light spell.

"Take some time to clean yourself up and eat," he advised, rose, and looked her over. "I will stop by your quarters in an hour or so to discuss the lesson."

Coura nodded in a dazed manner, as if she still could not understand what took place.

He accepted that and turned to walk toward the palace, allowing the awaiting mob to bombard her with praise, including Lavine, whose voice he heard above the others. Evern's time to compliment his daughter would come later when he concluded the rest of his business.

Those working in the training ground glanced at the crowd, and some even wandered over to investigate the noise, yet a familiar figure stood alone with his arms crossed. Detrix had been observing on the opposite side of the space once the spar began and kept to the rear so as not to distract anyone. A wide grin stretched across his face as Evern approached.

"I can no longer deny your blood runs in her veins," the commander began with a shrug. "Such ferocity in combat is one of your specialties."

"You do not seem surprised."

Detrix's amused expression relaxed into a casual smile, which Evern returned. "I have been noticing her growth for a while now, so it is less shocking for me than for yourself."

"Why the test then?" Although he wished to analyze Coura's development anyway, it was Detrix who suggested the sparring session and the addition of a second opponent to raise the difficulty.

Instead of answering right away, his fellow commander gestured for them to move inside. "There is something I would like to show you."

***

After a much-needed bath, Coura rushed to visit the mess hall for a brief meal then hurried to the third floor in order to meet her father on time. Dozens of people hung around the training ground for a while to converse about how she managed to beat both Lavine and Evern. The whole affair left her flushing with pride, especially since Lavine seemed to enjoy entertaining the crowd by commenting on various moments from his perspective.

Her mind continued reeling from the experience as she arrived at her room to find the door partly open. When she pushed it farther to enter, she spotted two figures inside. Evern stood near the window next to someone wearing the Yeluthian bronze armor; however, when he glanced at her with a smile, she realized no one was in the metal suit.

"What is this?" she asked while closing the door.

Her father waved a hand at the unmoving object, which glimmered as sunlight shined on its polished surface. "What do you think?"

Coura tilted her head without comprehending his question. "Of what?"

Evern chuckled before glancing over the armor. "Commander Detrix observed our lesson in the new training ground, and he informed me of your progress too. He had this delivered as an official offer for you to join his company."

Coura looked between him and the empty suit without hiding her disbelief. Her mouth hung open while her mind attempted to understand what this meant. "I'm already a member of his company."

"Technically, you belong to Asteom. Detrix merely requested for you to participate in the scouting party. Your lack of proper training prevented you from being eligible for a position among our people, at least until today. I never asked you to be under my command because it is a spot you needed to earn for yourself; favoring you would also not sit right with our people, myself included. Detrix hopes to invite more humans to become official members of his company stationed here; however, I can say for certain he has kept an eye on you for a long time."

She didn't know how to respond, prompting another blush, so she lowered her eyes and dipped her head. "I'm honored," she managed to reply against the mind-numbing daze.

Evern closed the distance between them to place a hand on her shoulder while using the other to raise her chin, allowing their eyes to meet. "Coura, you should not disregard the effort you put into getting yourself this strong, skilled, and intelligent in combat. I am so proud of you for that work ethic and for learning to not let your emotions dictate your actions. Detrix, as well as many other Yeluthians, admire such growth."

"Thank you." By that point, Coura mirrored her father's wide smile before he removed his hand.

"I must share something else with you as well," Evern continued in a less enthusiastic manner. "Detrix asked me to pass this message along. Whether you are aware of it or not, he has been using your presence in his company to attract any remaining demonic creatures in the area. I learned none have appeared around here ever since our initial encounter. He would like me to apologize on his behalf for the selfish decision and assure you it will not happen going forward."

Coura recalled several instances in the past where that reasoning seemed to explain the commander's actions, such as why he always sent her out at dusk, ordered three or four soldiers to accompany her on her assignments, and requested she never wield magic without permission. Despite her past vexation with the overbearing attention, she came to understand their need to take precautions.

"I suppose I trust him to utilize what he can," she concluded.

Evern nodded. "I will relay your response to him this evening at dinner. As for the suit, I believe you should thank him for that in person."

His proud smile returned as he took his exit, leaving Coura alone to put her thoughts together.

For a few minutes, she simply admired the metalwork of her gift. One part of her longed to try it on, if only to feel its weight shielding her body, yet the other hated the idea of smudging the smooth, shiny surface.

I never needed to wear armor before, she noted with a sigh since the fact reminded her of her demonic connection. *No one bothered to give me more than a uniform or leather padding during my training or the scouting flights.*

Coura faced the armoire containing her clothing, pulled the wooden doors open, and shoved the hanging shirts and pants aside so the coat of her uniform could be visible. With a huff, she dropped onto the bed where she looked between the bronze and crimson and sorted through her mixed emotions. It had been months since she was reminded of how unique her position remained as a trained soldier of Asteom, a mage from the Magical Arts Academy who never graduated, and an officially recognized Yeluthian.

If I accept Detrix's offer, what will that change? Father made it sound as though the scouting company plans to stay and continue their search, but will the assignment be permanent? Would I ever be ordered to leave under their authority? I refuse to abandon my home. I also can't forget I'm technically stationed under General Terrell, so he should know about this. When I get a chance, I'll speak to the commander...

A knock at the door startled her enough to jump, leading her to wonder how much time she spent pondering the situation, and she called for her guest to enter.

"I was hoping you'd be here," came a familiar voice before Byron stepped inside. As he began to offer a greeting, he paused at the sight of the bronze suit before raising an eyebrow at her.

Coura waved a hand to dismiss the subject, resigning to let the matter sit in the back of her mind for the moment. "Detrix had it delivered as a proper request for me to join his company."

"Really?" Byron closed the door and crossed the room to assess the untouched armor. He appeared to want to ask a question, yet his next comment sounded like an attempt to not pry. "I would imagine this is quite a distinction among the Yeluthians."

"I guess." Although it proved tempting to share what took place earlier in the day, she pushed past her vanity to focus on the purpose of his visit. "Did you need me for something?"

As if waiting for the opportunity, he turned away from the distracting metal suit with an almost cheerful expression. "Emilea sent me to invite you to a dinner party at Lady Katrina's home. Did you hear the news yet?"

She shook her head, uncertain of what to expect.

"High Priest Jurek finalized Marcy and her former husband's divorce yesterday morning."

Coura's eyes widened in surprise before she found herself smiling along with Byron. "You're kidding! I was under the impression she would need to return to Dala to meet with their priest."

This time, Byron shook his head before crossing his arms and leaning against the windowsill. "That had been the ultimatum last year when neither her ex-husband nor the priest who married them would budge on the separation. It's all a matter of egotism, and

Marcy simply wanted freedom from her old life. Well, Jurek attempted to explain her intentions in order to use guilt against the priest; however, not every religious leader is as virtuous as they claim.

A lot of time passed between letters until Jurek had an opportunity to go south and visit. In the end, it came down to a bribe. Marcy, with a couple unnamed benefactors' help, raised enough to buy the priest off without letting her ex-husband know. If the man ever does find out, it'll be too late."

For as well as the problem resolved, the means it took for Marcy to gain her freedom and continue paving a path for a new future left a sour taste in Coura's mouth. "I wish it didn't include paying the priest who continued the trouble. Those men get a slap on the wrist for trying to ruin someone's life."

"I'm sure everyone feels the same way," Byron went on, allowing his smile to wane and reflect his agreement. "That's all in the past now. Katrina and Lord Donovan are hosting a celebration of sorts the day after tomorrow and asked Emilea and I to invite anybody close to Marcy. They'll be speaking to their friends too since plenty of people were aware of the conflict."

"You mean we must surround ourselves with flocks of loud, overdressed lords and ladies?"

When Byron nodded, Coura groaned and dropped her head into her hands, causing him to chuckle.

"Just remember, this is for Marcy. Besides, there should be enough guests you're familiar with to keep you company."

"Is Cintra going?" she decided to ask with no shortage of mischief.

Aside from glancing away, Byron revealed nothing about his relationship with the seer. "She's staying in Verona until the celebration is over."

"That's nice of her."

He prepared to take his leave before Coura could pester him further, so she chose to leave the subject alone.

He shared little about his relationship with Cintra to anyone, but Emilea brought her up once during a break in their training when

Coura mentioned the woman's ability to see visions of future events. Particularly, she wondered if such an ability acted like a goddess gift. Emilea dismissed the notion since she knew several light mages with similar magic they could channel, though the academy frowned upon using such a spell. When Coura later considered this, she remembered the old widow named Marie from Neston who used her foresight to observe the changing weather or their next harvest season. That same woman also saved the entire town, including Paulina, the night the demon bonded with Coura.

Over the past year, she learned Byron and Cintra wrote to one another, leading the former to request time off in order to visit Fester more often. When the seer did stay in Verona, it was at Emilea and Clearshot's home, and usually for a week at most.

The couple found it amusing, so Coura left Byron alone despite her curiosity. She had enough to deal with regarding her own attempt at a romantic relationship anyway.

***

Every door and window in Lady Katrina's home had been thrown open, allowing fresh air to circulate through the crowd mingling inside. Of course, Marcy remained the center of attention during the day and stayed in the sitting room where she could relax without needing to constantly stand. Grace procured a chair in the same space when she arrived with Emilea and Clearshot, but the pair moved outdoors not too long after, leaving her at the mercy of the surrounding ladies. They fawned over Marcy, complimenting her bravery in the face of distress and congratulating her for escaping her ex-husband, as if the divorce became a life or death situation.

How the woman managed to remain polite by thanking them, smiling, and laughing throughout the morning amazed Grace, who did the same when the nobility's attention turned to her. Yeluthians made regular appearances in the city and around the palace, yet the lords and ladies always acted to impress her when the opportunity arose. At the moment, she desired to go to the yard as the inside of Katrina's home filled to the brim ever since she arrived. Unfortunately, a pair of women planted themselves directly in front of Grace, preventing her from slipping away.

I should know better than to remain in the middle of the group, she thought while repressing a tired sigh. *Perhaps the discussion will distract me from Mother's letter...*

The message she received earlier that week continued to float around her mind, preventing her from relaxing and enjoying the atmosphere. Ever since her last encounter with her parents where they argued about her position in Asteom and her future in Yeluthia, she actively avoided bringing up the subject. The two hadn't visited since, yet they decided to write letters frequently in order to brag about their discussions with King Arval on her acting as ambassador, what other positions appeared the most desirable, and who her potential suitors are.

Each of the six men they chose came from households active in the kingdom, whether they led community groups or served in the army; however, her parents only described the actions, not their personalities.

I suppose an arranged marriage goes smoother when the participants do not consider the other's character, she reflected bitterly. *At least no one is acting on their behavior. Without my being in Yeluthia, there is not much Mother and Father can do.*

Whether or not Aaron kept his word about defending Grace's position, she didn't know. Her friend never returned to their previous conversation during the past couple years, so she assumed he hadn't heard additional details; either that, or he didn't believe she needed to learn who he spoke with.

Before she could sink into her rising worries, the woman to her right laughed. The somewhat obnoxious gesture drew her attention, and she forced herself to mingle until she could find an appropriate moment to leave the stuffy room.

The discussions taking place usually came to bore Grace since they often revolved around similar topics and people, but one piqued her interest enough for her to turn and listen.

A lady she learned was Katrina's neighbor fanned herself with a napkin and showcased a deep frown. "What a mess in the north. Honestly, why discuss such unpleasant news now?"

The person she addressed proved to be a younger, more masculine-looking woman with a no-nonsense expression.

"They're looking for solutions, Brigetta," the second stated in a tone befitting her tough appearance. "No one wants another war."

Grace continued listening as the two shared what they learned from others in Verona, ranging from an invasion into Nim-Vala, sending spies across the border to assassinating their king, remaining stagnant along the perimeter, and attempting another peace treaty. By that point, more individuals in the room began chiming in their own opinions and tidbits of information.

"We don't need a war, so why should they attack?" someone demanded in an arrogant manner. "Our mages and the Yeluthians are more than enough to squash any resistance."

"Are you sure about that?"

"Of course! It's the most peaceful approach."

"Reasonable, maybe. A peaceful approach would be to establish an alliance or propose a treaty where we leave each other alone."

A few people snickered at the notion before a lull fell over the group. During the pause, one of the older ladies shared a piece of information a bit hesitantly.

"There's talk of an arranged marriage to create an alliance."

"His Highness wouldn't dare wed a Nim-Valan," a hefty brunette in a maroon dress muttered loudly enough for those nearby to hear.

Most of the room agreed, though Grace steadily dismissed the conversation afterward when it devolved into whose daughter would be the most heartbroken should the king marry another woman.

Aaron did not appear bothered by the idea when he mentioned his mother's intentions, she recalled. *I am sure he has always understood that is what would happen. Still, I wonder if he feels the same way I do about his options. Does he care about his potential suitors aside from their positions and appearances?*

While she contemplated what her friend might think of an arranged marriage to a Nim-Valan princess, she considered her own, conflicting emotions on the subject before a new idea dawned on her.

If he does not wish to wed someone from the northern country, would he consider...me? I am not too much younger, and we know each other well. From his perspective, he would be marrying to stabilize our peoples' alliance, and I would be forging a bond with royalty. Mother and Father could not possibly consider removing me from Asteom then, and Aaron and I could live our normal lives with one less concern.

The more she considered the concept, the better she felt about the proposal until she wished for nothing else in that moment than to share it with her friend. Imagining his relief and encouragement lifted her spirits, and she grew confident in herself for the first time in months.

*

Although her mood improved, Grace eventually grew weary of the sitting room when the ladies began discussing the idea of a ball in the palace in order to flaunt the capital's young women to the heir. She believed Aaron would hate the notion based on his previous behavior at the private dinners, yet an event like that could allow her to share her suggestion of an arranged marriage between Asteom's king and a member of Yeluthia's royal blood line. If she couldn't find him before the group's anticipated gathering took place, she vowed she would use it to speak with him.

The excitement allowed her to slip into the hallway unnoticed where she decided to get some fresh air. Plenty of people had moved outside throughout the afternoon, filling the backyard with pairs and trios engaging in their own conversations. As she wandered around the area, Grace spotted Emilea's white sundress and instinctively shifted to head in that direction.

Three others stood around the master mage, and she soon recognized Coura and Marcy beside a third, dark-haired woman. When Emilea noticed her, the rest turned to look at the newcomer before smiling as Grace joined them.

"You finally stepped out of the house," Coura commented with a smirk. "I don't know how you can tolerate being in there for more than a minute or two."

"I suppose my years of practice are the reason," she responded and returned the grin. Then, her eyes drifted to the stranger in their group.

Emilea noticed her gaze shift. "Have you met Lydia? She's Byron's primary assistant, basically his second-in-command."

Grace curtsied and introduced herself, to the dark mage's chagrin.

Lydia was not pretty by any means, and her boney figure suggested she'd never held a tool or weapon in her life; however, she seemed friendly and proved her intelligence during their following conversation about the newer training ground. She then inquired about the Yeluthians' transition to living in the dormitory building, a subject Grace had answered multiple times over the past couple weeks.

"I must say, listening to you talk about your work in the palace is far more entertaining than the majority of what the noblewomen like to chat about," Marcy added with a shake of her head. "They're nice people, but sometimes…"

"It becomes a bit dull?" Emilea finished for her.

"Immensely!"

While the two laughed, Coura rolled her eyes, though Lydia offered a sympathetic smile.

"It is not all boring," Grace felt compelled to mention as she remembered the final topic in the sitting room before she took her leave.

The three sets of eyes stared at her, as if expecting her to elaborate. She opened her mouth to do so, yet she grew inexplicably shy about mentioning arranged marriages, especially since it had been prompted by the ladies' conversation on Nim-Vala.

"They would like to organize a ball," she said instead without fully committing to the response.

"Another one?" Emilea asked and tilted her head. "After what took place last time, I wonder why?"

"I suppose it's because the nobility weren't involved with that," Coura added before Lydia expressed her agreement.

"Only we mages could sense the malicious presence, and even fewer people understood who had been behind the problem."

Marcy began giggling and put a hand over her mouth. "Sorry, but it's really not that serious. Katrina and her friends seem to be bored and are hoping for an excuse to stir drama by making it about King Aaron. They've been toying with it for weeks."

Coura raised an eyebrow, but Lydia voiced the next question. "What do you mean?"

"With the conflict to the north and an increase in demonic creatures to the south, they like to distract themselves by fantasizing about a grand wedding. Many have daughters or relatives around his age, so they'll continue throwing suitors at him until he decides to marry."

Grace nodded to show her agreement for the reasoning, causing Emilea to scoff.

"It really is a game to these people," the master mage commented. "I suppose that's one condition for royalty: You never can avoid being the center of attention."

A pause followed her words.

"Perhaps he likes it," Marcy added with a hint of mischief. "He has the authority to choose anybody to wed, even a commoner. The men I used to know craved that kind of power over others, even their own family members. This presents the perfect opportunity to manipulate those around him."

The harsh notion startled Grace. She prepared to defend her friend, but Coura spoke first.

"Aaron isn't like that. Anybody who thinks otherwise is just plain ignorant."

When no one responded, she crossed her arms and looked away, though her cheeks appeared slightly heated. Grace decided the reply sounded like enough to put the doubt to rest and dismissed her previous urge to argue; however, she caught Emilea and Marcy share a look.

What is going on?

"Are you ready to head back to the palace?" Coura asked Lydia, who also seemed confused by the shift in the conversation.

The dark mage nodded, so the two congratulated Marcy once more before departing from the garden. Grace considered leaving as well until she heard the remaining women snicker.

"You were right," Marcy told Emilea at a lower volume. "I didn't imagine it would be so obvious."

"What would be obvious?" Grace chimed in. She didn't feel comfortable being on the outside of their joking, but when Emilea explained the cause of their reaction, she wished she remained oblivious.

"Those two have been enamored with each other for a while. Marcy and Katrina didn't believe me."

"You do not mean…"

"In any case, it's their business," the master mage stated, yet her lingering smile revealed her amusement. "I'm not going to waste time worrying about them."

Grace went cold and excused herself to wander inside and through the entryway where she began to return to the palace alone.

Coura has feelings for Aaron, and he reciprocates them? I suppose I never considered this because of their differing lives. Then again, I rarely see them together anymore. This should not mean much since he is royalty and she is a soldier.

Despite the facts, she found herself wondering if she could continue with her plan to discuss an arranged marriage with Aaron in order to save herself from the future her parents lined up for her in Yeluthia.

If he chooses Coura, I will be forced back to my kingdom and into a life I would not be happy living. Aaron understands this, so I refuse to panic until I am able to speak with him. Right now, that is my only option.

The Inner Circle

The capital of Nim-Vala had only ever been referred to as such by the townsfolk in Muld and by Finn until he and Will reached its enormous gate, then the spy called it the inner circle. The wall surrounding its perimeter consisted of bricks the size of a person's head stacked one after the other in a sturdy fashion to stand over four stories high, making it the tallest building Will had ever laid eyes on. The grayish coloring proved to be a testament to its lengthy history, one that had him interested in the city's founding.

As the pair passed through the metal doors cracked just enough to let a horse-drawn cart through, the walls followed them for a few steps before ending, as if to emphasize its capability to stand firm against any opponent. The guards inside proved to be just as imposing with bodies that reminded him of plow oxen packed into Nim-Vala's black uniforms. Will wasn't able to distinguish one from the other because their features appeared to be the same: inky hair combed back and tied at the nape of their necks, beards trimmed to their chests, eyes stretched enough to prevent their color from being identified, and skin lacking any color, presumably from being under the structure all day.

I wonder if their people think everyone from Asteom looks the same, he mused while Finn spoke on their behalf to the man posted behind a wooden booth of sorts littered with papers. Some words were discernible, but most became lost due to their back and forth conversation. At last, Finn gestured for Will to follow, and they continued forward onto the main street.

The sheer wave of noise distracted him for a minute. Animals in pens or cages vocalized their discomfort or lack of attention while their owners tried to match the volume by shouting at everyone who passed by. Farther inside, the farmers and vendors either hosted a booth to display their wares or laid a blanket on the ground instead. The environment felt odd to Will; however, he didn't get a moment to soak in his surroundings since Finn continued at a brisk pace without giving anything a second glance.

When they reached the buildings, the Nim-Valan finally slowed, and only because the people around them moved leisurely in carriages or on foot while wearing the gowns and suits of the rich. This area reminded him of the western main road in Verona with its luxurious gardens, expansive homes, and enticing aromas, though he noted two differences.

Firstly, and most noticeable, instead of being limited to a district the homes and their lawns practically overlapped with one another and spread into the road. Will waited for them to reach the end of that section, yet the end never came. In fact, he saw the grass expanding as they went on.

His second observation related to a lack of gates or fences to provide any sort of protection against intruders. He caught men who appeared to be guards standing watch just outside the paths leading to the widest buildings, but other than that, the area remained open to the public.

Will attempted to figure out the reasoning until Finn startled him by pivoting to turn onto a cobblestone walkway toward one of the estates. This home displayed a spear-bearing guard, who merely nodded to Finn once the two came into view. The Nim-Valan spy's posture suggested he was familiar with the place, so Will keep his head down to avoid appearing too out of place.

Once they stepped inside, all pretense of composure melted away.

Decorated walls showcasing paintings matching the dining hall in Asteom's palace adorned every surface against a polished, wooden floor. On side tables sat vases and metal artifacts whose hints of gold and silver caught the eye despite the lavish art surrounding them. Farther ahead, several openings teased rooms beyond.

This is just the entrance? Will thought in disbelief.

In seconds, he became too preoccupied with studying the space, so his feet slowed instead of keeping up with Finn. A gentle bump against his right shoulder abruptly returned his mind to his body. He glanced in that direction to see a young woman draped in furs down to the ground. Her raven hair had some sort of product in it to press the locks down against her head in a sleek manner, which matched the slender body barely visible underneath the exterior, dark coat.

While Will's mouth hung open, she shot daggers at him before hissing what he assumed to be an insult, then she asked who he was and what he was doing there. He clamped his jaw shut, considered how to respond and if he could even pass as one of their people, and hesitated to reveal information to the stranger.

Thankfully, a hand fell on his shoulder, and he heard Finn's voice a second later. Will understood part of the reply, but the key words remained a mystery. The woman said something along the lines of, "Keep the rabbit away from me," before raising her chin and spiriting herself out the front door. His guide moved through the nearest opening after, preventing him from learning what the exchange had been about.

Every room Will saw after proved to be similar in design. The pair didn't notice any other people, though Finn kept in front and consistently glanced in every direction. Soon, the Nim-Valan stopped in front of a chestnut-colored door, and after a brief survey to confirm they were still alone, he addressed Will in Asteom's language at no louder than a mumble.

"We're here. Through this door is your patient. I can stay to assist you, but don't speak until I give you permission."

"Why not?" Will asked just as quietly.

Finn frowned, yet his brown eyes danced with amusement. "The woman you ran into is the daughter of the administrator, his second child. This is their home, though we shouldn't encounter anyone else. The administrator spends most of his time in the king's company and his wife with her fellow ladies. Their firstborn child is who you will be treating. None of the servants wish to be near the illness; however, the rumor is that it only affects certain people. Besides the one waiting inside, it'll just be us."

Upon hearing the fragments of information, Will's nerves jumped. "That doesn't explain why I can't talk. Is it because of my accent?"

"Partly. Mostly because I told her you couldn't hear, so communicating is tough."

There it was, the lie Will would need to build upon if he was to keep his true identity hidden.

He released a frustrated sigh in response. "Fine, but be prepared for a lot of gestures. I don't know what to do if they don't have the proper medicines."

Finn left his comment at that in favor of opening the door. Unlike the other rooms, this one seemed simple by comparison. The walls had been left plain white, the floor looked scuffed, and the wooden furniture appeared worn and chipped in various, noticeable places. In a bed wide enough for two people, a figure lied covered by a fluffy quilt up to his neck. His face had grown nearly as white as the walls, though shadows under the eyes and the pink flush of his cheeks contrasted the paleness.

At their entrance, a woman in a charcoal-colored dress popped up from one of two chairs placed at the bedside. "Finn, you're back!" she exclaimed with enough emotion to convince Will she was being genuine.

Finn's behavior also supported that theory, as he outstretched both arms to embrace her.

"I'm sorry," she muttered, face buried in his chest. "My lord is getting worse with each passing day. I tried what you suggested, but…"

"Who knows what could have happened if you weren't here for him," Finn replied with more sincerity than Will had ever heard the Nim-Valan use. "I brought a medicine man who may be able to help."

The two broke apart so Finn could introduce him and explain his pronounced lack of hearing. In accordance with that facade, Will stared at them as though he were curious what they said. The woman gave him a shy wave, then she addressed Finn again.

"If he begins to feel ill, call for me at once."

"Of course." After a kiss on her forehead, Finn dismissed her.

Will considered what their relationship might be as he watched the door close behind the woman.

"Since we're practically alone in here, just keep your voice down," came a request that forced him to focus on their situation.

If this illness doesn't affect everybody who comes in contact with it, I would assume she and Finn are safe. I should monitor myself too, just in case.

Will crossed the room to stand over his patient with a critical eye. Diagnosing the problem became one of his areas of expertise over the years, so he planned on taking charge immediately. He started by asking Finn general questions about the man in order to analyze if any daily activities could be behind the illness.

His new assistant revealed his patient's name, which was Yukin, and that the man was in his late twenties. Yukin's father had been training him to act as one of the king's advisors, and outside of that, the young lord spent most of his free time reading in the garden and painting.

Next, Will narrowed his questions down to Yukin's condition. Finn answered them all with an odd sense of confidence, stating the man began with symptoms of a head cold, such as a fever and coughing, then a pain arose in his joints, leaving him unable to stand for long periods of time. Lastly, he lost his appetite and fell asleep for most of the day.

Will filed these characteristics away before beginning a physical examination. What he found perplexed him.

"Can you tell what's wrong?" Finn inquired afterward when Will returned to his chair to contemplate his results.

"Yes, or at least partly," he hesitated to share. "Back in Asteom, there's a sickness in the east called wind lung. Because the area is flat, the people living there face strong winds and often dust storms when the ground is dry enough. Those forced to work outside during these storms are exposed to the dry, dirt-filled air, and when it enters their lungs, they get infections. That is some of what I'm seeing here."

"How is it treated?" Finn practically demanded with a longing in his voice.

Will shook his head, let his eyes drop to his hands, and paused.

"There isn't a cure?"

"Every instance I'm familiar with has been treated by a light mage."

At that, Finn fell silent.

Will inhaled a shaky breath and prepared to face his main limitation once more. "A healing mage has the ability to use their energy as they would a sort of sensory organ and feel what is wrong within the patient's body. Then, they can correct the issue. When they train, they study how to go about doing that, whether through burning away an infection or easing a fever and so on. With issues like this that aren't familiar to me, I'm going in blindly, except for hints I gather from the outside."

"Can't you treat one symptom at a time until they're all gone?" the Nim-Valan asked next.

Finn's lack of understanding made Will rub his right temple in an attempt to stay patient. "I would assume that's what that woman tried before. The problem is, unless the major issues are resolved, we would essentially be pulling leaves off a weed instead of digging it up at the roots. If the source isn't stopped, it can continue to produce more symptoms until..." He caught himself before he could finish the sentence. "Anyway, that's where I'm going to start."

***

As he leaned against the brick siding of Clearshot and Emilea's home, Byron gazed upward to soak in the rays of sunlight that found their way through the cloud-filled sky. The end of summer had always been his favorite time of the year because of its beauty, warmth, and tendency to linger through the first couple weeks in fall. That day started out better than he imagined given his tight schedule to return to the palace before the next council meeting and need to leave Cintra alone once again.

The home's owners left a day earlier and were familiar enough with the seer to trust the property to her while they went away during that brief amount of time. Byron spent the past three nights outside Verona as well and would be escorting Cintra to the road splitting south while he followed its opposite end north toward the capital.

Their relationship hadn't devolved since they admitted their true feelings for each other; if anything, he became more comfortable with her as a lover than a friend, but her dual, conflicting desires threatened to tear him apart whenever either brought them up. To his relief, the front door opened then to prevent him from diving into that subject.

"Sorry to keep you waiting," Cintra apologized as she closed the door, locked it behind her with a silver key, and walked over to hand the item to Byron, who promised Emilea he would return it at their meeting that afternoon.

He slipped the metal into his pocket before readjusting the pack hanging off his shoulder and offering an elbow. "We'll make decent time if nothing interrupts us."

The genuinely sweet smile resulting from his words projected a sense of ease to melt his heart. Some of that emotion was due to Byron's complaining the previous evening about having to hurry in the morning, but he figured she hoped to avoid a grueling trek considering her only pair of shoes were heeled boots unsuited for an arduous journey.

She accepted his arm, shifted the bag she carried along her back, and the two took off on a leisurely stroll through the woods.

"You really couldn't ask for a better day," she commented once they left the reddish building behind. "The weather around here isn't so different from Fester, but sometimes it gets so blazing hot that all I long for is to sit in a cool pond during the afternoon."

"That's why I enjoy staying in the north during the summer months. Even East Hoover had been more forgiving than Fester."

"Which city would you prefer to live in?" she asked in a carefully neutral tone.

Byron attempted a smile, though he sensed what direction their conversation was heading in. Somehow, a subject as simple as the weather always brought them back to their problems. "It's hard to say considering I taught for years in one, work my current job in another, and entertain a partner in the third."

The only sounds for a while were the chirping birds and rustling in the canopy.

"I enjoy Verona," she continued at last. "There's plenty of activity, and so much to do and see. The festivals you brought me to were lovely. I wouldn't mind…"

Byron bit his lip when she ended that sentence, then he listened as she began talking about a new topic.

I introduced Cintra to the city through dozens of visits, and Emilea does the same when she has the time, he reflected with half his attention on the woman beside him. *Still, she's plagued by that vision and fears it will bring about her death, even though she entered the grand hall twice now. Nothing happened, but nothing has changed. I suppose I would be paranoid too if I possessed foresight and couldn't see anything but that scene whenever I tried looking into the future. It's difficult to remain patient when our life together is right over the horizon.*

Around the noon hour, the pair saw the split in the road up ahead populated by travelers and animal-pulled carts, signaling their departure from one another. Some people passed them in both directions when they approached and stopped just before parting. Cintra stared at him with her gem-like, blue eyes as the wind played with her unbound hair; in that moment, she appeared perfect to him. He had seen that image many times over the past year, yet each time he experienced it, he cherished it more than the last.

"You should stay," he blurted out without considering the words.

The sapphires' shine dimmed, and she dipped her head. "You know I would if it were safe."

"You *will* be safe with me. I love you, Cintra. Nothing can come between that."

"I know," she practically interrupted while shaking her head. "I love you too, but my visions have never been wrong."

Byron paused, recalled what she had told him about it on multiple occasions, and tried a reassuring smile. "You believe what you saw takes place inside the palace, correct? You could live in the city without ever stepping foot into it alone."

"What about you?" she countered. A crooked smile revealed her bitterness. "Would you sacrifice the luxury of the palace to be with me? What if you retire from being Master Byron Rinod for a simple, safer life?"

This time, it was his turn to glance downward to avoid her gaze. She heard enough of him defending that position, as well as the people he cared about in the capital who relied on his abilities and insight. To repeat the sentiment would serve no other purpose than to leave them both feeling worse about the situation.

Byron pressed his lips to Cintra's a moment later until she broke away for a final embrace, then they went their separate ways. It took about half a day to reach Verona from the woods, and he spent the remainder of the time alone considering the future they desired.

It's not fair for me to demand so much of her without being willing to sacrifice a part of myself. I understand that; however, the only part I can offer is my time, which would involve retiring as the palace's master mage.

The idea didn't concern him as much as he thought it would. *Lydia is doing a fine job taking on the responsibilities I assign to her. In fact, she's done just about every task I normally do except attend the king's council meetings and the additional work derived from those discussions. Would she be willing to shadow me from now on to prepare for... It's too soon to try for this afternoon's meeting, but I would like to hear her opinion on assuming the full responsibility and transitioning into the role.*

For how smooth and relaxing the first half of the day had been, the latter proved to be chaotic and challenged Byron's patience. He expected the council meeting to stretch through the evening meal since their main priority would be to figure out what to do about Nim-Vala, an item Aaron tabled until even Byron knew they were stalling for far too long.

What startled him, and frankly irritated him beyond belief, was the addition of several noblemen he didn't know too well who all seemed keen on being involved with the conversation regarding a potential war. Their lack of factual information showed when the king recapped where Asteom stood with soldiers along the border. Then, he opened the floor for suggestions. The newcomers took turns offering different perspectives on the same idea: attack Nim-Vala before they strike again.

Byron vowed to prevent any rash decisions until the council received a break to consider the details thoroughly while he listened for new information. The one piece General Casner let slip happened to be that he received a response from their spies across the border about a revolution of sorts spreading from the northern half of Nim-Vala. With every opinion laid out in the circle, the room quieted so each individual could contemplate the options.

Essentially, what these people want is for Asteom to send troops across the border while their country is preoccupied with the conflict to the north, Byron concluded and scratched his chin. *The only result I can discern from that course of action would be to challenge them. We wouldn't be going over for resources or to take and hold land for any reason other than to provoke a war. Justice for the victims who were killed in General Casner's company shouldn't be the priority considering the consequences of adding pressure along the border.*

Aaron echoed those thoughts before motioning to continue holding the border and wait for more news from Nim-Vala. All except three of the noblemen agreed. While the discussion turned elsewhere, Byron noticed the king's lack of energy or real investment in what was being said after.

The generals mentioned the positive feedback they received for the newest additions to the palace, then everyone shared their enthusiasm for the Yeluthians' participation in the scouting routes across Asteom. General Casner mentioned the demonic creatures appearing to the south and General Tio's name, but nobody felt the need to do more than they already had been doing for the Dalan base. Finally, around the time when Byron's stomach began to tighten with hunger to signal the end of the meeting, one of the noblemen threw in a comment no one expected.

"Your Highness, the people are growing nervous about Nim-Vala to the north and demonic creatures to the south," the lanky man drawled as he leaned forward with eyes set on Aaron. "What would you say to offering them some reprieve?"

For the first time that afternoon, Aaron showed interest with a raised eyebrow. "What do you mean, Lord Jacov?"

"Well, the people could use an event to distract them from their fears, just as the festivals help keep morale up throughout the year. Until the Harvest Festival, they will be toiling away under the shadow of conflict."

The nobility like to dance around the subject like wolves baiting their prey, Byron observed and frowned.

He wasn't the only one to notice.

"Get on with it," General Tont grumbled and swept his hand around the table. "The rest of us would like to eat before sundown."

Lord Jacov apologized yet held an unbothered expression as he leaned back. "Have you given any more thought to a wedding, Your Highness?"

Although Aaron didn't visibly show emotion at the question, Byron figured it took all of the young man's self-control not to roll his eyes. Whenever the notion had been brought up in the past, he immediately dismissed it for other matters he deemed to be far more important.

"I appreciate your concern, but now isn't the time to be planning a celebration when we're on the cusp of a war," he answered, to no one's surprise.

Still, the lord pursued. "Of course, but what I mean to suggest is not so personal. You see, the citizens are in need of encouragement. They could use a national event to strengthen their patriotism, and what better way to do that than to flaunt our alliance with the angelic race?"

"You mean to suggest an arranged marriage with a Yeluthian?" Emilea was the first to ask.

The man shrugged. "Why not? Asteom is more familiar with their kind now than we have been in decades. People from all across the country see angels flying above to protect our land. We should be united."

"You also intend for that excuse to encourage pride in Asteom in case of a war," General Garvish added, though not with malice.

"I prefer to utilize every part of a hunted animal. Let nothing go to waste that we can't use for our benefit. Isn't that right, Your Highness?"

While Aaron appeared to be contemplating this, High Priest Jurek hesitantly raised a hand.

"The preparations will take weeks to arrange, especially choosing the bride from afar. We would need King Arval's input and permission as well."

"I can recommend several individuals whose daughters assist in their kingdom's business," the lord offered.

Byron suppressed the urge to scoff. *Of course he's familiar with those who hold power in Yeluthia. I'd be shocked if they didn't promise him a reward for setting one of their daughters up with a king.*

"What about the ambassador?" General Garvish proposed next. "She's around the same age and has been living in Verona for long enough to know our customs. Besides, you two were friends before the late King Hernan's passing. What could be more perfect than-"

"That's enough," Aaron interrupted at a lower volume but with a firm tone. "I will consider what you all presented today relating to Asteom, Nim-Vala, and Yeluthia. Are there any final items to discuss?"

No one answered, so he dismissed the meeting. Steadily, the chamber emptied, though Byron was one of the last to leave despite his appetite. Part of him lingered on their final topic with the curiosity of an old hen.

I always assume business outweighs personal pleasures, yet after today I believe there's more to Aaron's indirect refusal of an arranged marriage. Lord Jacov proposed a fair argument. I see no reason for King Arval to turn down the proposition in order to unify the people during a time of conflict, and Grace is the best option given the location and their relationship. If anyone else occupied the throne, this would be settled already.

That comment answered his question regarding the king's hesitation, reminding him of Aaron's continued infatuation with a particular person.

Another royal figure would be married by now to get the ceremony out of the way or because both parties are willing to go through with it. I try not to pry in his or Coura's lives, but Emilea fills me in on what I miss. The real concern is if their relationship is destined to go further than doe-eyed infatuation. I trust Aaron to assume his position above all else, and I want to trust that Coura will understand too, but they're so young. Besides, if she accepts Commander Detrix's offer to become a Yeluthian soldier, she could be sent anywhere. The wife of a king is never expected to do much other than make appearances. That could be why I'm so nervous; a life stuck inside the palace walls, dressed up, and mingling with people would be torture for her.

Naturally, Byron's stomach led him to the dining hall while his mind had been distracted. Although he planned to bring the meal to his room, a group of dark mages gestured for him to join them at their table. The idle conversation sounded simple enough to participate in, postponing the internal strife he used to project his own troubles.

***

Terrell proved to be busy enough that Coura needed to schedule a time to meet through the man's assistant general in order to discuss Commander Detrix's offer. In her eyes, becoming a member of the Yeluthian's company while staying an Asteom soldier remained an option as the angels were being permanently stationed in Verona and across the country. That had been the most prominent factor when it came to reaching a decision.

I will only accept Detrix's offer if I can continue to live in Asteom, she concluded after contemplating what she desired most. *The alliance brought us together, and I consider myself proof of that. There's no reason to tear me away from my home either, especially since I know this place better than any of them. If King Arval wants his soldiers stationed here for the future, why would he pull me away from being part of that change?*

When the day came to meet with her supervising general, Coura explained all this. Terrell listened without interrupting, though she sensed his mind wandering elsewhere. He accepted her offer to remain a soldier between his troops and the Yeluthians' and didn't bring up any questions or potential conflicts, leaving her to wonder if he simply dismissed her in order to save time instead of attempting to fully understand the situation.

In whatever case, she would freely share his verdict with Detrix so the commander could decide based on Asteom's authority over her position. Given his lax attitude and their relationship over the past year and a half, she had little doubt he'd be upset.

Coura returned to her quarters afterward in order to craft a message for the Yeluthian commander. That way, he would be able to meet with her on his own time instead of dealing with her pestering. They were in no hurry to finalize the process, so why bother him more than necessary.

As she stepped inside her room, Coura noticed a slip of paper under her foot and picked it up before closing the door. Only one person had letters delivered to her room because he was unable to roam alone anymore, or he never had the time.

If you're free this afternoon, I'd like to see you in the garden. - Aaron

She tossed the parchment into the nightstand drawer to join several others like it, released a long, nervous sigh, then left for the eastern side of the palace.

With Marcus now in Dala under General Tio's command, Aaron often sent for her when he needed to talk or escape from his responsibilities. Sometimes their meetings proved to be a pleasant experience reminiscent of their first year as friends. Conversations remained casual, they joked with each other, and she felt no pressure to make a positive impression on him; however, the king of Asteom recently began showing a romantic interest in her more often, and Coura wasn't certain how to handle the attention.

I'll never regret kissing him first, she reflected as she descended the stairs and moved out into the queen's garden. *I care about him immensely, but in a different way than I do about anyone else, like I have a responsibility to ensure his physical and mental well-being. Is that what a serious relationship entails?*

Whenever she acknowledged those emotions, Coura's chest tightened and her breath shortened with an anxiousness stemming from both fear and elation.

I also can't forget the fact that Aaron's royalty...

Before Coura could dive into the messier side of their relationship, she reached the opposite end of the garden where only the king and his invited guests were allowed. Two guards stood in front of the lone entrance, and they bowed their heads while she passed by. Internally, she wondered if anybody cared how close the two were becoming.

Aaron knelt in front of one of the dirt patches with a miniature shovel in hand and a sack of flower bulbs at his side. He wore tan, patched-up clothing similar to those the servants used, which told Coura all she needed to know.

"The ground must be soft enough for planting," she commented and took a seat at the nearby bench.

He continued digging and turning over the soil for a few minutes, then he rose, stretched, and brushed the dust off his pants before facing her with a tired smile. In that moment, he appeared as nothing more than an ordinary gardener. "I wouldn't say it's ideal, but the sooner I attempt to till the surface, the less work I'll need to put in later."

Coura nodded and continued to observe his progress on that particular spot. Ever since his mother's death and the public opening of the garden, he assumed full responsibility of managing the private area only available to him and his guests. She figured Aaron wished to honor the late queen's memory by keeping this part supervised by someone in the royal family. If he ever requested assistance, she wasn't aware of it.

They started a conversation after, and Coura soon shared the news about Commander Detrix's offer, as well as General Terrell's approval for her to join and still remain part of his troops. Aaron's reaction seemed similar to Byron's in that they both paused with neither enthusiasm nor disapproval and moved on from the subject.

It really is my decision then, she realized. *My guess is they're worried what they do or how they respond will impact that.*

When their talk died down, Aaron finished the section he worked on, set the tools aside, and stood to observe his progress. "I've never tended to anything like this before," he commented absently with his back to her.

Coura smiled while recalling how she heard him mention that multiple times over the years, but she didn't reply right away. He continued looking over the area, so she moved to go to his side and inspect the dirt.

"You could have fooled me. In fact, you should settle for gardening instead of ruling an entire country."

He laughed at her sarcasm before tilting his head to stare at her. "I did have a purpose for requesting you join me here that didn't involve your compliments on planting flowers."

Coura sensed the direction of their next conversation and glanced away. "Really?"

"Yes, but I hate to admit I'm a bit terrified to bring it up."

Here it comes…

Her heart beat faster when he turned to face her, prompting her to do the same; however, she found herself eager to discuss their relationship instead of dismayed.

"It's no secret I believe you are one of the most amazing people I've met in my life, as well as one of the only women who acts sensible around me."

She raised an eyebrow at that but restrained a retort requesting him to clarify what he meant. It felt obvious by his vulnerable expression that he was utilizing their developed friendship to speak openly, so she refused to judge him for it.

After a pause, he went on at a lower volume. "I hoped you would be here today so I could ask how you feel about me, because if I'm being honest, I believe I'm in love with you."

Coura's eyes widened a bit in alarm, yet her lips instinctively stretched into a smile and her cheeks heated into a blush. A hand flew up to cover her mouth as she glanced away, mostly because she considered how ridiculously giddy she probably appeared. Despite that chagrin, the instant, genuine joy sparked by his confession shed a light on her own uncertainty from earlier.

"I love you too, Aaron. I think I have for a while, but I wasn't-"

Before she could bumble a response, he wrapped his arms around her to pull her into a tight embrace, which she returned a second later. A new warmth filled her chest and remained even after Aaron broke away while continuing to keep her hands in his.

"You don't know how glad I am right now," he commented and chuckled weakly.

Coura squeezed his hands, as if to convey how the positive sensation was mutual. For those precious minutes, her world seemed perfect.

"Now that the worst part is over, there's something I need to tell you," he continued, albeit in a bashful manner.

"What else is there?"

"I've been meaning to do that for a while, but I never felt prepared for your answer. I would have waited longer if it wasn't for the members of my council. They're pressuring me to find a wife, and…"

Coura's smile faltered when he hesitated. "What are you talking about?"

"Since I'm king, they're hoping to secure the throne in case anything were to happen to me. I can't blame them because of what took place in the past, but the ladies and their mothers must be aware of this. They're pestering me more than they ever did. If I hear about how my father already married when he was my age, I think I'll cry." Although he meant the final sentence as a joke, his resulting wince didn't sell it.

Coura released his hands and stepped away as the nerves returned. Dozens of thoughts swarmed her mind, causing her to doubt the moment they shared earlier. *Marriage? Securing the throne? Is that all this is?*

Either Aaron realized how incoherent his words sounded or he noticed her uncomfortable behavior, for his expression grew concerned. "I do love you. That's the truth."

"Then, what's the rest?"

He paused before answering. "I intended to warn you about what being together with me entails. Our relationship is special, so I'd like to maintain and develop it together. In order for that to happen, you can't expect it to remain a secret."

"Why bring up the ladies and marriage?" Coura asked next.

"Because I've seen what desperate women will do. They threw themselves at my father to further their own interests, even after he married my mother. Hiding my feelings in public gives them every reason to pursue me. Besides, I would like to marry you, and before you respond, just know I spent the past couple years considering it. I wouldn't make such an important decision without understanding what it involves."

As Coura continued to stare at Aaron, a heavy weight fell on her shoulders at his off-putting proposal. While he realized his feelings for her and spent time evaluating the details, she acted on a whim without bothering to reflect on what he had to face. She became embarrassed by her seemingly premature confession and ashamed by her inability to commit despite the implications. This left her certain of two things: Aaron deserved a fully thought-out response for both his pride as a royal leader and as her friend, and she needed to figure out what kind of life she wanted.

"I can't give you an answer," Coura admitted and met his hopeful gaze. "It wouldn't be fair to you for me to accept right now with how sudden this is."

"I understand."

His following, downcast expression cut at her heart, yet she forced herself to stay firm in her explanation. With as much dignity and sympathy as she could manage, Coura closed the space between them, raised a hand to his cheek, and pressed her lips against his in their familiar, parting gesture. Then, she took her leave of the garden.

*

That evening, Coura planned to deliver her written message to Detrix's quarters, and possibly discuss the offer in person; however, one of his soldiers, a man she became familiar with during their scouting flights, stopped by her room before she had a chance to leave.

"It would seem we have another assignment," he informed her after they greeted one another. The Yeluthian handed over a folded set of papers that Coura began leafing through. "Dala still requests our aid in dealing with the demonic creatures plaguing the south, so the commander is sending a hand-picked squad to deal with the issue personally."

"Thank you for these," she replied when it was clear that was all he had been permitted to reveal at the moment.

The soldier gave a curt nod before turning on his heel and walking away amid the few people going about their own business. After closing the door, locking it, and tossing the papers on her desk, Coura dropped onto her bed to stare up at the ceiling.

I heard how frequent the sightings and attacks were for months, and from multiple people in the palace. Father mentioned once how King Arval sent some of his troops, but there must be more trouble than we originally thought. If there wasn't, Tio would be reluctant to ask for this much intervention from the capital. Could it be…that demon from the forest, Terran? I never doubted our encounter, yet after Detrix, Byron, Emilea, and their company found the source of some demonic creatures, the council put the subject to rest. Even though the scouting parties continue observing the woods across Asteom, I should have been persistent in proving the demon's existence. What if he is actually the cause of what's taking place now?

Another, forgotten notion crept forward from the back of her mind. *He said he wanted to use me, or rather, use whatever Soirée did to me for himself. I'm no closer to finding out what he meant now than I was before, though the Sie-Kie witch reminded me of my damaged center. I should make sure to explain to Detrix how I might end up being the demon's target. As much as I hate acting as bait, I can't think of another way to draw Terran out. Then again, until I figure out a solution to my problem, I'm essentially a target wherever I am, including in the palace.*

Coura sensed a headache approaching and closed her eyes as the seemingly endless trail around the demonic creatures' presence continued. The concern remained regarding her association with Aaron and if the source of the attacks would act through their interactions somehow. She then recalled how Hendal manipulated his way to power with Soirée's help and the possibility of him unwillingly accepting demonic energy as well. He would be a threat if her hunch proved true; however, without someone like the *shimla* and her ability, they couldn't tell.

Nothing in Verona requires my immediate attention, she decided in order to put the matter to rest for the time being. *I'm making assumptions based on nothing set in stone. Once we are in Dala and observe the situation, then we can go from there.*

A Second Encounter

The next three days of treating the ill man were brutal. It became apparent after the first night that Will arrived just in time, for Yukin's fever spiked and he shifted between wheezing and coughing to the point where Will needed to force several concoctions down his throat just to get him to relax into sleep again.

The following morning proved to be better, though he sent Finn into the city for ingredients the home didn't possess, and the Nim-Valan spent the morning and early afternoon explaining what could only be found in the northern country. Once they became organized, Yukin went through the same conditions as the night before, yet he took more time to settle down. While Finn slept in the chair at Yukin's bedside, Will stayed awake to mix medicines, hoping the similar ingredients would act like those he grew accustomed to using. As the hours passed, he had a rising suspicion tomorrow would be their final chance to save the man's life; that seemed to be enough motivation to keep him up until sunrise.

At Finn's urging, he slept for a couple hours, ate whatever food the woman waiting on them brought in, then tried his new potions. His mixtures went right when Yukin's eyes opened that afternoon.

"F-Finn?" he whispered as Will placed a cool rag on his forehead.

Will prepared to call the Nim-Valan over until he remembered his supposed lack of hearing and bit his lip.

Fortunately, Finn heard his name and rushed to kneel on the opposite side of the bed. "I'm here."

Yukin smiled weakly, obviously feeling the drugs' influence. "I…w-wasn't sure…where you w-were…"

"Sleep. We can catch up when you're well enough."

As if the words acted like a spell, Yukin's body relaxed, and his breathing eased.

Will released a sigh of relief when he felt certain the young lord slept. "That's a positive sign," he commented with his own smile at Finn.

The Nim-Valan appeared doubtful, but Will grew tired and ready to accept whatever luck came their way. He instructed his new assistant on what medicines to give when and how to change the cooling rag before slouching in the chair for a well-earned nap.

*

What he intended to be a brief rest ended up lasting until sunrise the next morning. Will regretted his position as every part of his body above his waist ended up stiff or sore, and he yawned before standing to stretch. Their patient remained asleep with steadier breaths and more color in his face while Finn had left the room.

When the sun fully rose, the Nim-Valan returned bearing a tray full of customary breakfast foods, such as hard-boiled eggs, buttered bread, and sliced fruit. Will ate his fill while Finn moved to sit at the bedside and decided to make conversation once he felt satisfied.

"How was he last night?"

"Better. He's more talkative and coughs less."

Will covered another yawn, rose, and took up the other chair. "I'm glad to hear that. At this rate, he should be able to get up and walk around in a couple days, which will strengthen the muscles in his legs."

Finn's eyes never left Yukin's face, but he dipped his head to acknowledge the assessment.

Something about his behavior ever since he visited Geneva left Will wondering about the man's past. He couldn't be more than a few years older, yet the old caretaker claimed he had been aiding Asteom citizens by bringing them across the border to start a new life. While they were together and unlikely to be interrupted, Will figured he could try his luck and see what the Nim-Valan would reveal.

"How do the people here view you?" he began, hoping the question didn't sound too personal.

It didn't spur a reaction. "What do you mean?"

"In Asteom, and even Muld, I heard the people in the capital are self-centered, focusing on their own lives and property instead of working to better the rest of the country. You don't seem like them is what I mean, and you gave no impression you're nobility. Is your master someone in the inner circle, or perhaps the lord of this house?"

Part of Will didn't expect a reply considering the information he requested could hinder the spy's duties, so it didn't surprise him when the space fell silent for long enough that he gave up and prepared to switch topics.

"Am I allowed outside this room?" he asked next. In the few days since they arrived, the only areas Will had been permitted to enter were Yukin's room and the lavatory one door over. Needless to say, he was due for a proper wash and fresh air.

At that, Finn stirred. "Let me escort you to the bathhouse and pick up new clothes. After, I can show you the garden area."

Will expected the aforementioned bathhouse to be private and as luxurious as the rest of the house, perhaps with heated water instead of the cooler river and well water he had used for the past year and a half. His wish was granted as the pair moved through an enclosed walkway with stone walls at the back of the estate to enter a steam-filled, humid room. A metal tub wide enough to seat Will four times comfortably stood above the ground to occupy most of the space. A meticulously crafted rock divider surrounded it, creating a circular bench where a handful of towels had been scattered around. The only other furniture appeared to be a standing shelf filled with folded towels, bars of soap, and bottles containing various cleaning products.

"We got here at just the right time," Finn said once Will spent a moment absorbing his surroundings. "Lady Chila prefers to soak in the morning, and for at least an hour each time. I will send a servant to drain the tub and refill it with fresh water, then they will deliver clean clothes to match mine. That way you can blend in with the rest of the household."

The Nim-Valan returned the way they entered, and soon enough a boy around ten years old stumbled inside carrying a bucket in each arm. The steam emitting from them proved to be enough to make Will tremble with anticipation. Once the water was replaced and the servant gone, he procured a bar of soap and sank into the bath, savoring every second.

Time crept by before he realized the temperature grew tepid and the air clearer. The boy had left behind the promised outfit, and after drying off and changing, Will felt completely refreshed, albeit different in the thick, leather clothing.

Finn loomed nearby when he emerged and gestured for him to follow.

With the servants wandering around that day, he took no chances by making a stray sound. The pair wound up outside where an overcast sky reminded them of the fall season. Flowers from summer wilted, and the trees' leaves began to change shades. Underneath one tree, they sat in a pair of metal chairs and waited until no one could overhear their conversation.

"Now I can answer your questions," Finn started with an upward gaze. "I suppose you earned it."

"I don't need you to feel obligated to return the favor. Geneva told me that's not how you work."

The brown eyes met Will's as Finn focused on him, then the man shook his head helplessly. "That old woman; she's something else. I suppose she told you how we met?"

Will nodded. "You saved her from trouble in Asteom."

"It's a part of my responsibilities. That happened a year after I began patrolling the border. My master is someone close to the king who likes to know who enters and exits the country. Most of the time, it's no one important, but on rare occasions, an enemy tries to escape."

"You stop them then?"

"Not exactly. Nim-Vala's politics are based on who pleases those with more power. If my master possesses that information to use as leverage, they gain others' favor."

Will paused, uncertain if his next question would be answered. "Who is your master? I don't need to hear their name or any details, but why are you here if you don't serve the lord?"

Despite his worry, Finn seemed prepared to talk. "I pledged my services to an individual who wishes to better Nim-Vala's relationship with Asteom. I'm sure you learned about the inner circle, but it's notorious for lacking empathy when it comes to the rest of the country. The people here focus on their own lives and property instead of working to better Nim-Vala as a whole. You won't spot petty thieves or beggars because only the wealthy can afford to live here, and they earn their wealth through various means under the king and his advisors. If you noticed the lack of gates or locks, it's because the rich tempt others to commit crimes so those less fortunate can be caught and thrown out of the city. The current system favors the cunning and powerful, and I wish to change that. As for the second half of your question, I'm playing an upper servant. Those beneath me are not allowed to leave the property while I can utilize my free range of the city."

"What about when you go to the border?" Will pressed. "How do you get away from your duties here?"

This time, Finn contemplated how to respond while wearing his impassive expression. "It's possible because of Yukin. He took me on knowing who I am and grants me permission to leave when I need to."

"He believes in your cause that much?"

The Nim-Valan didn't answer and focused his attention elsewhere. "There's more you might become involved with if you stay. This illness is affecting numerous households and could even reach the palace. If someone finds out you're a fraud, it could jeopardize your life. Once Yukin is recovered, you have no obligation to remain in the inner circle."

Why he felt a desire to make that clear at the moment, Will didn't understand; however, those words signaled the end of their discussion. The two moved inside, returned to the nobleman's quarters, and found the caretaker preparing to leave as Yukin slept.

"Forgive me," the woman begged while showcasing an ecstatic smile. "My lord is recovering well thanks to the medicine man."

Her eyes locked on to Will before she mouthed words of gratitude. Then, Finn extended his hands for hers.

"Madaline, would you give us time for another checkup?"

The woman bobbed her head up and down. "Of course, Finn. Anything for you and your guest."

With that, she took her leave of the pair.

"You care about her a lot," Will commented without thinking while the Nim-Valan sat beside the lord.

"Madaline has become like a sister to me. We look out for each other, and she takes on my duties when I'm away."

Will prepared to respond when another voice, a gentle tenor about the same pitch as Finn's, joined the conversation in the Nim-Valan language.

"*That* has been far too often, you know."

Both Will and Finn turned to the supposedly sleeping figure. One of Yukin's eyes opened to stare at Finn a second later. Will threw a hand up to his mouth once he realized the lord would not only know he could hear, but also that he could speak Asteom's language, yet neither person paid him any mind.

"You're awake," Finn commented with more emotion than he ever showed.

Yukin pried open his other eye to reveal their darker color in between adjusting blinks. "Yes, because of your friend over there. Why don't you introduce me, then we can discuss what's taken place."

Finn waved for Will to approach, which he did without attempting to hide his sheepishness.

"This is Will. He's one of the refugees who crossed the border last year with the group I spoke to you about."

Although Yukin wasn't able to sit up yet, he extended a hand by way of greeting. "It's a pleasure. I'm sorry we had to meet under such circumstances."

"The pleasure is mine, My Lord," Will replied, figuring it would be in his best interest to act polite.

Yukin's eyes widened and fell on Finn again. "I'm surprised he has any personality left given how many days he spent with just you."

Finn's mouth parted to show how the comment startled him, prompting Will to cover a chuckle that drew the young lord's attention.

"Honestly, Finn lets his image bleed into his character too often."

He said something else Will couldn't readily translate, though it led to him and Finn laughing, so Will took it as a positive sign. After, Finn resumed control of the conversation.

"If you're well enough for introductions, you'll be well enough to obey the medicine man's orders. I needed to tell your sister he can't hear, or else she would have shrieked about his appearance."

"I see," Yukin replied in a thoughtful manner. His resulting smile looked kind and mischievous all wrapped in one. "That's for the best. Chila likes to toy with the new servants and flirt with any man possessing a pulse. It wouldn't take her long to realize you're not from Nim-Vala."

"With your permission, I wish to put Will in the guest room nearby, just in case," Finn interjected. "I already let him know about the illness spreading and gave him the option to stay or return to Muld."

Yukin addressed Will then. "Without a doubt, you are welcome. I'll obey your instructions until I am healthy enough to properly reward you for your service. Afterward, the decision to remain or not falls to you. As for the guest room, you will find it two doors down and to the left when you exit. If you need anything, there is a bell to ring, and Finn will be the one to answer. Otherwise, you are free to enter here when you need to."

Will thanked the young lord for his hospitality and repeated the daily medicine list to Finn since it seemed the Nim-Valan spy wasn't prepared to leave Yukin's side. "Come find me if his condition changes," he concluded.

When both Finn and Yukin agreed, he opened the door and slipped into the hallway; however, before he could close it all the way, he caught Yukin raise a hand, which Finn clasped and pressed to his lips. The two gazed at each other with such intimacy that Will found himself blushing while noiselessly closing the door.

He stood a bit stunned for a moment before walking to the guest room, entering, and lying on the bed. What he just witnessed proved enough to steal his thoughts away from the new, glittering atmosphere of another decorated space.

They're lovers?

Finn's determination to travel to the capital with an experienced healer and his resolve when working with Will all made sense once the two let their guards down. The idea of helping Yukin had never been political but personal, and he found himself smiling despite the slight unease their surprise raised.

*

Will wasn't needed until the next morning when Finn came to find him for a medicine restock. Even though nothing changed on the outside, he analyzed what the Nim-Valans did and said over the course of the day, adding few words otherwise. Neither addressed if he behaved any differently, and the two shared no personal moments for him to catch again.

While he stayed for the recovery period, several servants regularly became visible. Wherever the rest of the family lived, it didn't seem to be within that part of the estate. Eventually, Yukin could walk and did so inside until Will gave him permission to leave. The weather neared mid-fall, so the temperatures dropped harsher than usual, or at least to him, and Finn showed up in his quarters one afternoon to mention just that.

"Have you reached a decision?" the Nim-Valan asked as he toyed with a part of his sleeve. "Cooler weather leads to more sickness. Yukin will send you to others if you stay."

Will released a sigh, one drawn out enough to earn Finn's full attention, before answering. He spent the past week considering what remaining in the capital would mean and ultimately remembered Geneva's words. "How can I not when there are people who would die without my help?"

"You think about others too much. I've found that's an Asteom virtue: never turning down a person in need."

"I guess you're right." Will grinned. "Is that why you're always helping us? Because our traits are rubbing off on you?"

Although he meant the comment in jest, Finn's stoic expression led him to wonder if the Nim-Valan took it to heart.

"Don't consider this a request from anyone else. Your life is at risk by aiding people who might be all too willing to turn you in if your identity is discovered. I don't expect to be paid back for what I do, and when I ask a favor, it's not because somebody owes me. If you stay, I will protect you as best as I can, but your direction is your own choice."

Will bowed his head. "I understand and will be where I'm needed, under your watch."

Finn grunted in affirmation, as if he expected such an answer. "Come to Yukin's quarters when you are prepared to leave."

*

As far as Will knew, the illness the young lord overcame was the same as what spread around Nim-Vala's capital city. He requested a medicine bag for the primary potions and ingredients in case they became necessary since he figured Finn or a servant of the household would be able to gather whatever he used up. Then, he packed under the pair's supervision. For how noble the cause sounded, Yukin didn't appear particularly pleased with what they planned to do, but he gave no reason for his concern.

Will trailed behind Finn outside the estate until they reached their first destination farther inside the city. He longed to inquire about the rest of the capital as he had yet to see a castle or building grand enough to consider a palace; however, once they reached their patient, his mind moved to his work.

The woman appeared to be in her late thirties with milder symptoms than Yukin's while her six-year-old daughter constantly slept with the rosy cheeks, fever, and limp limbs. Their caretakers were treating them correctly, except the potions they used proved to be too subtle, so Will nonverbally instructed them on how to mix the proper amounts before mimicking what convulsions or fits they might have and what to do in that case. He expected to be staying the night at the very least in order to monitor their progress until Finn thanked those in the room, accepted a pouch of coins, and ushered Will away. Finn's only explanation was that they had to trust the household to follow their directions or else they would be wasting their time on two people instead of more.

***

The flight to the southern base spanned three days at the Yeluthians' strict pace and took more of a toll on Coura than she was willing to admit. In the documentation, Detrix requested they wear their bronze armor to show the citizens across the area who they were and as a means of intimidation for whoever controlled the creatures. The night before their departure, she spent plenty of time figuring out how to put the armor on to avoid potential issues in the morning. The clasps proved easy enough to manage alone, yet the added weight strained her body since she had yet to become accustomed to it. This applied to her wings as well, as she soon found out.

By the second day of straight flying, every part of her felt sore enough that, if she weren't around the others, she would have frequently stopped to rest. Not only did her limbs and back soon grow weary, but her head seemed heavier than normal, especially the higher they climbed.

I hope I'm not catching a cold, she thought absently.

In order to distract from the physical pain and discomfort, Coura found she would rather contemplate the issue with Aaron, the commander's possible responses to her message about staying an Asteom soldier, or anything else floating through her mind. Nothing resulted from the effort, yet soon enough Detrix signaled for them to land when the Dalan base came into view.

As Coura knew from her previous visits, additional clothing would be provided, along with a room and a meal upon their arrival that afternoon. Detrix dismissed the group to clean up, eat, and settle into their spaces until they could be summoned for their assigned routes. The details for each individual would differ, that much she was aware of, but no one explained the specifics throughout the journey.

Still, she remained adamant about speaking to the commander, and even Tio or Calin, about her involvement. They all marched inside the base behind a handful of well-versed Dalan soldiers, who began leading them up the stairs to their reserved quarters. Detrix didn't follow. Instead, he shifted to head down the hall, presumably to the general's meeting room, so Coura hurried after him.

"Commander," she called before he noticed another set of metal-clad footsteps.

He half-glanced back at her without stopping. "What is it, Coura?"

"Sir, there's something I need to tell you…"

Before she could elaborate, Detrix interrupted while halting his steps.

"You assume the demon from your and Evern's encounter is involved with the creatures' frequent appearances," he said with an edge to his voice.

It startled Coura more than his correct guess regarding her intentions. "That's right. How di-"

"You also worry that, because it revealed itself to you specifically, it will do so again?"

She pressed her lips together in a silent confirmation.

With an exasperated sigh, the commander shook his head and eased up. "I think you forget who you are speaking to," he began, though this time while offering a slight smile. "My king, your father, and the leaders of Asteom took great care and caution when organizing this mission, *especially* since you are here. I suppose it is also worth mentioning we would have rather had you here instead of at the palace, given the increasing range of the sightings. What we decided is, even if the risk is great, it will always be present."

Coura lowered her eyes. "I suppose I underestimated you."

After a pause, Detrix spoke again at a quieter volume. "I do not want you to assume you are here only for that reason, or else I would not have requested you join my company. I consider your presence valuable, no matter what kind of monster we may be dealing with. If that were not the case, you would be brought farther north and placed under guard in case the enemy does come after you. You proved your skills on multiple occasions, which is why you are a member of this group. Do not forget that."

His words lifted her spirits enough for her to meet the commander's eyes and nod. As long as he was aware of the potential danger, she felt satisfied. "Thank you, sir."

Detrix placed a hand on her shoulder and instructed her to catch up with the others. Then, he sympathetically chuckled at her pained wince.

"I apologize," he said before removing the added pressure from her tender shoulder. "If you were not sore from your first flight with our armor, that is when I would be concerned! Now, get upstairs, relieve yourself of the burden, and find a bath to soak those muscles."

Coura groaned but obediently left her supervisor alone to take his advice.

The following day, she woke late in the morning feeling predictably terrible. Some stretching and massaging released a significant amount of tension, though her back was unable to receive sufficient treatment. Meanwhile, a dull pounding sprouted under her temples, and a soreness started at the back of her throat to signal the start of a head cold. Coura contemplated remaining in bed after breakfast until somebody came for her, but she didn't get the chance.

During her meal, Detrix's second-in-command named Roane joined her to explain their upcoming route. He would be leading her and a set of brothers she had yet to meet west to the area north of Medina where the road met the Western Woods. Apparently, Tio reached out to the Sie-Kie earlier and sent troops there already; Roane, Coura, and the other two Yeluthians would be assisting their people along the perimeter. The four were one of the final groups to set out, and she had no doubt Detrix arranged that to give her time to recover.

She returned to her room with the intent to find Marcus after a nap but slept through the afternoon and awoke only late at night with a growling stomach.

*

The second flight stretched into three days so the four would reach their destination on the evening of the third and prepare camp. A pair of Sie-Kie scouts already waited for their arrival and promised they would return in the morning with additional instructions. Nothing about the area suggested they would run into trouble, which Coura mentioned, to her companions' agreement.

Despite the severity of their assignment, she looked forward to being around the familiar faces of the Sie-Kie. She understood how their people worked together based on how they handled demonic creatures in the past with strategy instead of brute force. Unfortunately, none of her comrades showed interest when she tried to share her past experiences involving the people of the forest.

"Our mission is to identify disturbances and kill any beings possessing demonic energy along the way," Roane explained as they waited for the scouts' return. "If we need to visit the Sie-Kie village, it will be for business purposes, not a friendly reunion."

Coura debated whether or not to address his ignorance but left it alone for the evening.

The next day proved uneventful until the two scouts returned around noon. By then, Roane and the older of the twins named Jerik started restlessly pacing and glancing into the noisy, colorful trees beyond. Before either could comment on the delay, one of the Sie-Kie spoke.

"The *shalma*, our chief, wishes to speak with you before your departure throughout the woods. He is designing a map to sort out the beasts' past locations, and he would like you to copy it."

"We were assigned to monitor around the Western Woods, not inside it," the Yeluthian leader replied a bit sharply.

The scouts exchanged a look, then the second shrugged. "I suppose it's your decision. The Dalan troops have taken up residence with our people in tents below the village or at nearby resting sites along the path leading north. We must know what you intend to do and where you will be positioned."

Roane didn't respond immediately and appeared to be contemplating the request.

Coura wondered what deterred him from accepting the offer. "What's wrong?"

"I would prefer to go to their village by myself."

"Why?" the younger twin named Lee asked before Coura could.

"The purpose is to gather information on the creatures, as well as to alert their people and the Dalan troops of our arrival. That does not require four soldiers, let alone alongside two Sie-Kie scouts. Besides, our position is still outside the woods and to the south, including this land before Medina. Their town should also be made aware of our presence."

"We could always split up," Lee suggested only to be chided by his brother.

"Roane and I can handle ourselves alone, but you are less experienced, Lee."

Coura didn't like how the Yeluthians continued to leave her out of the conversation, even if she couldn't work by herself, and vocalized her own thoughts. "Let me go see the Sie-Kie. I already told you I'm familiar with their people and the environment."

She expected someone to protest, yet the three fell silent. Her eyes, as well as Lee and Jerik's, soon focused on their leader, who evidently had to make a decision.

"Here is what we are going to do," he began in a more relaxed manner. "Lee and I will accompany the scouts and plan to stay with their people for two days in order to gather what information they have available. Jerik and Coura, you two will remain posted here until we return. I want an extra set of eyes at this entrance to guard the path south, and once Lee and I finish, we can head to Medina for their report. Is that understood?"

"Yes, sir," Coura and Jerik grumbled together with obvious displeasure at being left behind.

Roane led Lee toward the Sie-Kie scouts, then the four followed the path into the trees and eventually disappeared into the greenery.

"Why does he always have all the luck?" the older twin muttered before storming in the opposite direction.

In the meantime, Coura reluctantly sat around their fire alone.

*

Over the next two days, the pair took turns patrolling the area from above in order to scan the landscape. They didn't discover anything noteworthy, so the rest of their time consisted of conversations, eating, and resting.

Jerik soon revealed pieces of his training under Commander Isan before being stationed in Verona with his brother. From what Coura could tell, the siblings remained close over the years and reveled in competing with one another. Their physical builds looked similar, yet based on Jerik's descriptions of his younger brother, she got the impression Lee relied on trusting in fate rather than attempting to chart his own course in life. Her theory proved true when Jerik mentioned how he requested to join Isan's squad and worked toward that goal, yet his brother shared no such intentions and had been selected by chance. She didn't push the topic any further.

The soreness in her back and shoulders eased drastically during the downtime, putting her in a better mood; however, nothing quelled the sting in her throat or gentle pounding of a headache behind her forehead. She warmed water often to gargle and drink slowly while wishing for an herbal remedy from the Sie-Kie.

On the morning of the third day, they stayed on the ground to watch for the moment when Roane and Lee would emerge. The sun rose and set, but their comrades never returned.

"What do you think is keeping them?" Jerik asked as he stood to stare into the shadows of the woods.

It was Coura's turn to prepare the evening meal, so she knelt by the fire to finish up when he addressed her. "Who knows. Maybe they hoped to avoid wandering around in the dark and will leave in the morning."

That seemed to be the likeliest option, so she didn't get worked up over their disappearance. Meanwhile, Jerik lingered nearby until she invited him to eat, then he scarfed down his food before returning to the edge of the fire's light to pace. Coura ignored his behavior in favor of sleep, trusting in Roane to act as a responsible leader. If not that, she had faith the Sie-Kie scouts and Barnelus would not lead the Yeluthians astray.

The next morning followed suit, except around noon Coura began to worry when their comrades still didn't emerge from the woods.

"Why are they late?" she mused and stretched in a warmer, sunlit spot.

Jerik stood farther ahead from her location and stepped toward the dirt path. "We should go look for them."

"Wait. If they departed this morning they wouldn't arrive until later in the afternoon." Logically, it made the most sense to stay by their camp, but Coura doubted Roane was the type of soldier to abandon formalities or forget to send them a messenger; either option provided various dilemmas she would be dealing with.

Jerik inched closer until he practically entered the woods. After a moment, he stomped back to where she continued watching him. "We cannot assume the worst, but what if I meet them halfway?"

"You'll be abandoning your position," she replied in an unamused tone of voice.

"Our job is to guard this area and the site, which you can do while I locate them."

Coura frowned once she recognized what he was trying to do. *Not only am I going to be left behind, but if I chase after him, it will be my fault if anything happens out here.*

While she debated whether or not to protest, Jerik already returned to his items to don his helmet and retrieve his sword before moving onto the road with an air of confidence.

"I will be back with Lee and Roane around the time the sun sets," he announced. Without waiting for a response, he charged into the woods.

Coura groaned in frustration yet hesitated to pursue him. Finally, when she figured she would be in trouble either way, she snatched her own blade and helmet from her bags beside the fire, put on the latter, and hurried under the cover of the enormous trees.

Jerik must have realized she tailed him, for he increased his pace so they were well along the path when she reached him. Even then, he continued at a brisk walk.

"You are abandoning your position?" he asked without looking at her.

Coura ignored the accusation. "What if they aren't leaving the Sie-Kie village today? Not only are we going to reach them after dark, but think of what's being left behind."

"The campsite is your responsibility." His words weren't necessarily meant to offend her, but instead sounded as if he dismissed the business to join his comrades.

"You're acting irrationally," she countered.

Before he could reply, a scream from farther ahead stopped both in their tracks.

"What was that?" Jerik asked. He appeared a bit startled, though he recovered once Coura continued at a jog.

"It sounded human," she commented and recalled the many creatures whose shrieks were definitely unnatural.

A second scream identical to the first reached them from their left, so they dropped their argument to locate the source. The pair slowed when a marking on the path caught their eye. Dark stains soaked into the dirt while ruby-colored blood painted the grass and bushes.

"Someone was attacked and dragged through here," the Yeluthian soldier observed and pointed in the direction of the most recent scream.

His eyes became fixated on the trees off the road while Coura inspected for signs of danger. She noticed a set of footprints leading to the blood, but no other clues.

"Whoever they were, they came from the north," she shared. "Why would someone be out alone?"

Jerik's head snapped to her. "Do you know of any animals in the area that could severely harm a human or drag their body away?"

"I've heard of wild dog packs and large cats that could be a problem, but they would have left some sign of their attack, like fur or paw prints. I don't see either, do you?"

He seemed like he had more questions, yet he only pressed his lips together in response. There had to be an explanation for such a clean disappearance, and Coura figured the obvious answer would probably be the correct guess.

"It's likely a demonic creature," she started while unsheathing her sword. "If that's the case, this is an unsafe place to linger."

Although Jerik readied his weapon too, he made no move to leave. She prepared to repeat her suggestion when a voice croaked off to the left. Because of the quieting forest dwellers, they heard it even at a great distance. The words couldn't be made out, yet they were undoubtedly filled with pain and weariness.

Did the victim escape? Coura wondered as they continued listening to no avail. *A demonic creature wouldn't let their prey go. That means this person either got hurt by unrelated means or this is some sort of trap.*

Before she could explain this, Jerik burst into the foliage to chase after the sound. Her resulting call for him to wait stayed in her throat, for it proved too late to stop the headstrong Yeluthian. Coura swore under her breath and again hesitated to follow. If it was a trap, they'd be running straight into a fight without anyone knowing where they went.

One idea came to mind involving leaving a sign for Roane, Lee, and the Sie-Kie or Dalan troops to signal what direction the two went in. She stripped off her helmet, set it upright in the center of the path, and carved an arrow with her blade to give some sort of indication. It looked crude and wouldn't last if an animal wandered over it, but for the moment, it was the best she could do before racing after Jerik.

Off the road, the trail the potential enemy used seemed conspicuous, as if it only meant to hide its presence in the open. A body had been dragged along the ground showcased by both the marks in the dirt and splatters of blood on the plants, which reminded Coura they were likely dealing with a creature intelligent enough to lure them away from the safety of the trail. Unfortunately, the victim's cries and Jerik disappeared, leaving her with nothing else to focus on.

I suppose since he moved far enough ahead I can let him trigger the ambush and surprise the source when the time is right. It's a coward's approach, but it might lead to an easier fight. Of course, then I have to hear him complain about me to the others. I'll let his fragile pride be the punishment if he can't handle it without me.

Combat became familiar to her throughout her life, especially against demonic creatures, and she mentally isolated herself from any emotions that could distract from their objective. A shadow passed by up ahead, causing her to slow to a crawl and listen. She picked up grunts and curses in Jerik's deep voice, uneven footsteps shuffling around, several bell-like clangs of hits to his armor, then the unmistakable thud of his metal-clad body hitting the ground. Upon hearing that, Coura forgot about her plan and stealth to sprint ahead until she stumbled to a stop in order to avoid breaking an ankle.

Jerik lied face down in an area unsuited for fighting, as a handful of saplings nestled around the wide trunk of a much older tree. Its roots reached above the surface to tangle in knots among the flora so frequently she would have to cautiously climb over each spot to get anywhere. She spotted another body among the plants next to Jerik's dressed in the Sie-Kie warriors' tanned clothing, but it too remained unmoving. When Coura reached her comrade, she instantly noted his missing helmet. No markings revealed what knocked him unconscious, but a dent the size of her fist adorned his chest armor.

Whatever did this is still out there, she reminded herself after the brief examination.

As her eyes scanned for any sign of movement, a rustling from behind had her preparing to spin around with her blade ready and defend against an attack. The source of the sound shoved her backward before she could react and with more strength than she expected, causing Coura to waste precious time catching her balance and raising her weapon to block a follow-up strike.

However, none came. Instead, standing with empty hands at his sides and wearing a brooding expression was the demon Terran. His appearance hadn't changed over the two years since their last encounter, though he regarded her with a greater amount of disgust than she remembered.

"You," Coura whispered in shock while her body went rigid.

I was right. I did encounter him before, not some human conjurer! I'm in trouble… There's no way I can take him on in a place like this, even if it was an equally fair fight. Jerik and the Sie-Kie man are hurt and at risk every second we remain here.

While her mind raced, Terran stayed as still as a statue, studying her with an unreadable gaze.

"What do you want?" she asked without concealing her internal irritation with the situation. As she spoke, she dove into her center of light energy in preparation for a physical or magical attack.

"So, you're pretending to be one of them?" came the oddly calm voice embellished by an uncharacteristically smooth tone. The demon's violet eyes lowered to inspect her bronze armor.

Despite the covering it provided, Coura felt somewhat exposed by the penetrating gaze. She kept silent since any retort that came to mind would provoke the demon.

"I've been hoping you would continue to stay out of my way until I require that tantalizing power you're carrying," he went on, allowing a bitterness to escape beneath the words. "My goal was to avoid bringing attention to you. Now, I face a dilemma: Do I kill you here and mask my existence a while longer to raise more creatures to do my bidding, or do I allow you to go free and reveal I am still in this country?"

In either option, I'm at his mercy, Coura reflected as a bead of sweat trickled down her temple. *If I question his intentions, he could decide I know too much and silence me. Letting me inform someone about this encounter wouldn't do much except raise suspicion about his appearance, and he wouldn't give me details about his plans.*

She opened her mouth to demand answers, such as why he hid in the Western Woods, but the demon summoned his blade before she made a sound. Terran's expression twisted into a sadistic grin reminiscent of another demon; the image spurred a shutter.

"I have a better idea. I will let you live to tell your superiors about me. I've been itching for a challenge ever since I stepped into

Asteom, so perhaps this will relieve that annoyance. Also, as the lone survivor here, I'm interested to see if they believe you this time."

Coura's eyes widened at the realization of what Terran prepared to do. Even as she cried for him to stop, the demon sidestepped to stand next to Jerik's body and poised the tip of his sword above the Yeluthian's throat.

"I hate these pieces of metal," he commented nonchalantly, and the crazed expression vanished. "A material that shields the body slows my opponents and negates damage. What's the point of a test of skill and endurance when one of us is purposefully restrained? Why not face an enemy in your best, most natural form?"

"It's a different story when you can heal," Coura spat back and lunged forward to strike before the demon could.

In either a feat of mental fortitude or the irony of her words, Terran didn't move a muscle. Her blade slid into his stomach, then she pulled it out in preparation for a second stab; however, he reached his hand toward her after.

Coura froze, fully expecting a spell in retaliation. Instead, she felt the energy in her center being pulled away. A sickening sensation filled her insides when she immediately recalled the moment Soirée stole her demonic power, leaving Coura unable to use dark magic. She leapt away and reached into her pool of comforting, Yeluthian energy, which remained ready to act on her command.

A second presence, what Terran reached for, lurked underneath, but it retreated when the demon lowered his hand after.

The violet eyes danced with delight at her reaction before his blade sharply lowered into Jerik's exposed neck. Coura gasped just as her comrade's body jerked awake. His eyes opened wide before both hands flew up to grab at the demon's sword; however, Terran released the spell on his weapon, then he stared her down.

"Next time we encounter each other, I won't need to restrain myself." The ominous words echoed in her mind while he turned to stalk into the woods beyond.

She shouted for him to wait and attempted to follow until Jerik's gurgling noises reminded her of his injury. With a curse, she threw herself to her knees at his side.

By that point, his eyes were closed, and his hands weakly tried to cover the wound oozing blood against his paling skin. Meanwhile, Coura shut her swelling emotions away in order to focus on saving the Yeluthian in front of her. She stretched both hands outward and reached into her center to call upon a shielding spell to surround them in case Terran decided to return. Then, she delved into her knowledge of healing magic she learned from Emilea, placed both hands on Jerik's throat, and let the energy go to work.

As the time passed, her eyes shut to ease her into a trance-like state after releasing the grip suppressing her power, and she prayed someone nearby would sense her light energy and come to their aid. The waning level of power in her soul space remained the only way she could measure how long the two were away. Still, the wound bled and tore open again and again while she struggled to hurry.

If I try closing it from one end to the other, he'll bleed out before I get halfway through, she acknowledged despite her frantic state of mind. *My ability isn't strong enough for much more than targeting the worst spot and patching it up temporarily.*

The struggle continued, though Coura realized she was losing him, leading her to pour another portion of herself into the spell against a growing sense of hopelessness. Then, a second wave of energy washed over hers so fluidly she thought she began hallucinating until the wound actually started sealing. In another few minutes, the healing was complete.

She peeled her eyes open before shutting them when her vision went in and out of focus. Hunger and fatigue, two results of a mage draining their energy, settled upon her body after. Multiple people patrolled nearby or stood around by that point, and their voices filled the area, alongside the natural sounds of the woods.

When someone put a hand on Coura's shoulder, the touch dragged her out of the inevitable exhaustion.

"Are you all right?"

She recognized Roane's voice and nodded.

The hand lifted away. "How is he?"

She prepared to respond until another person answered.

"We managed to close the wound, but he lost a lot of blood; some of it is in his lungs. All we can do now is wait."

Coura opened her eyes again and saw Lee sitting across from her. Tear streaks decorated his cheeks, yet nothing in his words hinted at any emotion except a touch of sympathy.

Roane turned to walk away after, leaving the pair to stare down at Jerik until the time came for them to move on from their location. A Sie-Kie man helped Coura to rise before draping her arm over his shoulder so she could limp toward the road, then to his village. She struggled to count how many people surrounded her because most disappeared and reappeared seamlessly within the forest environment; however, she noted Roane going on ahead while Lee stayed behind with Jerik, who would soon be lifted into the treetops.

When she reached the space below the hidden community, a rope slithered to the ground. Coura's stomach dropped at the idea of climbing in her condition, but to her relief, the Sie-Kie man took that into consideration with a swiftness rivaling any craftsman she had seen knot rope. He folded the additional length in half and over itself before wrapping part of it around her waist and the rest through each of her legs so it created a seat to suspend her as she held on. Even as the villagers above pulled her up, she didn't understand how he manipulated the material in such a way, causing her to smile at another demonstration of the Sie-Kie's ability to innovate.

A woman waited on the upper platform to take her arm as soon as another removed the rope from her legs. From there, her caretaker led her into a hut for guests, stripped the armor off, and left Coura to collapse onto the blanketed floor.

*

The next morning, Coura woke stiff, sore, and certain she caught a head cold. Every joint hurt or ached, and her forehead, sinuses, and throat had mild pressure building behind them. Still, she dragged herself to her feet to change into an ordinary, tan dress laid out for her before leaving in search of breakfast and her current superior in order to tell him what she and Jerik faced yesterday.

Many of the Sie-Kie recognized her from her previous visits, especially the warriors, so she wasn't surprised when they greeted her and wished to talk while she stayed in their village. Because of this, she soon heard Barnelus, his father, and whoever led the Dalan troops posted in this area met with a Yeluthian in the wide meeting space near the center of their treetop home. Coura thanked the young man she spoke with and tried to ignore how rude she sounded by abruptly ending their conversation there as she hurried to the aforementioned hut. The guard posted in front spotted her at a distance and held open the cloth that acted as a door so she could slip inside.

Roane alone stood in the plain area while Barnelus, his father, and three other men dressed in ordinary clothes, or not the traditional Sie-Kie pieces, all sat on cushions in a circle. None appeared startled by her intrusion, so Coura moved to occupy one of two open spaces.

"Your timing is excellent," Roane began with a glance her way. "We were waiting for you to fill us in on what took place in the woods and how Jerik managed to have his throat sliced open."

Coura avoided wincing at the Yeluthian leader's bluntness and dove into a recount of the previous day. She explained how they had been waiting, then she shared Jerik's insistence that they search for Roane and Lee, the cries they both heard, and finally Terran's appearance. "I would've chased after him, but Jerik..." The sentence was cut short as she attempted to clear her sore throat before leaving it at that.

"What an interesting layout of events," the *shimla* muttered.

"What do you mean?" she asked hesitantly.

"Allow me to elaborate," Roane picked up. "Lee and I reached the village without issue and were informed of the demonic creatures plaguing these woods. Over the months, they picked away scouts and travelers, so I offered our group to investigate this. The escorts we encountered at the perimeter departed to find you and Jerik."

Coura lowered her eyes. "We never met them at the edge of the woods."

"That would be because the demon or its creatures attacked the pair first."

"We found one dead by your location," Barnelus explained. His face appeared grim enough to tell Coura he knew the scout personally. "We have yet to recover the second body."

A heavy silence filled the room as each person considered the situation in a thoughtful yet anxious manner until the chief spoke again directly to Roane, and in an oddly controlled tone of voice.

"Although I'm not certain why this new demon wished to split up your group by murdering the men sent to reunite you four, it's clear it intended for us to learn of its existence; Coura said so herself. Now, what should we do about this?"

"We must warn General Tio!" one of the three strangers exclaimed, causing a second to jump to his feet.

The Sie-Kie leader nodded, as if he expected their reaction. Then, he glanced at Roane. "What will you do?"

"I am not certain," the Yeluthian muttered and raised his eyes upward. "Jerik is in no condition to travel, though he is stable enough. I am told he may recover after a few days under a healer's watch. I doubt Lee would be willing to leave his brother, especially after exhausting his magic. Aside from their conditions, these woods need protection now more than ever with a demon lurking nearby. I am even hesitant to allow travel through them anymore."

The Dalan men grunted with displeasure at that, and the *shimla* nodded a second time.

It's too dangerous to move outside the village, Coura noted as she caught Barnelus' eye. *Their people need to fortify their defenses if Terran plans on staying here. Then again, he might not remain in one place if we raise our guard in this area of Asteom. Tio still needs to know, along with the other generals in Verona, but it's a gamble to send soldiers away from here because of the demonic creatures.*

She repressed a weary sigh while the muscles in her shoulders tensed. "I'll go."

Roane shook his head. "You leaving this village so soon is out of the question."

"There's a chance the demon won't attack again or will leave the Western Woods altogether now that we found his location, so-"

"I am referring to your physical condition," Roane interrupted, to Coura's surprise. "Commander Detrix informed me this is your first assignment with armor, and I remember what that does to the body. Like Lee, you also drained most of your reserved energy to keep Jerik alive and need the time to recover. It would be cruel to let you do more than you can when we have other options."

As he spoke, his tone sounded more considerate. Coura longed to cave into the offer to relax, yet she understood his final words were practically a lie.

"Any other route would waste too much time. Anyone besides us could be followed easily and attacked inside or outside the woods. You need to stay for Lee and Jerik and help protect the Sie-Kie. I'm the most expendable, as well as the most experienced when it comes to demons. Let me return to Dala with the news."

Roane didn't seem pleased with her persistence. When he asked the others in the room for their opinions, the Sie-Kie expressed their trust while the Dalans supported a messenger with wings taking the shorter trip, which became enough to persuade him.

With her mission set, Coura excused herself in order to prepare, and everyone else remained to discuss their next course of action. Whatever that would be, she wouldn't know unless someone needed her to be informed. The general and Commander Detrix would most likely understand the fortification and leave matters to the Sie-Kie until their people requested assistance. She kept that in mind as she ate, dressed in the previous day's clothing and armor, and sought the basic supplies for the brief trip. By midafternoon, she felt ready to leave.

Since there were no breaks in the canopy, she would need to climb into the treetops and burst through the thinner branches and leaves. It wasn't an ideal method to reach the open sky above, but she had to try what she could. She manifested her wings, shouldered the pack her caretaker brought so it wouldn't be in the way, and leapt to climb from branch to branch until it became safe for her to pump her wings into a launch.

Insight

Although no one seemed particularly serious about organizing a ball the last time she heard about it, Grace found the event taking traction as the days passed. She didn't see Lady Katrina, Marcy, or Emilea lately, so she had no idea who took the reins on the preparations, but evidently someone convinced Aaron or a member of the city council to host a social gathering for the noblewomen. To her relief, the focus remained lighthearted instead of on the heir, yet Grace knew no one would forget to throw their daughters or favorable young ladies at her friend.

The idea of an arranged marriage stayed with her ever since she originally considered how she and Aaron could solve their repeatedly dismissed dilemmas. As if to emphasize the significance of her decision, her parents sent a letter the previous week to prattle on about her duty to serve Yeluthia.

As she sat on the edge of her bed, she reread the message before tossing the paper aside to rise and gaze out the window. *I have not seen Aaron in a while. Hopefully the situation with Nim-Vala did not become worse; I heard the issues to the south require attention, though I would feel I could trust the gossip more if it came from Marcus or another, familiar source.*

Moments like that weighed heavily on her heart, reminding her of how little she could do when trouble arose, as well as the danger such threats posed to the palace.

To avoid recalling her mother and father's words on the subject, she figured she might relax outdoors and departed for the queen's garden. More than anything, she longed for a friend to talk with and lean on, yet her close circle had spread thin again.

The weather proved to be warmer than normal, attracting plenty of people to the fountains and pools reserved for such an occasion. Grace avoided the majority of wandering soldiers and mages in order to find a quiet space to sit. Those who noticed her waved, bowed, or offered a greeting, though none requested to accompany her or attempted to converse.

I suppose I could visit Lady Katrina sometime this afternoon and join whatever dinner or party they plan to attend, she thought after wondering how to spend the rest of her day. *There always seems to be some event happening in Verona anyway. At least it will keep my mind off...*

A faint ringing in her ears distracted her until she closed her eyes and shook her head. After a minute, it returned.

Grace repressed a groan. *Why can I never seem to catch a break? I am being dramatic, but I can never do much to ease my nerves. My friends left the palace, Aaron is busy enough that I would hate myself for keeping him from helping his country, and I cannot get a moment of peace away from my parents.*

She expected her headache to grow worse from the additional thinking; however, the sound remained without any pain. This startled her, and she realized the sensation stemmed from her center of power.

What is this? It is becoming irksome.

After a moment, she recalled where she recognized the feeling.

This is similar to when I met Coura! How could I forget our opposing energies? Still, that only happened when she possessed the demon's power. I never noticed how my body adapted to this because the creature's energy soon spread throughout the palace; I just became accustomed to the irritation after a while.

Grace's breathing picked up once she understood this, and she moved to her feet in order to hurry inside.

That was the last time I encountered demonic energy, which means it returned here. What I sense is too dull to be another creature, though. Could this be one of the animal-like beasts I heard stories about?

As her feet carried her toward the center of the structure, the sensation steadily faded until she considered if she had imagined the experience. Nothing suggested the power bothered anyone else too, so she slowed to a stop.

How odd... I could not identify the source because the presence remained so faint, yet I know what I felt. Would the light mages understand? Perhaps I should find King Arval or one of his commanders and explain it to them.

Her persistence brought her to the council's meeting chamber, which proved to be empty, and she searched for one of the leaders to no avail. Next, she looked for Aaron in order to inform her friend of the possible threat; however, she learned he was in the middle of a business gathering in the private dining hall. When the posted guards inquired about the severity of her request, she reluctantly dismissed the pursuit and returned to her quarters.

If I get the opportunity, I will mention this to Aaron, King Arval, or another Yeluthian. The sensation was similar, but I am not fully confident it acted hostile, or that it even was demonic in nature.

After wrestling with her personal concern for the safety of those in the palace and her certainty in the potential issue, she decided to lessen the additional stress by trusting her instincts and avoid causing more trouble.

***

As much as Coura tried to ignore her body's discomfort, by the time she spotted the Dalan base in the distance, she realized how much she needed a break. A part of her remembered when she was able to go without sleep, food, or water for days thanks to the overflowing amount of demonic power she once carried and longed for that ability to ease her journey in the present.

The past three days pushed her to near exhaustion since her power already became limited without a full recovery. Being in the air also worsened what started as a minor headache at first into a consistent pounding, which made her vision blurry at some points. Along with her body's soreness, it ached from the frigid air above, and her nose dripped despite her constant sniffing.

In short, Coura was miserable from the moment she left the Western Woods.

She descended from the clearing between the base and the city to land in front of the bridge in order to avoid startling the soldiers guarding that area. They didn't hide their concern, though they recognized the bronze armor, so she stripped off her helmet to inquire about the general's location. In what felt like a few seconds, she entered the space reserved for meetings and stood in front of General Tio, Commander Detrix, and Calin, who appeared bewildered by the sudden interruption.

"Coura, what are you doing back at the base?" Detrix asked after Calin greeted her and Tio poked fun at her messy hair.

"Roane, the Sie-Kie's chief, and the Dalan troops stationed in the Western Woods sent me to deliver a message," she started. At that, the three dropped any pretense that her arrival was just a leisurely visit to listen attentively while she explained the details from their arrival to the scouts' disappearance and finally Terran's attack.

Only Calin could hold his composure throughout; Tio's face paled despite his furious expression, and Detrix had the opposite reaction, showing apprehension as his cheeks flared with unspoken anger. When she finished, the general growled a response first.

"*Now* it all makes sense! These beasts *are* being controlled. If I knew earlier, I'd have demanded we search for it from the start!"

"I expect this is all part of the creature's plan," Calin pointed out.

The words had no effect on Tio, who continued to raise his voice in frustration and file through several papers on the table. While the pair fell into their work, Detrix stared at Coura with an unreadable expression.

I suppose it would be unprofessional to say, "I told you so." I bet he's thinking about my warning and the danger my being here possesses. Terran made it clear I'm a target, one he wants to use in the future. This encounter means I won't be sent off on my own anymore. What's worse, the commander also mentioned bringing me north and placing me under guard. Her heart sank at the idea.

Detrix must have sensed where her mind went because he dipped his chin slightly in a nod. "For the time being, I am ordering you to remain in the base under one of the Dalan soldiers' supervision."

He looked over his shoulder at Tio for permission, and the general, too distracted by his emotions, merely waved a hand at the request. Coura longed to protest but thought better of it.

If anything, this will give me time to rest, she justified and let her shoulders slouch.

As she began turning away to exit, Detrix stepped forward to seize her arm. He raised his free hand to her forehead a second later and jerked it away before she understood what was happening.

"I thought your face looked gray," he explained and released her arm. "Your energy level is low, and you have a strong fever too. Go to the healer's quarters now. Stay there until I send someone for you."

The seriousness of his tone accompanied by the way he studied her as she left made Coura wonder what he planned to do. In any case, she went straight for the medical station. A female light mage instructed her to sit on one of the nearby chairs in order to analyze her condition; however, Coura didn't expect the following reaction.

"What a fever! I'd imagine your head is killing you too. How long has this been going on?"

When she revealed the answer, the woman shrieked.

"Why haven't you been in to see a healer yet? This isn't at the point where you can wait for it to go away on its own anymore. I'm shocked you didn't faint on your way here!"

"I didn't think it was that bad," Coura mumbled awkwardly.

That earned her a strained lecture as the woman crossed the room, returned with four potion bottles, and measured them out. All the while, a dozen or so people in the station glanced over at the noise. Coura ducked her head to avoid their eyes, accepted whatever medicine the healer gave her, then stripped off her armor and fell into bed.

*

Every time she stirred, Coura noticed a man sitting nearby with a book in hand before an assistant gave her a light meal and potions that put her to sleep. Someone removed her armor from the room as well, but nobody would reveal where it was.

They're probably worried I'll attempt to leave. Based on her previous stay in Dala, she didn't blame them for considering that.

At the moment, she lied still with eyes closed to savor the morning sunlight and noise. Four days passed since she admitted herself to the station, and sleep vastly improved her condition. Nothing hurt enough to make note of while her mind became more alert than it had been in weeks. She longed for a bath and change of clothes and planned to argue for them with the healer, though the same woman looked after her during her stay with a belligerent attitude. Only with her blessing would Coura be released.

Even then, Detrix gave the impression I'm going to be transferred somewhere safer so they can focus on catching Terran. Maybe I can convince him I'm still useful as long as I'm with additional soldiers. It's so embarrassing to be sent away just because I attract trouble.

She rolled from her side to her back, placed both arms behind her head, and opened her eyes to stare at the ceiling. For a minute, she contemplated that idea.

"Looks like you're awake," came an amused, male voice.

Coura turned her head to see Marcus sitting nearby instead of the regular guard. His appearance changed from when they last met since he grew out a beard and put on more muscle in his upper body. Despite his familiar smile, she noticed how his time in Dala hardened his facial features.

He's practically a younger copy of his father, she thought yet remained attentive enough to keep that comment to herself. Instead, she pushed herself into a sitting position and attempted to comb her hair with her fingers as Marcus rose to come closer and sit on the edge of her bed.

"Is there ever going to be a time when you're visiting Dala and *not* winding up in the medical station?" he teased.

She grinned in return. "I'm glad to see you too."

"I'd love to catch up, but I was told you should be allowed to get out of bed, if you're feeling up to it."

Coura looked around nervously for the healer before answering. "Were you ordered to watch me today?"

"Sort of." He glanced at the wall and licked his lips. "I relieved the soldier who had the pleasure. I figured you would prefer to be guarded by someone you trust and can talk freely to about what happened. Also, without my intervention, they intended to keep you here until Commander Detrix says otherwise. Knowing you, there was bound to be an issue with that."

She couldn't keep herself from chuckling. "I don't know what you're talking about."

Marcus' laughter joined hers before he rose and shrugged. "You can thank me later. For now, I suggest you get cleaned up and eat something other than bread and soup. The woman hovering over you said to come back for a final check-up. After that, find me in the training area."

Coura agreed and watched him leave, grateful for the opportunity to escape the healers and their potions. After visiting her original room for clothes and washing in the bathing area, she stopped by the crowded mess hall for a meal before returning to find her loyal caretaker waiting to test her body and mind for sickness. A few minutes later, the woman released her.

The training ground at the center of the base didn't seem as busy as the dining area, but it still contained enough people to leave little space for standing and gawking. To her relief, Marcus noticed her and jogged over with Calin following behind.

"Let's get a seat in the shade," he suggested and gestured toward the surrounding garden.

Shortly after, the three were on the grass under the cover of an apple tree. Beads of sweat decorated both boys to show they had been working together before she arrived.

"How are you feeling?" Calin asked her to initiate the conversation.

"Better. I'm curious what Tio and Detrix are up to now." She assumed they were aware of the appearance of another demon and didn't elaborate.

The two shared an anxious glance, but it was Calin who continued speaking. "Unfortunately, there's not much to do except alert the rest of the country. Without the demon's location, we've been ordered to hold our defenses where we're positioned. Marcus and I supervised all over the place and made sure security is fortified. The angels are helpful, though, so we can spend more time at the base under the general in case trouble rises around here."

She raised an eyebrow. "That's it?"

"Not all of it. Commander Detrix sent a pair of scouts to the capital as well. Once they learn what's been going on, we expect they'll come up with a plan involving the Yeluthians' magic or the ancestral weapons. Those were what the commander claims worked last time."

The recollection of what it took to stop Soirée in the past made Coura tense. *I only sealed her away in the demonic realm, and the spell Detrix used on Hendal eliminated the dark power he carried. Nothing we did actually killed a demon. Would I need to repeat the process in order to stop Terran?*

She crossed her arms and shoved her doubts aside for the time being. "Fine. What do they expect to do with me then? I warned Detrix before; I'm like bait for the demons and their creatures."

Both Calin and Marcus averted their eyes.

"They can't really believe keeping me here is the best option!"

"It's not," Marcus replied firmly. He plucked a piece of grass and rubbed it between his fingers to distract from her glare. "To put it simply, it sounds like Commander Detrix doesn't know what to do with you. He obviously trusts you, just not what might happen if you remain here. Everyone is focusing on their own duties, and protecting you can be a full-time assignment sometimes."

Coura narrowed her eyes while the shadow of a smile danced on his lips. *As much as I hate to admit it, he's right. I also get the feeling Detrix is concerned because he's friends with Evern, so the situation is more personal than just my being in his company. I'm his responsibility while I'm here, which became more than he's willing to handle right now.*

While she considered this, Coura noticed Calin watching Marcus with a bit of impatience. "Is there more?" she asked when neither continued.

"There is," Calin added and gave up on breaking his fellow soldier. "Marcus has been ordered by General Tio to escort you to Verona where you both will await further instruction. He believes throwing you at their mercy is a better decision than leaving you stuck inside the base lounging around instead of being productive."

Coura could vividly picture the general saying those words and relaxed. "I can agree with that, but why send Marcus along? Why not let me fly to the palace?"

"Because both he and Commander Detrix are concerned with you traveling alone. That, and it would be easier to hide you on the ground. Two people are more conspicuous on the road than one in bronze armor soaring through the sky. Besides, Marcus needed to return to the palace anyway. If there's information to be sent to Dala, we essentially have a messenger already in place."

That must be why he's acting like this, she realized as her eyes fell on Marcus again. *He longed to escape from his father by working with someone else in a new environment. Now, he'll be forced to interact with the very person who drove him away.*

"When do we leave?" she asked after.

Calin offered a reassuring smile. "As soon as possible. With how mild the weather is acting, it shouldn't take more than a week on horseback."

Coura automatically winced at the idea of riding for hours until she remembered how painful the flight to Dala had been. *Perhaps I could suggest a slower canter, or a cart to ride on the entire trek...*

*

The journey to Verona was as uneventful as the flight had been to Dala, if not more so since Coura and Marcus only had each other as company for the majority of the trip. There weren't many people on the roads, and those who were kept to themselves, projecting weariness and caution. Despite the solidarity, Marcus made appropriate conversation throughout the passing days to prevent Coura from feeling lonely. Mostly the two discussed their lives prior to reuniting in Dala and some of what took place with their mutual friends. She grew worried when he inquired about Aaron considering how uncomfortable her last encounter with the king had been, and when he dropped the subject almost immediately, she believed he caught on that something happened.

Afterward, they started to reminisce as they passed through Umbrich and Sindaly before camping outside the latter. Marcus was familiar with using horses for travel, so he took the lead once they entered the capital city, guiding them toward the northern side where the stables were located. His burlier animal carried her Yeluthian armor and appeared relieved when they removed the burden. Her friend dropped the two, equally heavy bags with a grunt, wiped his forehead, and gazed around for the stablehand.

"Well, we made it," he commented nonchalantly. "Once our horses are taken inside, we can head back to the palace."

"What are you going to do first?" Coura asked while shouldering the armor. Each individual piece wasn't terribly heavy on its own, yet putting them together became enough of a reason for the previous strain on her wings.

Before Marcus could answer, a pair of dirt-covered, brown-haired boys ran across the salle to collect their rides and papers, then the two scuttled away to brush down and feed the new additions. Coura started to leave until her friend extended a hand toward her to gesture for one of the bags.

"To answer your question, I'll go meet Aaron or one of the generals to request they summon an emergency council meeting," he began as he hauled the one pack she offered over his shoulder. "They should already be aware of the situation thanks to whoever Commander Detrix sent ahead, so I shouldn't need to re-explain our main issue."

Coura nodded and contemplated going along. "Do you want me there too?"

"That depends on what you intend to do otherwise. I figure you plan on speaking to your father or seeing King Arval, but I would bet they'd be at the emergency council meeting. If not, I will request it."

"All right, I'm going to drop my bags off and then join you," she concluded when they approached the bridge leading to the double doors of the palace.

***

"Well, you sure know how to take advantage of people in a horrible situation."

Yukin's comment as he weighed a tan pouch in his hand had been meant for Finn, but Will wasn't completely blameless either. The young lord dropped the coin-filled bag into his desk drawer with a clink, closed and locked it, then addressed the pair standing before him. The trio hid in Yukin's private study, complete with all the elaborate furnishings, instead of his bedroom this time. Anywhere else would risk their conversation being overheard, according to Finn, yet Will wondered what made this meeting special.

"That would be, what, the ninth or tenth payment?"

"Tenth," Finn supplied while inspecting his fingernails.

Yukin released a weary sigh. "I suppose there is nothing I can berate you for. The people are recovering, you're accepting fair compensation, and our medicine man is safe."

Will glanced at Finn when the young lord didn't continue and found him giving Yukin a skeptical gaze with one eyebrow raised.

"You didn't bring us here for praise, so what else is there to discuss?"

"He's right," Will added. "If this is about me or something I did, I should…"

Yukin raised a hand for them to be quiet before fixing Will with a sympathetic expression. "Trust me when I say I would never let either of you go out blindly if there is danger I'm aware of. No, what troubles me is that I received word from my father. Someone at the king's estate requests your services."

"What?" Finn replied while Will found himself going rigid.

"One of his daughters has fallen ill with the same sickness, and no one has been able to help."

362

Finn cleared his throat with an unusual amount of chagrin. "Is it Elena's daughter?"

Yukin nodded, and the two shared a knowing look before he continued, addressing Will specifically.

"You've been allowed to roam free and speak minimally, but this time we need to be extra wary. I must go along as your master. Finn will not leave your side at all during our stay. Also, I suggest we return to the ruse that you lost your hearing and are mute as a result. There's a risk one of your previous patients will call us out on it, but I would rather deal with that issue later instead of allowing someone to catch your lack of fluent Nim-Valan."

They all agreed to the terms and planned to leave the next morning in one of the family's carriages.

*

The journey to the king's estate proved educational, as Will learned more than he ever imagined just through Yukin's commentary. Instead of a castle, the king owned single- or double-story homes, which connected to one another through hallways, outdoor walkways, and bridges. Every building was located at the center of the capital, a brief ride from the lord's property; this shocked Will since he figured he had already passed inside the enormous, enclosed inner circle.

Servants and gardeners slipped around the traffic to go about their business while posted guards stared down every guest entering over the road. Yukin pointed out the various locations, including the throne room, which remained open to the public, before they moved away to stop before a brick structure of a white color.

Then, the nerves rose.

Will followed Yukin, who dressed in a violet and gold tunic, black pants and boots, and a white cape clasped at the neck. Meanwhile, Finn and Will wore the same outfits to signal their allegiance to the lord's household. A duo of guards escorted the trio to a room where they stood watch at the lone entrance. Inside, the scene looked reminiscent of his first encounter with Yukin.

A girl lied in a bed large enough to swallow her up inside a bundle of blankets while a woman he assumed to be her mother sat at the

363

bedside with both hands on top of her daughter's chest. Unlike Yukin's fair complexion, the woman and child had unique, dark brown skin that contrasted with the white walls and bedsheets. As the young lord bowed deep and dramatic to the king's wife, Will found himself reminded of Clearwater the longer he stared. It wasn't uncommon to interact with people showcasing that complexion in Asteom as they were said to have immigrated from beyond the Mintelian Mountains, but plenty crossed by boat to trade with the fishermen and craftsmen.

"Yukin, how wonderful to see you are well again," the woman named Elena commented and rose at the gesture.

The young lord took her hand, kissed it, and placed it against his forehead. "The pleasure is mine, Your Grace. Allow me to introduce the medicine man who saved my life. Will lost his hearing, so he doesn't speak or respond unless you use hand signals."

The king's wife turned to Will with compassionate, amber eyes before smiling to reveal pearly, straight teeth.

At that, he scrambled to bow as respectfully as possible. Upon rising, he became promptly ignored. She made a hasty exit with Yukin after informing Finn of the medicines', tools', and ingredients' locations and mentioning he should speak to one of the guards if they need additional items. Then, Will went to work.

By evening, the girl's symptoms settled enough for them to rest without needing to monitor her in shifts throughout the night. It became difficult to tell because of her skin color, but the reddening cheeks were no longer as prominent, and although she coughed every now and then, there were no violent fits.

All the while, the duo of guards remained at their posts. Finn ordered them to call for a servant when Will signaled they would be done for the evening, and a man led the pair to a guest room with two beds, two tables, and nothing more. Another set of guards took up residence in front of the opening, preventing Will from discussing the day with Finn. Before he knew it, he fell asleep.

At some point, he was roused from his dreamless slumber by Finn and a panicked servant, so they hurried to find the girl mumbling in a hysteric, fever-driven state. Will calmed her down with some medicine and a cool rag, but the servant sent him away right after despite his wish to remain at her bedside.

The next four days followed the same pattern while his patient steadily healed. Elena never made an appearance when Will was present in her daughter's room, and Yukin only stopped by once to whisper a message to Finn. He caught the two holding hands as they did so before forcing himself to focus on his current task. On the fifth day, the girl could sit up and eat on her own.

It became difficult for Will to instruct her without using words; her fear and weakness were at the forefront of her recovery, which remained that way until Finn caught on and vouched for Will's abilities despite his limitations. That afternoon, her mother visited and wept silently while her daughter slept, so Finn led him back to their quarters.

The following morning, she woke hungry and ready to move. Will ignored his concern to help her walk until she could do it on her own. Again, Finn had to remind her Will couldn't hear because she would order them both around and grow upset when Will wouldn't obey. It proved to be a meticulous dance he had to perform for her; however, if it meant she'd be fine, he was willing to endure the discomfort.

"How is the little princess feeling today?" Yukin asked in a playful manner as he entered the room and sat in the chair beside the girl's bed.

The young lord hadn't been in the room to visit her since their arrival at the king's estate, and his presence visibly bothered Finn, who stood with his arms crossed next to Will on the opposite side of the bed.

Yukin's attitude cheered up the princess, though, and soon her mother arrived to do the same.

This should mean we're finished here, Will noted with some relief as Finn gestured for the three of them to take their leave. *Not that I don't enjoy the royal estate, but I'm ready to have my voice back.*

With weary legs, he trudged behind the guards and fell onto the bed once they reached their quarters. It was late afternoon, and his stomach already started growling to signal the time for the evening meal, which a servant usually delivered to whatever room he and Finn shared.

To his surprise, that night proved to be a new experience.

"We'll be waiting out here for you when you are prepared," one of the guards announced from the doorway.

Finn's affirmative grunt had Will sitting up to face the Nim-Valan with a curious expression. Both understood how risky speaking to one another would be, even in their own room, so there were no other options for Will except to rise and exit with their guards.

The men didn't make conversation or appear that interested in the guests, but as the four approached a different wing of the estate, the sounds of festivities reached them, like the breeze before a storm. Soon, well-dressed men and women hovered in the hallways to chat in the familiar manner of the nobility, and Finn cleared his throat to get the guards' attention.

"Pardon me," he started with a cool gaze across the area. "I believe we should be fine on our own now."

The men exchanged a dubious look.

"Our orders are to return you to Lord Yukin," one replied in a flat tone to show his displeasure.

"Unless the seating arrangements changed, my lord will be on the eastern side of the dining hall," Finn continued impatiently. "I have been to dozens of meals at the king's table and never once required supervision. If you wish to remain attached to us, then sow yourselves to our backsides."

He proceeded to take Will's arm and storm ahead, leaving their escorts behind. After a moment, the two reached the entrance to the hall. Will felt thankful he had someone to pull him forward since the sight blinded him momentarily.

All the walls were covered with a gold paint that reflected the light of mounted candelabras and a chandelier hanging above the center of the enormous space. No pictures tarnished the purity of the coloring, and the flooring, which appeared to be marble, looked polished enough to where everyone's reflections were clearly visible. Half a dozen tables stretched from one end of the space to the other, all filled with chattering lords and ladies while their personal servants or bodyguards stood behind to dart their eyes around in a defensive manner.

If Finn hadn't taken the lead, Will would have been lost in seconds. They crossed to the farthest end through men and women who paid them little to no attention until Yukin's violet tunic stood out against the rainbow of other colors. The young lord greeted the pair with nothing more than a dismissive wave in between a conversation with a handful of women around their age, so Finn shoved Will down into one of two empty seats.

They didn't have to wait long before the meal was served on platters, allowing each individual to claim their share, then the conversations continued. If someone played music, it became drowned out by the noise. It wasn't until Yukin leaned over to speak to Finn that Will could relax.

"Did you miss these parties?" he asked at a raised volume matching everyone else's. A hint of mischief sparkled in his eyes, but the rest of his face showed nothing except a touch of boredom.

Meanwhile, Finn frowned, sent a sharp glance at Will, then returned his attention to Yukin. "It's loud enough now that we can share more without being overheard. Just place the napkin over your mouth if you have a question."

Yukin smiled when Will's eyes widened.

Is he talking to me? He must be, considering he wouldn't speak like that to someone he's familiar with. Several questions did arise, mostly general ones about the structure of the capital city, its relations with the rest of the country, and if they knew the king, yet Finn went on while still pretending he addressed Yukin.

"King Syrus is across the room at the center of the main table."

When he paused, Will squinted, trying to make out the other side of the area. He caught a vague glimpse of a hefty figure covered with glimmering pieces of jewelry and surrounded by several ladies.

"He's a lover of all things shiny," Yukin added. "Just look at this room! It serves to bring him attention."

For some reason, Will couldn't help but remember his first encounter with the current king of Asteom and wince. *Aaron never wanted special treatment. In fact, he hated being acknowledged with embellished items or titles. Then again, the two countries are strikingly different in many other ways.*

"The king has six wives," Finn continued as he plucked up and inspected a piece of cheese left on the dessert platter. "Elena, the woman whose daughter you saved, is the king's fifth wife, and the girl is the youngest of his twenty-three children. They aren't necessarily important except for his pleasure since neither will likely succeed him, so when Elena's daughter fell ill, he shrugged it off. She was the one who sent for you after catching wind of your work. Luckily, she's an ally."

"You mean, a secret lover?" Yukin teased. Despite the information spinning in Will's mind, he thought he noticed a faint hint of jealousy from the young lord.

Finn ignored the comment, returned the cheese, and went on. "I brought you along as a means of earning her favor for the lord's family, nothing more."

Will heard Yukin mutter, "She already has *your* favor after all," and noticed the Nim-Valan look away. This provided him with some much-needed time to turn over everything in his head.

Based on the king's behavior, I can see why the rest of the country suffers. As long as it's not right in front of his face, he dismisses any issue that could lose him the possessions he considers precious. I would be willing to bet he doesn't even know I'm here to help his daughter, or at least he didn't know until someone informed him. That makes me wonder how much slips under his nose. Finn did mention he was sent to find one of the advisors who has been causing trouble, the one who initiated the attack on the campsite and almost killed me.

Some part clicked then as he put the pieces together. He snatched the napkin in front of him to raise it to his mouth and speak without making eye contact with either individual beside him.

"Your master is somebody living in the king's estate, aren't they?" he tried to ask at a quieter volume.

He felt rather than saw both heads snap to him.

"My first guess is Elena, considering she is the only person we've seen since I've been here. Whoever they are, though, they must not like the advisor you were on the border looking for. That's when you found me and my companions."

This time, he set the napkin down and turned to face Finn with what he hoped looked like an innocent, dumb expression to fool anybody who might have noticed the trio. Behind him, Yukin snickered and drank from his goblet. Finn's narrowed stare would have intimidated either of them if they weren't as familiar with it. At last, the Nim-Valan let out a sigh powered by an internal irritation and answered.

"You're clever, more so than I gave you credit for. Yukin and his family are some of Elena's preferred company, which provides excellent cover for her intentions to order around one of the family's servants. If you tell anyone, even by accident, I'll have to kill you."

Will grabbed one of the remaining cheese cubes, slipped it into his mouth, and raised the napkin to his lips. The pride resulting from his correct assumptions was like a delicious wine that paired well with the treat.

"I think we can trust him," Yukin added with less humor. "I do, and you're going to need his insight on magic if you're ever going to catch the man you're looking for."

The discussion ceased when a pair of women fluttered over to steal the young lord away. His parting wave must have been a sign he would not need them to stay, but Finn remained firmly planted in his seat, even though Will hesitated to rise. His next explanation became the start of another, private conversation, which Will found odd since nobody could be used as a cover for speaking to the medicine man lacking his hearing.

"King Syrus is the first ruler in Nim-Vala to hand pick his advisors. Usually the king takes someone from each of the noble households to make it fair for everyone to be represented; however, he selected those he'd grown close to throughout his life and turns a lot of the business to them, so all he has to do is give his final approval. The people living here aren't pleased with him, even those with the representation."

"It also allows for the advisors to propose their own agendas," Will muttered with a hand above his mouth.

Finn nodded. "Exactly. The man I've been tracking looks to spark a war with Asteom and somehow convinced the king to neglect any propositions of peace. That's pretty easy to do when you live within the defensible inner city. What's odd is how the advisor is dragging citizens of the outer circle closer, naming them barbarians despite their citizenship to Nim-Vala, and using them to attack across the border behind the king's back."

"He wants it to seem as though Asteom is attacking Nim-Vala unprovoked, when in reality the supposed barbarians are hoping to prompt a war so their lives will improve from the results."

Finn gave him a sidelong glance. "That's right. Your ability to understand the entire picture is remarkable, you know."

Will blushed as the compliment startled him, and Finn continued.

"What's even more suspicious is we are unable to pinpoint what the man's goals are. He isn't loyal to any home but his own, has no other family members we know of, and the servants there won't talk. Any time they are asked a question, they freeze like mice and reject what's being assumed. Elena has been inquiring about his past and an heir, but all we know is he seems to be a long lost relative of the Olim family who were said to have died out decades ago. In fact, he took on the last son's name, Lupin, which some believe is a dark omen considering the boy supposedly died at the age of eight without a given cause."

Will memorized the limited information regarding the king's strange advisor and started to glance around for anyone suspicious. "Is he still here in the hall?"

"No. Neither I nor Elena, Yukin, or his father have seen or heard from the advisor for two weeks. I believe he went to the border again, but circumstances have kept us tethered to the inner circle."

They sat in silence long enough to bury the topic for the moment, and soon they left the dining room altogether in favor of some well-deserved, and well-needed, sleep.

Even though he grew physically exhausted from the evening, Will struggled to fall asleep as he found himself considering his friends and family in Asteom. Many questions about their safety sprang up, and he became homesick for the first time in months; however, this time Clara nor any of the other light mages were there to comfort him.

He was completely alone.

A Memorable Evening

A knock at the door drew Coura out of the nap she almost slipped into. She sat up, rubbed her eyes, and gazed out the window to gauge the time. *The sun is still up, so it hasn't been too long*, she reflected with a yawn.

It had been six days since she returned to Verona, and between the sessions she attended, she needed to stay inside the stone walls under the council's orders. None of the members seemed surprised by her position at the center of the problem, and most avoided speaking to her directly when discussing the demon and its creatures. Only Byron, Emilea, Aaron, Marcus, and surprisingly General Tont requested her input. Even Evern didn't address her, though she understood it was to limit her involvement.

The meetings bored her immensely considering no one attempted to suggest new ideas; they believed the best method to protect the country would be to fortify their defenses and follow up on any additional sightings of Terran. In a way, their strategy was based on protecting the more vulnerable areas of the country, such as towns and cities possessing open farmland or those less populated places in the woods, and acting solely against the creatures. With less activity in the northern half of the country, they would be able to afford sending troops to those places.

King Arval gave his permission for additional soldiers to move as well, mentioned he would request for Commander Detrix to return to Verona and join in the discussion, and suggested they search for the remaining ancestral weapons. That was where they left the matter.

The knocking came again more fervently, so Coura got to her feet to open the door. On the other side stood Marcus, appearing as lazy as she felt with arms crossed and a tired expression. "Yes?"

"Are you busy?"

She shook her head.

"I was wondering if you'd be interested in a walk through Verona," he began with a tilt of his head. "I need to get out, and I'm sure you do too."

"What about the restrictions?" she halfheartedly asked. No one on the council forced her to stay inside the palace, but the last thing she needed was to get in trouble again.

Marcus' lips spread into a crooked smile. "Those were loose orders to make sure you don't go off alone. To be honest, I'm shocked you listened for this long."

Coura smiled too and shrugged. "If I don't get blamed for it, I'll come along."

"Great, let's go."

Together, they moved to the grand hall, across the bridge, and through the main road populated by hundreds of people on business of their own. Their talk remained short, but she got the impression Marcus just needed to be around someone instead of sitting alone. She didn't mind it at all since she kept to herself outside the council meetings and meals in the mess hall.

Then again, I've been away from others in the past, enough to not rely on their company. Not that I didn't want to be around anybody, but... It was better to be alone. The thought didn't bother her as much as she expected it to.

The autumn weather fell upon the city, though it showed most along the western main road where the wealthiest citizens maintained gardens and trees, which changed colors with the seasons. Coura suggested they go there, so the pair went over before it grew too late to see the environment. They must not have been the only people to consider this, for the street became busier than she ever remembered it being. Gates were thrown open to welcome guests into the homes for parties and private dinners, sending wafts of delicious-smelling aromas and whispers of string music and pipe flutes throughout the area. It proved to be a beautiful experience, one that made Coura consider the lifestyle despite the nobility's overwhelming characteristics.

Along the way, they recognized Lady Katrina's home and spotted a gathering in front of the metal gate. As they neared the property, someone waved in their direction; Marcus waved back and hurried over, leaving her to follow. To Coura's relief, the group turned out to be all familiar faces. Clearshot had been the one to wave them over with Emilea by his side in a sapphire gown. Next to them stood Byron and Cintra.

I remember her visiting Verona often, but Byron never mentioned if she's staying in the city for a while. At least he looks happier when she's here.

The woman wore formal clothes similar to Emilea's, making Coura wonder if the group had been invited to one of the current parties. Of course, Lady Katrina lingered by the gate's opening dressed in the fanciest outfit consisting of a deep scarlet gown and a matching, feathered hat. Tucked behind and to the side hovered Marcy in her dress of muted gray. She always looked stunning and had embraced Katrina's overbearing devotion to turning her into a noblewoman despite her past.

"What's the occasion?" Marcus inquired when he and Coura slid into the circle. If Byron or Emilea had an issue with her being away from the palace, neither commented on it.

"There's an event we were invited to," the latter began until Katrina gasped and made a shooing motion with her hands.

"Emilea darling, it's not just any event!"

"Excuse me," the light mage apologized and rolled her eyes. "There's a *special* dinner in the private dining hall this evening for the noblewomen."

Katrina glanced around and showcased a broad smile. "What an honor! Truly, I can't remember the last time I was invited to dine with the king."

"Aaron organized this?" Marcus asked skeptically with a raised eyebrow.

Emilea shook her head and answered before Katrina could jump in. "No. In fact, I'm not certain he'll be showing up tonight. When I gave him the invite, he grimaced."

Half of their circle chuckled at that before she continued.

"Katrina requested my help to organize an event for the ladies where they can dine and gossip to their hearts' content."

"Thankfully, that leaves us men out of it!" Clearshot exclaimed with a glance at Byron. "No offense, but the food is never worth having to tolerate the guests."

Katrina pouted and wagged a finger at him. "You wouldn't be welcome there tonight anyway. Isn't it obvious? It's time our young king chooses a bride."

Coura's heart sank at the lady's words. She tried to appear unbothered by it even though no one paid her any attention.

"You can't be serious," Byron added.

"Why not? There's been talk for months about the lack of a queen and a proper heir. Some are even arguing for an alliance marriage with one of the Yeluthians. This is their chance to brag about their daughters and offer them to the king."

Why didn't I hear about this? Coura wondered as they transitioned to another topic. *I guess it could be like Katrina said, and it's only meant to be a dinner for the nobility. Still, would Aaron actually attend? Will he move on that easily? I haven't spoken to him since our last encounter in the garden.*

The idea of him surrounding himself with flirty women, and enjoying it, made her sick. To tune out those feelings, she focused on listening to those around her instead of her own concerns. It wasn't until a guard came around to light the street lamps that they were reminded of the time.

"We're going to be late if we don't leave soon," Emilea told Katrina, who claimed to have forgotten her fan inside and spun around to retrieve it.

Clearshot took the opportunity to lean closer to Marcus. "With the women away, Byron and I are grabbing a few drinks. Care to join us?"

Marcus hesitantly glanced at Coura.

"I don't care," she muttered with indifference.

"Sorry," he replied and faced Clearshot again. "I haven't had an opportunity to visit Aaron since we got back. If he isn't planning on attending this dinner, he might need a distraction."

"Fair enough."

The clicking of Katrina's heels on the cobblestone walkway drew their attention. "I forgot where I put the darn thing," she explained while fanning herself dramatically. "Luckily I own plenty of spares. It's a real collection-"

"I'm sure it is," Emilea interrupted. "You're also forgetting the dinner should be starting about now."

"Yes, yes! Marcy, take care of yourself tonight."

As the others moved out into the street, Coura caught Marcy's eye. "You're not going along?"

Marcy hugged herself, shook her head, and opened her mouth to respond when Katrina's giggling cut in.

"She has another matter to attend to by the name of Lord Theodore." Her coy tone and Marcy's following blush visible even away from the torchlight was all they needed to figure out her prior engagement.

Coura could only wish her friend well before they turned to stroll toward the main road as a group. She put distance between herself and the lady in order to avoid drawing attention to herself, yet Katrina focused solely on Cintra, looping her arm around the other's and preening the seer's unbound, blonde hair.

"With Marcy preoccupied, you'll need to keep me company. We're lucky the invite is for any woman in the home, or else we would have to bend the rules a bit."

From where she walked, Coura noticed how nervous Cintra looked. The woman's normally relaxed, confident demeanor seemed anxious as she stood straight due to the visible tightness of each muscle. Just watching her made Coura uncomfortable.

Behind them, Byron observed Cintra with a strange expression. Eventually, he noticed Coura's gaze and met it while wearing a thin smile. She raised an eyebrow, glanced at Cintra and back again, then waited; however, her former mentor turned away after. That became enough reason for Coura to worry since she knew he was hiding something from her about his relationship. By that point, Clearshot led Byron toward one of the busy taverns as the rest went to the palace before splitting apart.

Coura returned to her room alone and meandered through her belongings mindlessly before realizing how she longed to talk to someone. She contemplated who would be available and remembered her parents.

When was the last time I spoke to Mother? If she isn't busy with Odell and Jackie, perhaps we can spend the evening together. After considering the idea, she decided to see if Paulina was available and would like to go into the queen's garden for a while.

***

The private dining hall grew livelier than it had been during any of the other times Grace spent the evening there, which was due to the fact that all the women present understood this would not be simply another meal with the nobility.

Every lady wore a gown, probably their finest, and matching jewelry, hats, and accessories, which they fussed over consistently enough to reveal their anxiousness. Meanwhile, Grace opted for the white dress gifted to her by King Hernan years ago when she first arrived in Verona. It needed a few alterations, but not too many that it would be more trouble than it was worth. Her opal necklace stood out brilliantly against it, raising her confidence.

She wound up entering a few minutes late once the various women were already present, so all eyes were drawn to her. In response, she held her chin high and entered with poise befitting her name. Everyone she spoke to showered her with compliments, though she brushed them aside in her quest to find Asteom's king.

Despite everyone else's enthusiasm, she believed Aaron might not even attend the gathering for several reasons; the most prominent being he hated socializing with people whose only goals revolved around creating a positive impression.

I also cannot forget Coura did not receive an invite, she reflected while gazing around the room at the familiar, decorated faces of the ladies. *I hoped to speak with him tonight and propose my idea for an arranged marriage. It has been a while since we discussed our troubles in the council's meeting chamber, but I know he is not avoiding me; his work should always come first.*

Despite her logical approach, Grace also understood she hadn't been actively seeking him out either. Her solution to their problems still seemed like the best way to help each other; however, upon hearing of her other, half-Yeluthian friend's feelings and how Aaron apparently reciprocated them, she grew nervous.

I do not believe it is my business, but I also must keep in mind how likely it is anything will come from their infatuation. They are my friends too. If I insert myself into his life, how would Coura react? Would she still wish to be associated with me?

Grace soon realized as she mingled with those nearest to her that someone would be upset with her, no matter what decision she made going forward. The notion solidified her determination to at least discuss the matter with Aaron when they encountered each other next.

Evidently, tonight's event would not provide that opportunity. No more guests seemed to be arriving, leading the servants to shut the doors in order to give the party privacy, and she gave up for the evening.

Someone nearby called her name, pulling her away from the previous thought. As she turned, she caught Emilea approaching with a broad smile.

"You look stunning," the master mage started by way of greeting. "White really suits you."

Grace thanked her for the compliment before the two chatted about the setting. Servants bearing trays with various, dainty finger foods and cups of wine rotated around the space to wait on the ladies, who paid them little attention. The chairs normally positioned around the tables had been removed to provide additional room, though the tables remained.

When their conversation paused, Emilea released a sigh and gazed around the area.

"The nobility will probably remain here all night, even if His Highness doesn't make an appearance."

"So, he is not planning to attend?" Grace inquired and felt a bit deflated when the master mage nodded.

"I doubt it, mostly because Marcus is back in Verona, and they might like to catch up. Also, he seemed to grasp the purpose of this event and wanted nothing to do with it."

Why must he make this so difficult?

Although she avoided muttering the question under her breath, Grace couldn't help from groaning.

If Emilea heard it, she didn't comment on the sound. "In any case, I expect most of the ladies will start to leave once they realize that. I intend to depart here shortly."

"I see. Then, I wish you a pleasant evening."

The master mage offered a warm smile before crossing the room.

After, Grace considered leaving as well. Her mind wandered to her options, such as seeking out the king and assistant general, but she didn't want to disrupt their overdue reunion. Another, less appealing idea was to look for Coura.

Perhaps I should find her so we can discuss the matter once and for all, one part of her suggested. *If she hears my reasoning, she may be willing to let Aaron and I be together. After all, Emilea, Lady Katrina, and Marcy never mentioned her feelings being that serious. It could just be a sense of admiration, like what the ladies express.*

The other part of her shuddered at the thought. *Coura openly despises how the nobility behave and is one of the most straightforward people I know. I doubt she would continue to harbor such emotions if they were not serious. Once I speak with Aaron, I will learn if he feels the same or not. In my mind, that makes the most impact.*

With a solid plan in place, she ignored her frustration with the situation and decided to retire for the night. The nearby conversations died down to reflect the guests' growing boredom with the lack of entertainment and gossip, so she figured they would soon depart as well.

Her feet led her to the exit where the doors remained closed; however, when she pushed against one, the wood didn't budge. In a confused daze, she stepped back to observe the knob and latches and found no sign they had been tampered with.

Is it broken? The only other explanation is that somebody blocked it from the opposite side...

The thought prompted her to glance at the next set where an older woman attempted to do the same with an identical result.

"How ridiculous!" the lady exclaimed and practically stamped her feet to display her annoyance. "Where are the servants? The guards outside should be able to hear us."

Her tantrum drew the attention of the majority of the room, leading everyone to shuffle closer. In the midst of the busying section, a figure parted from the crowd to approach her. The young man did not appear older than Grace, yet he wore the tan outfit of the servants to show his position. Still, she noted how unkept and matted his inky hair looked, which she found odd given the normally strict regulations from their masters.

"It's about time," the lady grumbled with a huff as she stepped aside.

Instead of inspecting the door, the servant faced the woman, allowing Grace to take in his entire appearance. His beady, dark eyes hid underneath a bushy brow to hint at his more mature age, though his clean-shaven face had tricked her into believing he was younger than she first gave him credit for. The baggy clothing also hid a lean build, not a skinny body.

In that moment, all the information she processed came together, and she realized the man was not an ordinary servant. She opened her mouth to yell a warning; however, her worst fear came to pass before her eyes.

The stranger in the servants' clothing lunged while sliding a knife out from his sleeve to stab the lady in the stomach before letting her drop to the floor. A chorus of screams started after that, but to

Grace's horror, not all were spurred by what she just witnessed. People scattered to reveal half a dozen other bodies in the same position as the first victim with blood staining the stone beneath them.

A staged attack?

Grace froze at the idea. The group had managed to seal the guests inside the private dining hall without anyone noticing due to their disguises and waited for the right opportunity to strike.

The nobility would never consider the palace servants betraying them. Then again, I do not believe these are the same people who normally attend to the kingdom.

She shouted at her legs to move when the man wielding the knife turned away. Although her fear threatened to paralyze her, she managed to shake away the sensation in order to fall to her knees beside the injured lady.

"L-Lady…ambassador…"

"Hush," Grace ordered as she placed her hands on the wound. Her light energy sprang forth to begin a healing spell, though she refused to remove her eyes from the fake servant.

As she worked, he stepped closer while raising the knife in an attempt to threaten her, yet he came to a stop instead of approaching or attacking. Grace made sure to meet his eyes and glare, as if the gesture would be threatening enough to scare him away. They remained staring at each other until his eyes raised to look at a figure behind her. Then, he began shouting in a language she didn't understand.

When a second male voice responded from over her shoulder, she jumped.

"Run…my lady," the woman under her hands managed to choke out in a raspy voice.

She shook her head without responding. The worst of the injury seemed to be taken care of, so she prepared to tell her patient not to act when the man in front of her mentioned Yeluthia clearly enough to stay her tongue.

He knows I am a Yeluthian? she wondered while gazing up into his face. *Is that why he did not harm me? Was the one he shouted at preparing to do so?*

Before she could comprehend the situation, the cold blade of a knife pressed against her throat from the stranger behind her. Every limb stopped responding as a chill swept through her body and made her spine shiver. Still, the killing blow never came.

The voice at her back barked what sounded like an order before using his other hand to tug on her arm until she rose to her feet.

If they will not hurt me, they must be planning something else, she thought. The memory of her previous time in captivity came to mind immediately after. *I would rather fight until my last breath than be taken away!*

The statement rang in her mind while she squeezed her eyes shut. After considering what she could do, which proved to be limited to using light magic, she decided to peer into the nearest man's mind in order to figure out who was behind the attack and use the information to her advantage. Her power leapt forth to shape the goddess gift's ability, allowing her to stretch her presence over the knife-wielding stranger at her back.

Who are you? she decided to ask in a forceful tone with the hope of being intimidating.

The question succeeded in startling her target, causing him to stumble backward, and he held no restraint with his resulting thoughts. Unfortunately, his raving all came in another language. Grace attempted to remember what she could, though only a few terms stuck out as names or places.

Yeluthian... Lupin... Perish...

She noted the three words since the man used them repeatedly before retracting her mind when he scrambled away. When she faced forward again, the second attacker had fled as well.

They look like Nim-Valans, but I am not familiar enough with the native tongue to be certain. I only hope some of what I picked up can be useful.

Her mind shifted to the problem at hand, which devolved into a mass hysteria among those trapped with her in the area. Most of the guests lied unmoving on the ground, which didn't immediately register with Grace. The remaining ladies hid behind a magical shield in the farthest corner of the room, reminding her of the only other light mage in the vicinity.

Emilea must be guarding the survivors, she realized before attempting to cross the space. Every wobbly step brought her in contact with an injured victim; however, as she watched the scene nearby, she knew she needed to assist the master mage.

Although the two fake servants she interacted with disappeared, the dozen or so others surrounded the wall of energy. Each dressed like the previous pair wearing the tan clothing: Their hair remained unkempt, and their shaved faces gave them a younger look. Her hope began to dwindle when the shield grew dimmer and steadily broke apart so the men could slip by one at a time.

A hot anger filled Grace's stomach as another woman's cry pierced through the groans, weeping, and frantic mumbling around her. One hand rose to prepare a spell while her inner voice projected to those who managed to sneak behind Emilea's shield.

Enemies of Asteom, leave if you value your lives! Run and await your deserved deaths someplace else!

Whether or not they understood her, she didn't know, but the order she yelled proved to have the same effect as when she addressed the first stranger. The group began shouting at one another as the men retreated from the flickering wall of energy while crying out in a fearful manner. Before the others could act, Grace manifested another shield to strengthen the master mage's defense.

That caused the attackers to rethink their strategy. One after the other turned tail and hurried to where a door parted from the wall, presumably one used by the actual servants during normal events. Within a minute, all that was left were the remains of their massacre.

Once she stood alone and the male voices disappeared, Grace felt every bit of her strength drain from her body. She dismissed her shield and began stumbling over to where the ladies huddled together. The sounds of pain and agony echoed in the room to fill her heart with sadness, and the resulting sights made her nauseous.

Find Emilea, she told herself in order to focus. *She can tell me what to do next and start healing the injured.*

Despite her optimism for the survivors, only seven women proved to be behind the shield. They wailed and wept upon seeing her, though her eyes locked on to the figure of the master mage kneeling on the floor. Three patches of scarlet decorated the front of her previously clean gown, her blonde hair became disheveled, and her complexion grew pale.

Grace hurried her steps until she could throw herself in front of the woman.

"Emilea, are you all right? Where are you hurt?"

Her voice wavered as she asked the questions, but her instincts kicked in to get her started on a healing spell. Despite what she saw as she approached, the master mage had been stabbed twice in the back as well, creating a pool of ruby liquid around her legs. Grace ignored the realization in order to pour all her energy into closing the wounds, which she succeeded in doing minutes later.

"I healed the injuries, so you should not lose any more blood," she explained, if only for her own sanity. Already, her head started to ache, and the room shifted in and out of focus.

Despite the work she did, Emilea didn't respond.

"Come on, there are others who need us," Grace practically begged while shaking the woman's shoulders. She repeated her words and similar phrases even when her voice began to crack and tears slid down her cheeks.

Then, she caved into her emotions, wrapped her arms around the limp figure, and sobbed.

***

Even before the guards posted outside the king's suite started banging frantically on the door, Aaron had a bad feeling about the evening. It all began when Marcus arrived to interrupt his impromptu nap and inquire about the event in the private hall. He hadn't given much thought to it since he planned on spending the time catching up on paperwork instead; however, he dismissed that work since this would be the first day the two could talk since before the assistant general's return, and he longed to hear if the Dalan base's atmosphere benefited Marcus.

His friend didn't waste time before pestering him about the ladies, or rather his potential suitors, until he showed irritation about the subject. If Marcus guessed it had anything to do with Coura, he didn't say, but the discussion shifted to a different topic then. Soon, they considered calling for a servant to bring them dinner, yet one of the armored soldiers reached them first.

"Your Highness, please answer!" the guard called while continuing to knock.

At the sound, Marcus hopped to his feet to stand in front of his king.

Aaron rose a moment later while the assistant general went to fetch the sword he discarded against the wall earlier. "What's wrong?"

For his safety, he let his friend unlock the door and crack it open with the weapon at the ready. Marcus relaxed a second later before swinging it inward farther, allowing him to observe the four, silver-clad men in the hallway.

"We received an emergency message from the guards on the east side of the palace," one explained with a strained expression. "Someone killed those assigned to monitor the private dining hall and used pieces of furniture to block the entrance to the space. It seems a number of unknown assassins attacked those inside. The messenger claims a team of healers is on their way, but they wanted to make sure you remained unharmed and are aware of the situation."

Aaron felt the blood drain from his face, though he attempted to keep his composure and ignore the urge to consider his neglected invitation. Instinctively, he took a step forward only to have Marcus grab his arm.

"Are you sure?" his friend asked at a lower volume while meeting his eyes and releasing his arm.

Although he grew a bit flustered beneath his rising temper, Aaron appreciated the concern Marcus showed. *It's going to be difficult to witness, and I'd be putting my life in danger if those responsible for it are lingering nearby. No matter what, I need to be there for my people and make certain we stay organized in order to collect as much information as we can about the incident.*

He could tell the assistant general and his guards would rather continue protecting him from the safety of his room, and he expected them to protest his decision to throw himself into the mess, but no one argued as he moved into the hallway.

"Stay close to me," Marcus ordered after two of the four soldiers took the lead, leaving the other pair to watch the rear.

*

Near chaos met the group at the entrance to the private dining hall as dozens of soldiers, mages, and servants all attempted to hurry in and out of the space through the two doors. Even more onlookers crowded the hallway, forcing one soldier accompanying Aaron to demand they part for the king. That piece of information had people backing away or entering the room while quieting.

Everyone knows I'm here now, he noted before straightening. For the time being, he wouldn't address anyone until he understood the situation. *Father used to say a kingdom is weak if its sworn protectors let fear entrap their minds. After all we've been through, I would hope the majority of the troops can use their experience to properly handle a problem of this scale.*

Aaron, Marcus, and their four guards reached one of the open doors and stepped inside.

As soon as he entered, his senses became bombarded by the current state of the space. The smell of iron struck him first while the surrounding conversations, groaning, and weeping filled his ears. What he saw completed the description of a massacre. The bloodied bodies of many noblewomen covered most of the floor, and dark stains marred the usually polished stone. Few on the ground moved, yet those who did looked horror-stricken to display their shock.

Marcus muttered a list of curses as the group crept farther into the hall. Various soldiers and mages inspected the bodies, assisted in tending to the wounded, or searched the area for clues, yet three, familiar faces caught Aaron's attention.

386

General Tont and General Garvish stood together with Grace in between them. The Yeluthian ambassador looked as pale as her white dress and hugged herself with a defeated expression. Meanwhile, the generals spoke to one another until noticing Aaron and his guards.

"Your Highness, I'm relieved the messenger found you," General Garvish began with a slight, half-hearted bow. "We weren't expecting you to leave your quarters."

"What happened here?" Aaron asked instead of addressing the man's unspoken concern regarding his appearance at the scene.

"It sounds like an orchestrated attack," General Tont began when his fellow general pondered the question. "One of the routine guards arrived to switch shifts and discovered the bodies of those assigned to monitor the event. The doors had been barricaded, so after finding backup, the soldiers who arrived first managed to enter."

"The Yeluthian ambassador has been filling us in on what took place," General Garvish picked up with a gesture to Grace. "It seems the Nim-Valans are behind this."

"What?" Marcus exclaimed as Aaron frowned. "How could they have entered the palace without being noticed?"

"We're looking into that, but my troops found the bodies of the servants who were supposed to be working this event. Lady Zelnar mentioned the attackers all wore the ordinary outfits, so I assume they've been hiding and waiting for this moment."

"I say the opposite," General Tont added and crossed his arms. "The details are too specific for this to be a chanced strike."

The pair stared at Aaron, as if waiting to hear his input; however, he dismissed the idea of discussing that at the moment.

"Is there any more information you can share about tonight's incident?" he pressed instead.

General Garvish scratched his chin while General Tont grunted, though the former answered.

"Not much, I'm afraid. Upon discovering this mess, the soldiers scattered to find healers, alert us, and pursue the enemy. Terrell left with a separate group right before you arrived in order to locate and hopefully restrain the criminals."

"And General Casner?"

"He hasn't shown up. We also didn't hear from the Yeluthians, though we sent a messenger to their quarters on the fourth floor, just in case."

"Good," Aaron mumbled while dipping his chin. "I suppose all that's left to do is deal with this room."

A pause followed his comment, as if the sense of dread they had been attempted to ignore crept upon them at once. The cries and moans subsided drastically since most of the injured were being taken care of and removed from the hall in order to recover in the medical station. This left a haunting silence over the untouched, unmoving bodies around the group.

"Your Highness," General Garvish started after. "I assigned my soldiers to manage the crowd outside in order to avoid distracting the healers or impeding their work. Since it's a given the news will spread, please allow me to manage those uninvolved with the massacre."

Aaron raised an eyebrow. "Is that too much for one person?"

"Perhaps, but until you are prepared to address the public, someone should inform the troops and raise our defenses in Verona."

"If you believe you and your assistants can handle it for the time being, you have my permission."

The general placed a fist on his breast and bowed before thanking Aaron and taking his leave. As they watched the man exit, General Tont cleared his throat.

"With Terrell searching for the invaders and Garvish managing the bystanders, I will supervise the recovery and cleanup here."

"Your main focus should be the victims," Aaron reminded the general, though he trusted the man's intuition. "Once they are safe, find a location for the dead and transport the bodies. It would be disrespectful to proceed with a pyre until their families are made aware of the situation."

He avoided going into too much detail, but fortunately General Tont understood the message. With no other orders to give, Aaron dismissed the man, who turned to monitor what progress had been made during their discussion. That left one, immediate problem left to fix.

From the moment he entered the hall, he kept part of his attention on Grace despite her reluctance to meet his eyes. His Yeluthian friend hadn't spoken a word, which reminded Aaron of her desire to remain out of harm's way.

"Grace, are you hurt?" he decided to ask first while projecting his concern.

She shook her head and glanced up at him; her eyes reflected mixed emotions to hint at a lingering sense of shock.

None of us need to stay, he reminded himself with a glance at Marcus.

His friend didn't chime in until that moment, and he leaned closer to whisper into Aaron's ear. "It's still dangerous for you to be here. I agree with my father about this being a coordinated attack; maybe there's more to their plan."

Reluctantly, Aaron nodded and faced the assistant general. *Somehow, the enemy managed to sneak into the palace and replace the servants without anyone noticing. Either this took weeks to do at a methodical pace or they intended to strike at once in a sudden move. In any case, we must be as cautious as possible, meaning I'll be locked away until further details emerge. I just need to trust in my council to inform me of additional changes.*

"Marcus, escort Grace to the medical station. You can come find me later."

Both his friends appeared displeased with his order, yet only the Yeluthian ambassador spoke after.

"Aaron, be careful."

"I will," he responded with as much of a reassuring smile as he could muster.

Still, she seemed bothered. "The generals know about the attackers' disguises, but I did not finish sharing my observations since you arrived."

"It can wait," Marcus interjected in a gentle manner to show his concern.

Although she let him take her arm, she continued with a surprised expression, as if she didn't realize the assistant general was present too.

"They recognized me as a Yeluthian and avoided harming me because of it. I am not sure what they intended to do since one held a knife at my throat, but I used my goddess gift to see if I could overhear any useful information. Their thoughts were in a different language; however, I picked up on Yeluthian, Lupin, and Perish. I figured you should know in case they are captured and interrogated, or if the words come up again."

Her rambling ended abruptly, though Aaron made sure to log the account away for the future.

Marcus started to lead her in the opposite direction then, so he thanked them before ordering his remaining guards to escort him to his quarters. Throughout their walk, he avoided glancing at the faces of the unfortunate victims lying on the floor, as well as the curious, frightened, and suspicious stares following him in the hallway.

I owe it to my people to do what I can in a safer location. Nim-Vala will pay for such treachery, that I can ensure, but the protection of Asteom comes first, starting with its ruler.

An Unexpected Rescue

The queen's garden didn't prove to be any busier than normal, allowing Coura and her mother to find a secluded spot near one of the ponds in the southeast corner. There, the two talked in private. Their conversation began as it usually did with Paulina sharing what she learned during her time in Yeluthia and Odell and Jackie's progress in school.

Coura's brother seemed to excel in his classes and became confident enough to volunteer whenever his instructor needed a designated leader or demonstration partner. Her mother found this humorous based on his previously shy behavior as a child, yet she admired his focus and dedication.

On the other hand, Jackie began to deviate from her usual interests in order to pursue painting and weaving. Coura knew her sister had always been interested in art, but over the years, she came to notice her parents urged their youngest daughter to become a scholar. Apparently, the girl always earned high marks in her courses, so they figured that was what she wanted to do for a living. Paulina took advantage of her eldest child's willingness to listen and complained for a while until she realized she'd begun rambling.

Then, to Coura's dismay, the woman turned the tables by asking about the palace and her position under Commander Detrix. That led to an explanation of her time in Dala, with a few details omitted, and her visit to the Sie-Kie village.

"I love hearing about your adventures around Asteom," Paulina admitted while Coura lied on her back with her head resting on her mother's lap. "The world felt so small when I was growing up, and living in Yeluthia disconnected us from the cities and diverse regions. I suppose you are familiar with the entire country."

Coura's eyes wandered to the clouds above before she closed them to enjoy the moment. Last winter, she decided she needed to inform her parents of her past, including what the demon did to her, for two main reasons. Firstly, she became an example of how harmful demonic energy could be and had been selected because of her mixed lineage. If any creatures like Soirée intended to kidnap or possess others like Coura, she hoped the targets would be better protected.

Secondly, hiding her past created a rift between her, Evern, and Paulina. What details she could share were for militaristic purposes, so they only held half the entire picture. Neither her father nor her mother ever requested further details, but their strained curiosity led Coura to realize they had been attempting to be respectful because they either felt guilty for not being around when she grew up, didn't believe they had a right to demand such personal information, or both.

So, she revealed her relationship with Soirée, what the demon's power did to her, how she chose to reclaim it when the rogue angels tore the power away, and why she bore the bruise-like markings for a few months. The pair didn't ask questions until she permitted it, and even then they remained understanding. After, Coura felt a sense of relief, and soon their bond grew stronger.

She reflected on that time-consuming conversation as she relaxed on her mother's lap. *I'm sure Evern guessed I'm not entirely healed after the ordeal, but I won't tell them about the* shalma's *observations until I can figure out what to do. I heard mention of the Mintelian village's soul cleansing ceremony on multiple occasions throughout the years, especially from Father. Perhaps I should look into it...*

A pair of approaching footsteps drew her attention before Paulina shook her shoulder gently.

"Can we help you?" her mother asked while Coura sat up and spotted the newcomer.

One of the palace's servants stood alone in the opening with his hands at his sides. Unlike the majority, this man appeared older and sported inky hair possessing several, messy braids. His dark eyes studied her from under eyebrows akin to a black-haired, fuzzy caterpillar before he gestured for her to go to him.

"What is it?" she inquired with a glance at her mother, who looked a bit worried.

When the servant didn't reply, she figured it had to be a private matter, which led her to remember Terran's attack and her current predicament. She repressed a sigh and rose before facing Paulina as the man turned on his heel to lumber away.

"I'm sorry to-"

Her mother waved a hand to dismiss her apology. "You know I understand," she commented with an honest smile.

Coura returned it, thanked her mother, then hurried to catch up to the servant. Her mind again wandered to his purpose and lack of an explanation before a shadowy figure moved out of the corner of her eye. Instinctively, she slid to a stop on the dirt path before spinning around. Although her body grew tense as she adjusted, she didn't expect any sort of threat; however, a second man nearly identical to the first charged with a cleaver in one hand.

Years of training with Marcus and Lavine prepared her for such strikes, though she responded too slowly, resulting in a horizontal slice across her midsection. Although a brief inspection showed it wasn't deep enough to have damaged any organs, it bled plenty to soak the lower half of her shirt in a matter of seconds and hurt enough to cause her to wince.

After wrapping one arm around her stomach to add some pressure to the wound, she retreated a couple steps before the stranger came for her again. This time, Coura anticipated his swipes and managed to dodge without earning anything worse than a cut on her right cheek when he went for her face.

He's not trained, that much I can tell, she noted in the midst of his attacks. *If I can avoid his blade with an injury, he never learned how to properly manipulate an opponent's weakness. So, who is he? Why is he after me?*

The question led her to wonder if her mother would be safe, which sent a jolt of panic through her chest. Instead of fleeing toward the palace, she spun around when an opportunity presented itself and sprinted for the private section she rested in mere minutes earlier.

Unfortunately, the second man either expected her to retreat or the two planned to surround her, for the first fake servant stood just beyond the opening. Coura growled a curse before opting to try her chances given her ability to avoid dying against the initial stranger. Without considering what weapon the person possibly carried, she forced her feet to move at a run straight for him.

This stranger bared his teeth in an ugly grin while removing a short knife from his pocket in response.

Don't worry about fighting him, she told herself. *I just need to get by, then I can figure out what to do next.*

As soon as the man's arm pulled back in a motion to signal a stab, Coura pivoted on her left foot in order to twist around and shift to his right. His resulting, baffled expression let her know he was untrained as well, though he unintentionally abandoned his lunge to stumble away. This brought his knife in contact with her right bicep, slicing her flesh in the process.

She ignored the new wound in favor of bursting through the opening where she slowed to a stop in front of Paulina. Her mother sucked in a breath before jumping up, obviously shaken by her daughter's appearance.

"Coura, what happened?" the woman shrieked after observing the crimson on her shirt, arm, and cheek.

Still, Coura focused on protecting them since she expected the pair of men to pursue her. With her free arm, she crafted a semi-transparent shield using her previously inactive Yeluthian energy and watched as the magical wall spread to cover the entire opening. On the opposite side, she spotted the shadowy figures of the fake servants, then they could hear shouting in some foreign language.

"Those men attacked me as soon as I stepped into the open," she explained when she abandoned her attempt to decipher the pair's conversation. "The guards near the garden's entrance probably mistook them for servants like we did."

A pause followed her words, so she glanced back at Paulina, whose face paled into a gray shade.

"Are you..."

"I'm fine," Coura reassured her mother and offered a pained smile. "I couldn't risk leaving you to find help, but they surprised me first. I'll heal myself once I'm sure we're safe; I only learned how to wield one spell at a time, so I can't drop the shield."

When Paulina nodded, she returned her attention to the silhouettes beyond the magical wall.

I also refuse to show any sort of weakness that will lead them to think they should stay around until I pass out, she thought afterward when she realized how lightheaded she'd grown. *If Mother hasn't mentioned it yet, then I can still be convincing.*

*

The strangers paced in front of Coura's shield for much longer than she expected, leading her to consider if they truly did blend in with the ordinary palace servants. Their incomprehensible yelling quieted into grumbles before one of the two left.

By that point, Coura began to feel faint, though she kept her head up and stood as straight as she could without releasing any pressure from the most severe cut. Blood trickled down her legs to create a noticeable puddle at her feet, drawing Paulina's attention; however, she told her mother to ignore the injury and remain calm. A part of her expected the woman to scold her or give into the inevitable, parental instinct to fawn over her, and that part grew with every passing minute.

Just when they started to discuss the approaching evening, the second man backed up before turning tail and sprinting away.

"Did you see that?" Paulina asked while stepping closer to the shield.

Coura prepared to tell her to stay back until they could be certain they were safe, but the headstrong woman hurried to stand in front of the wall of energy and peer at the opposite side.

"The area is empty."

"We should wait, just to be safe," Coura replied.

Although her mother shot her a disapproving look, they remained silent for another couple minutes when noise from near the palace reached them. Then, she lowered her trembling arm and allowed her spell to fade. A gentle breeze floated through the opening but nothing else.

She focused on her Yeluthian energy next in order to close the wound along her midsection before Paulina retreated to her side.

"You didn't see anyone?" she asked while straightening. The cuts on her face and bicep had stopped bleeding already, so she dismissed them for the time being.

Her mother shook her head. "It is getting dark, though. What do you suggest we do?"

Coura studied the woman for a moment before releasing a sigh. *I'm beginning to hate being a victim, especially when I'm not doing anything wrong. I can see Mother is concerned, but she never usually makes my business her problem because she knows my life is different than it would be if I left Asteom.*

"I'd better report this," she admitted and rubbed the side of her nose. "The generals need to hear about those men pretending to be servants, and how they got away with it."

Paulina tilted her head. "I believe we should find your father before that."

"Why?"

"You look exhausted. Let him share this information so you can change clothes and rest."

"Won't he be busy?" Coura countered while considering the idea. If she alone had been attacked, the strangers would either choose to hide or flee the palace, making it safer for her to remain in her quarters for the time being and eliminating any time restrains.

Meanwhile, her mother mentioned Evern's routine involving guarding King Arval until after the evening meal.

"I would guess they returned to the fourth floor already," Paulina concluded. "No matter what you decide to do, we need to get inside."

*

The many, strained voices and amount of traffic in the hallways alerted Coura and her mother of trouble as they exited the garden area. Bits and pieces of new information echoed around them to reveal another issue: Multiple attacks took place that evening.

Neither shared their thoughts aloud, yet Coura sensed the fear stemming from Paulina as they reached the nearest staircase and ascended. What she didn't expect was the strain on her body from the blood loss. By the time the pair reached the second floor, her lightheadedness had her leaning against the wall to catch her breath. Twice more she needed to pause their trek to avoid tripping over herself or passing out, but they reached the fourth floor and hurried to locate King Arval's quarters.

A portion of the built-up stress fell from Coura's shoulders when she spotted her father standing at attention in his bronze armor. He placed his back to his superior's door in order to observe the entire hallway at either side, allowing him to notice his wife and daughter's arrival.

At first, Evern's expression reflected his curiosity; then, his eyes widened a bit when he could identify the scarlet covering Coura's front side. Still, he refused to move from his position or call out to them until they came near enough for them to converse at an appropriate volume.

"What happened?" he demanded while grabbing Coura by the shoulders and inspecting her from head to toe.

"I'm fine," she replied before figuring she should start at the beginning. "Two men pretending to be servants separated me from Mother…" She proceeded to fill her father in on what transpired in the queen's garden and ended with the pair's decision to find him.

"I figured you would be able to speak with the generals so Coura could clean up and rest," Paulina added after the recounted experience.

Evern turned his head to glance behind at the door he guarded. He remained that way for a moment before dipping his chin and lowering his gaze.

"What is it?" his wife asked a second before Coura could.

"Not too long ago, King Arval received a report containing information about a planned attack in the private dining hall."

As Coura listened to her father recount what one of the generals shared, her body grew tense, and her old wound ached when she considered her visit to Lady Katrina's home earlier that afternoon.

Katrina, Emilea, and Cintra dressed up to attend... Wait, I never got an invite, so why was I targeted too?

"Are the guests all right?" Paulina inquired once Evern finished speaking.

"I am not certain, but the description did not bode well. The messenger hoped to relay what took place to King Arval and make sure we remained safe; however, I neither sensed nor saw any suspicious activity near our location. Commander Isan stood with me until we decided he could stay inside to discuss this matter with the king."

"What about Commander Detrix?" Coura pushed when her father fell silent.

Evern met her eyes with an unreadable expression. "He has been in the training ground and offered to check in on the new complex housing our soldiers. I would imagine he will return here once he learns of what took place."

Coura pressed her lips together but didn't question the situation any further.

I don't understand, she admitted to herself in the silence of the otherwise empty hallway. *The strangers' attack wasn't by circumstance or else they would have gone after Paulina too. Could it be because I possess magical energy? Also, they argued in another, unfamiliar language. I don't know much about the land outside Asteom, so I'd be ignorant to blame Nim-Vala for this. Besides, there's the massacre in the dining hall to consider.*

None of the three uttered a word while they lingered outside King Arval's quarters as each seemed to be wrapped in their own thoughts. Evern excused himself to share his wife and daughter's appearance with his supervisor and fellow commander, leaving Coura alone with her mother. Neither could come up with much to talk about in the meantime until footsteps echoed from farther down the floor.

As multiple male voices joined the sound, she prepared for the possibility of another ambush until they could clearly spot three figures in bronze armor. Detrix led the trio, though Coura didn't recognize the other two Yeluthians, and he offered a polite but strained smile.

"Where is Evern?" he asked after they halted.

Paulina pointed to the nearest door without a word while Coura tried to ignore the three sets of eyes studying her bloody clothing.

"I see," the commander muttered before ordering his subordinates to patrol the floor.

Each soldier nodded and moved to pace in opposite directions while Detrix knocked on his king's door. A grunt from the other side signaled for him to enter.

When Coura stood alone with her mother again, she contemplated what she could do to help their situation. Her heart pulled her in the direction of the dining hall where she would be able to study the aftermath herself and possibly connect that incident with the men in the queen's garden. The other part of her knew she would most likely be in the way if the victims needed medical treatment, which most would based on her father's report.

"Just be patient," came her mother's voice to draw her attention.

The woman offered a sympathetic smile as she reached out to touch Coura's cheek and continued. "I worry there is not much we can do at the moment, so try not to stress yourself out."

Coura thanked her after a pause before they heard the doorknob turn. The pair watched as Evern slipped back into the hallway, looked them both over, then scratched his stubbly chin.

"You two can follow me," he said and gestured to the right. "I will escort Paulina to our room then walk with you to yours, Coura."

Although she didn't protest, Coura sensed a bit of tension underneath her father's words. The trio passed a Yeluthian soldier on the way down the hall, and Evern stopped in front of a door to the room she knew her parents shared.

"I hope this situation will be resolved sooner rather than later," Paulina mumbled while she placed a hand on the doorknob.

Neither Coura nor her father added to the comment, so the woman entered the space, waved, then closed the door. Then, Evern continued down the hallway.

The blood caking Coura's torso and arm began to irritate her skin, though she refused to scratch at those parts until she could wash herself. *I wonder if I'll be allowed to go to the bathing chamber tonight. Maybe I can sneak away after Father leaves me alone.*

While she considered this, Evern said her name in a serious enough tone to have her thinking he'd read her mind. His footsteps didn't stop or slow, so she hurried to his side so they could converse.

"Detrix brought an updated report from King Aaron," he began at a quieter volume as they reached the descending staircase. "It seems an unidentified group orchestrated the attack on the private dining hall and went after you, but they also attempted to break into Verona's prison at the edge of the city."

"What? Why-"

"They do not know," her father interrupted. By that point, they landed on the third floor where more people wandered around to limit their privacy. "Three were involved with the prison, four have been apprehended within the palace, and six hid or fled outside the palace's perimeter."

"Let's wait until we can talk in my room," Coura suggested when she noticed others' unwanted attention shifting to the armor-clad Yeluthian.

Evern's silence usually meant he agreed, so she left it at that. No one bothered the pair as they went on, and within a few minutes, they stood opposite from one another in her quarters.

Coura let her weariness show then by dropping onto her bed. "The guards only captured thirteen suspects?" she asked to pick up their earlier discussion.

"That is correct, but it sounded as though Asteom's king and his council are not certain of many factors."

"What do you mean?"

Her father's eyes rose to the ceiling. "I doubt those were all the intruders. The true number will probably never be known if some escaped. Detrix mentioned those captured refuse to speak, leading the generals to assume they are from Nim-Vala. After what you mentioned about the two arguing in the garden, I must agree.

Next, the incident in the prison does not line up with what took place inside the palace nor with what happened to you. Until the generals and King Aaron learn what motivated these incidents, I am afraid that part is a mystery."

While Evern explained the new soldiers' assignments for the evening, Coura focused on his second point.

What do I have in common with the people in the dining hall and the prison? she asked herself first. *As far as I heard, only the noblewomen were invited to the gathering, except for Aaron. That eliminates any connection with me. The attack across the city confuses me the most. I've visited it a handful of times to see Hendal, nothing more.*

An unexpected shiver slid down her spine until she admitted the key piece of information she neglected to consider. *We both shared a connection to Soirée. Terran and the demonic creatures targeted me because they can sense the damage she did. Perhaps the same is true of Hendal, though I needed to speak with the* shalma *in order to learn that. How does a demon relate to Nim-Vala if that is actually where the attackers came from?*

"What is wrong?" her father inquired to tear her mind away.

With a sigh and an inkling he wouldn't be pleased with her train of thought, Coura informed him of her conclusion, including her visits to the prison, the conversations with Hendal, and the possibility of the former high priest possessing demonic energy because of a damaged soul space.

"I can't guess why the private dining hall was attacked, but Emilea mentioned Aaron had been invited and chose not to attend because our friend Marcus returned with me," she added. "Either that, or the enemy has a different goal."

To her surprise, Evern's expression softened. "I appreciate you telling me what you did. Although I do not agree with your actions, this sheds some light on our problems. I plan on reporting it to King Aaron and the generals immediately. For now, I order you to remain here. My soldiers will stand guard outside until we can be sure you are safe."

"No," Coura snapped as her father prepared to leave. When he ignored her outburst, she jumped to her feet. "I can't just hide inside my room!"

"You can and you will," came his cold response. "This issue is much greater than I imagined, and I wager my fellow commanders, the generals, and both kings would agree."

"The demon *is* involved," she stated without letting his tone and protective behavior shake her resolve. "You understand that, right?"

He didn't reply, yet his hand hovered over the doorknob.

"I shouldn't stay here when innocent people might get hurt. Detrix and General Tio used me as bait in Dala and the Western Woods; Hendal might unwillingly be doing that too. We're more of a danger in the same location."

"What would you do, then?"

Coura lowered her gaze to avoid her father's when he turned to face her again. This time, he projected a melancholy sense of concern, as if he already figured out her next course of action.

"I'll leave the capital and head south, back toward Dala. Their base can house and protect me."

Evern shook his head. "That would merely postpone another interaction," he elaborated when she tilted her head.

"Then, I suppose I could go west…"

"No, you should move east. I believe rectifying your problem is most important at the moment."

Coura raised an eyebrow while her stomach dropped. "Where are you sending me?"

"I heard your account, and Paulina can fill in any gaps," he explained and seemingly pieced together his suggestion. "If you truly wish to leave, you should visit the Mintelians in the Ghurun mountains and proceed with the soul cleansing I recommended in the past. The former high priest might benefit from the same process."

He isn't pushing for me to go, Coura realized during the following pause. *I could stay and obey his order; it would be easier on me but more of a risk to everyone else. The damage to my center attracts demonic energy, no matter where I hide. I think it's safe to assume that problem will only get worse before it gets better.*

"What about the Nim-Valans?" she asked after. "My departure would lessen the likelihood of another ambush, but their people don't possess the ability to use magic."

"Your question is one I cannot answer right now, though this is due to the fact that multiple parties are involved in the recovery efforts. If their people do not wield light or dark energies, why should they target you or the prison? What was the point of harming those in the private dining hall, and what is their ultimate goal? These are questions for later and ones I will raise; however, I promise to do so in front of Yeluthia and Asteom's leaders."

Coura dipped her chin to contemplate his words. After a moment, she heard the door open, and her head snapped up.

"Wait," she started before he could slip into the hallway. For the first time in months, she felt utterly helpless as the weight of her new journey fell on her shoulders. "Where will I find the Mintelians?"

Evern closed the door once more, crossed his arms, and pondered the foreign subject. "What I recall from years ago may not be entirely accurate, and I do not know anyone who has been through the process or traveled to one of the villages. The humans in Kercher built various paths through the mountain range in order to access the Mintelians for communication and trading purposes. I would imagine those roads are strictly guarded, so I would go to Kercher and speak with the leader of the messengers to request a guide."

"I can manage that much," Coura muttered before thanking him.

After reiterating his promise to share her intentions with King Arval, the commanders, and Aaron, her father cast one last look over his shoulder as he stood in the open doorway.

"Be careful," he warned with a stern expression. "Not much is known about the humans in the mountains. If you need assistance, send someone for me. Otherwise, your mother and I will wait to hear from you."

In response, Coura managed a smile, which she hoped hid her nerves and genuine fear of the future outside familiar territory. The door closed behind her father afterward.

*

It took Coura a matter of minutes to change clothes, fill her pack with the regular travel supplies, and select a map to tear out of one of the texts on her desk. Then, she focused on how she could sneak away before her tightening stomach reminded her she would need food.

I'll visit the kitchen on my way to the training ground, she decided while buckling her sword around her waist and wrapping a cloak around her shoulders. Bringing her Yeluthian armor or Asteom uniform would only slow her down and connect her with either group when she went to get Hendal, so she departed while considering her plan further.

I won't be able to fly with him, but I suppose I can afford a horse or bargain for a similar beast. That's another stop before I leave Verona.

Because of the frantic energy causing the entire structure to buzz, no one paid her any mind, allowing her to slip into the pantry. There, she procured several items that wouldn't perish for a few days until the amount satisfied her.

Her body automatically moved north toward the exit into the non-magical combat area next. Along the way, she reflected on the news from her father and Detrix and wondered about those she knew had been present at the noblewomen's gathering, as well as her friends who would assist with or lead the recovery efforts. Her feet began to slow when she considered checking on them; however, a brief reminder of her purpose for leaving steadied her resolve.

Fortunately, no one showed her attention as everyone in the hallways seemed to be searching for the intruders or on guard duty. This gave her the opportunity to slip outside unnoticed in order to circle around to the front and exit into the city. The soldiers who gathered near the main stable cast her dubious gazes, but no one bothered to question her business.

The haunting silence and murmurs in the shadows revealed the commotion in the palace already influenced the citizens. People hurried through the streets while avoiding the many soldiers marching through on patrol; some even stopped those in the crimson coats to demand information or beg for protection. What they heard, whether an exaggeration or not, Coura couldn't guess.

When she reached the stables at the perimeter of the city, she found half a dozen guards monitoring the area. Two took her aside when she approached to interrogate her about her whereabouts and purpose for visiting, so she told them as much of the truth as she could, which consisted of her desire to head east under Commander Evern's order. To avoid creating any suspicion, she pretended to play dumb about the attacks before offering to postpone her task in favor of assisting with the search.

Neither soldier seemed inclined to accept, most likely because they would be expected to supervise the new recruit, so the pair released her. She approached a stablehand inside to inquire about a horse and managed to purchase a decent animal she could afford without spending all her coin. The man prepared a chestnut-colored mare, then Coura departed for the far end of the main road.

Once away from the more populated buildings, she snuck between the alleys comprised of less dense structures, found a fence along the way, and tied the reins so she'd be able to return for the horse later.

"That should be enough," she muttered to herself while removing her bag to prop it against the wooden post.

After wiping her forehead with the back of one hand, she contemplated her next steps and glanced over at the prison's entrance in the distance. *I would imagine it's been reinforced after the earlier incident, and I doubt the guards on duty will let me waltz away with Hendal. That means I'll need to enter, break him out of his cell, then escape before they can seal the main door.*

The thought of committing to such a bold tactic made her anxious, yet a jolt of excitement reminiscent of her rebellious days as a student shot through her body, prompting a grin. Without letting her mind wander too far from the situation at hand, she closed the distance between herself and the prison. The soldier posted at the front proved to be someone she had spoken with on multiple occasions during her previous visits and waved when he spotted her.

"Hey, it's been a while," he said by way of greeting as she came nearer. "Were you sent to investigate the incident here too? The last person just left after dragging the scum away, though he couldn't tell me any details or about what went on in the palace."

Coura prepared to dismiss his assumption until she realized it would be the perfect excuse for her to appear and wish to enter.

"I'm fortunate General Terrell chose me for this location; not too many people seem familiar with the prison," she replied.

To her relief, he didn't look doubtful and let her inside so they could finish the investigation for the night.

The main hallway appeared as ordinary as she remembered, though twice as many guards stood around to converse. None extended a longer greeting than a wave, which she returned before continuing to the descending stairs. In the basement, the usual supervisor Irvin grunted as she went straight to Hendal's cell without a word.

"What are you doing here?" the prisoner asked with a yawn after sitting up upon her arrival.

Coura remained silent while glancing him over. Although he wore woolen socks, pants, and a tunic, she figured he would survive until they could procure some better clothing options. Next, she glanced to the left and right to find both of the metal gates wide open and the spaces empty.

Then again, I don't remember there being any other people around him, she thought absently before shouting over her shoulder as desperately as she could muster.

"I need help! Hurry!"

It wasn't in her nature to sound as helpless as she attempted to be, but it proved to be enough for the soldier, who rushed over while she faced the wide-eyed ex-high priest.

"What's going on?" came a gruff reply when he reached her side.

Coura silently drew her sword, spun around, and aimed the tip at his pale throat, barely cutting off his question. The motion was so fluent he hadn't realized what she did until the blade pressed against his skin and drew blood.

"What in the-"

"Get in the cell," she ordered in her most serious tone and gestured with her chin to the open gate on her right.

"You think I'm afraid of some girl holding a sword? Why even bother? You'll be caught before you get past the stairs!"

Despite his shouts in protest, the guard complied. He took his time backtracking into the designated space, and when he was nearly pressed against the farthest wall, Coura demanded he relinquish the keys he possessed. After attempting to deny it, she had to twitch the blade in order to scratch his throat gently and intimidate him into giving up the jingling set kept in his pants pocket. She stepped away to close and lock the gate as he leapt forward and pushed against the metal bars.

"You'll never see the light of day again after this! They'll lock you up just like they did with him!" The man spat in Hendal's direction before proceeding to rant about all the punishments she would endure.

It didn't matter to Coura. After all, she was already trying to avoid the worst trouble. Next, she hurried to unlock the other closed gate to free the former high priest.

"Come on," she said without meeting his eyes.

It was a miracle he didn't stop to question what they were going to do or create a fuss over leaving his jailor locked up. He just followed behind in silence except for his heavy footsteps. As they reached the staircase, the guard cried out for them not to abandon him, and those words echoed.

"We're going to need to run for it," she decided when they could hear voices at the top of the stairs. "If you get left behind, I'm not stopping to return for you."

If he gave a response, she didn't hear it as she bound ahead. The several men ranging from middle-aged to gray-haired stood closer to the stairs compared to when she left them. If she had to guess, Coura figured they were debating what took place in the basement and who should go down first to investigate. Their lack of a plan and knowledge of her intentions created the perfect opportunity to fly through the hallway toward the entrance. Based on their startled exclamations and the sound of weapons being drawn, they were expecting to act as a barricade instead of handling a pair of fleeing criminals.

The regular guard at the front and another man became the final obstacles blocking the exit. Coura shouted at them to draw their attention, ran closer, and threw the jailor's set of keys in one of their faces. They both backed away, as if it were a weapon of some sort, leaving the metal to drop and clang on the floor and Coura to flash by with Hendal hopefully behind.

The cold evening air hit her face like a bucket of water, which she used as a signal to stop and spin around to face the opening once more. After reaching into her center for the Yeluthian energy, she cast a shield sealing the entrance and keeping the guards from pursuing. No matter how hard they pounded on or struck the magical wall, it would not budge until she dropped the spell, which would be when they moved outside the city.

Meanwhile, Hendal also halted a little ways away, doubled over, and panted with hands on his knees. The time to explain what took place in the palace and why they needed to leave would come when they were on the road, so Coura started jogging to where the horse waited. She checked the saddle and straps again before turning around when the former high priest's breathing told her he was standing behind.

"What's going on?" he asked, suspicion teeming in his voice. "Why did you do all that? It couldn't have been for me."

"It wasn't," she replied and stripped off her cloak to toss it over to the man. "I can fill you in on everything later, but right now we have to at least get out of Verona, unless you want to get caught and thrown back in that cell."

Hendal dipped his head with a grunt. "I take it this mare is for me?"

At least he's still able to use his head.

Coura stepped away, allowing him to approach the shying horse, gently lay a hand on its neck, and take a minute to mount on his own more easily than she would have given him credit for. When he finished and threw on the cloth covering, she secured the reins just in case he had any ideas of running away before leading the mare into the city.

Plenty of commotion met the pair the closer they got to the palace, and additional guards surveyed the streets, but it wasn't until they reached the western main road that a horn from the prison sounded the alarm.

That took a lot longer than I expected it would, Coura thought with some relief and dismissed the shielding spell, which continued to pull from her center until that point.

Everyone on the road glanced west in response, and most of the people hurried inside or farther down the path and out of Verona. When the search for the escapees would reach that area, she planned to be deep within the woods and heading east.

Glossary

CHARACTERS

Aimes Occaily – an older, former seaman from Clearwater who joins Coura during her venture to defeat the demonic creatures roaming Asteom

Aaron Vanstriann – heir to the kingdom of Asteom and son of King Hernan and Queen Freia

Assistant General Calin – leader of the Dalan base under General Tio

Barnelus Dagger-Diver – son of the Sie-Kie's *shimla* and their people's lead hunter

Bryn Leetle – a light mage who survives the ambush along the border

Byron Rinod – a master mage who wields dark magic and acts as Coura's mentor, an instructor at the Magical Arts Academy, and eventually the academy's representative in the palace

Califer Beackdal – former master light mage in Asteom's palace

Captain Harvey – leader of the Nim-Valan army who visited Asteom's capital

Cintra Amaldi – Byron's childhood friend who lives in Fester and works as a seer

Clara Waterton – a light mage who survives the ambush along the border and befriends Will

Commander Detrix – one of King Arval's trusted soldiers in Yeluthia

Commander Isan – one of King Arval's trusted soldiers in Yeluthia

Cornelius "Clearshot" Bayporter – a distinguished soldier who specializes in archery and Byron's close friend and comrade; he is married to Emilea and has two children: Mace and Lexie

Coura (core-ah) Galdwin – a dark mage and soldier with the ability to wield demonic energy and manifest black wings

Drake Telkanar – a rouge Yeluthian working with the traitor in Verona

Elena Taymor – wife of King Syrus, one of Nim-Vala's six queens, and Finn's master

Emilea Bayporter – a master mage who wields light energy and acts as the palace's lead healer; she is married to Cornelius and has two children: Mace and Lexie

Evern Galdwin – commander of Yeluthia's army; he is married to Paulina and has three children: Coura, Odell, and Jackie

Finnley (Finn) – a Nim-Valan spy who assists Will and the light mages across the border

General Casner – commander stationed in Verona who is sent to the Nim-Valan border

General Garvish – new commander stationed in Verona

General Terrell – new commander stationed in Verona

General Tio – leader of the Dalan base

General Tont – commander stationed in Verona and Marcus' father

Grace Zelnar – Yeluthia's ambassador sent to Asteom's capital; possesses a goddess gift that allows her to speak mind to mind with others

Hector Lauple – a rouge Yeluthian working with the traitor in Verona

Hendal Duers – Asteom's former high priest

Jaspire Uskinor – leader of the rogue Yeluthian group assisting the traitor in the palace; possesses a goddess gift that allows him to heal from a distance

Jurek Younder – Asteom's new high priest

King Arval – leader of Yeluthia

Kline Galbourough – a rogue Yeluthian working with the traitor in Verona

Lady Katrina Neneme – wife of Lord Donovan Neneme and friend of Emilea

Lavine – Yeluthian soldier under Commander Evern who befriends Coura

Lissa Quentile – a light mage who survives the ambush along the border

Lupin Olim – King Syrus' mysterious advisor

Lydia Teller – a dark mage and Byron's second-in-command

Lyla Kroft – Wesley's apprentice and future priest of Kercher

Marcus Tont – an assistant general in Asteom's army and Prince Aaron's closest friend

Mary-Ann Weavu – a light mage who survives the ambush along the border

Marcy Kilguire – a woman from Dala who joins Coura during her venture to defeat the demonic creatures roaming Asteom

Nullan & Elenor Zelnar – Grace's parents and political leaders in Yeluthia

Paulina Galdwin – she is married to Evern and has three children: Coura, Odell, and Jackie

Soirée (sw-our-ae) – a demon who appears like an adult woman who forms a soul-bonding with Coura

Terran – a demon who appears to Coura during a scouting mission in search of Soirée

Thelma Boncarl – a rouge Yeluthian working with the traitor in Verona

Urvin Tsansa – a rouge Yeluthian working with the traitor in Verona

Verdic Ulshritz – former priest in Kercher and Hendal and Wesley's uncle

Wesley Ashre – priest in Kercher and Hendal's nephew

William "Will" Shairp – an herbalist from Clearwater who focuses on medicinal potions

Yukin Crowmald – a Nim-Valan lord and friend of Finn who Will treats and allies with

Zelma Vulan – a light mage who survives the ambush along the border

LOCATIONS

Clearwater – the southernmost city in Asteom primarily known for fishing

Dala – a city in southern Asteom housing a military base led by General Tio

East Hoover – northern town housing the Magical Arts Academy

Kercher – an eastern city known for housing messengers between Yeluthia and Asteom

Magical Arts Academy – often referred to as the MAA, this school houses primarily light and dark mage trainees and is located in East Hoover

Medina – a town located in the southwestern section of Asteom and the site of a demonic creature's massacre

Neston – Coura's hometown located in the forest south of East Hoover

Nim-Vala – country north of Asteom

The Valley Beyond – open area between a series of tunnels connecting Dala, Clearwater, and Fester

Verona – Asteom's capital city

Western Woods – an extensive forest covering most of Asteom's western coast and home of the Sie-Kie people

Yeluthia – also referred to as the City of Angels, this kingdom consists of a people who are closely connected with light energy, allowing some to manifest wings and thus giving them the nickname angels

MISCELLANEOUS

Ancestral weapons – items gifted to Asteom's royal family consisting of two, golden swords, daggers, and bows; crafted with a sealing spell to protect against demonic energy

Chi-alve (key-al-ve) – term for soul space or center of power

Goddess gifts – special abilities used by certain Yeluthians involving telepathic communication, long-range healing, portal manifestation, and other spells

Mintelians – a secluded people who live in the Ghurun mountains and value artistic trades

Shalma – Sie-Kie's term for witch, or one who uses magic

Shimla – Sie-Kie's term for chief

Sie-Kie (sih-kai-e) – a tribe living in the Western Woods who value tradition over magic

Summa and Izina – god and goddess worshiped in Kercher

About the Author

Courtney Lillard was born and raised in Appleton, Wisconsin as the middle of five children. Growing up, she loved music and theater, and participating in both allowed her to develop a deeper interest in the arts. She graduated from Quincy University in 2015 with a B.A. degree in Broadcasting and Public Relations Communications and from Western Illinois University in 2018 with a M.A. degree in Communication Studies.

Aside from writing, Lillard is a fan of reading fantasy stories and the classics. Her other hobbies include cooking, playing video games, and doing puzzles, at least until her cats knock the pieces off the table.